KT-556-523

THE DATING DETOX

Gemma Burgess moved to London at the age of 22. She started working as an advertising copywriter, and applied herself more wholeheartedly to having a good time. Eight years later she decided to distil some of her experiences into *The Dating Detox*: the book for women with confidence, wit and style but absolutely no clue whatsoever how to know the real thing when they see it. (Love, that is.) She lives in London.

To find out more about Gemma go to www.gemmaburgess.co.uk

GEMMA BURGESS

The Dating Detox

This novel is entirely a work of fiction. The names, characters and incidents portrayed in it are the work of the author's imagination. Any resemblance to actual persons, living or dead, events or localities is entirely coincidental.

AVON

A division of HarperCollins*Publishers*
77–85 Fulham Palace Road,
London W6 8JB

www.harpercollins.co.uk

A Paperback Original 2009

1

First published in Great Britain by
HarperCollins*Publishers* 2009

Copyright © Gemma Burgess 2009

Gemma Burgess asserts the moral right to
be identified as the author of this work

A catalogue record for this book is
available from the British Library

ISBN-13: 978-1-84756-191-6

Set in Minion by Palimpsest Book Production Limited,
Grangemouth, Stirlingshire

Printed and bound in Great Britain by
Clays Ltd, St Ives plc

Mixed Sources
Product group from well-managed
forests and other controlled sources
www.fsc.org Cert no. SW-COC-1806
© 1996 Forest Stewardship Council

FSC

FSC is a non-profit international organisation established
to promote the responsible management of the world's forests.
Products carrying the FSC label are independently certified
to assure consumers that they come from forests that are managed
to meet the social, economic and ecological needs
of present and future generations.

Find out more about HarperCollins and the environment at
www.harpercollins.co.uk/green

All rights reserved. No part of this publication may be reproduced, stored in a retrieval system, or transmitted, in any form or by any means, electronic, mechanical, photocopying, recording or otherwise, without the prior permission of the publishers.

For Anika and Paul

Prologue

Nine months ago

I knew the second I walked into this party that it wouldn't be any fun. Every person here looked around when we walked in. Then they welcomed Rick and ignored me. That was two hours ago and now here I am, in my stupid librarian costume, sitting in the kitchen alone, trying to enjoy myself and failing. Very. Badly.

My friends aren't here, which doesn't help. They're all having dinner together in a pub in Westbourne Grove. I wish I was with them. But I have to be here. My boyfriend Rick is here. He is friends with the guy who's throwing this party. Or he knows a guy who knows him. Something like that.

Where the hell is he, anyway? I haven't actually seen Rick in ages, but I don't want to be one of those socially-needy girlfriends. Especially after last night. Hell, people at this party are unfriendly. Perhaps they don't get that I'm dressed as an ironic geek.

The theme is 'Come As Your Childhood Ambition', and I'm surrounded by sexy nurses and Pink Ladies and ballerinas and air hostesses. (Aspiring to jobs that don't come with a revealing/girly costume doesn't seem to have occurred to these women as five-year-olds.) I should have come as Prime Minister or something. But I really did want to be a librarian. The men are dressed as Indiana Jones and Luke Skywalker and knights and things like that.

For God's sake, I'm 28 years old. I can handle an unfriendly party, can't I?

We're in a large flat just off Kensington Church Street, and it's packed. It's just the kind of party I usually love. Lots of people having loud conversations and being funny and silly. I don't know anyone, so I ought to just flick the insta-banter switch, go forth and jazz-hands myself around the party, conquering friends. I tried to do that earlier, but they just seemed to not hear me, or look through me. Or something. So I don't want to try again. If only my friends were here.

I wonder how much longer I can sit in this stupid kitchen, pretending to read and send non-existent texts. This is so not me.

I wish I didn't look so dowdy. I'm wearing a tweed skirt and carrying a pince-nez and a stack of books. I felt terribly chic and witty when I was getting ready, now I just feel drab and lost. I could go home. But that might upset Rick. Plus, they're his friends, and I would really like to get to know them better. I've never really met any of them before.

Seriously, where the sweet hell is Rick? He seems stressed tonight. I know his work is crazy at the moment. He was texting me about it the other night. Seeing him less is probably good for our relationship anyway. I just hang out with my best friends when he's busy. Or hang out by myself in the kitchen at parties where everyone's a bit weird and unfriendly. That's good fun too. (Sigh.)

'Are you a teacher?' says a guy who just walked into the kitchen. He's dressed as a cricketer. (How imaginative.)

'Librarian,' I say, and add, in my best librarian tone, 'Shhhh!'

He frowns slightly, gets a beer out of the fridge and says 'Freeeeeak . . .' under his breath as he walks away.

See?

I repeat my mantra ('posture is confidence, silence is poise') to myself and smoke another cigarette.

That's it, I'm going to look for Rick. Kitchen, living room,

2

dining room, balcony, second balcony . . . no, no, no, no, no. Just people who look around at me, see that I'm not interesting enough to bother with, and turn back to each other to keep talking. Fuck me, I hate this party . . . Sheesh, this place is packed. So many doors. He wouldn't have left without me, would he? Maybe he's near the front – oh, here—

Oh my oh my oh my oh my God.

Rick, on a bed, with nothing on but his judge's wig, straddled by a near-naked Pink Lady. It's Frenchy. I can tell because she's still wearing her Pink Lady jacket and it's got 'Frenchy' embroidered on the back.

They're having sex, holy shit, they're having sex. It takes a few seconds before they even notice I'm standing in the doorway. Then they both look around at once. (People look so odd when they're having sex. No wonder I've never understood the whole porn thing.)

'Fuck!' says Rick, and then lies back on the bed, pushing the girl off him. She giggles and nearly falls off the bed.

I need to get out of here. I need to get out of here now.

I back out of the doorway as quickly as I can, stack of books and pince-nez in my left hand and my dull little librarian's bag over my right shoulder, and dash for the front door.

I feel sick. I can't breathe. How could he? How could he do that to me? I've got to get out of here. As I open the front door, I hear people behind me whooping. They must have seen him with the Pink Lady too. They're all laughing. I hate those people. I hate them.

How could he do that? Is he even going to follow me? Is he even going to say anything? How could he do that? When I'm here, I'm at the *same fucking party*? How could Frenchy do that? She was always my favourite Pink Lady.

That's not a rational thing to think. Be rational, damn it. Pull yourself together.

How the hell do you get out of this mansion block shithole?

3

I feel sick. I feel like throwing up. I am definitely going to throw up. Where can I . . . ah, a plant pot. Lovely.

I lean over the pot, bend the plant out of the way, and start dry-heaving. Up come my three vodkas and the peanut butter sandwich I ate before I left home. I can see my teeth marks in the bread. Gross. I must chew my food more.

I stand up and wipe my mouth. My hands are shaking and tears are running down my face. How could he, how could he? Why hasn't he followed me? Has he even called me? I'll check my phone . . . no, nothing. What happened between us arriving at the party together and him shagging someone else? Did I do something wrong? Who the hell shags at parties anyway? She must have seduced him. I hate her.

I'm going to call him. Maybe it's a huge mistake and he's hammered and thought she was me. That would be . . . no, that would not be good either. Please, please let this not be happening.

He doesn't answer the first time I call, so I try again. On the seventh ring, he answers.

'Yes?'

'It's me . . . I'm . . . How could you do that, Rick?'

'Pretty easily,' he says, and starts laughing. His voice is muffled. What is funny about this? What? Is he talking to someone else?

'Who is she?'

'No one you know.'

Is he even going to apologise? 'I'm so upset . . .' I say. He doesn't say anything. 'Did you plan this? Why did you even . . .' (I start crying, but try to hide it) '. . . ask me to the party?'

'I didn't ask you to the party. Don't give me that shit. You asked what I was doing and assumed you were coming too.'

I'm still crying silently, trying to quieten my shaky breathing. Typical lawyer, trying to point score even when completely in the wrong.

'I . . . I . . .' I can't talk. 'How could you d-d-do this to me? It's so h-horrible of you . . .'

4

I hear him sigh impatiently. I don't know what to say now and my stammering seems to have kicked in, so I don't say anything. Please, please let him apologise. I want to go back in time and stop this from happening. Dear God, if it is even the tiniest bit possible, please send me back in time right now to stop this from happening.

Or just make him ask me to forgive him.

Or even say sorry. Once.

Instead he just says: 'I can't deal with this. I just ... I don't love you and I don't want you anymore ... I gotta go.'

You know when you jam your fingers in a drawer and you know a split second before the pain hits that it's going to hit, and your chest has that weird icy seizure? That's what I have right now. And then he hangs up, and the pain hits me, and I'm standing outside some mansion block on Kensington Church Street with a stack of books and my pince-nez and my handbag and I squat down – which isn't easy in heels, you know – and bury my face in my hands. I can't breathe. I want to vomit, but nothing is left in my tummy. I can't bear this. I can't bear to wake up tomorrow and have this as a memory.

Fucking, fucking, fucking bastardo. Never again. I will never let this happen again.

Chapter One

Well, I thought I'd discovered the secret to never getting dumped again. And then Posh Mark came over to see me last night. And now I'm back in the bearpit of the singles.

Yet again.

The whole thing is just horrific. Not as horrific as the Rick/Pink Lady night all those months ago, I grant you, but horrific for the fact that it is now my sixth – SIXTH! – break-up in a row, with me as the breakee, and now I have to go and do it all over again. No, not today, I know, but eventually.

Oh God, the idea is so exhausting.

These are not particularly positive thoughts to have before you've even opened your eyes on a Wednesday morning. I sit up in bed and survey the detritus of last night: used tissues strewn around my pillow in a halo, chocolate wrappers all over the bed, a fag pack spent and crushed on the floor. Mon dieu, quel cliché. I flop back down on the bed and close my eyes again. I want to cry, but I actually can't be bothered.

OK, I'd better tell you the background so you can get up to speed.

Break-Up No.6: Posh Mark. We met a few months ago in January, at a theme party ('80s Movies'). He was wearing a girlish flowery dress, a frizzy wig and carried a watermelon around all night.

7

Wouldn't you have given him your number? Exactly. (I was wearing khaki shorts, a white-fringed jacket and little white cowboy boots like Sloane Peterson. If you're asking.)

So I made eye contact, he came over, I did my flirty thing, and then he asked me out.

Posh Mark was definitely not a bastardo. I realised that on our first date, at Eight Over Eight (sexy Far East vibe and delightful first date place, and my God do I know a lot of them). Posh Mark lived in Holland Park (expensive, leafy area of London, jam-packed with the sedate rich), was warm and affectionate (if a bit clingy with the hand-holding), liked to read (sports biographies, but whatever), didn't work in any of the 'arsehole' industries (law, banking, medicine) and greeted everything I said with an open-mouthed, utterly delighted smile (rather like a Labrador, and I do love an appreciative audience).

Crucially, he seemed to fit the criteria. Which was, basically, no bastardos. You see, after the Rick-shagging-a-Pink-Lady fiasco (Break-Up No.5) – and the weeks of utter, utter misery interspersed with binge-drinking that followed – the criteria for men I'd even consider dating changed slightly: they had to be too nice to dump me. Which – if anyone is taking notes – is not a reason to go out with someone. Posh Mark was also the opposite of Rick in every way he could be. Polite, easy-going, tall and very, very nice.

We fell into a complacent co-dependency pretty fast. He called every night, texted every morning, discussed weekend plans by Wednesday, and was generally a Boy Scout of a boyfriend. My cup runnethed over. No, I didn't want to be with him forever, but I decided not to think about that right now, thank you very much. And after the soul-destroying storm of Rick, he was a wonderful protective harbour.

Brutal honesty: he was (whisper it) a tiny bit dull and, um, thick. But he'd worn the Nobody-Puts-Baby-In-The-Corner costume. He obviously had a funny, clever side somewhere. And hot damn, he was nice. As mentioned.

8

And so we come to last night. He came over to see me un-expectedly. He said that he needed to talk. (Cue familiar stomach curl.) He said that when he met me, he was bowled over by how 'rahlly sahriously lovely, basically' I seemed. He said that I was 'so fun to be with, rahlly, rahlly so . . . yah, so fun' and his friends loved me, which was, obviously, gratifying to hear. Then he said 'I just feel like you're, ahhh, rather reserved.'

Huh?

'I just . . . After this much time one should know, you know, whether it's going to work or not and . . . I don't feel like we have rahlly gotten to know each other, Sass, and maybe, uh, it's because you were only recently, uh, single . . .'

Don't you mean permanently single, I wanted to say. And it wasn't that recent. The Rick thing ended almost six months before I met Posh Mark. Six ghastly months.

'Annabel thinks perhaps, uh, you're still in love with him. With your ex.'

Annabel can blow me, I thought. Slightly chubby Sloane-ista with a pashmina so permanently attached to her jowls that I've nicknamed her Pashmina Face to myself. She probably wears it at the beach. She's also one of Posh Mark's best friends and, naturally, comes complete with a blatant agenda. And I'm not in love with fuckfeatures Rick.

'So perhaps we should just, you know, be mates.'

Mates? Oh God.

'What do you think?'

I didn't think anything very much, actually. And I'm not great at talking about feelings. Not lately. In fact, I never said anything to Posh Mark about how I feel (or don't feel). I thought he'd like it that way.

'I'm . . . I'm . . .' I'm not able to finish a sentence? I felt helpless. I didn't want Posh Mark to go, but I couldn't think of a reason why. Because I don't want to start again? I wondered if I could say that. Probably not.

9

Slumping down on the couch and burying my head in my hands seems a better option than speaking. Despite a tiny voice in my head saying 'you're not actually surprised, are you?', a much louder voice told me he was a lovely non-bastardo who had made me feel happy(ish) post-Rick, when I thought nothing would, ever again. And now I have to start all over. So I cried.

'I'll miss you,' I croaked through my hands. And I will. He stroked the inside of my arms for hours when we watched DVDs and had perfectly muscley arms just built for spooning on a Sunday morning. (Does that sound shallow?)

'I'll miss you too, Sass. Rahlly. I feel ah-paw-leng doing this to you. I've had such a bloody good time with you, sahriously.'

I smiled into my hands. I love the way he pronounces appalling. So posh. And he pronounces my name with the longest-drawn-out 'a' sound you've ever heard. Saaaaarrrrhs.

'Since the night we met. That hilarious pahty . . . Hugo made me take him out for a big night at Da Bouj, you know, in return for the outfit that you loved.'

Pause. The way he abbreviates Boujis to Da Bouj is irritating, but—

Outfit?

'The 80s costume, you know. With the watermelon. From *Girls Just Wanna Have Dancing*, or whatever it was, yah? It was all his idea. Well, he saw someone else wear it at a party up in St Andrews once, basicallah. And you were dressed as *The Breakfast Club*.'

Well, if I needed distracting from the idea that I'm being broken up with for the sixth time in a row, then voilà.

For the rest of the night, through him saying goodbye, and me calling Bloomie and Kate to announce that dating someone who isn't a bastardo won't prevent you from being dumped, falling asleep in a haze of nicotine and mild hysteria, and waking every two hours for a self-pitying-but-not-really-heartbroken little weep, I thought about that sentence.

Did I actually fall in love, no, sorry, in LIKE with someone

10

because he wore a funny costume that his friend saw someone else wear at some rah party in fucking Scotland? What the hell is wrong with me? And he didn't even know that Sloane Peterson was in *Ferris Bueller's Day Off*.

Enough thinking. I pull back the duvet, scattering tissues and wrappers across the bed, and shuffle to the mirror. I don't look that great, but I've certainly looked a lot worse.

I will try to look as ace as possible today, so that the world rewards me by doing something really ace for me. That's sartorial karma, you see. I'm a firm believer in it.

Chapter Two

Shampoo, condition, scrub with exfoliating gloves and body wash, brush teeth, shave armpits, then shave legs (one razor in each hand so each leg is done in about seven seconds – that's an as-yet unpatented time-saving move I invented when I was 14). Towel, hairdryer once-over, moisturiser, deodorant, perfume.

Throughout my morning routine, my brain is on a loop titled 'disbelief'. Because I just cannot believe it's happened again. I picked the nicest guy I could fucking well find and it fucking well happened again.

Let's start at the beginning.

Break-Up No.1: Arty Jonathan. I was 22, and had been living in London about a year. (No one ever dates in their first six months of living here; they're too busy avoiding psycho flatmates, drinking in bad chain bars and getting the wrong District line tube.) I met Arty Jonathan at a workmate's party one night in Café Kick in Shoreditch, which was cutting-edge-indie cool at that time, rather than yuppie-indie cool as it is now. Arty Jonathan was gorgeous in a shaven-headed, mockney kind of way. He teased and flirted and flattered me, and I became helplessly giggly in his presence. He said he was an 'avant garde' artist – which meant he'd secure deadlines for shows at a 'space' and then throw something together last minute out of whatever rubbish he found on the way there. Avant garde, I now know, is French for pretentious, and any

12

mention of the phrase makes me want to laugh hysterically. He'd had various jobs over the previous few years (producing indie films that never got greenlit, managing bands that never got signed) and had lots of stories that made me laugh.

You're right, of course: he was a talentless cockmonkey. I'd like to blame inexperience, or perhaps I'm just a bit thick, but he seemed interesting . . . I think I was probably looking for someone unlike every good public school boy I'd known at university. And his self-belief was stupendous. I'm a sucker for a confident man.

Looking back, I cringe at how green I was to be impressed by a dude like that. I was an art groupie for an artist who hadn't really created anything. I'd sit quietly in the Bricklayer's Arms in Hoxton, buying way more than my fair share of rounds, listening to Arty Jonathan and his friends gossip about Young British Artists that I'd never heard of and they didn't actually know. We'd snog. He'd draw doodles for me. They made jokes about the establishment, some of which were very funny, even though I didn't know what the establishment was yet. Then, after about two or three months of this, and just as I was starting to wonder why Arty Jonathan never did any of the things he talked about doing and notice that he recycled all his best lines and jokes, he ended it. He looked at his watch when we were walking towards the Barley Mow one Saturday lunchtime and said: 'I have to go to King's Cross. My girlfriend is arriving from Leeds in an hour. We're going to Paris for the night.'

I was sledgehammer-stunned by this, rather than heartbroken. There is a difference. What hurt more was that he was a bit of a freeloader, and in fact, two days before he dumped me, he'd 'borrowed' £200 off me. He said his bankcard was broken. But clearly, he wanted the money to take his girlfriend to Paris. And I was too timid/stupid/polite to ask for it back. I just nodded and walked away as quickly as I could and never contacted him again. (I've never liked confrontation.) My friends from university started to move to London soon afterwards, so life improved immeasurably, and I tried to chalk it up to experience. At least it knocked some of the naivety out of me.

God, Arty Jonathan was a long time ago. And yet here I am. Single. Again.

What shall I wear today?

Unsurprisingly, given my newly single status, mild heartache and general blues, I feel like being an Urban Warrior today. I throw on blacker-than-black opaque tights, black boots, a black dress and a black motorcycle jacket with studs. Hair in a ballet bun, some scary black undereyeliner and a few careful minutes with my eyebrow pencil. (I'm obsessed with my eyebrows. They are my bête noire.)

Outer Self is thus prepared for the day. Check with Inner Self. Inner Self is not as prepared. Inner Self would like to curl up at home and watch *Gossip Girl* on the internet all day, despite fact that Outer Self is old enough to play a mother on *Gossip Girl*.

I eat a banana, standing up in the kitchen(ette), noting happily that my never-home flatmate/landlord Anna has left the dingy little 60s-era front room as pristine as ever. I've rented a room here for years. The shower is dreadful, the carpets are worn and the furniture hasn't been changed since Anna's parents lived here in the early 70s. But Pimlico is a good area: no real personality (it can't decide if it's posh/scuzzy/boring) but it's about 15 minutes from Oxford Circus, home of practically every flagship high street fashion brand and tourist hell. My room is very quiet and light, Anna and I enjoy a good flatmate relationship (friendly without being in each other's pockets), and it's très, très cheap. She could actually get more for it, even given the shittiness of the place, but she doesn't seem to care. Most of Anna's time, when she's not away for work, is spent with her boyfriend, who I've never met. I get the feeling she's hoping to move out soon and in with him.

I give the kitchen a quick once-over with a dishcloth, ignore the huge pile of my unopened bank statements on the breadbin, grab my lucky yellow clutch and head out the door to the tube. I would try a skippy-bunny-hop on my way out the door, but I don't think I can manage it today. Sigh.

I swing into the newsagents to buy *Grazia* for a little pick-me-up. As I'm waiting in line, a 20-something guy walks in. He's wearing rugby shorts and a T-shirt with 'I taught that girlfriend that thing you like' written across the front. I lower my gaze behind my sunglasses and check him out. Big strong thighs, good chunky knees like huge walnuts. Mmm, the rugby-playing man. Shame it comes with a predilection for obnoxious T-shirts and 'boys-only' nights out that end with pissing in the street.

Break-Up No.2: Rugger Robbie. He played rugby – obviously – with some of the guys in my newly-arrived uni crowd, and after three months of random snogging, we started going out. Rugger Robbie was a classic Fulham rugby boy: easy-going and actually very sweet. You know the type: intelligent but not introspective, good humoured but not humorous. (Yep, the antithesis to Arty Jonathan.) We mostly hung out in our large group of friends; we were all earning money for the first time in our lives, and life was one long party. (Which was fortunate, as Robbie and I would quickly have run out of conversation at one-to-one dinners.) He shared a horrifically messy flat off Dawes Road with three other rugby guys, and got so shit-faced with the rugby boys every Saturday night that once I met up with him at the Sloaney Pony or Crazy Larry's, I'd have to carry him home practically straightaway and take off his shoes and jeans for him. One time, I woke up to find him pissing on the curtains. 'At least I got out of bed,' he said apologetically the next day. For some reason, this didn't bother me at the time.

I liked Rugger Robbie despite his habit of getting apoplecti-cally drunk because he just seemed so straightforward and familiar after the strange, intimidating pretensions of the East London crowd. And he had a really, really good body. (Ahem.) So I settled into it and decided he was an excellent boyfriend, and was quite content with life. Until, after about three months of properly being together, he said, 'I'm going to Thailand for Christmas. I'll call you when I get back.' And then texted me in mid-January:

I met someone else in Thialand I'm sorry I'll see you around

Dumped via text. With a misspelling. Or typo, to give him the benefit of the doubt.

Sure, it was no great love affair – Rugger Robbie never really made me laugh and frequently responded to things I said with 'you're bonkers'. (I'm so not, but since he had no imagination, I blew his fucking mind.) But I'd grown quite fond of him, so it hurt. That's the thing about being dumped. Even if you don't care about him that much, it still hurts. Because if you don't care much about the dude and you're still dating him, he must not care about you far, far more to actually go to the trouble of dumping you.

I did have boyfriends at university, since you ask, but they hardly count. It was so much easier then. You'd see them in lectures or at parties and get a crush, and know them via their friends so you could weed out freaks, and flirt for ages and then finally snog, and once you snogged three times, boom! You were going out. Then you'd both agree it was over and move on to someone else. It was easy. Not anymore.

Oh fuck me, again. I can't believe it's happened again.

As I walk up towards Victoria station, *Grazia* tucked underneath my arm, I decide to call Bloomie. She gets to work by 7 am every day, because she has a high-flying job. In a bank. (Note: despite high-flying job in aforementioned arsehole industry, Bloomie is not an arsehole.)

'Mushi mushi?'

'You know, Bloomerang, you're not Japanese.'

'You better now, Sassafras, my little drama queen?'

'Dude, I give up. If you pick someone interesting, they're a bastardo and they'll dump you. If you pick someone kind, they'll be boring and, apparently, they'll still dump you. What. The. Fuck.'

'So you are better, darling?'

'*Yes*. I'm *fine*. I'm just fucking over . . . this . . . shit.'

Sometimes when I'm upset I get dramatic. It makes me laugh. And that kind of makes me feel better. Even when I'm lost in Break-Up Memory Lane.

'Sass, darling,' Bloomie whispers. I don't think talking on the phone is really approved of in her office. 'I thought we agreed last night that it was better you stopped toying with Posh Mark? You would have thrown him back into the sea sooner or later.'

Bloomie is one of my best friends, and manages to say 'dahling' at least four or five times a minute. It's not pretentious from her, for some reason. She grew up in Chicago, as her dad's American, but her parents moved to London when she was about 16, so her accent is a bit of a mongrel between East Coast USA and posh London. She's been exactly the same since the first time we met, on the first day of university.

Bloomie is also a total alpha: always leading the way, immensely more self-assured, together and tougher than I am, and sometimes – and she knows this too – rather spiky. But she's utterly lovely and funny, of course. Why else would I be friends with her? And since I'm the kind of person who's quite happy standing on the sidelines smoking fags and making quips rather than leading the pack, we fit together very well. Together with Kate, who I'll tell you more about later, we've seen each other through about 19 boyfriends, 16 holidays together, probably over 250 coffee-and-fags-and-shopping Saturday afternoons, and truly countless hangovers, yet we still don't run out of things to talk about.

'I must be doing something wrong. I've been dumped six times in a row, Bloomie!'

'Darling . . . it's just really, really, really, really fucking bad luck.'

Suddenly the reality of both statements hits me. I really have been dumped six times in a row. And it can't just be bad luck. I must be an absolute loser and no one will ever love me again. (Why would Bloomie say I am a drama queen? I mean really.) So I start to cry, ish. Mostly I snuffle into the phone. Bloomie makes soothing noises for a while, and then she clears her throat and says abruptly:

'Darling, seriously, I have to work. Let's have a drink tonight. We can talk about this properly . . . I'm not being, you know, negative, but I don't want to see you get into a post-Rick spiral . . .'

How could she remind me of that? 'Sheesh, of course I won't. You're on for drinks, though.'

'Good, darling, that's the spirit. I'll ask Katie too, and email with detes later. Sayonara.'

This perks me up, naturally, and I stride, like the Urban Warrior my outfit makes me, to the tube station, with a cheeriness I don't really feel. Despite my heartbreak/ache/mild graze, I can't help but notice a few good-looking men as I walk through and down to the Victoria line. They're all heading towards the District line. I wonder where they go.

Where was I? Ah yes. Now, on Break-Up Memory Lane, we come to a large speedbump.

Break-Up No.3: Clapham Brodie. I met him in the Bread and Roses pub in Clapham just after I turned 25, following a long dry spell during which I had an excellent time and met no one I really fancied. At all. I had lots of flirtations, of course, and still went on a few dates – just to keep my tools sharp. When none of the guys tried particularly hard to keep seeing me after one or two (or three or four) dates, however, it was actually more depressing than if I'd actually liked them, if that makes sense.

18

But I really liked Brodie. Damnit, he was cute, with perfect teeth, like an American. And he really made me laugh.

Clapham Brodie was a product manager, whatever the hell that is, and lived in Clapham. (Clapham is an area in South London that is popular with young people because it's quite affordable, quite safe and quite nice . . . oh God it's boring.) All his friends lived in Clapham, and every restaurant or bar he ever went to was in Clapham. 'I will never leave Clapham,' he said on our first date. 'It is the centre of the universe.' He was full of quips that tickled me, though looking back, I'm not sure he was joking about that.

So. Clapham Brodie. Very funny guy. He kept up a running patter of playful silliness that I adored. We had long, giggly dinners at Metro and the Pepper Tree, where he made up food voices ('don't eat meeeeeeee!' squeaked pasta, 'who are you callin' chicken?' barked stirfry – I know what you're thinking, but it was funny at the time). We danced to 80s music in Café Sol on Fridays and bad dance music in Infernos on Saturdays (if we were drunk enough to consider it), and spent Sundays in the Sun pub, people-watching and making up voice-over conversations for strangers. I found him hilarious, if a tiny bit deluded about his own intelligence (he once corrected my pronunciation of hyperbole, incorrectly). And we never talked about anything serious, ever. I'm not a particularly serious person, so that was fine by me.

After a few months of what I considered to be a rather nice relationship, I heard him refer to me as 'a friend . . . with benefits' when he was talking to his mates in a bar. A cold chill ran over me, but I was too chicken to bring it up that night. (The ol' fear of confrontation strikes again.)

'How do you . . . uh, feel about, us, what's going on with us?' I asked his teddy bear Ivan the next night, as we watched DVDs in his bedroom. (Clapham Brodie liked to chat via the medium of the teddy.) 'I am bear. I feel ggrrrrrrrrrrreat!' growled the toy.

(Ivan was Eastern European.) I glanced at Clapham Brodie. He kept his eyes on the TV. I decided to try again, in a silly way he might respond to. 'Do you think . . . are we . . . you know, officially going steady? Like, swinging hands?' I asked in an American accent that I hoped belied my hopeful tone. Clapham Brodie put the toy down and looked at me. 'I was wondering when this would come up . . .' he said, and promptly dumped me. If I hadn't asked him, he would have let us keep wandering on for months. Friends with benefits infuckingdeed. Bastardo. I was quite upset about Clapham Brodie, I must admit. The ability to be silly is so attractive and rarer than you might think.

Shall I just tell you about Break-Up No.4 quickly? Go on, then. We're nearly done in my Tour O' Heartbreak.

Break-Up No.4: Smart Henry. A bit less than a year after Clapham Brodie, I met Smart Henry at a BBQ in Putney. (People who live in Putney have to bribe you to come and visit them by offering you food.) I was there with Bloomie, who was dating the BBQ host, a man now known as The Hairy Back. Smart Henry was The Hairy Back's cousin. Smart Henry lived in Putney too, in a grubby little terrace. He was very tall and thin and scruffy, and always wore a battered tweed jacket that had belonged to his father, which made him look like a genteel English professor-in-the-making. Smart Henry seemed to have the perfect combination of indie cred (he freelanced for the *NME* and reviewed films and bands for the *Guardian*), genuine braininess (he had a degree from Cambridge) and politeness (he stood up when I approached the table, and always made sure I had a drink), with just enough silliness to surprise and satisfy (he'd frown at me when I teased him and say funny, mock-patronising things like 'you're smarter than you look', or 'that's a spanking for you'). He always called me by my real name – Sarah – rather than Sass, which everyone has always called me, ever since I can remember.

Smart Henry was also older than me – 32 to my 26 – which

was refreshing. Enough of these boys, I thought, I want a man. He was nonchalant about everything, and suggested cool, grown-up things to do – like see arthouse films, or go to new restaurants no one else knew about yet, or art fairs where we'd drink brandy out of his hipflask and make up faux-expert reviews. He was a bit serious and detached, but I put that down to age. I was happy.

Then just less than six months after we met (a record long relationship for me), Smart Henry announced he was moving to the States to go to Harvard for an MBA as he was 'fed up with earning fuck all' and wanted to 'make some serious coin'. So he broke up with me, and I went home and cried.

Was I really devastated? I don't know. Yes. I think I was. But I was tired. I felt like I'd been dating for decades. It seemed like they always really liked me until they got to know me. And each time I met someone new, I tried to be as positive and open and hopeful as I could be. Each time I got so damn fond of them and I'd wonder if I was falling in love. I thought they were having fun. I certainly was. (Though then again, I find it pretty easy to have a good time. It's one of my better qualities.) But each time it went wrong.

Of course, over the years I also met a lot of guys who were almost great, with one fatal flaw. I don't think I'm being too picky, either. Would you date someone who had a horrible snake-tongued kissing technique, or who ate with his mouth open, or talked about money all night, or admitted to an extensive Crocs collection, or who said stupid things like 'Global warming, I'm not sure I believe in it'? ('It's not the tooth fairy,' I replied. "Believing" makes no difference.') Well, I wouldn't. One date was enough. Sometimes I ignored them afterwards, sometimes they ignored me, whatever: a disappointing mistake is a disappointing mistake.

Oh, Smart Henry. I hope you're making some serious coin now. You cockmonkey. If I'd only known what was ahead of me. The next guy was Rick.

21

I can't bear to think about him right now. I just can't. Anyway, I'm almost at work.

I get out of the tube at Piccadilly Circus and start walking up past Burger King to my little corner of Soho. I love it at 9.30 am. The streets are scuzzy, and fresh air mingles with the smell of last night's sin, but the sun is shining in its absent-minded London way, and Soho looks all small and personal. Not big famous naughty Soho. My nice little Soho, with my favourite little hidden coffee shop, where they know what I like without me having to go through the whole 'latte but with a bit less milk slash macchiato but with a bit more milk' thing.

I work in a tiny advertising agency on a little road just near Golden Square, just around the corner from Piccadilly Circus. My first ever boss, Cooper, left the (big, glossy, soulless) ad agency we worked at to start it, and after a few months of witnessing the Machiavellian politics at the big agency, I scurried off to join him. It's a fun job, not a real job like being a doctor or a teacher. But I like it. Anyway that's all I'll say about work for the moment. The only thing more boring than hearing about other people's jobs is hearing about other people's dreams.

Chapter Three

'I had the most bizaaaaaaaaaaarre dream last night!' chirrups Laura as I walk into the office. She's a Mac monkey – that is to say, a very junior designer. Very kooky, very sweet, constantly stunned and excited by everything.

'Really?' I say, turning on my computer and settling at my desk. I sit in the far corner, facing the room, back to the wall, so I can see everything that's going on. If I slouch in my seat, no one can see me from behind my monitor. It's the perfect place to hide on a day like today.

'I dreamed that you were marrying Mark Ronson! Can you imagine? Mark Ronson? Hahahaha! And you were wearing this fabulous fabulous long long dress in a sort of creamy Thai silk, you know, like oh, what's it called, like, uh, oh . . . Hmm. Oh no, that's not it, not Thai silk, I mean the other one. The heavier one but with a shine but not like cheap shine, like, expensive shine?'

'Satin?'

'Yes! And it was sort of gathered here and here, with a big thingy here, and we were in a big church and Coop was there, but he was painting the walls, no, they weren't the walls, they were the puzzle windows, you know? The puzzle see-through windows? With the – the colouredy light, you know?'

'Stained glass?'

'Yes!'

I let Laura's streaming dream commentary ebb and flow around me. Coop isn't in the office this week. He's been in Germany, meeting some old clients to sweet-talk them into being new clients. This is extremely lucky, as I feel vague and distracted all morning. I edit some copy I wrote yesterday, cheer myself up with Go Fug Yourself, and over lunch take a very serious look at topshop.com, shopbop.com and netaporter.com. Soul-cheering retail therapy from the comfort of my desk. I don't buy anything, obviously. Anything purchased the day after a break-up will be forever afflicted with the taint of heartache. And for me, netaporter.com only exists so that I can recognise the designer knock-offs when they hit Zara and H&M.

'Sass, my job needs a quick proof,' says a flat male voice.

Ah, yes I didn't tell you – I'm what they call a copywriter. Theoretically, I help think up advertising, erm, ideas. (If that's not an oxymoron.) We're a tiny agency, which means there's not the usual creative team structure there is in big places, and I do just about everything else to do with words, too: posters and websites and emails and leaflets and all the millions of little things that you read every day that someone has to write. And proofread.

'Now,' the voice adds.

I look up. It's the senior art director. Andy. He's in his late 30s: short, scruffy, with a pot belly and curly, slightly dirty hair. He dresses like many creative hipster hobbit clones: dirty skinny black jeans, battered studded belt, yellow 70s-motif T-shirt with too-short sleeves revealing arms with the muscle tone of a toddler. Most of the time you'll find him spouting predictable counter-culture snob-pinions in a loud mockney voice.

He's also fundamentally sexist and uneducated, which makes him prone to saying things like 'Jane Austen? Mills and Boon in a corset, innit?' which is, obviously, stupid on about ten thousand levels. It's odd, because he thinks he's so daringly creative and maverick – shades of Arty Jonathan – but of course, he's just following a different party line. Lots of art directors, of course, are brilliant and funny and original, like Cooper. But quite a few of them are like Andy. (It goes without saying that I'd never date someone like him, doesn't it? That's probably another reason I spend so much time in bars: I'm never going to meet someone via work.)

'What job?' I say, getting up from my desk and following him. He's already walked away from my desk, knowing I'll follow. Arrogant bastardo.

'Shiny Straight,' he says, sitting down on his chair with a spin and a sigh. He's referring to one of the shampoo brands we work for.

I nod, and look down at the copy on his screen. He can't even be bothered to print it out for me to read properly. It's an A5 ad insert that goes into magazines like *Cosmopolitan* and *Elle*. (Yeah, those annoying leaflets that fall out when you're reading . . . someone has to write them. Sorry.) But I've never seen this ad before.

Reading it briefly, I can quickly see that it's all wrong. The strapline (the big type at the top) is new. The supporting copy (the smaller type below that talks about the product) only uses one of the three key words the client requires us to use. The whole thing sounds weirdly formal, not girly and friendly the way it's meant to. It doesn't even have a clear call to action – that's what we call the line that tells people what to do (like go online to register for a freebie, or use the leaflet as a discount voucher, or whatever). It's just a jumble of lines I've written before, put together all wrong. And there's a punctuation mistake. It's a mess.

(Did I say it's boring hearing about people's jobs? Too bad, dudes. I have the conch. Heh.)

'I've never seen this before,' I say, looking up at him. He shrugs.

'Where is this copy from?' I try again, blushing slightly. I find his obvious contempt hard to deal with. I repeat my mantra:

25

posture is confidence, silence is poise. (It's not a particularly clever mantra, I know, but it stops any nervous babbling when I'm confronted with a difficult situation. And it really does make me stand up straight.)

'I wrote it,' he says breezily. He means he copied and changed things from my previous work, the douchebag. 'And Charlotte approved it.' Charlotte is the account manager. She's in charge of making sure the good people at Shiny Straight are happy with everything we do, and prone to giving me briefs that say things like 'it's bespoke and tailored and personal', not realising these all mean the same thing. She is not responsible for writing. If anyone is responsible for writing in this 12-person agency, it's Cooper, or it's bloody well me. 'Just proof it, Sass. It's not a big deal.'

'Why, um, was that?' I ask, trying to look calm as I stare at the dreadful copy on screen. 'Why didn't you ask me?'

'Last-minute brief. Didn't have time to include you. I've read enough of them to know what to say,' he says. 'Anyway, it's the design that counts. Words are bricks, as they say.'

I glance over at him, my scalp prickling with anger, and see him looking at his design underlings with a smug smile.

'Well, I can't, um, approve it,' I say. My cheeks are burning. 'I can't approve that copy.'

The entire creative department – Andy, his two art directors and a freelance illustrator – is looking over. Laura, who they put over on my side of the room because she's a girl and they love their little boys' club, is staring at me. Even Amanda, our receptionist/Office Manager (she prefers the latter title, always in caps, so I tend to call her Amanda The Office Manager in my head) says 'one moment please!' and puts her caller on hold so she can devote all her attention to what's going on.

I want to tell him that it's crap copy, and words aren't bricks, and he's an arsehole, but I can't. As you know, I hate confrontation. Plus, I think everyone else really likes him, though I have no idea why, so they're all probably laughing at me.

'Well, I'm not staying here all night waiting for you to write the fucking thing. So proof it, or I'll just get Charlotte to.'

'Cooper . . .' I hesitate. I'm sort of friends with Cooper, more than anyone else is anyway, and everyone knows it, so I try to never use him as a pawn in this sort of battle. I wonder if that's why I always lose them.

'Cooper would probably prefer we didn't miss the deadline with the printer. Which is in ten minutes, by the way. So just fucking proof it. Fix the essentials.' He's being openly hostile now.

I take a deep breath. I can feel tears sneaking into my eyes. Why do I cry whenever I'm angry? This is the last thing I need today. It's not that important. I'll just give in. I lean over the computer, fix the punctuation mistake (an errant apostrophe in 'its') and look up at him.

'There. That wasn't so hard, was it?' he smiles. His lips are dry and cracked. And I know if I got within two feet, his breath would smell of coffee and badly-brushed teeth.

I turn around and walk back to my desk. Andy snickers and covers it up with a cough.

Who cares? It's only a stupid ad.

But copy is my job. I could have written the shit out of that. And they should have briefed me.

Ignore it.

Now a crap ad is going out. What if Cooper sees it? What if the client realises how crap it is?

It doesn't matter. At times like this, I really miss Chris, the art director I worked with at the big agency. He was talented *and* nice. Which shouldn't be as unusual a combination as it is.

I hide behind my monitor at my desk as our little room goes back to normal, and get an email from Kate. She can't join us for drinkydinks tonight, so we're catching up tomorrow night instead.

I don't know why I just said drinkydinks. I'm sorry. I'm not quite myself today.

27

Andy leaves me alone for the rest of the day, talking instead to his art minions about Doom, or some other sociopathic computer killing game, and how good he is at it.

I try to work, but my mind keeps wandering. I'm sure that by now, you know what it's wandering back to. Dumped again! Six times. Etc.

OK, let's get it over and done with.

The man I caught shagging a Pink Lady.

Break-Up No.5: Rick. I didn't even really fancy him at first, honestly. We met outside the Westbourne in Notting Hill one sunny Sunday afternoon in late summer two years ago. From that very first meeting, he pursued me with an intensity that was hard to resist. I mean, he *really* pursued me. Sarcastic texts, funny emails, more wordplay than you could shake your innuendo at, flirty flattery . . . As you can imagine, I was a bit of a skittish dater by this stage and tried hard to see the potential bastardo in any man. And I thought he was too slick, too arrogant, too charming, so I tried to stay away from him when I could, and was sarcastic and flip when I couldn't. That seemed to interest him even more. His flat-mate worked with Bloomie, and they were friendly and somehow we seemed to run into him a lot at bars and parties. Loads of women were always after him – I wouldn't call Rick the most handsome man I've ever dated, but he had charisma. And he always made a beeline for me, which was flattering, obviously.

So, after about four or five months of Rick's charm offensive, during the dark, endless depths of January when it's really, really depressing to be cold and single, I said yes to dinner. We met up one Thursday at Notting Hill Brasserie, where the food and wine and ambience combine to make you feel important and happy and interesting, all at once. And we talked till they closed. It was the best first date I'd ever had. He bared his soul, and I bared mine, and I realised that what I'd thought was slick arrogance was just hard-earned confidence (he'd won several scholarships to school and university) and genuine charm. We found each other interesting, and funny, and smart – at least he kept telling me he thought that . . . I now think he was lying, of course. But I thought he was wonderful. We kissed, and sparks went off in my chest. At the end of the night he said, 'I know what you're thinking. You're wondering if I'll call tomorrow. I'll do better than that.' He called me the minute I got home and we talked till I fell asleep. I was smitten. (I mean smote. No, smitten.)

For the first three months, I was in dating heaven. Rick was sharp and witty and worldly and attentive and all those other attractive things that make a girl flexible at the knees. But then, almost overnight, he started to, well, be not quite so nice. He stopped emailing and texting first (an absolute must, and yes I am a feminist, dash it, but all the same), and didn't suggest meeting up as much as he used to – in fact, he would wait for me to gingerly bring up the subject and then say 'let's play it by ear' to see if something (someone?) more exciting came up. He never asked how I was, or what I had planned that week. He'd ignore my call on a Thursday and not return it all weekend while I tried to remain positive and think, 'It's cool! He doesn't have to see me! I love me-time!' and then on Sunday afternoon would text me to come round for, well, not-particularly-interesting hangover sex and a DVD. Which he chose. So it was something like *Sin City*. Or *Death Proof*.

A bastardo, in other words. A Class-A bastardo cockmonkey that I should have ditched the minute he turned sour, like milk. But I didn't. I tried to pretend I was fine and happy, and made excuses to my friends and myself: he's working, he's stressed. I felt him pulling away, dimming the addictive, warming spotlight of his adoration and I couldn't bear it. We'd been perfect! He knew me, I knew him! I spent days and nights racking my brain, thinking how to make him go back to adoring me like he had at the beginning. I analysed every text and email, and hoped and hoped and hoped that everything would go back to being good. Don't look at me like that. You've probably done it too. Everyone has one person they really lost their head over. And he was mine.

Why, you ask? Because I thought he understood me? Because I thought I understood him? Because of my immature, impossibly hopeful disposition? Because all my previous relationships paled in comparison? Because each successive break-up had left my self-esteem in tatters? Or because all my previous disappointments made me determined to hang on to this one potentially perfect happiness if I could?

I don't know. There are a thousand possible reasons. None are really good enough.

And you know what's even worse? Even during those six torturous weeks of him acting like this, we'd meet up once a week or so – me, sick with nerves obviously – and it would be bliss again. He'd apologise, blame work for being too busy to see me, we'd have a bottle of wine and talk and laugh and sparkle and I'd adore him more than I ever had before, despite the days of confidence-eroding worry beforehand. I'd feel totally secure, blissfully happy, utterly content. And it was during one of those nights when I told him I loved him.

I know! Don't look at me like that. Trust me, I know I shouldn't have said it.

I hadn't planned it, it just popped out. It's not the kind of thing I'd ever, ever have said if I'd been in the least bit in control of myself. I'd never said it to anyone else. Maybe I felt so happy and relieved that the sparkly secure feeling was there after a particularly long week with almost no contact from him. Maybe – probably – I subconsciously thought I'd prompt him to say he loved me too, and we'd go back to being sparkly all of the time. Who knows? The female brain is an annoyingly mysterious thing. Even to us. At the time I thought I meant it, by the way, but I realised pretty soon it wasn't love . . . it was more like addiction.

And no, of course he didn't say it back. He just smiled, and kissed me. (We were in his kitchen cooking spaghetti bolognese, which I hate but every boyfriend I've ever had thinks he can cook better than anyone in the world.) In a split second I realised he wasn't going to say it back, because he didn't love me, and never had. I wanted to run away and cry, but instead I poured another glass of wine and kept smiling. It doesn't matter. Everything will be fine. Just hang in there and be positive and show him what a good girlfriend you are.

And the next night was the 'Come As Your Childhood Ambition' party.

For weeks – months – afterwards, I kept getting hammered and crying. I honestly felt like I should look like a human raisin, I cried so much. I turned 28 just two weeks after he dumped me. That birthday was a real low point. Bloomie organised a dinner for me and I had to keep a tissue folded in my palm to mop up the tears that just burst from my face, even when I didn't think I was crying. I then got as drunk as I could, threw up, and had to be taken home by 10 pm. God, that was a pathetic period of my life. I hate that me. I fucking hate her. After every other break-up I'd bounced back pretty fast, with the help of the magic trifecta of friends, clothes and vodka, ready to head out and have some fun again. But not this time. Recovering from Rick was like recovering from a debilitating illness. I needed liquids (vodka), darkened rooms (bars) and rest (vodka-induced comas).

I don't even know why Rick affected me like that. He just did. It was – oh God, it was a car crash.

In comparison, the Posh Mark break-up was like skinning my knee.

Rick never called me to apologise, by the way. In fact, we didn't even have the excruciating/satisfying/sad ritual of giving each other's things back. His flatmate gave Bloomie my eye make-up remover and various underthings I'd left at his house. (He had left nothing at mine. He'd refused to stay over after a few token efforts at the beginning. Another bastardo sign, by the way. The home game advantage is huge.)

I'm really not a victim, though you probably think I'm an absolute basket case after everything I've told you. You know, I secretly wonder – and sorry for using you as a shrink, but I can't afford a real one – if, after six months of rampant partying post-Rick misery, I actually went out with Posh Mark not because he was nice and wouldn't dump me, but because I expected it to fail. At least if I didn't like him that much, it wouldn't hurt. Hmm. Bloomie calls those kinds of relationships 'emotional blotting paper': they prop you up after a relationship Hiroshima until you get enough time and perspective to recover and start thinking about dating someone you actually like. And waking up wrapped up in nicely-muscled arms is better than waking up alone. Sort of.

Oh fuck me, I can't imagine doing it again. Or rather, I can imagine it, but I just can't face it. It's so depressing to think about. So many mistakes. And I don't want to go through it all again. Meeting someone, liking them, going out with them for dinner, waiting to see if they'll call again . . . it's exhausting, and it never works out for me. I'm obviously romantically-challenged. I just . . . I want out of this game, I really do.

Chapter Four

At 5.30 pm, I leave work as quickly and quietly as I can – noting on the way out that today's Urban Warrior sartorial theme clearly failed miserably and I should rechristen it Andy's Urban Victim – to head down to meet Bloomie in a bar about ten minutes' from South Kensington tube station. I'd like to get a black cab, but can't quite justify it. (I spend an inordinate amount of time justifying the expense of black cabs to myself. My two go-to excuses are that it's late so the tube could be dangerous – which it never really is within Zone Two – or that I'm wearing very high heels.)

On the number 14 bus on the way down the Fulham Road, I try to talk myself into being in a good mood. Despite the universe throwing every happy loved-up person in London in my path tonight (how can they all find love and not me? How can the drab little beige thing in front of me be calling her boyfriend to say she'll put dinner on for when he gets home? Why, damn it, why am I unable to achieve that?), it's not actually that hard. I'm cheery by nature, I love after-work drinks, I love Bloomie and I love the place where we're meeting. It's a restaurant called Sophie's Steakhouse, but we only ever go to the bar part. It's not quite a pick-up joint, but not all couples; not too rowdy, but not too quiet; not too cool and not too boring. In short, it's the perfect place for the freshly single.

I push past the heavy curtain inside the front door, and see the usual young, rather good-looking West London crowd. There are some gorgeous men in here, as ever, though I know they're probably a bit rah-and-Rugger-Robbie for me. A few floppy-haired Chelsea types in red corduroy trousers (where do they sell those things and how can we make them stop?), a couple of older business-type guys waiting alone in suits for wives or girlfriends, and I can sense, but not see, a group of five guys having an early dinner in the restaurant part, as they turn around to look at me as I come in. I know it's only because, well, I'm female, but still. It's gratifying. Especially today.

Bloomie is, as usual, about half an hour late, so I kill time reading the fun bits of the paper someone else has left behind (you know, the celebrity bits, and the movie and book reviews). As soon as she arrives we start as we always do: with a double cheek kiss and a double vodka.

Things move swiftly from there. I don't want to get hammered tonight as it's only Wednesday and payday isn't for another ten days, but quite soon we start going outside for cigarettes (neither of us smokes, except in situations of extreme stress, like last night, or drinking, or, um, gossiping on a Saturday, or sometimes on the phone), which is a sure-fire sign we're here for the long haul.

Before I know it, I'm slapping the table with one hand to emphasise my point (which point? Who can say? Any point! Pick a point, please) and making dramatic absolute statements that start with 'I will NEVER' and 'There is no WAY'.

From drink one to two we talk about Posh Mark, from drink two to three we talk about Eugene (the extremely lovely guy she's been dating for a few months. She calls him The Dork because who the sweet hell is called Eugene?), with a quick side-wind into talking about Bloomie's recently-redundant-and-leaving-soon-to-travel-the-world flatmate Sara, from three to four we talk about the state of the economy. (Just kidding! We talk about Posh Mark and Eugene again. Obviously.) And then drink five hits.

And the thoughts that have been percolating in my brain all day tumble out.

'Bloomie. Bloomster. Listen to me. I can't do it again. I can't do it again.'

'What? Drink?' Bloomie is writing The Dork a text, with one eye closed to help her focus.

'No – I mean, yes, I'll have another drink . . . um, yes, a double, please. I can't . . . I can't date anymore, I can't do it, I'm useless at it and I can't do it.' I'm hitting the table so hard to emphasise every point that my hand starts tingling.

'Get a grip, princess.'

'Seven years of this shit, Blooms. Six failed relationships. I don't want to do it anymore. I just want it all to go away.'

'It's seven years of bad luck, that's all. Wait!' Bloomie throws up her hands melodramatically. 'Did you break a mirror when you were 21?'

'I mean it . . . I can't do it again. The whole dating thing is fucked. You see someone for ten minutes in a bar and they chat you up and ask you out, and boom! You're dating, but how can you possibly know if they're really right for you?'

'Well, you hope for the best,' shrugs Bloomie, with all the confidence of someone in a happy relationship.

'No. I can't bear it . . . The nausea, the hope, the waiting for him to call, the nausea, and on the rare occasions that everything is really good and he likes me and I like him, the nausea of waiting for him to dump me. As he will, because he always does, no matter who the fuck he is. I've done it too many times, and I look back on them all and feel so angry at myself for dating them in the first place . . . And have I mentioned the nausea?'

Bloomie looks at me and frowns.

'Is this really about Rick? Because I swear to God, that guy was . . .'

'No,' I interrupt quickly. 'Of course it is not. I am over him. I really think, I mean I know, I know I am over him.'

'OK . . .' she says doubtfully. 'Why don't you just concentrate on work for a few months and not worry about it? That's what I did after Facebook guy and it was the best thing I could have done. And after Bumface. And The Hairy Back.' These are her ex-boyfriends. She pauses. 'I always concentrate on work, actually.' She starts to laugh. 'Imagine if I hadn't had such a shit lovelife! I'd never have had any promotions.'

I look at her and sigh. I've never had a promotion.

'I am a failure at my job, Bloomie. Today was . . .' I close my eyes. I can't bear to think about work. I've told Bloomie about my inability to deal with Andy before, and she suggested ways to handle it, but I'm just not able to tackle things like she does. (I believe the technical term is 'head on'.) 'It's nothing, it's not worth even discussing. I should just quit my job. I'm so bad at it. I'm a failure! At everything!' Oh, there goes the drama queen again. Sashaying away.

'Hey. Come on. You're great at your job,' she says loyally, reaching a tipsy hand out for my shoulder. 'Though I wish you'd be as ballsy with them as you are with us.'

I raise a doubtful eyebrow at her. 'Being ballsy with my best friends isn't exactly hard. It's the rest of the world that's difficult.'

'I had a bad day too,' says Bloomie supportively. 'You know, this is the first time I've left work before 8 pm in a month. I hate it.'

She so doesn't hate working late, but I'll leave that. 'Really? Are you OK? What's happening?' I take a sip of my drink. I'm hungry, but the drinks here are expensive, and dinner will have to wait till I get home.

'Don't you read the papers, darling?' she says, laughing. I notice, for the first time, the bags beneath her eyes, and that her nails are uncharacteristically bitten. 'It's more that nothing good is happening . . . I just need to keep my head down and not lose my job.'

'Oh, um . . . yes,' I say, stirring my drink. When it comes to the world of finance, I'm clueless. Have the banks started collapsing again? I always picture them tumbling down piece by piece. 'I'm sure you won't lose your job, Blooms.'

'Yeah, yeah, it'll be fine,' Bloomie says, making a batting-away motion with her hand. 'And The Dork is an excellent distraction. That's what you need. You need a Dork to distract you.'

'No,' I say, and sigh deeply. 'I can't make the right choices no matter what I do . . . It will never work out for me. Never. And I don't want to try anymore.'

'I know you,' says Bloomie, laughing. 'You say that now, but tomorrow you'll see some hot dude in a bar and think, yes, please.'

'Exactly! I even walked in here tonight checking the guys out and wondering which of them might ask me out. I really do think like that, and I've been single for less than 24 hours. What the hell is wrong with me? I'm in a vicious circle where my life revolves around dating, but dating is bad for my life. It's called an addiction!'

'No, it's not. It's called being a single in your 20s.'

'Well, I'm over it,' I say. 'I'm sick and tired and fed up with the whole fucking thing. As God is my witness, I am not dating anymore.'

'You're not religious, Scarlett O'Hara,' says Bloomie, poking her ice with her straw. 'You're not even christened.'

'OK then, as Bloomie is my witness . . .' I pause for a second, and slam both my hands down on the table so hard that the bartenders look over in alarm. 'Yes! Yes! I will officially cease and desist from dating and everything to do with it from this moment forth. No more dating, no more dumpings. Officially. For real.'

'No men?'

'No men.'

'No sex?'

'No sex.'

'No flirting?'

I pause for a second. 'No obvious flirting. But I can still talk to guys . . .'

'You need to draw up a no-dating contract, then.'

'Do it,' I say, taking out a cigarette and perching it in my mouth expectantly. 'I'm cleansing my life of men. It's a total testosterone detox. A dating detox. Shall we call it Dating Rehab?'

Bloomie snorts with laughter. 'No let's make it happier than that. We'll call it the Love Holiday!' says Bloomie happily, looking through her bag for a pen.

'Love Holiday? That sounds like a Cliff Richard movie. No, it's a . . . it's a Sabbatical. A Dating Sabbatical.'

'What if you meet the man o' your dreams?'

I roll my eyes. 'Come on. What are the odds of that?'

Bloomie cackles with laughter. 'When will you know it's over?'

'Six months. That's the average Sabbatical, right?'

'Dude, seriously. That's a long time to ignore real life, even for you.'

'That's the point . . . OK, three months,' I grin.

'Right, I need some paper. I'll ask the bartender. Another drink?'

As Bloomie heads towards the bar, I gaze around, looking in delight at all the men I won't be dating. I feel deeply relieved to have the whole issue taken away. I can't believe I never thought of this before! I am brilliant! High-fives to me!

Chapter Five

The next morning I wake up with a predictably dry and foul-tasting mouth. I open one eye, noting thoughtfully the crusty-eyelash sensation that means I demaquillaged imperfectly, and discover a piece of paper on my right breast. Naturally, dear reader, you're one step ahead of me – I'd expect nothing less – and you know already that this piece of paper will be the list that I remember reading (with one eye shut, due to mild vodka-induced double-vision) as I went to sleep last night.

THE DATING SABBATICAL RULES
1. No accepting dates.
2. No asking men out on dates.
3. Obvious flirting is not allowed.
4. Avoid talking about the Sabbatical.
5. Talking about the Sabbatical is permitted in response to being asked out on a date. Until then it would just intrigue them and be another form of flirting and in fact be taken as a challenge.
6. No accidental dating, ie, pretending you didn't arrange to meet them just for a movie or something when you blatantly did.
7. No new man friends. It is just as confusing. And it would open up opportunities for non-date-dates, ie,

new-friend-dates, which are just the same as dates, when you get down to it.

8. Kissing is forbidden. Except under extreme circumstances, ie, male model slash comic genius is about to ship off to sea to save the world and as you say goodbye he starts to cry and says he never knew true love's kiss.

9. Actually, if you meet a male model slash comic genius who is about to save the world, you can sleep with him. Otherwise keep your ladygarden free of visitors as it will complicate matters. None. At all.

10. No bastardos.

I signed it and Bloomie signed it. Our signatures have, unsurprisingly, slightly more flair than usual. In fact, I've added an 'Esq' to mine. Hmm.

What the hell is a ladygarden?

Shampoo, condition, fuck shaving the armpits, brush teeth extra thoroughly, no one will see my legs, to hell with exfoliating, towel, where the fuck is the moisturiser, who cares, deodorant, perfume. My sartorial motivation today is comfort. So I turn to some very old Levi 501s, a soothing, eight-year-old grey T-shirt I call Ol' Grey, a brown cardigan, woolly socks and Converses. I look like a Smashing Pumpkins fan. A male one. In 1992. This isn't working. Normally, when I doubt my outfit, I give myself the 'if I think it works, it works' speech, but I can't make this one fly.

I take everything off and think for a moment. What else is comforting? Living in the 70s would be comforting, I think. No email or mobiles, you could smoke everywhere, and use a typewriter. How simple. So I put on some very flared blue jeans, a ribbed white top, my Converses again, pull my damp hair into a side plait, lace a mildly retro silk (polyester, whatever) scarf from H&M through the belt loops and tie in a side knot, and consider myself again. Ah yes. Vaguely Co-Ed 1972.

This will do fine. Thank fuck I work in advertising and can wear anything I want; if I had to put on a suit right now I'd slash my wrists . . . Make-up . . . hmm. My eyebrows are being blatantly annoying, and I don't have the patience to deal with them today. Lots of mascara, some bronzer and blush to fake good health, lipbalm. I add a beige checked men's coat I bought in a charity shop and voilà. Slightly watery-eyed, but not bad. I check my watch. It's taken me twice as long to get ready today as yesterday. This is the reason that I don't drink. (Much.)

On the tube on the way to work I ponder the Dating Sabbatical. Obviously, it's kind of a silly idea. But also so easy. An easy way to put off dealing with being back in the singles game.

I could go on a Dating Sabbatical and nurse my afore-mentioned bruised heart – OK, OK, so it isn't bruised and I didn't really give Posh Mark much thought at all yesterday. (Jeez, you're a tough crowd.) But my heart is very shy right now and it doesn't feel like coming out to play for awhile. It would rather eat chocolate in the bath and read Jilly Cooper's *Polo*.

I open my lucky yellow clutch to take out the Dating Sabbatical Rules for a quick review, and pull out a bunch of receipts from drinks last night adding up to over £60. Yikes. I mentally add this to the spreadsheet I keep in my head of incomings and outgoings. (No, it's not a foolproof way to plan my finances, but it works for me. Ish. Since I don't earn much money, I have to make some sacrifices to spend as much as I like on what I consider essentials, like clothes and vodka and black cabs. So I don't belong to a gym, never get my hair done, and spend almost nothing on things like, you know, food. I eat a lot of baked beans, tinned tuna, bananas and toast.)

I get to work, the perfect coffee in hand, and email Bloomie: *Duuuuuude. I'm still in.*

She replies:

Ha, really? Fine. You can test it tomorrow night at Mitch's party.
I reply:
Roger that.

I hide behind my computer all day. Andy doesn't look at me once, and though I'm meant to talk to him about a new brief, I decide to send him an email about it when he's out at lunch. I just can't face him today.

I'm meeting up with Kate for dinner. She's the third in our trifecta from university, but is slightly more absent from our social lives over the last year or so as she's in a ridiculously stable long-term relationship. We meet near her work in Mayfair at The Only Running Footman, a pseudo-rustic pub. It's packed with finance-type people drinking away their worries but we find a seat in the restaurant bit downstairs. I notice quite a few very good-looking men here. Shame I'm on a Dating Sabbatical and not looking, I remind myself.

Over burgers and beers I explain the theory of the Dating Sabbatical to Kate. She nods very seriously and poses relevant and poignant questions, all of which I answer with what's becoming rather slick aplomb, till—

'Alright, Sass. This all seems like a very *you* thing to do. But what if you meet someone you actually want to go out with?'

I pause, chip in the air.

'How do you mean?'

'What if you . . . you know, you meet someone you really, really fancy and want to go out with?'

'A guy? That I fancy? And want to go out with?'

I'm flummoxed. This idea hadn't even occurred to me. I haven't met someone I *really* wanted to date in years. I just sort of do it as it seems like something to do. And if they've gone to the trouble of asking, unless I find them ugly or sleazy or loserish or I'm positive they're a bastardo, then I think I should say yes, and then just see what happens. (Though this approach, as history shows, hasn't really worked out.) But I can't exactly tell Kate that. It sounds stupid.

'Hmm . . . well . . . I guess I never *want* to go out with anyone till he asks me out. I might think someone across the bar is hot, or whatever, but I just don't think about it much more than that till he's made the first move. Why waste the energy?'

'That seems kind of . . . reactive,' says Kate carefully, dunking a chip in the huge dollop of English mustard at the side of her plate. It's really weird how much she likes English mustard.

A little more about Kate: very pretty, very short and thus kind of adorable. Probably my sweetest friend. She and Bloomie and I have been close friends since about day one of university, when we met in halls, got hammered together on cider and discovered a shared love of Jeff Buckley (yep, such clichés). She grew up in a little town in Cambridgeshire, going to Brownies and riding horses, and still has that milk-fed prettiness such girls always get. Boys always loved her. Men love short women, have you ever noticed? I'm on the tall side, by the way. And I've never had a boyfriend tall enough to wear three-inch heels with. (Does my dating agony ever end, I ask you?) Sorry, back to Kate. She's an accountant, though I don't really know why, as she read Italian and French at university. She even spent a year in Florence. She's always been a bit of a control freak, the person who makes plans weeks in advance and panics when things change unexpectedly. Perhaps that's what accountants are like.

Kate lives with her boyfriend, a guy called Tray. Bloomie and I referred to him as Tray Nice when we first met him, then Tray Serious. Now it's Tray Boring. He's perfectly nice, but brings nothing to the conversational table. It's not that I don't like talking to him, exactly. It's just that I like talking to everybody else a lot more. I guess they must have some crazy connection to make Kate stay with him for three years. As my dad always says, no one sees the game like the players. (He is a bottomless well of sporting/relationship analogies.) She seems pretty happy these days – a bit quieter and less prone to silliness than she used to be, and we don't see her as much as we used to, but happy.

'Did you like Tray before he asked you out?'

Kate squints in thought. 'I don't know . . . I just thought he seemed very intelligent and sort of . . . kind. Kind and interesting to talk to. And I'd decided I wanted that in my next boyfriend. Yeah, I guess I did like him first.'

'And sexual chemistry?'

'Oh, yes, yes, all that too,' says Kate quickly. 'And you know, I really was intent on having someone kind. I'd met so many, uh . . . bastardos. Remember Dick the Prick? And The Missing Link?'

I start laughing. Dick the Prick was a guy she met when she first moved to London, but he cheated on her and she dumped him. The Missing Link wasn't awful, but he wasn't particularly nice either. He was thick and pretty.

'So after all your bastardos you decided to proactively find a clever non-bastardo?'

'Uh . . . yes.'

'That's just like me and . . .' I pause for a second to remember his name '. . . Posh Mark! He was kind!'

And thick, I add silently. Fuck me, I'm callous.

'Yes, but I'm not sure how well suited you and Posh Mark ever were. Tray and I have a lot in common. I enjoy his company. He's very intelligent,' she adds. Again.

Hmm. She sounds a little Stepford Wife-y and she's not meeting my eye, but I decide to agree with her.

'You're right. Lucky you, darling. So important to have someone kind and intelligent.'

There might be something wrong here, but I'm not going to push it. Kate doesn't talk about her feelings unless she wants to. She has that nice reserved thing going on; not in a cold way – she'd do anything for any of us. I think it's shyness. You never know if she's really great or utterly miserable until she wants you to. I wish I wasn't such an open book. My mother can read my mood by how many rings it takes me to answer the phone.

'How are you feeling about Posh Mark, anyway, Sass?' says Kate. I rang her on Tuesday night and bawled, embarrassingly.

'Oh, fine,' I say truthfully. 'He was, you know, a life raft. Better than drowning in a sea of self-pity and vodka.'

'Nicely put,' grins Kate. 'So where's off the list now?'

'Eight Over Eight, because that was our first date place,' I say, taking a thoughtful bite of my burger. 'And Julie's, because we used to go there for brunch when we stayed at his place.'

'Are there any brunch places near your place that aren't tainted by ex-boyfriends by now?' Kate says, laughing. She professes to not understand why I refuse to go back somewhere that reminds me of someone who dumped me. Especially as the list is getting slightly ridiculous.

'None,' I reply honestly. 'Pimlico is one big no-go zone for me these days. I may have to move.'

We move on to gossiping about people we know, and talk about the party at Mitch's place tomorrow night. The guestlist seems to be snowballing, with lots of people I haven't seen in ages. Yay. I siphon off the back part of my brain and leave it to go through my wardrobe and plan an outfit. We finish our burgers, pay the bill and decide to go outside to finish our beers with a fag.

'God, I miss smoking,' sighs Kate.

'Mwhy mdya qvit?' I say, talking with my cigarette in my mouth as I light hers. So classy.

She takes a drag and exhales happily. 'Tray hates it, and he IS right. It does kill you.'

'Yes, he is right. It does.'

There seems nothing more to say. See? Even saying his name halts conversation.

'How's the world of accounting?' I ask.

'Scintillating,' says Kate crisply. 'At least I'll never be out of a job, no matter what happens to the economy.'

'Why?'

'Accountants are always needed. We're like prostitutes. One of the world's oldest professions.'

This, from Kate, is outrageous. She's in a funny mood tonight. Funny odd, not funny haha.

'Oh well, that's good,' I say, starting to laugh. 'What are you doing on Sunday? I've probably got the flat to myself all weekend as usual, so we could have an all-day movie fest. We'll start with *Sixteen Candles*, then *Overboard*' – did I mention I have a thing for Goldie Hawn? I totally do – 'then *Dirty Dancing*, then *Pretty Woman*, then *13 Going On 30*. Holy shit, that film makes me cry.'

'*13 Going on 30* makes you CRY?'

'Yes. Whenever Jennifer Garner cries I lose it. I don't know what it is. I saw her cry on *Alias* once, and I had only just flicked over from another channel, so I had no idea what was going on, and I cried my arse off . . . though we could sub in *Old School* and end on a high. Marvellous film.'

'Marvellous,' agrees Kate happily. 'Don't you feel, though, that chick flicks are all the same?'

I splutter in mock outrage.

'The SAME?'

'Yah, you know . . . the same. They all kind of suck.'

'So? Christmas kind of sucks and is always the same, too. Do you hate Christmas?'

Kate starts to laugh. 'No . . .'

'Actually, chick flicks DON'T suck. In fact, Katiepoo, the chick flick is a formula designed to satisfy, but always with small subtle variations. The girl is somehow identifiable. The guy is somehow unattainable.' I start to warm to my argument. 'There is fashion. There is a dancing scene. There is some kind of klutzy friend, though sometimes the heroine is a klutz too. Then somewhere along the line, there is a fear that he's messed up forever and has to prove himself to her to win her love.'

Kate nods. 'Yah. I picked the plot up. When I was six.'

'In fact, forget Christmas. Chick flicks are like all my favourite things in life – burgers! Really high heels! Weekends in New York! Sexual encounters! Every single one is different, but has the same essential components and is – hopefully – equally pleasing!'

We both laugh. OK, we cackle. The two-beer buzz is delightful.

'Uh . . . ladies. May I trouble you for a lighter?'

Deep voice. American. Male. Late 20s. I glance at Kate's face, but she's staring at Mr America behind me. I turn around, getting out my lighter at the same time.

'Sure,' I hand it over and he grins and lights his cigarette. Extremely cute, in a jock kind of way. Baggy pale blue jeans, Ralph Lauren Polo T-shirt, short floppy American-banker haircut. He must be fresh off the boat. American men wear very bad jeans till they realise every other man in London wears his jeans darker and tighter. Then they all buy Diesel jeans. (They never change their hair.)

'Thanks,' he leans back and exhales, a small smirk on his face. 'So you like chick flicks as much as sex, seriously?'

'It's awfully rude to eavesdrop.'

Kate's phone rings. 'It's Tray – back in a sec . . .'

Hmm, I have to wait for Kate and talk to Mr America. I could wait inside, if I was going to be really strict about this not dating men thing . . . But he's so cute. Preppy, Ivy League and cute. Damn it, come on Sass, I chide myself. I should not be noticing this shit. I decide to finish my fag and put the Dating Sabbatical to the test. I run over my mantra in my head, more out of habit than need. After all, I'm not able to date him, so there's no need to feel nervous. But he is kind of good looking.

'Personally, I can get behind any John Hughes movie, so I'm with you on *Sixteen Candles*. But I'm not sure about *Overboard*.'

I look back at him like I'm surprised he's still there. (Am I breaking Rule 3? Obvious flirting? Nah, this isn't obvious yet.)

'I heart Goldie Hawn. She's brilliant.'

'Sure, but give me *Private Benjamin* any day.'

'Oh, I love that film! "Go check out the bathroom, it's FABULOUS!"'

Mr America laughs. 'Yeah, I can see that you'd like that line.'

I grin, and our eyes meet. He's very confident. Sexual frisson, bonjour.

'So . . . I loved your little speech there.'

'The chick flick speech? I was just being silly . . .'

'I like silly.'

Why can American men say lines like that and get away with it? It must be the accent. This one's particularly cocky. It's terribly attractive. However, I never know what to say back when someone's coming on to me so openly, so I just smile and take a drag of my cigarette.

'Could I get your number . . . perhaps we could have dinner sometime?'

I pause and smile. Shit. Time to put the Dating Sabbatical into action.

'I know a lot of movies. I could quote 'em to you all night.' He grins. Perfect teeth. Another attractive American trait.

'I'd love to, but I'm not dating right now.' (There, that was easy. Rule 1: no accepting dates, and Rule 5: talking about the Sabbatical is permitted in response to being asked out on a date.)

'I don't get it. You've got a boyfriend?'

'No, I don't. I'm just – I'm not seeing anyone at the moment.'

'Did someone just break your heart?'

I laugh. 'No! I've just . . . I'm . . . I'm not dating right now. I'm taking a break from uh, seeing guys.'

'You're gay?' His tone is disbelieving.

'No.'

'You're just . . . not dating.'

'Yup.'

'For how long?'

'Three months,' I say airily. 'Possibly, probably, longer.' I don't want him to think he can line up a date for three months' time. Especially since I'd probably say yes. Saying no to this date is hard enough as it is. (See? Dating IS an addiction. Thank betsy I'm detoxing. Every time I say no, it will get easier. Just say no.)

'That's, like, pathetic. Some guy must have really done a number on you.'

This riles me. 'Oh, please. I'm just not dating right now.'

'Hey! I'm not going to fight with ya about it!' He stubs out his cigarette and throws two finger guns at me. 'Your loss.'

He storms back into the bar just as Kate comes back. 'That was Tray . . . I've gotta go home. What the hell happened there?'

'Rejection,' I say happily. 'My first Dating Sabbatical rejection in action. His response was "YOUR LOSS".' I imitate the finger guns, adding a 'peeyong' shooting sound for good measure. Kate and I collapse with laughter and head down towards the tube.

Chapter Six

Right. The morning routine. I snooze till a delightful 8.25 am, and then take a long lazy shower with no shampoo or conditioner as I want fresh hair for Mitch's party tonight and a double-wash makes my hair flop like it's pre-product-1972, brush teeth, scrub with exfoliating gloves and body wash, shave pits and legs, blah-blah, you know the rest already.

Today Outer Self is channelling Tough Nu Wave Cookie, so I throw on pointy blue shoes, skinny white jeans, a sleeveless black turtleneck and a black blazer. As I pop up the collar of the blazer and roll up my sleeves, I wonder if I look a bit odd and decide not to think about it. I realised a few months ago that I really haven't changed my fundamental approach to dressing since I was 13. I pick a theme and keep adding things till I get there. (Favourite outfit when I was 13: DMs, black opaque tights, jeans shorts, a black belt with a peace sign buckle, a white T-shirt and a black blazer. Would definitely wear the same outfit now, minus perhaps the peace sign belt.) Brush hair vigorously to make the day-old grease look like shiny newness and throw it into a dishevelled chignon thing. Win the daily Battle Of The Brow. Inner Self is thus ready to face day two of Dating Sabbatical. I grab my lucky yellow clutch and run downstairs.

As I head into the kitchen(ette) to grab a banana and a tin of tuna, I see Anna curled up with her duvet on one of the 60s settees.

'Morning Anna!' I call. She moans in reply and I look back around at her. 'Are you OK?'

She raises her head and I see her eyes. They're all swollen and pink like a newborn puppy. Yikes.

'Don and I broke up,' she says, reaching for a box of tissues hidden somewhere in the duvet.

'Oh . . . dear . . .' I say, and come over to perch on the side of the settee. His name is Don? No one has been called Don since 1955. 'Is there anything I can do?'

'No, no, I'll be fine,' she says, snuffling into a tissue. She looks up at me dramatically. 'He has a wife, you know. I'm not sure if she's the separated kind.'

Double yikes. Even I wouldn't get into that situation. I look at Anna whimpering on the couch. She's very pretty, about 30 or so, one of those tall girls with long brown hair and long elegant arms. I swear my upper arms are abnormally short. Anyway, back to Anna. I don't know what to say to make her feel better. 'That's not . . . um . . . good.'

'I'm just so tired of it,' she sighs, blowing her nose. 'The reason I went for that prick was that I was tired of game-playing single guys. He said he was unhappy and separated, and I thought that he'd be perfect for me, or else I wouldn't have done it, I'm not that kind of person . . . and then last night he told me they were going to try to work things out . . . And none of my friends understand, they're all in long-term relationships or married . . .' Oh Jeez. Anna and I aren't close enough to have this conversation.

'Um, oh . . .' I say. 'You'll be fine, Anna. Have a nice hot shower and get dressed and you'll feel better.'

She shakes her head, staring blankly into space. I can see she's having conversations in her head. Unhappy ones. I try again. 'You really will, Anna . . . I know how hard it is. I've been dumped six times in a row.'

'Really?' she says, looking over at me with new interest. 'How the hell have you survived?'

'Um . . . I just sort of kept going and hoped for the best, I guess. And well, right now, I'm officially not dating. I'm on a Dating Sabbatical. I can't make the right decisions, so I'm not making any at all. I can't date men, accidentally or on purpose, for three months.' I pause. 'Like a nun.'

'I love that idea,' she says. 'It's the only way. Nothing else works. Nothing. You can try as hard as you like to be careful and you'll still fuck up. I had my first boyfriend 18 years ago. I'm so tired of it all . . .'

'Exactly,' I nod. This is kind of sweet, we've never had a conversation like this. 'I should leave for work, Anna . . . are you OK? Do you have plans tonight? My friend Mitch is having a party if you'd like to come . . .'

'Oh, thanks, but I'm heading up to Edinburgh to see my mum,' she says, pulling herself up into a sitting position. 'I'd better get up too. The good people at Unilever won't survive without me.'

I wonder what she does. I should probably know. 'OK, well, have fun,' I say. I lean over and give her an awkward hug. Her face smushes into my collarbone. Sigh. Bad hugs suck. 'Hope you feel better soon.'

'Thanks,' she says, getting up off the couch. 'Maybe I should try my own Dating Sabbatical.'

I turn to smile at her as I head out the door. 'Maybe you should!'

On the way to work I reflect on last night's loss of my Dating Sabbatical virginity. Mr America had been confident, cute and funny. Just the kind of guy I always like. He'd also revealed himself to be an utter brat with a bit of a bad temper. Without question a cockmonkey, a bastardo classico.

If I'd agreed to go out to dinner with him, I would have been charmed by the good looks, impressed by the confidence, seduced by the banter – and dumped in a few months when he got tired of me. I know it, because that's what has happened every time before.

Well done me. I can handle the Dating Sabbatical. In fact, I can *thrive* on it.

I feel terribly happy all of a sudden. Strong and happy. I skippy-bunny-hop a couple of steps, and high-five myself. No, I really do. (A self-high-five involves jumping in the air and clapping your hands together, with the back of one hand facing you and the other coming up to clap it from below. It looks funny, but it feels great. I highly recommend you try it.) A guy walking by flinches instinctively as though I was going to hit him and I get the giggles. Day Two of the Dating Sabbatical is going to be good.

I get to work with my tailored-to-my-personal-tastes coffee, and, seeing that Andy isn't in yet, sing 'Gooooooood morning!' as I reach my seat. Laura looks up and narrows her eyes.

'You look soooooo different today! What is it? Oh, oh, oh, I meant to tell you – though how could I have told you before when I didn't see you! And last night I left work and I thought I saw you! Only it wasn't you. And it looked just like you and I was thinking, what is she doing in Hackney? Because obviously you live in Putney!'

'Pimlico?' I say. 'So . . . what do you need to tell me?'

'Oh! Yes! Coop wants you. In his office, well, it's not an office, but you know, at his desk. Because he's here.'

'Thank you, Laura,' thunders Coop from the other side of the Chinese silk screen that separates his desk from us. It's silly, really, as he can hear everything.

I walk around it and sit down with a cheery morning face that I'm pretty sure will annoy him. Coop was very good looking back in the 80s, I think. He had a moderately successful New Wave pop group. Then, the 90s saw him partying hard with Oasis and Blur (well, perhaps not with them per se, but certainly near them), which aged him and made him look a bit craggy and bloaty. He got into advertising at about that time too. These days he's in love with a German woman called Marlena, a former model and fledgling jewellery designer, who eats, lives and breathes organic and forces him to do the same, so he's the picture of mildly irritable health.

Coop's habitual manner is distracted and grumpy, but the minute he actually concentrates on anything he's rather fun to be around. I think it's because creating ads is one of the only things he really enjoys. And he seems to think I'm good at my job, which is always nice, and I think as a result I'm more confident around him than I am with anyone else at work. (As one of my primary school teachers wrote in an end of term report once: 'She responds well to praise and approval.' Heh.) And over the years he's been lovely every time I come in crying about a break-up, though he always pretends he can't remember anything about it afterwards.

'You. Wordgirl. Explain what the hell has been going on here with these scamps.'

When he says scamps, by the way, he doesn't mean lovable little rascals; he means creative ideas. I sit down next to him and talk him through the scamps. As I do, I hear Andy get in. Odd how even his voice makes me shudder inside.

'Anything else to report?' he asks, looking through the scamps one last time.

I shake my head. 'Nope.'

That's a lie, but he's not looking at me and can't tell. Thankfully. He'd worm the Andy story out of me in about one minute.

'Good. Good to know you're here when I'm away. Safe hands,' he adds, writing something in the notepad he carries everywhere. 'Do you have any holidays booked over the next few months? Weekends away?'

'Nope,' I shrug. 'I'm not dating,' I add helpfully.

He looks up, frowns, and ignores me. 'May need you to help entertain the Germans a few times. They'll be coming back and forth from Berlin.'

'Me? With potential clients?'

'Yes, and you'll present all the award-winning work you're about to create.'

He goes on to explain everything. The Germans, it turns out, head up a huge personal care company called Blumenstrauße – tampons and toothpaste and razors, oh my! – and they're launching four of their most popular products in the UK next year. We're going to work with them for a few months working out launch plans, and if they like us, we'll get the business. Sort of a pitch-by-fire. I realise quickly that this pitch is a very big deal. It could be the making of this agency, and Coop's career.

'That's brilliant, Coop,' I say. 'I can't wait.'

'Thought you'd like it,' he says. 'Actually, wordgirl, I want you to head up this one.' Me? I'm speechless. He glances at his watch. 'I'm late for a thing. Call a company meeting, tell everyone about the pitch, and that there's going to be a lot of work for the next few months. Lots of late nights, and no neglecting existing clients.'

I have to bear bad tidings? And create another scene after Wednesday's drama with Andy? 'Um . . .' I say, trying to think of a way to get out of it. The dog ate my public speaking voice? 'Why not email everyone? Better coming from you?'

'No,' he says, standing up. 'People never read those emails properly. Nothing beats being told in person. Scott already knows.' That's the senior account director, a smooth-talking Ken-doll type. 'He's with Shiny Straight today at a strategy roundtable. Anyway, I want you to answer any questions about the Germans and whatnot. I'll be back later.'

I go back and hide at my desk for a minute, thinking. I have to call a company-wide meeting to tell everyone to kiss goodbye to their social life? I can feel panic rising in my chest. Why, why would Cooper make me do this? I can't do it. I really can't.

I look at the clock. It's still early. I'll just wait till everyone has their breakfast and coffee. Then they'll be in a better mood. I email Amanda The Office Manager about the brainstorm and Google Blumensträuße. Lala. Procrastination. Panic-led procrastination. I feel a bit ill. Maybe I am coming down with something.

At 11 am I can't put it off anymore. Cooper could be back any second. With a nauseous feeling in the pit of my stomach, I send an email to all staff to meet in the creative room immediately.

As the accounts people wander in, looking around for Cooper, I clear my throat and walk over to the centre of the room.

'Cooper isn't here, but he asked me to . . .' I start. No one is listening. In fact, the account managers are chatting away about Charlotte's new manicure. Andy is on his mobile. His underlings are looking at something on YouTube and snickering. Amanda The Office Manager is picking her breakfast out of her teeth whilst Laura is twisting her hair and snipping off split ends. She'll end up with hair like a haystack, but now isn't the time to tell her that.

'Everyone!' I say louder. Laura glances up and quickly drops her hair and the scissors. Everyone else continues as they were.

I pick up a spoon and empty glass left over from breakfast on Laura's desk, and clink them together. The first few clinks don't quite connect, but the last three are quite loud. Everyone stops what they're doing immediately and looks at me. I feel the blood rush to my face. *Just get on with it.* I lean against Laura's desk, faking a nonchalance I certainly don't feel. Posture is confidence, silence is poise.

'Hi, everyone . . . Uh, as you know, Coop's been away for the past week in Germany . . . and the good news is, we are pitching for a huge German toiletries company that's about to launch in the UK.' The words all tumble out of my mouth in a rush, and I pause to clear my throat and calm down. Everyone is looking at me and – surprisingly – actually listening. 'We want to handle it all for them: from strategy for the launch to packaging to branding and online and offline campaigns and well, everything. If we win, it'll immediately double and eventually triple the size of the agency, so it's a pretty big deal.'

Everyone snaps to attention. For the next five minutes I answer questions about the German company. It takes Laura to get to the point. She's probably the smartest person in the room.

'When is the pitch? And what do we have to do?'

'The work starts today,' I say, and I can hear a few people groan under their breath. Oh fuck. I really, really do hate telling people things they don't want to hear. 'Brainstorm at 3 pm. All staff are invited, compulsory for creatives. Now, um . . . there'll be weekly meetings with them rather than just the one big pitch. Coop knows the, uh, head guy, and he's, um pitching us as the kind of agency that works as a partner, not a supplier . . .' I look around. Everyone's still paying me total attention. Gosh.

I clear my throat. 'The good news is that there's no one else competing with us for the job – yet. The bad news is that if they're not happy, we will lose them straightaway. Which means the pressure is going to be pretty consistent over the next few months. Coop wants everyone to help. So there'll be a lot of late nights and possibly weekend work . . .'

I hear even louder groaning. Oh shit. Mutiny.

Andy speaks up. Oh double shit. 'We can't do that on top of everything else. It's not possible.'

'Well, it has to be,' I say to the wall, as I don't dare to meet his eyes.

'I'm already here till eight every night,' he says. 'My team and I work harder than anyone else. We need extra support. I know a couple of freelancers. I'll call them.'

'No,' I say, looking at his chin. 'Everyone in this agency works hard, Andy. If you and your team didn't spend half the day looking at YouTube, you wouldn't have to stay late to get the work done.'

I see the account managers smiling at this.

'It's creative research,' he says loudly. 'We need stimulus. We actually create things, you know . . .'

God, you're pathetic, I think.

Suddenly I don't feel intimidated by him. Right this second, I don't care if he – or any of them, actually – likes me or not. I am in charge of this pitch, and I am not going to let some charm-challenged man-boy fuck it up for me.

I stand up and look him straight in the eye. 'Well, for the next month, you and Danny and Ben are going to have to get your creative stimulus outside working hours. This is the most important thing to ever happen to this agency. I don't want creative to be responsible for losing this account, and I'm sure you don't either.'

He stares at me without speaking. I stare back. He looks away first. Fucking hell! Yeah!

Danny raises a hand. Gosh, what am I, a teacher? 'Yes, Danny?'

'One of the clients at my last agency was Johnson & Johnson. I know the market. I'd like to be involved.'

'Great.' Dude, what part of 'Coop wants everyone to help' don't you understand, I think. Then he flickers a little smile at me and I realise he might actually be speaking up to show support to me, and give two fingers to Andy. Double gosh.

Charlotte clears her throat and raises her OPI I've Got A Date To K-Night!-manicured hand. 'I'd really like to be involved too, my team will be able to manage all my existing clients.' Her 'team' – two account execs (recent graduates that she works like dogs) – glance at each other in anguish. 'Is that OK?'

Even Charlotte is treating me like I'm in charge? 'I'm sure that's fine. You'll have to run it past Scott, though.'

She nods. Everyone is looking at me expectantly. What do I say now? Class dismissed? 'OK, well, see you all the boardroom at 3 pm.' The office disperses quickly, but the rise in buzzy chatter shows how excited everyone is about this pitch. Shit, it really is a big deal, you know. And Coop asked me to be in charge, kind of.

As I walk back to my desk, Laura beams at me and I wink back. I feel pretty good. In fact, I feel great. I sit down and realise my heart is racing with excitement. I just can't believe how well that went. I look over. Andy is loudly inviting his team out for coffee. And a Sass-slagging session, I expect. Laura and I are not, obviously, invited.

I'm busy for the next few hours doing work for existing clients, and when Coop comes back and looks over to me with raised eyebrows, I just nod back with a little smile. Everything is fine, dude. Totally fine. The 3 pm brainstorm goes equally well. Apart from Andy loudly denigrating every idea I have, and coming up with none of his own. My brain is 100% dedicated to the task at hand. Men, love, dating – these things are no longer worthy of my time and energy.

As the meeting finishes, I stand up and say 'Thanks everyone', mostly to genuinely thank everyone but also as I want Andy to know that he hasn't beaten me. He ignores me. I grin at Cooper on my way out and he gives me the thumbs up back. I choose to take it as a message of solidarity. Thank God he's back from Germany. It's so much nicer sitting in the office without big bad Andy dominating it.

With only a few hours left till the weekend, I settle down to one of my favourite regular jobs: a monthly chatty email to teenage girls about their spots for a skincare client of ours. (When they sign up to the social networking bit of this skincare site, they'll get an email a week for a few months. It's mostly skin-related stuff, and some period/hormone/hygiene/boy talk. And the odd discount and competitions and prize draws.)

Let's see . . . Discover the power of perfect skin. Discover the joy of perfect skin. Imagine perfectly soft, deeply clean skin. Finally, perfect skin could be yours. Picture perfect skin, every day. Transform your skin, and your life. Yikes, that's a bit much. Let's go with the first one. Discover is a nice strong active word, and alliteration is always a positive pleasure. Plus, it's not promising perfect skin. You can't really promise something like 'Perfect skin, guaranteed'. You have to just talk about how good it *could* be to get perfect skin. Otherwise – according to the neurotic marketing manager at the skincare company, anyway – someone who uses the stuff and gets a spot could sue. (Really, who would bother?)

The power of positive persuasion. That's what I'd title today. Coop positively persuaded me to take a bit of a lead role in telling everyone, and I positively persuaded everyone to get behind it.

As I start writing the rest of my peppy teenage copy, I get lost in an odd, reflective mood. Poor teenage girls, I muse. I found it quite tough being a teenager. I was attacked by a shyness bug from 14 through 17, and had a slight stammer/babble problem when I did talk. It's not exactly unusual: apparently Kate was shy, too. (Bloomie never was, unsurprisingly.)

Some girls must be born knowing how to make life happen exactly as they want it to. I assume they're not the ones reading these skincare emails, but I've seen them on the King's Road in Chelsea: dewy-skinned, pouty little 16-year-old madams with the air of cream-fed, much-adored cats. I was not one of those girls. When I was 13, my parents moved from London to Berkshire, and I changed from a bookish, liberal little Notting Hill school where everyone was a bit keen and giggly and geeky like me, to a rather posh, uptight, sporty, country one where the lustrous-haired pouty missies ruled the roost. They looked at me, recognised my stammering inadequacies instantly, and dismissed me. And of course, when someone doubts you, the more you doubt yourself, until you're unable to talk at all, or at least I am.

That's when I started the mantra. 'Posture is confidence, silence is poise.' The idea was that if I looked confident and poised, I'd feel confident and poised. And people might think I was about to say something brilliant. And then, if I did want to say something, they might actually listen, which might stop me stammering.

In other words, fake it till you make it.

Thanks to my mantra, I survived school. Then I went to university, where I met kindred spirits, particularly in the form of Bloomie and Kate, and discovered I didn't really need the mantra anymore. Everything is so much easier when you have friends who think you're funny. Inside every shy girl is a loud showoff dying to get out.

I still grasp the mantra like a security blanket in times of need. Which is basically, when something intimidates me. Like work. Or a bad date. Or, now that I think about it, every time I ever saw Rick, towards the end.

Hmm.

The mantra certainly worked this morning. Everyone acted like I was, well, not to sound too dramatic, but like I knew what I was talking about. But that's not because of the mantra: I really did know what I was doing, and everyone else knew it too. Fuck fake it till you make it. I made it. I fucking made it.

I just had a good day at work. Not just a good day.

An awesome day.

Thinking this, I stare at the wall for a few minutes till I realise it's ten to five and my copy is due at 5.30 pm. I push everything else out of my head and finish the email copy, proofread it, and send it to the account manager. Oooh, the adrenaline rush of a deadline met.

I know I'm breaking my don't-talk-about-work (or dreams) rule, by the way. Don't worry. It's nearly the weekend. All I usually think about on the weekend is what to wear and where to drink. (And in the olden days, who to date.) As I head down to the tube, I skippy-bunny-hop a couple of steps. Then right outside the Crown pub on Brewer Street, I run smack-bang into Cooper coming out of the door with his pint, almost knocking him over in the process. I never go to the Crown. Smart Henry broke up with me there.

'Coop! I'm so sorry!' I exclaim, laughing. 'I was running for the tube . . .'

Cooper grins at me. 'You were skipping, actually.' I laugh even more, and turn to look at the guy he's with. About 35, very nice grey suit, slightly too-long hair. Rather chiselled cheekbones and bluer-than-blue eyes. I quickly compose myself and look back at Cooper, who introduces us. His name is Lukas, and he's about to move to London from Berlin to be the UK MD of Blumenstraße. (That explains the Euro haircut.)

'Oh, fantastic,' I say. 'We've been talking about your company all day.'

'I've been talking about it for eight weeks, since I joined,' Lukas says, smiling at me and holding very thorough eye contact. 'Please, let's talk about something else. Like . . . what you would like to drink.'

Is he flirting? 'Oh, um, I'd love to, but I have to get home. I have plans tonight,' I say. (Rule 6: No accidental dating.) 'Thank you, though. Lovely to meet you. I'll see you soon.'

'Yes, you will,' he says back. 'Very soon.' His German accent is mild, and gives his words a nice clipped sound. 'Have a good night.' Definitely flirting. Slightly sleazy. Probably a bastardo.

'See you Monday,' says Cooper.

I hurry down to the tube, running over everything that

happened today again, and realise I should try to put work out of my head and think about what to wear tonight. Normally I'd have had that sorted by about 10 am. God, what's happening to me?

Chapter Seven

The party is just getting underway when Bloomie and I get there at about 9 pm. On the way, I reread the Dating Sabbatical Rules, and then fold them up and tuck them safely in my lucky yellow clutch. I've resolved to never be without them.

Mitch lives in the far back end of Chelsea, almost in Fulham, in a fully party-proofed little flat: there's a tiled, wipe-clean kitchen, a living room with – this is key, I'm sure you'll agree – no carpet, and a not-particularly-nice back garden that can't get ruined. Despite cosy appearances, it fits over a hundred people with the appropriate social lubricant (gin, vodka, beer, wine). Right now, only about 15 people are in the front room, mostly playing that never-ending party game, No My iPod Playlist Is Better, and a few more are in the kitchen. Bloomie dashes off to join them and unload her goodies.

I see Mitch supervising the iPod war, kiss him hello, and then feel obliged to kiss everyone else in the room hello, which means I'm basically tottering around darting my head about everyone's face like a little bird for the next three minutes. Finally, I finish working the room and get back to Mitch.

Mitch is one of my best friends, but forget any ideas you might have about me secretly falling in love with him or vice versa: he spent the first year of university chasing after Bloomie and I, then resigned himself to best friendship, and now professes to find us physically revolting. He's a banker, like

Bloomie, but I'm afraid he probably *is* an arsehole, at least some of the time.

He's also a complete tart, but since he never leads the girls to believe it'll be anything more than just sex, he gets away with it. Just.

'How've you been, Special Forces? I heard about you and Posh Mark.'

'Mmmm,' I say. Special Forces is his nickname for me – because of SAS/Sass. Except when I'm really drunk. Then he calls me Special Needs.

'Tough luck, though he was too thick by half. But for fuck's sake don't talk to me about your feelings. DO talk to me about this intriguing Sex Vacation.'

'Dating Sabbatical.'

'Whatever.'

'Big crowd tonight, Bitch?' I ask. It's not a very clever nickname, but it makes us laugh.

'Don't change the subject . . . But about seventy or so, I should think,' Mitch says, scanning the tight-white-jeans-encased bottom of a girl in the iPod group. He turns to me. 'I'm a trendsetter, you know. These parties are totally recessiontastic.'

'Huh?' I say.

'Houseparties are the new going out. Front rooms are the new Boujis Beer is the new Cristal.'

'Oh, right.'

'Where's Gekko? I need to talk to her about a work thing later.'

'Kitchen.'

Mitch calls Bloomie 'Gekko' in a rather sweet Wall Street reference – she says she hates it, but I'm not sure she does. He walks through to the kitchen, high-fiving and low-fiving people all the way. Mitch is good at collecting people. Most of the crowd tonight will be our university friends, and then satellite friends from everyone's work, school and extended family. Being part of this insta-crowd makes living in London a lot easier: an ever-evolving gang without too much effort. My first year in London, pre-Mitch and Eddie and Bloomie and Kate joining me, is barely worth talking about. I call it The Lost Year, the one before I went out with Arty Jonathan. I spent most of my time getting drunk with the other new, green Londoners in horrible chain bars, and taking nightbuses back to Mortlake, an area in South London that you can only get to by buses and sheer willpower, where I shared a manky little flat with four strangers. Then, thankfully, the old group all moved to London and I quickly phased out my new friends for the cosy reassurance of my old ones.

'Sass! I hear you've become bitter!' says Harry, a podgy architect who's been involved in a passionate conversation about Jack Johnson for the past few minutes. He was skinny on the first day of university. His shirt now strains against his gut so tight that I can see the cavernous shadow of his belly button. I smile at him and don't say anything. He adds cheerfully, 'Sworn off all men!'

The rest of the iPod-battlers look up and grin.

Holy shit, my friends are gossips. Looks like news of my Dating Sabbatical has hit the streets. Rule 4: avoid talking about the Sabbatical.

'I'd rather swear off them than under them!' I reply cryptically. I've made better comebacks, but I decide to pretend it was a killer riposte, raise a knowing eyebrow at Harry and swan off to the kitchen to find Bloomie.

Despite work very nearly getting in the way of a timely sartorial decision, I managed to come up with a rather soul-cheering outfit. It's a rather short fitted black mini dress with sheer black tights and ankleboots, and my hair done in a rockabilly-quiffy-ponytail thing. (Yes, yes, why I am dressing as a Robert Palmer girl meets Elvis when I ostensibly don't want to attract attention is a mystery to me too, but old habits die hard. Anyway, 'drop your style standards' isn't one of the rules.)

Bloomie is standing at the counter, a cigarette jammed in the corner of her mouth like a cowboy as she manhandles a bottle of vodka, a bottle of blue Curaçao, a punnet of blueberries and a blender lid. Eddie – one of my other best friends in London – is standing next to her, holding two bottles of Morgan's Spiced Rum, a bag of bananas, a coconut and some mango juice. This is the point of Mitch's houseparties, by the way. We all bring various ingredients, he borrows blenders from everyone who has one (are you kidding? I don't own an iron, dude, let alone a blender) and we make up cocktails and name them. Yes. It's dangerous.

'This is it, kids,' announces Bloomie as dramatically as you can with a cigarette in the corner crease of your lips. 'Prepare to experience the most mind-blowingly awesome cocktail since the Knickerless Bloomer.' That, obviously, was the name of her cocktail at the last party (white rum, coconut milk, Malibu, strawberries and a pinch of cinnamon).

'No fucking Malibu this time,' calls Mitch, as he leaves the kitchen with a round of shots for the iPod brigade. 'Every cocktail Gekko makes has fucking Malibu in it. It's like being at school. And stop fucking smoking in my kitchen.'

'You wish, Bitch, my darling . . .' says Bloomie, very obviously more concerned with arranging the ingredients on the counter.

I lean over and kiss Eddie hello. Eddie and I dated for two weeks at university, and broke up for heartfelt reasons now forgotten. (He doesn't make the list as one of the official break-ups, obviously.) Eddie's been in a long-distance relationship for the past two years with a girl called Maeve who lives in Geneva, of all places. They see each other once every two months, and he doesn't even talk about her much. I secretly suspect he's just lazy and doesn't want to bother to play the field. Eddie's an engineer. What he actually does all day, I just don't know. Builds things?

'What's shaking, Edward?' I ask.

'Not much,' he says. 'My sisters are in London tomorrow night. They're going to Spain on Sunday. Wanna help me entertain them? Dinner, somewhere cheap and cheerful in Notting Hill?'

'Good luck finding that,' interjects Bloomie.

'Love to,' I say. 'Love the lovely sisters. How's Maeve?'

'Good, fine, she's fine. Now, do you know how to open a coconut?'

'"Open" a coconut?' I repeat.

'I'm making a tropical punch.'

'What a stunning idea,' I say.

'Not original enough for you, my little creative bunny? Fine. Here's a twist for you: when someone drinks it, you have to hit them in the face. Get it? Tropical punch.'

I start to laugh. 'Take my fag, darling,' Bloomie interrupts. This darling means me, I know, so I reach over and take it from her mouth, and she immediately whirls around and throws her hands in the air. 'Everyone! I have a secret weapon! I have a pestle and mortar and I shall be muddling blueberries with sugar as the base for tonight's winning cocktail!'

The crowd in the kitchen laughs and whoops. After a few minutes of muddling, and some blending of ice, vodka and Curaçao, she pours the cocktail into about 15 of the many double-shot glasses Mitch purchased specifically for his parties. She raises her glass: 'A toast to the Blue-mie Moon!' and drinks it. We all repeat 'the Blue-mie Moon!' and follow suit. (If this drink takes its inspiration from the mojito, then it's a long-distant, slightly inbred, unpleasantly blueberry-skin-filled cousin.) The night has begun.

An hour later, and we've had Mitch's Marvellous Medicine (tequila and crème de menthe; disgusting), the Molasses Fiend (this one was mine, and if I may say, it was a toffee-espresso delight), a Deep Deep Burn (Tabasco – need I say more?) and a Bite Me (butterscotch schnapps and Baileys, garnished with crushed up bits of Crunchie). Eddie has been banished outside to wrestle with the coconut and a large cleaver, and someone new has discovered, as someone new always does, that blending lemonade and ice leads to tears.

Bloomie and I have taken up our customary early-party position perched up in the big kitchen window, so we can hold our fags outside and comment on activities inside at the same time. It's a delicate operation in a mini dress, but the adroit placement of a teatowel over my thighs sees me through. The best thing about sitting in the kitchen window, of course, is that it's low-effort socialising: everyone comes in when they arrive to say hello and try a cocktail or five before situating themselves near the booze-and-ice buckets planted strategically around the living room, stairs and garden.

I tell Bloomie about my night with Kate, and the finger-gunning Yank. She cackles with laughter.

'I also had some rather good stuff happen at work today,' I grin, and waggle my eyebrows.

Bloomie whoops. 'About fucking time, darling. Did you bitchslap them back into place?'

'Something like that,' I say. 'I won't bore you with the details . . . Where's The Dork?'

Her face goes gooey with happiness. 'On the way. He just texted me. He had to have dinner with his sister tonight. She's pregnant. Her name is Julie. She lives in Paris. She sounds really nice.'

I am shocked. This kind of babbling is entirely unlike Bloomie and utterly delightful to see. We smile at each other, but before we get caught in a sickly-sweet moment I quickly turn my smile into a manic, scrunchy-nose-frowny-pig grin and turn my face back into the kitchen . . . just as an utterly divine man walks in from the living room.

He's very tall, with broad shoulders and dark hair. And his eyes are locked directly on my scrunchy-pig face. Shit. I quickly try to set my face to pretty, but it's too late. He's already glanced over me and back to the group of people he walked in with. Good thing I'm not in the market to get attention from men, I say to myself.

Bloomie swings her legs back in. 'Mitch's cousin is here!' she says to me. That's Mitch's cousin? I think. Mitch is blond and skinny. She hops down from the window sill with the careless aplomb of someone wearing jeans, and skips through the crowd shouting 'Jake!'

I ease my way down delicately and decide, Dating Sabbatical or not, I can't quite face meeting a good-looking man named Jake who just saw me looking like a pig and will therefore dismiss me without a second thought.

Instead, I turn to see what the current mixologist is up to. It's Fraser, another old friend from university. He's looking his usual prematurely middle-aged self in corduroy trousers and a slight belly, and is pulling Valrhona chocolate powder, Ben & Jerry's ice cream, full-fat milk and a bottle of brandy out of an Ocado delivery bag. We kiss hello.

'Help me!' he says. 'How the bugger do I work this godawful contraption?'

'It's a blender, sweetie,' I say. 'Holy fatgrams, Batman, what the sweet hell are you making?'

'Dessert cocktail. Had one on a date the other night. Ruddy nice, actually.' Fraser's dad was in the army and Fraser talks just like him. Gruff, with very abbreviated sentences and archaic curse words.

'The cocktail or the date?' I ask.

'Cocktail. Date got blotto and threw up. Waste of a night, actually. Think I was boring her.'

'No way,' I say. 'Not possible.'

It's entirely possible, if he started talking about the history and structure of the British Armed Forces. He's such a lovely guy, but this is probably the fiftieth bad-first-date story I've heard him tell.

'She clearly has a drinking problem, Fraymund,' I say, as we finish measuring in the ingredients and press blend. 'Onwards and upwards. Now, what are you going to call that? The Muffin Top? The Spare Tyre?'

Fraser laughs. 'I was going to call it the Dessert Cocktail.'

'Good call,' I say. We pour the thick concoction into the glasses and ring the large bell Mitch also bought specifically for these parties. (He takes them seriously. Did I mention that?) Everyone without a drink crowds round and takes a glass, and Fraser leads the toast ('The Dessert Cocktail!'), then writes the name of the cocktail on a chart on the wall. It's delicious, though – unsurprisingly – sickeningly rich. The crowd gives it a seven out of ten. I then show Fraser how to take the blender apart ('Cripes, it's like a ruddy rifle,'), blast it with the hose in the sink and leave it upside down on a teatowel to dry, next to the other blenders waiting for their next chance to shine. Fraser starts talking to two girls standing next to the chart about the merits of full-fat milk, and I collect all the used glasses in the kitchen and run them through hot soapy water.

'This is far too complicated. Whatever happened to good old-fashioned drinking?' says a voice behind me. I turn around and – you've probably guessed it, but it's true – the scrunchy-pig-face guy is talking to me. What did Bloomie call him? Jake. I assemble my thoughts quickly.

'This is drinking on a more evolved level. It's taken years to iron out the kinks.'

During the last four seconds, I noticed a few more things about him. He's about six foot three, I'd guess. Slightly crinkly-round-the-edges eyes. Teeth almost straight and very white. Eyelashes dark but not too long. Lips look like they get sunburnt a lot. In short, attractive as hell.

Go-go-Gadget mantra. Posture is confidence, silence is poise.

'Looks like a slick operation to me,' he says.

I nod nonchalantly. 'The last remaining kink is that as the

night goes on, the names and scores become hard to read. So we never really know who the winner is.'

'Hmm.' He looks over at the chart. 'Well, I came prepared and I am ready to conquer.'

Fuck, I shouldn't even need my mantra, goddamnit. You are on a Dating Sabbatical, missy. And remember Rule 3: no obvious flirting.

'What do you have?' I ask.

'Passionfruit. Vodka. Pineapple juice. Ginger.'

'How intriguing. Do you have a name yet?'

'Let's think of one as you help me make it.' He looks over at me and grins. Fuck, I adore a bit of charming bossiness. No, really. I do.

'OK.'

I busy myself chopping and scooping passionfruit into the blender, and he slices the rind off the ginger. Working side by side like this, we lapse into silence for a few seconds and I desperately try to think of something offhand and witty to say. All I can think about is how close he is to me and it's making me feel all hot and tingly and flushed. Hey – stop that. I know what you're thinking. Of course I won't break the Dating Sabbatical Rules for the first guy I'm really, truly, seriously attracted to (in ages, by the way, like, years). Wait, why am I trying to think of something to say? Rule 3, damnit, remember Rule 3.

'I need something,' he says abruptly.

'I'm sure we've got it. People bring every possible ingredient . . . I mean, someone even brought a puppy last time.'

'A puppy? In a cocktail?' he exclaims, turning to look at me straight on for the first time.

I nod up at him, trying to ignore the buckling feeling in my tummy. 'It was tragique, but tasty. The mutt-tini.' Is that obvious flirting?

'Mutt-tini. Nice. I was going to say cockerspanieltail, but I can see I'll have to improve on that.' He grins at me and the buckling doubles. I feel like I'm sweating. Am I sweating? Suddenly, he spies Bloomie's pestle and mortar. 'Fucking bingo!'

He grabs it, throws the chopped ginger in and starts smushing it into a pulpy juice.

'Honey!' I say.

'Yes, sweetpea?' he shoots back.

I giggle. Foolishly. (Is that obvious flirting? No. Just politeness.) 'No, HONEY. You need honey in this. With ginger.'

'Gosh, you're smarter than you look, aren't you?' Jake says admiringly.

I make a dumb blonde face, bat my eyelashes and chew my little finger. (OK, OK. I admit. That was verging on obviously flirtatious. I straighten out my face and try to look serious.)

'OK, honey . . . ginger . . . passionfruit . . . pineapple juice. I have a feeling it's going to be too sweet . . . Shall we taste it and find out?'

'Oh no. You can't do that,' I say sadly. 'No tweaking. It means people have to really think about the ingredients before they arrive.'

'How fascist.'

I giggle again. Shit, I'm acting silly. Oh hell, the tingly tingles . . . Good banter, good looks . . . and he doesn't seem to be angling towards asking me out. He's flirting, but in such a delightfully playful way. It's so annoyingly attractive.

I need someone to intervene. There must be a hint of bastardo there somewhere. I'll locate it soon, forget about him immediately, and continue to adhere to the Rules.

'How about lemon juice? Or lime juice?' I suggest.

'Yes, yes, yes.'

We chop and squeeze two lemons and two limes and add the juice to the mix in the blender. He glugs in about a third of a bottle of vodka, I add the ice, he slides on the lid rather dextrously – big hands, surprisingly strong-looking fingers, badly-bitten thumbnails, what the hot damn am I doing fantasising about being manhandled like a blender lid – and presses blend. He smiles at me and I smile back. Mmm. (Argh! Sexual frisson extraordinaire. Arrêtez.)

'The name!' I gasp. 'You have to name it before the blending is done!'

'Hot Diggity! The Hottentot! Too Hot To Handle!' Jake shouts, then hits himself in the forehead with his free hand. 'NO! God, that film was diabolical.'

'What?' I laugh helplessly at the panicked look on his face. 'Ummm . . . ummm . . . the Gingersour? The Throatwarmer? The Linda Lovelace?'

'Filthy stream of consciousness . . .' he replies disdainfully, switching off the blender. 'Forget all that. I hereby christen this cocktail the Minx. I think it will be sweet, refreshingly zesty and rather hot.'

I'm trying to figure out if he kind of means me, and if so what the appropriate response might be, when Mitch appears bearing a tray of used double-shot glasses behind us. 'Alright children, let Mummy through, washing up here . . . Thank God I bought three hundred of these fuckers.' He dumps them all in the soapy washing-up water. I assemble some clean dry glasses, and Jake fills them, rings the bell and raises a toast to the Minx. It's a very good cocktail: a mix of citrusy sweetness with a warm gingeriness.

'Mmmm. Not bad for a beginner,' says Mitch, pouring himself a second and going through a sniff-sip-ponder wine-tasting rigmarole. 'It must be in the genes, cuz. Shame you missed Mitch's Marvellous Medicine. It was the best so far.'

I look over at Jake and shake my head, mouthing 'No, it wasn't'. He grins and, as Mitch looks quickly from him to me, trying to figure out what's going on, Jake quickly starts talking to cover it up. 'I had some excellent help,' he says. 'Jesus is in my heart and helps with everything I do.'

I snort with laughter. I try to think of something witty to

say back, and realise I really am, without a doubt, obviously flirting now, that he's flirting back, that I'm planning on how to obviously flirt more, and wondering where he lives, what he does, what his neck smells like, how long it might take him to ask me out and what I might wear on our first date. In other words, I'm hellbent on breaking the Dating Sabbatical Rules and they've only existed for 48 hours.

I walk over to the fridge and get three bottles of Corona out to buy myself a second to think. I am almost breaking all the Rules for a tall handsome smartarse. The kind of guy I always get caught by, the bastardo kind who makes me laugh and then breaks my heart when he decides he doesn't want me anymore. He's like Rick. A better-looking, taller, funnier Rick. That's all.

Right. Time to find Bloomie and get far, far away from this temptation. I hand over the beers, take a deep breath and say 'Must dash, boys . . .' to Mitch. I try not to look at Jake, but can't resist sneaking a glance as I walk away. He's smirking at me. See? Smartarse.

Chapter Eight

The party is really warming up now, with people spilling out of the living room into the back garden. Someone has won battle of the iPods (Marvin Gaye). I see Fraser talking to his flatmates in the middle of the living room and decide to say hi.

'Here she is!' exclaims Ant as I walk up. I snogged Ant once, when I first met him, under the influence of tequila and . . . uh, tequila. Regretted it instantly. He would be handsome if he wasn't so sleazy. And mildly monobrowed. He now seems rather happy with himself. 'The girl everyone's talking about! She's taken a vow of spinsterhood!'

'You're all talking about me?' I say. Great. Looks like I'm a laughing stock, then. 'How dull your lives must be.'

'A serial dater like you, renouncing all men? I'm surprised it wasn't in the *News of the World*.' Ant laughs like a hyena, and the other flatmates, apart from Fraser, join in.

'When did your Dating Sabbatical start, Ant? About eight years ago?' says Fraser. I smile at him gratefully. Now that is a riposte.

'We were just talking about the recession,' says one of the flatmates earnestly, a rather sweet geek called Felix who I think has a thing for me. However, he laughed along with the rest of them so I'm not going to be nice to him.

'How fascinating,' I reply. He looks crushed and I feel bad. I shouldn't pick on geeks. 'I'm a bit clueless about it, I'm afraid, Felix,' I add.

'It's bloody boring stuff,' agrees Fraser.

'You won't be clueless soon, when you have to pay for your own meals every night,' says Ant. 'No more steak dinners à deux for you.' I hate to say it, but he has a point. Dates have been a good source of meals for the past few years. Of course I always make an effort to pay, but they never let you. Certainly not on the first date. I wonder if Jake likes steak. I could cook it for us both at home. In my kitchen. Perhaps, if we all become really poor, we'll have to share baked beans on toast. No, scratch that. Baked beans are not a date-friendly food. I could . . . oh, I could make an omelette. I wonder if he likes eggs.

I'm interrupted from my – utterly ridiculous and very non-Sabbatical-compliant – reverie by Mitch, who approaches the group with his arm thrown around the neck of the white jeans girl.

'Don't talk to Sass, darling. She's a MAN HATER,' he stage-whispers. The girl giggles, hiccups, and seems to throw up slightly in her mouth.

As everyone falls about laughing, I smile/grimace at Mitch and wait to see if I'll think of something witty to say. I don't. I wonder if Mitch told Jake about the Sabbatical already. Oh God, I shouldn't care. Suddenly I feel very tired. I decide to avoid all men for the rest of the night, and walk over to talk to Tory, a girl Eddie worked with years ago. She's nice enough, but she talks about sex almost constantly. It's kind of weird. I think he invites her to parties because she's guaranteed to score with someone. She's party insurance. (Is that mean of me? Oh well.)

'So, no dating for you, Sassy, yeh?' she grins, after a bit of basic chitchat. 'I heard all about it. I'm going to do it too!'

'Really?' I say. I hate being called Sassy. 'Er, wow. That's great.'

'Yeh. Just sex, you know? The whole emotions-and-talking thing is just . . . such a waste of time,' she says, taking a long swig of her drink and casing the room.

I nod, and excuse myself to go to find Bloomie. I manage to stop at only two groups as I walk around the party, and have a moderately entertaining banter with them. However, my paranoia is now switched on and I'm convinced everyone is laughing at me. I can't see Jake anywhere. Not that I'm looking for him, I meant because I'm trying to avoid him. I finally find Bloomie in the backyard with Kate – who I didn't think was coming, so it's a rather nice surprise – and Eugene.

'Hello, princesses,' I say, kissing Kate and Eugene. He's not really a dork, obviously. He's in his early 30s, works in finance with Bloomie – they met in a conference call, of all the romantic stories – and is half-French, though he grew up mostly in London and has no trace of an accent. He still has that skinny, sexy, floppy-haired French guy thing going on. He can wear big square scarves knotted around his neck and still look pretty hot, which is an incredible feat when you think about it.

'What's news here then? Everyone in the rest of the party is talking about me, apparently.'

Kate nods. 'You or the economy. And you're more fun.'

I sigh. 'Sheesh. How you doin', Eugene?'

'Smashing,' he grins, and looks at Bloomie. She giggles and grins back. What the sweet hell is that about? Other people's relationships are mystifying.

'Where's Tray?' I say, as though I suddenly noticed his absence and was upset by it.

'Oh, he's at home,' says Kate, looking over to the house as if it was unexpectedly fascinating. 'He's . . . working. Do you have a cigarette, Sass?'

I glance over to exchange a quick look with Bloomie, but she's still gazing at Eugene. Kate's staring into space. I wonder what Jake is doing, and involuntarily look at the kitchen window. I only see Ant emptying a bottle of Diet Coke and a bottle of rum into the blender and pressing blend. Dickhead. I get out three cigarettes and light all of them, in my mouth, at once, then hand one each to Kate and Bloomie. An old trick from university. It's so not cool that it's almost cool.

'Wow, you guys . . . you're like the Pink Ladies,' says Eugene.

Oh, for God's sake. 'Wrong thing to say, darling . . .' says Bloomie, laughing. He looks perplexed. 'I'll explain later . . .' she adds, and they smile at each other happily. I wait for them to talk more, but they seem to be communicating through the medium of loving gazes.

'Young love, huh, Katie?' I say, turning away from the happy couple.

'Mmmm,' Kate says absently.

Gosh, what a bunch of funsters.

Bloomie's BlackBerry rings, and the expression on her face changes from happy to stern so fast it's like she's swapping those comic/tragic drama masks. She hands Eugene her drink without speaking, answers it and barks 'Susan Bloomingdale . . .' as she walks away.

'It's 11 pm on a Friday!' says Eugene, half to himself.

'It's probably the States,' I say. 'She works with the San Fran office a lot, right? Don't you do the same sort of job, anyway?'

He shrugs in his nonchalant Gallic way, and looks quizzically at us. Well, at me. Kate seems to have checked out for the time being, and is here in body only. 'I'm an analyst,' he says. 'And I'm not obsessed with it.'

'Neither is Bloomie,' I say loyally, and slightly untruthfully. 'She kind of gives everything 100%, that's all.'

Eugene nods. 'Well, if you'll excuse me, I'm going to the kitchen to get a drink. Can I get you anything?'

'I'm all good,' I say, glancing over at Kate, who's still mute. 'She's all good, too.'

I stand in silence for about 30 seconds, waiting for Kate to speak.

'Kate,' I say, taking a drag on my cigarette. She doesn't respond. 'Kate, I'm pregnant.'

She's in a trance. I sigh and look around the back garden. Everyone else is talking loudly or drinking messily. The noise

79

levels of the party seem to have doubled. The Killers are playing very loudly and I hear a whoop from the living room that probably means Mitch is doing The Worm across the carpet. The first houseparty of my Dating Sabbatical is suddenly turned up to eleven, and I'm completely unsure what to do with myself. I'm not even sure if I'm having fun anymore. Everything was fine till I met Jake.

'Hello, trouble,' says a voice behind me. I turn around. Oh, my God.

It's Rugger Robbie. My ex-boyfriend. Break-Up No.2. Fucking hell, I haven't seen him in years. I thought he moved to Brisbane to be with the girl he met in Thailand. The girl he left me for.

'Robbie!' I smile, kissing him hello. I can't pretend to be upset about it all, five years later. Especially when I'm not.

'You look fantastic!' Rugger Robbie says, looking me up and down very obviously. 'How are you?'

'Thanks,' I say. 'I'm great.' He doesn't look fantastic, so I can't say it back. The fit rugby body has become a fat rugby body, and his face looks like someone has pumped it full of air from the cheekbones down.

'So, Sass, what are you up to these days?' he asks jovially, staring at my boobs. It's most off-putting. 'Still living in London?'

'Yep,' I say. 'Are you back here on holiday?'

'From where – Brisvegas?' he asks. God, people who say Brisvegas are irritating. 'Nah, I came home about six months ago.'

'Is Kerry with you?' I ask politely. That was her name.

'Oh, no,' he says, eyes flicking up to meet mine. 'We broke up. I'm living with Riggsy and Martin again, just off Fulham Palace Road. It's just like old times!'

'How fun,' I smile. I wonder if he's still pissing on curtains. 'Well, nice to see you, I'd better see if Mitch needs any help with, uh, something.' I glance at Kate, who still seems to be in some kind of waking coma. What the fuck is wrong with her?

'Hey, uh, can I get your number?' Rugger Robbie asks. 'I'd love to take you out for dinner sometime. We should catch up.'

'Should we?' I snap, and then catch myself and smile sweetly at him. 'Afraid I can't, Robbie. Take care though. Come on, Katie.' Before either of them can reply, I grab her hand and we stride towards the house purposefully.

'Whoa, Thelma and Louise!' exclaims a guy standing outside the door. He's wearing a T-shirt with an absolutely huge Abercrombie & Fitch logo. 'Serious faces, laydeeeez! It's a party! Aren't you having fun?'

We stop and look at him.

'Make me laugh, then,' I say.

'Uh . . .' he says, looking for inspiration to his friend next to him.

'Too late,' I say and we walk through.

'Wow, that was a bit harsh,' says Kate.

'I'm just not in the mood right now,' I say, leading Kate up to a small cabinet in the hallway. 'It's been a very, very long week, and I deserve a party, and I don't think I'm going to be in the mood to party till . . .' – I lean down, slide open the door and pull out half a bottle of Jagermeister – 'I'm Jagerunk.'

Kate's eyes light up. 'That's been there since the last party?!' she exclaims. 'Brilliant!'

We walk into the kitchen, grab a few clean double-shot glasses, and start pouring out Jagermeister. It's pretty heaving with people, and in the corner I can see Fraser enthusiastically snogging Eddie's henna-ed workmate Tory. It's a bit early for that, isn't it? He's really putting his shoulders into it and everything. Ew.

Two guys are standing next to the fridge looking at us.

'You know,' says one very loudly, turning to the other, 'my life really HASN'T changed that much since winning the lottery.'

I turn around and look at him and start cackling with laughter. 'Dude . . . that's the best line I've ever heard,' is all I can manage to say, wiping the tears from my eyes. 'For that, you have to do a shot.'

'No problem!' he grins. He's kind of shiny, with lots of moles on his face. He and his friend step up to the kitchen counter next to Kate and I, and we all do a shot simultaneously.

'Oh, that was probably a bad idea,' sighs Kate.

Bloomie and Eugene appear, holding hands.

'No more work calls all night! Ooh, shots? Without me? What do you think you're playing at?' asks Bloomie.

'You're up,' I say, and in another minute, we've all done another.

'Now, THAT one was a bad idea,' I say to Kate.

Mitch lands with a massive thump at our feet after doing a triple roly-poly across the living room and into the kitchen, and pretends to do the breaststroke across the kitchen floor on his tummy. He looks up at Bloomie and I and smiles. 'Gekko and Special Needs. My two favourite girls . . . That was the Triple Axel Extreme Roly-Poly . . . I always nail it.'

'Bitch is into extreme sports,' explains Bloomie to Eugene.

'Why aren't I one of your favourite girls?' says Kate in an injured tone.

'The Extreme Roly-Poly is nothing compared to the Extreme WORM!' shouts Mitch from the floor.

'So, do you come here often?' I turn back around. It's mole-faced lottery winner guy. From a great line to a shit line in sixty seconds.

I look him straight in the eye, and say in a tone that means 'fuck off': 'No.' He exchanges a glance with his friend and they walk away.

Bloomie picks up the bottle of Jager. 'Another!'

Rugger Robbie charges into the kitchen. 'Hi, gang! Shots? YES!' He comes over, putting a sweaty hand around my waist.

'I'm out,' I say, moving away from the group so Rugger Robbie's hand falls away. My throat, stomach and indeed head all feel rather warm. Bloomie pours herself, Rugger Robbie, Eugene and Kate a shot, then leans over and pours another shot in Mitch's mouth. He gurgles appreciatively. Robbie offers me the dregs of his shot. I shake my head and try not to make eye contact.

Harry bounds into the kitchen. 'My turn for cocktails! I'm making a Sticky Surprise.'

I exchange glances with Bloomie, and we head to the living room, followed by Eugene and Kate. The Irish guys have cleared all the furniture to one side, and are holding a rhythmic gymnastics competition cheered on by the whole crowd. At the moment, one guy is doing an absolutely beautiful routine with an invisible ribbon. He dips and jumps, swirls and turns, and it's breathtaking, till Mitch runs in from the kitchen and rugby-tackles him to the side of the room.

The Jager has just hit my central nervous system, which is not an unpleasant feeling. Someone turns the music up, and Bloomie and Eugene climb onto a coffee table and start dancing. Kate takes out her phone, reads a text and heads towards the garden with a stressed look on her face. Hmm, something going on there.

Then I look up to see that Jake has just walked in from the garden and is looking at me. We make eye contact. I look away quickly.

Ignore him. No, that's rude. Say hi. No, ignore him.

I look back at him, as if seeing him for the first time, and acknowledge him with a quick nod. He nods back. It's so swift that it makes me smile.

As he starts to walk over to me, I evaluate my Jagerunkness. It's certainly given me a kick, but that's why I did them. I can handle it. Don't I have a mantra for potentially indimitating situations? I mean . . . portently intimidating situations? I mean . . . what?

'Mistress of the Minx cocktail,' he smiles. 'Having fun?'

'I . . . yes. Yes, yes, I am.' Where the fuck is my mantra?

'You're a very silly girl for drinking Jager like that, did you know that?'

83

He was watching me doing Jager shots?

'It's been a bad week. And don't call me a silly girl. I am a silly WOMAN.'

'A very silly woman.'

'Mmmmmm,' I say. He has very nice eyes. And I really do like his shoulders. At least I don't have that buckling tummy feeling anymore. I don't feel much of anything, actually. Bzzzzzjagerbuzz. 'I think I ought to go home.' I do? Do I think that?

'Probably,' he agrees. 'I believe you just did two enormous shots of a 70-proof drink in less than three minutes. Where's your partner in crime?'

'She's there,' I say, pointing at the coffee table, and look up to see Bloomie, but she and Eugene have disappeared. Outside for a snog and a cigarette, I expect.

'Shall we go sit outside and have a little chat while you sober up a bit?' asks Jake.

I look up at him and frown.

'No. Nooooo. Nonono.'

'Sheesh, don't overreact. It's not like I'm asking you on . . . a date.'

This sobers me slightly. I look him straight in the eye. My powers of deduction are drunk. He doesn't seem to be making fun of me, but his eyes are laughing.

'Your eyes are laughing,' I say.

'What?' he says, and starts laughing out loud.

I'm not sure what to say, so I don't say anything at all, but smile at him. Shit, I shouldn't be smiling, that's like flirting. I try to scowl instead and end up making what I fear is a very odd face.

'I feel glazed,' I say. Where did that come from?

'You look glazed,' he nods, then leans in towards me slightly. 'But you—'

At that exact second, Kate walks up to us quickly. 'I've got to go home, sweetie, I've got a cab outside . . .'

Thank God. I can't remember the Dating Sabbatical Rules right now, and I probably couldn't even read them if I got the damn sheet out of my clutch, but I'm pretty sure I'm close to breaking them. I look over and see Robbie in the kitchen screaming 'BEER BONG!' I've got to get out of here.

'Can I come?'

'Of course! But, like, I'm really leaving now. No long goodbyes.'

'I'm ready. I'll text Bloomie goodbye,' I nod. I look up at Jake. His eyes aren't smirking anymore. 'Uh . . . bye.'

'Bye.'

'Bye.'

We carefully step around an Irishman doing an impressive routine with an invisible hoop, over Mitch, who's passionately snogging the white jeans girl, and head out the door.

Chapter Nine

For the first time in what must, realistically, be years, I'm not waking up the day after a party thinking about the guy who asked me out last night, the guy who dumped me, or the guy next to me. I'm not nursing a sad heart, hoping for a text, or waiting for a kiss. I'm not planning what to wear if he – whoever he might be – asks me out, or dealing with someone else's hangover.

I'm just lying here, all by myself, in the middle of the bed, arms and legs reaching to each corner like a starfish, stretching and sighing happily.

I weigh up the benefits of getting tea and toast to bring back to bed versus the effort required, and decide it's worth it. I only have minor desert-floor mouth and, in fact, don't feel too bad at all. Sleeping for eight hours can cure anything, seriously. I'm back in bed, starfishing and munching, within a few minutes.

This is great.

Of course, I can't lie. After a few minutes of happy contentedness, I am kind of thinking about Jake. I'm kind of thinking about the fluttering in my stomach when I was standing next to him in the kitchen.

You know, here's all it comes down to: he is possibly the sexiest man I've ever met. I mean, really. And perhaps it's all Kate's fault for talking about fancying someone, because I haven't been attracted to someone like that in years. Maybe ever. I normally evaluate the attractiveness of a guy in a sort of detached way, ie, nice hair, bad shoulders, good teeth, etc. But last night was different. I reacted to Jake like a chemical thing exposed to another, um, chemical thing. (Fill in the blank. I can't.) I had a genuine tingly feeling every time I was near him. I have a mild tingly feeling just thinking about him now.

My phone beeps.

Breakfast, the usual place, at 11 am?

From Bloomie. Yay, she's taking Saturday off work, for a change. I reply.

See you there.

I wonder whether he was teasing me at the end of the night about my Dating Sabbatical.

But – and here's the best part – I don't wonder if he'll call. He can't, since he doesn't have my number. I don't want him to, since, after all, I know very well it'd go wrong in the end and I'd be dumped and miserable, again. I can't break the Dating Sabbatical, especially not for a guy like him. He's too arrogant to be really nice and too smartarsey to not be a bastardo. When I remember all that, Jake flits out of my mind as easily as he flitted in, and I feel at ease and in control again. I smile smugly. I have outwitted the first stumbling block to the Dating Sabbatical. High-fives to me.

My thoughts turn to the weekend stretching ahead. I've got a stellar Saturday planned: coffee with Kate and Bloomie and a tour of the vintage stuff on Portobello Road, followed by a walk across Hyde Park with coffees and an intense inspection of H&M and Zara in Knightsbridge. That should do us for a few hours. (Never attempt Topshop on a Saturday: only the Oxford Circus one is any good, really, and it's colonised by gangs of petrifying teenage girls.)

Shower, soap, shave, scrub, dry, moisturise . . . I'm feeling kind of smug and pleased with myself, and so decide to take tranquil inspiration from Manhattan Mommies. I wear caramel quilted ballet slippers, white jeans, a gold belt, a white vest and a caramel cardigan. (Isn't it strange how everything I wore on Wednesday felt perfect, but would be so wrong today?) I tie the silky (polyester) scarf through a little loop on my lucky yellow clutch for a bit of flair. Hair is clean and straight. My eyebrows do exactly what I tell them to. Outer and Inner Selves are serene and content, walking hand in hand down Madison Avenue.

On the way to Notting Hill I get a text from Mitch.

Did you get the number of the bus that hit me last night?

I reply:

Don't call her a bus, darling, she seemed lovely.

Mitch texts:

Harhar. Joe wants your number. I know from last time you fucking crucified me that I'm meant to ask you first so I am. Reply asap I'm not your sexretary

I reply:

No. I'm not dating at the moment.

I think for a second, and then text again:

PS Which one was Joe anyway?

Mitch texts:

A&Fitch tshirt

I reply:

Oh God no. No no. Talk later dude. Thanks for last night.

Hmm, how odd. I wasn't nice to that guy and yet I made enough of a good impression for him to pursue asking me out? Weird. My phone beeps again.

Hey trouble. Ant here. Wld U like to go 4 a drink 2moro night? :-)

Ugh, txt spk is almost as creepy as monobrowed Ant. What the hell? I think for a few minutes and then reply:

Hello Ant. I'm flattered, but unable to, due to aforementioned Dating Sabbatical commitment.

Ant texts:

Come on. A drink isn't a date.

I reply:

I'm sorry. I can't. I took a sacred vow.

My phone rings. It's Ant. I hate it when people ring just after texting you. I'm not sure why it's so rude, but it is. I turn it to silent and jump off the No. 52 bus. I am so excited about today. I've got £150 in my purse, earmarked to burn on clothes. That's quite a lot when you're shopping at H&M and Zara, you know. (Do not speak to me of credit cards. I got into several thousand pounds of debt at 23 – £4,893 to be exact – and, after a huge and nasty kerfuffle with my bank and my parents, it took years to pay off. Even thinking about that makes me feel sick. So I prefer to just not think about the whole money thing. That's why I never open bank statements.)

Kate's already in our favourite booth in our favourite little Westbourne Grove café when I finally get there at a few minutes past 11 am, and so is my large latte-with-less-milk-slash-macchiato-with-extra-milk. A triple espresso is waiting for Bloomie, who turns up 30 seconds after me. Hot damn, Kate is a planner.

'You look natty!' exclaims Bloomie. She is looking extremely pretty this morning: very pink of cheek and bright of eye. Lots of sex, I expect. (Mmm. Sex. I'll think about that more later. I'm going to miss it. Why was I so phenomenally attracted to Jake? Is it my body just being annoying, as it knows it can't have any action at the moment? It's quite unlike me. Hmm.)

'Thanks sweeeedie,' I say, sliding into the booth and pulling my coffee towards me. 'How did we all pull up today?'

'Smashing, actually,' grins Bloomie. 'I had to make it up to Eugene for the work call last night.' She stretches and yawns. 'I can comfortably say I excelled myself.'

'Ew,' I say.

'Fine,' says Kate, scanning the menu.

'I don't know why you're reading that, Kate, my girl,' I say. 'You're obviously going to have a BLT with a pint of English mustard on the side.'

89

'And you're obviously going to have a plain ciabatta with your utterly minging Parma ham,' she retorts, folding it with a flourish. 'Oooh, that reminds me.' She flips open a diary to the 'notes' section (does anyone actually use that section?) and writes down 'ciabatta' on a multi-columned list.

'What's that?'

'Supermarket shopping list.'

'Is that in order of aisle?'

'Yes.'

'Fucking hell.'

'Can we order, darlings? Dying here,' interrupts Bloomie.

We order. Bloomie fills us in on what happened at the party after we left – all hell broke loose; apparently that Irish crowd are chaos merchants when it comes to houseparties – and I tell them quickly about talking to Jake last night, skipping over the tingly attraction part and making sure to add that I am definitely not interested due to the wonderful, wonderful Sabbatical, and about waking up this morning and feeling so happy to be in bed by myself. I also tell them about the texts today. On cue, my phone beeps.

From a mystery number:

Robbie here! Hope you don't mind but Mitch gave me your number! Would you like to go for a drink on Tuesday! We should catch up! I've missed you're laugh!

Ugh. Fucking Mitch giving my number to ex-fucking-boyfriends. And his grammar is appalling. I show them and delete it without replying, and then show them Ant's text.

'I barely spoke to him,' I say, mystified. 'I think he's a dick.'

I tap a quick text to Mitch:

I said don't give out my number! The curtain pisser is stalking me!

From Mitch:

He's with me now. Took your no. without asking me. And he just read that text harhar.

Kate and Bloomie collapse with giggles.

'Screw him,' I say. 'He dumped me five years ago.'

'Right on, sister,' says Bloomie supportively. 'But you were so obviously just killing time with him . . .'

'I was?' I say. I don't remember that.

'You never answered his calls when you were out with us, remember . . .? Maybe I'm wrong, I just didn't think you were that smitten.'

'Hmm,' I say. That's interesting, I don't remember that. Nonetheless, he did dump me via text. And he's nowhere near as cute as he used to be. And I'm on a Dating Sabbatical and not interested. 'Why the hell is sleazy Ant trying to ask me out, though? And some Billy guy wanted my number . . .'

'Simple economics,' says Kate, the accountant. 'It's supply and demand. You are not available, so demand for you is high.'

'No, no. It's her pheromones. She is giving off some crazy look-but-don't-touch, hey-big-boy aura. That's what it is,' says Bloomie.

'Are you still drunk?' I ask her.

'Probably,' she nods, sipping her espresso. 'I adore Jake, by the way. He's just the kind of man I can see you with.'

I'll ignore that. She's a bit too direct sometimes. 'How come you know him and I don't?' I ask.

Bloomie thinks. 'Skiing that March when you had to work, I guess. And he was at that party at Fraser's that you didn't go to – the one just after you and Rick broke up, when you couldn't get out of bed.'

I'll ignore that, too.

'He moved here like a month ago or so.'

'Where from?'

'Edinburgh, maybe? I don't know.'

'He doesn't have a Scottish accent, though,' I muse. I catch Bloomie throwing Kate a knowing look.

'Why don't you ask him all these questions? Mitch could arrange a set-up,' she smiles.

'Well, unfortunately I'm on a Dating Sabbatical and therefore not interested,' I say airily.

'Very unfortunate!' agrees Bloomie with a grin, which turns into a yawn. 'I'm fuuuuh-king shattered.' This is an imitation of Posh Mark. Bloomie loved his accent so much. 'Saahriouslaah.'

'You cannot imitate my ex-boyfriends when I am on a Dating Sabbatical,' I say firmly.

'It's not in the Rules,' says Bloomie. 'Tragic'lah.'

Kate dunks the whole of the end of her BLT in the English mustard, and says quietly, 'I have something to tell you guys.'

'I swear to God, darlings, I can't sleep with The Dork next to me. He's so fuuuuuh-king sexy, I want to attack him all night. And now I'm so tired and I have to go to work later—'

'Shut *up*, Bloomie!' I mutter, seeing that Kate has started to cry.

'I'm thinking about leaving . . . I'm thinking about . . . leaving . . .'

'Leaving Tray?' I say.

Kate nods. Great big tears start running down her face. I scrabble for some tissues. Stupid lucky clutch, nothing useful is inside.

'I just can't bear it, and I have been feeling so . . . trapped, and then after dinner the other night talking to you, I don't know, I think when I met Tray I just did what you're doing, but instead of opting out of dating I just chose the safest, most boring route possible . . . and now I'm so safe . . . and so . . . bored . . . and I'm living with him . . .'

This is all a bit convoluted, and hard to hear through the sobs. I haven't seen Kate cry in years and years, it's kind of scary.

'How long have you been feeling this way?' asks Bloomie. We are both suddenly patting and stroking Kate as though she is a dog.

'Months.' Kate takes a deep shaky breath. 'Months. But there was Christmas, and then his birthday, and then we had a holiday booked . . .'

'You can't stay in a relationship just because you have holidays booked,' says Bloomie.

'And then I went home and suddenly it was all I could think about, and I talked to Mum and she said that it wasn't bad to feel this way . . .'

'It's not!' we chorus.

'And then I have days where I think, he is so kind and so smart, and I could do worse, and every other man in the world would just break my heart the way all those arseholes did before. And so what if I don't fancy him and he doesn't like to talk and doesn't enjoy the things I enjoy? I need to grow up and start realising that life isn't all excitement and fun.'

It's not? I think to myself.

'He doesn't like to talk?' says Bloomie.

'Oh, no, he does . . . I mean he just doesn't like, um, talking as much as I do. He likes to come home from work and . . . not talk. And I know he's stressed about his job and all that, but God! He doesn't TALK. At ALL. All NIGHT. And his idea of a good holiday is hiking and he never fucking laughs.'

It's very unlike Kate to swear, and she's almost only talking to herself now. 'But like, that's OK! I'm such a bitch for judging him!'

'Oh, darling, you are not a bitch,' says Bloomie. 'Of course you want to be with a guy who is, you know, a real partner. And someone to laugh with, someone who likes at least some of the things that you like, someone who just accepts you and adores you.'

Kate nods and sighs. I look at Bloomie incredulously. Acceptance and adoration? That sounds amazing. I've never had that. Ever. I can't imagine having it. I wonder if Bloomie has that with Eugene. I wonder if I'm even capable of it. I shake myself quickly. This is not the time to think about my stupid dating inadequacies. Kate needs us.

'Katie . . .' I say. 'Have you spoken to Tray about any of this?'

'Are you kidding?' she says. 'I'd break his heart. And when it comes down to it, I know there's only one answer. I have to leave him . . . I don't want to marry him. And I don't think he really wants to marry me, as he never mentions it either. Fucking hell, even the idea of it makes me feel like I'm drowning . . . so what were we thinking moving in together?'

Bloomie and I are nodding in unison.

'And, oh, guys, this is such bad timing. My company is imploding and everyone is walking around scared stiff of being made redundant. It's so awful. If I cared more, I'd hate it, but I don't. I feel completely detached from everything. Completely. I feel like I got this life by accident . . .'

Oh dear, she's spiralling. I know that feeling. When you can't find anything nice to think about, so you just think about everything that's shit in your life and get more and more depressed.

'Katiepoo, don't spiral,' I say.

'Huh?' says Kate.

'I thought you said you were like a prostitute? Never out of work?'

'I've been trying to tell myself that, too . . .' She shakes her head in despair.

'Wow, you guys have weird conversations . . . Katie, you can deal with work later,' says Bloomie decisively. 'Deal with Tray now.'

'Yeah, well, I mean, obviously, I need to end it and move out before I waste any more time . . .' She starts crying again. 'I feel fucking trapped, guys. I can't stay with him, but I can't bear the idea of hurting him either. And . . . where will I live?'

'You don't have to decide today,' I say.

'You can live with me!' exclaims Bloomie. 'Sara is moving out!'

'Really? When does she move out? I could stay with my sis for a few weeks . . .' says Kate, then checks herself. 'No, no, wait. I can't discuss this now. I can't make a plan for what to do after I – if I – leave him. It feels so callous.' She blows her nose about four times. 'I'm not going to think about it again today. Until I decide what to do there is no point. Right. What are we doing now?'

God, she's controlled.

'Are you sure? Are you sure you're OK?' I say.

'I'm fine!' she says, checking her reflection in the mirror next to the table.

'Really? Do you want to talk about this some more?' adds Bloomie.

'No!' Kate says briskly. 'That's enough. I'm sorry for burdening you with my shit. Let's go shopping.'

She really does seem fine now. No trace of the tears from 30 seconds ago. Bloomie gives a barely perceptible shrug. She'll talk more when she's ready, I guess.

Chapter Ten

The restorative power of a good shop can never be under-estimated. I know that sounds shallow, but it's true. The next few hours pass in a lovely daze of walking, shopping, coffees, cigarettes, chocolate (for energy) and the trying on of lots and lots of clothes. By about 2 pm I've bought a short black dress (yes, I have four of them at home, what's your point?), a weird but lovely boiled wool blazer, a white wifebeater vest with the perfect neckline (you know how hard they are to find) and a new pair of jeans. They're super-super-skinny, which I thought I was over. It turns out I'm not. High-fives to me, and high-fives to awesome cheap fashion. I didn't even spend all of my budget. All the more for black cabs and vodka, I think happily, moving the money around in the spreadsheet – OK, let's be honest, it's an abacus – in my head.

At 2.30 pm I get another text from Rugger Robbie:

Playing hard too get?

Ugh. Delete. How can he not know the difference between 'to' and 'too'?

Kate seems fine, though kind of distracted. I'd bet she wishes she hadn't talked to us at all; I think sharing emotions makes her embarrassed. How retro.

'You alright, darling?' I say, as we leave H&M in Knightsbridge.

'Fine! Fine. Honestly. Fine.'

'Your stiff upper lip is quivering,' I say.

Kate laughs despite herself. 'Well, thanks for, uh, talking.'

'Anytime, you know that.'

Bloomie clears her throat. 'And Sara moves out in three weeks . . .' Kate nods and looks away. Bloomie changes the subject. 'Well, I'm utterly shattered, darlings. I have to work for a few hours, then have a wee powernap before tonight. One of The Dork's French cousins is having au revoir drinks in somewhere in Notting Hill. Want to join?'

'I'm meeting Eddie and his sisters for dinner around there. I'll text you afterwards . . . Katiepoo?'

'I might drive up and see my parents, actually,' says Kate. 'I need to think. Come on, let's get the tube.'

I decide to walk home. It's one of those breezy strange March days in London, when the sun has decided to pretend it's in the Côte d'Azur in mid-summer. I love unexpectedly sunshiney Saturdays in London. Everyone laughs more and talks louder and smiles at strangers more than usual.

Serene contentment, consumer's euphoria and sunshine intoxication? Hot damn, this is the best I've felt in months.

In the past five days, I reflect, I've recovered from a break-up, had a great day at work, enjoyed a party where I didn't pull (or find my boyfriend cheating on me, for that matter) and made some outstanding wardrobe additions. Jake floats into my head, and floats out again just as easily. He's a bit handsome. But I'm not dating. So it just doesn't matter.

And it's all thanks to the Sabbatical.

Maybe my flatmate Anna really should do the Sabbatical. Maybe Kate should, after breaking up with Tray, obviously. In fact, maybe everyone should. Maybe I should launch it as a club. What would a strapline for the Dating Sabbatical be, I wonder happily to myself. Opting out is the new in? There's no sex in this city?

I put on my iPod, start walking in time to the beat (Tom Petty, 'American Girl') and sing along out loud all the way down

Sloane Street. (No one can hear me. People don't walk down Sloane Street. They just jump in and out of blacked-out Rolls-Royces to Chanel and Louis Vuitton and Chloe.) I can't wait to get to work on Monday and work on the German job, I think to myself. Then I start laughing at the idea that I am actually looking forward to work.

Still singing, I take a short cut through Belgravia (Carl Douglas, 'Kung Fu Fighting'), avoiding the Pantechnicon Rooms, a wonderful pub where I used to go with Smart Henry and can therefore no longer visit, cut over Eaton Place (Beach Boys, 'Don't Worry Baby') and walk down Elizabeth Street just as my favourite song of the moment comes on: Jay-Z, '99 Problems'. No one's near enough to hear me, so I start singing along and nodding my head and moving my arms like I imagine Jay-Z would. If you don't know the song, please Google it. The first line says it all.

At the precise moment I'm singing this line rather loudly, a tall man walks out of one of the posh bakeries on Elizabeth Street.

It's Jake.

I do a textbook double-take, stop and say 'Oh – hi! Hey. Hi,' take out my earphones and start to giggle nervously.

'Jay-Z,' he says, and smiles.

My giggles trail off in a gurgle and I nod, feeling very hot suddenly. 'Yup.'

How smiley his eyes are. 'Fancy running into you here,' he says. I am having trouble looking straight at him. I decide to put my sunglasses on. Then I wonder if that is rude, so I take them off. Then I drop my iPod. Dash it, compose yourself, woman. And stand up straight. (Posture is confidence.)

'Indeed,' I say. I can't think what to add, so I just close my mouth and look at him. (And silence is poise.)

'You ran away awfully fast last night,' he says. I really do like his eyes. And his lips. Oh, there goes my tummy again. Breakdancing around my torso.

98

'Oh, you know, it was like, almost curfew, and I thought I might get grounded.'

'Wow, over-protective parents are like totally bogus, huh?'

'Totally.'

I smile at him. He smiles back. After a couple of seconds of this happy silence, my stomach goes all calm. That's new.

'I love this bakery,' he says eventually. 'It's outrageously expensive, but worth it. I couldn't actually afford the deposit for the baguettes, but I've promised them my first-born child, so that should keep them happy . . .'

'Good thinking,' I reply. 'They also take souls, if you're ever down this way again.' I peer into the bag. 'Four baguettes? Are you sure you can afford to carbo-load like that?'

'I know, a minute on the lips, a lifetime on the hips . . . I'm doing my flatmate a favour. She's having a dinner party tonight. I'm in charge of bread and wine.'

'Yikes. Like a priest.'

'Yes, yes, you're right. I am just like a priest. In so many ways.'

'Mmm . . .' I smile at him. There's a pause, but it's a happy pause. I love this easy, silly conversation. Fuck, I forgot about Rule 3: No obvious flirting. Has it been obvious? Oh, I can't tell.

'Now, I was about to skive off from my priestly activities for half an hour and have a drink at the Thomas Cubitt. There's an outside table that is calling me to sit on it. The little tart. Can I . . . interest you in joining me?'

I would love to. I would love love love to. Um. He smiles down at me. I like . . . everything about his face.

'Come on, Minxy. Don't be a silly woman. All that singing and walking . . . you deserve a drink.'

This is true. But what about Rule 6: No accidental dating? I can't break the Dating Sabbatical now. Not when I'm doing so well.

'I'd love to but . . . I can't. I have to . . . I'm having dinner with some friends tonight and I have to go home now and then I have to . . . do that.'

'Ah . . .' he says lightly. 'Well, that sounds fun. Anywhere special?'

'Um, Notting Hill somewhere. Then joining Bloomie in a bar, I think. I don't know. I have to call Eddie.'

'I'd better get home anyway. Claudette is vibrating with stress at a level only dogs can hear.'

I nod and start backing away. 'OK! Have a great night!' Whoops, too much enthusiasm.

'You too.' He smiles at me and I smile back and then turn around and walk away.

I hope he's not looking at my arse.

Actually, I hope he is. And that's not against the Rules.

When I get home, I'm so energised by the Jake banter, I decide to do something I haven't done in ages. I get out my laptop and start writing. It's a silly short story, an urban fable of sorts, about a frog in a forest. I don't know what I'm doing with it or where it's going, but I write for an hour. I don't even re-read it – I will just delete it if I do, I know – I just write and write, and when I'm done, I save it in a folder called 'Ideas' that I keep for similar little bits and pieces. I see that it's the first thing that I've saved in it in over a year. Since I first started dating Rick, in fact.

Chapter Eleven

When I first met Eddie's twin sisters, they were nine and I was 18. Now I'm 28 (which doesn't feel vastly different from 19, except I've got a better wardrobe and I get hangovers now), and they've gone through all the gazillion dramas of adolescence, and are grown-ups. It's bizarre to think about, and makes me feel quite motherly.

We're eating in the Churchill Arms pub on Kensington Church Street, just a tiny tipsy wander from the Windsor Castle, where Posh Mark is probably drinking right this second. With fat Annabel Pashmina Face. Eurgh. London is a minefield of ex-boyfriend-places. Thank God I'm on the Sabbatical or I'd end up moving to Crouch End just to get a drink.

I've taken a black cab, as (justification incoming) I'm late, and frankly I suffer with the tube day in day out, and weekends should be relaxing and fun, you know, oh, and of course, I'm wearing extremely high heels so walking is simply not on the agenda. (They're pointed black stilettos, actually, with my new super-skinny jeans, a cream silk top, an old Lanvin-via-H&M fake black pearl and ribbon necklace topped off with a black trench, and I've blowdried my hair all big and glossy like Kim Basinger in *Batman*. Theme: 'Vicki Vale'.)

I skippy-bunny-hop out of the taxi and stride into the pub, which is as kooky a place as an old man's pub can be, decorated with a gazillion chamber pots and Churchill portraits. The place is packed, as usual, with a combination of old men, American students and youngish people like us. I almost walk right past Eddie and the twins: in the two years since I last saw Emma and Elizabeth, they've grown up. And out. And out again. I can barely refrain from commenting on their 32DDs, and realise that I am just a few small sashays away from turning into a mad old bat.

'Emma! Elizabeth! Oh my goodness! Look at you!' Yep, mad old bat. We all kiss hello and I lean over to the bar and, seeing that everyone else has a fresh drink, order a vodka for myself. Yum.

'Alright, darling?' grins Eddie. He looks a little watery-eyed. The coconut cocktails last night must have worked. Or maybe someone tropical punched him.

'What the sweet hell happened to your sisters?' I smile at them. They're all glossy brown hair and carefully applied eyeliner, and are sipping from their wine glasses just a tiny bit self-consciously. 'I only saw you two years ago, and you've grown up so much . . .' They look politely bored. I change tack. 'So tell me about your trip to Spain!'

They both start talking excitedly at once, and it's easy to chatter back. They're nearing the end of their gap year – both spent the past six months in Austria working as 'chalet biatches' – and are planning an extra-long summer in Spain at the family holiday house before starting university in autumn. We move on to talk about their plans for university, and then to the fantastic parties that await them there. I tell Eddie about Mitch's spectacular performance as I was leaving last night.

'You're so MEAN for not inviting Mitch tonight, Tedward,' pouts Emma. 'He's so fit.'

I choke on my vodka. 'You're just his type, darling,' I say. 'I'm sure you'll see him again soon.'

We have a couple more drinks and head to the Thai restaurant out the back of the pub, where we tuck into large servings of bog-standard but, at about £6 a person, extremely wallet-friendly,

Thai food. You might be wondering – well, maybe not, but I'll tell you anyway – whether the whole Jake thing is popping into my head during all of this, and my answer is no.

I mean, mostly no.

I mean, no.

In fact, I'm mostly not thinking about him as I refuse dessert (the super-skinny jeans don't really allow for it). Eddie grins.

'I thought you would let yourself go, now you've sworn off men,' he says.

'You've sworn? Off MEN?' says Emma, mouth agape. 'Why?'

'Um . . .' They're too young to understand. They'll think I'm crazy.

'Was your heart broken?' says Elizabeth sympathetically.

'Um, no, no . . .' I say, playing with my table napkin. 'It just got really . . . complicated. Going out with people. With boys – guys. Men. And I don't seem to make the right decisions, ever. So I have decided to stop making any decisions at all by not going out with anyone. That way, I can't get it wrong.'

The girls blink at me. This seems utterly incredible to them.

'I'd LOVE to be asked on a date,' says Emma. 'It must be SO exciting. All we get are snogs at fucking parties.'

'Hey,' says Eddie warningly. At what – the swear word? We all frown at him and keep talking.

'Yes . . . dates are exciting,' I agree. 'But there are a lot of real fucking bastardos out there.'

'Hey!' he says again. We frown at him again and continue.

'How can you tell?' says Elizabeth.

'Um . . . bastardo traits . . . let's see. Well, he might be aggressive, or he might be mean, or he might be selfish. Which can show in um, lots of ways that are surprisingly hard to spot and easy to ignore. Or he might not be a real bastardo, but he might just not like you that much, and you might like him more, and he'll dump you, and it will hurt. Or you might get involved by mistake, and he might turn out to be a bit stupid, or weird, or cheat on you, or be really boring, but by then you've become attached, and so you still always, always end up getting hurt. Every time.'

I'm waving my glass around as I spout all this tipsy wisdom. They're nodding very seriously, eyes wide open. Suddenly I feel like I'm telling five-year-olds that there's no Father Christmas.

'I mean, not ALL men are awful, of course . . .' I say quickly. 'There are loads of really amazing guys out there, and they want to meet someone too . . . because that's the whole point of everything, isn't it? To fall in love. And have a first kiss every day, and lie in bed being silly and giggling.'

They both nod vigorously. I'm quite taken aback with how romantic and Pollyanna-ish I am being. Do I really think that stuff? What *is* with all this dating and worrying? I feel tired just thinking about all the guys I've met in the past ten years. What on earth have I been doing with my fucking time? And what would it be like to lie in bed being silly and giggling with someone lovely? I suddenly realise I've been gazing into space, thinking these thoughts, for several seconds and look back at the girls. They're both staring at me with their mouths open. I smile and they smile back, but they have a slightly scared look on their faces. Yet again, mad old bat.

'Christ, I'm bored with this conversation,' says Eddie, trying to grab the attention of one of the harried Thai waitresses. 'Let's get the bill and go to a bar.'

Bloomie has texted suggesting we join their drinks at Montgomery Place, a cocktail bar that's a short walk, or an even shorter cab ride away. Obviously we get a cab.

A large group of 30-something Kensington types, French and English, are already dominating the long, narrow bar, so we order our drinks and squeeze in. The twins start being chatted up by some French guys almost immediately, and Eddie starts talking to Eugene, which gives me a few minutes to tell Bloomie all about running into Jake this afternoon.

104

'NO!' she exclaims. 'It's a sign!'

'A sign? Like, gag me with a spoon,' I say.

'God, you're 90s. Are you Brenda or Donna, do you think?' she asks. 'You're not Anthea.'

'Oh God, no, not Anthea. I was always totally Kelly!' I say. 'Until she became, like, a boring bitch, in the later years. But now I'm probably Serena, ya know? In fact, you can start calling me van der Woodsen.'

'It's so nice to see you back to your old self, darling,' she says, smiling at me. 'After Rick I was . . . I was really worried. And Posh Mark . . . you really didn't seem terribly happy with him, either.'

'That's the beauty of the Dating Sabbatical!' I crow delightedly. 'I am back to my old self! In fact, I'm better!'

We're interrupted by a rather handsome French guy.

'Excuse me, Bloomie,' he says, pronouncing her name very carefully. (I won't bother to spell things the way he pronounces them. You know what a French accent sounds like.) 'May I meet your friend?'

'Of course!' grins Bloomie, and introduces us. He's a family friend of Eugene's. His name is Benoit.

'Love your pullover, Benoit,' I say. He's wearing a red pullover draped over his shoulders and tied in a knot across his chest, with a white shirt and ironed jeans. I believe it's known as ironic preppy chic. But he probably doesn't intend it ironically.

'Oh, thank you. I like your tranch,' he replies. (OK, I had to explain how he pronounced that one. It's funny.) He's wearing cute little wireframe glasses. We talk about Paris – where he's from, though he lives in London now – for awhile, and Bloomie gets pulled away by Eugene for some apparently life-and-death question (snogging, as far as I can tell). Benoit and I chat about where we work, where we live, and then I'm almost out of small talk, when he says:

'One of my favourite French restaurants in London is close

to your house in Pimlico. La Poule au Pot. I would love to take you there for dinner.'

'Oh! Oh, gosh . . .' This is a statement, not a question. What do I say? (Just say no.)

'Are you free on Wednesday? I will pick you up at your house.'

Thank God. I can respond to that.

'I'm not free on Wednesday, Benoit . . . That sounds very nice, but—'

'You have a boyfriend!' he exclaims. 'Of course.'

'No, no boyfriend. I am not dating at the moment . . . I am not, uh, going to dinner. With anyone.'

Benoit regards me impassively for two or three seconds. 'OK.' He shrugs, turns around and starts talking to the person behind him.

Wow. I can't help laughing. This Dating Sabbatical is making me the most unpopular person in London. And it also seems to bring out the bastardo side of men.

'When you're laughing by yourself, you look completely crazy,' says a voice behind me. I turn around quickly. It's Jake.

'Stalking is a federal offence, you know,' I say.

'This isn't America, Minxy. We don't have federal offences.'

He leans over and kisses me on both cheeks. It's the first time we've actually touched. Warm cheeks, freshly shaven, with a lemony warm smell. Mmm, lovely crinkly eyes. But what the sweet hell is he doing here? Didn't he say he had a dinner party? I won't ask. Is it hot in here? I'm taking off my trenchcoat.

'Jake, darling! What a surprise! I thought you had a dinner party!' exclaims Bloomie, charging over and kissing him.

'I did,' he grins. 'We've eaten, and Claudette decided she didn't want us to mess up the flat any more than we already have, so we decided to come out for a few drinks. I live just around the corner.'

'How was the bread?' I ask.

'Exquisite,' he says. 'Can I get you a drink? And let me introduce everyone . . .'

The other survivors of what sounds like a rather hellish evening are standing at the bar, looking relieved. Jake introduces the two guys, Barry and Sam, two girls, Claire and Yvonne, and the very glamorous but uptight Claudette, who seems to be barely on speaking terms with any of them.

We all start drinking and talking. His friends are funny, he's funny, I think I'm holding my own (with the help of Bloomie, who keeps feeding me openers for my best lines, not that I'm flirting, oh no), and I'm not letting myself think about the jumpy-yearny feeling in my stomach, or the fact that I'm in a perpetual cold sweat.

Pretty quickly, the French group and Jake's group and Eddie's group all start mingling and talking. Then, somehow, Jake and I are left alone at the bar together and, instead of feeling nervous or fluttery or hot, everything goes tranquil and quiet and happy inside me. Just like the calmness today outside the bakery, but even more so.

'I like the trenchcoat. You look like Kim Basinger in *Batman*,' he says.

'That's exactly what I was going for,' I say, elated.

'How'd you recover from your Jager-binge last night?'

'Not bad,' I say. 'I think I'm allergic to it, you know. It makes me drunk. It's weird.'

'Yeah, that is weird,' he agrees.

We sit in silence for a few seconds, smiling at each other. Mmmm.

'Do you like Homer Simpson?' he asks abruptly.

I think for a moment.

'Well . . . yes. I must do. I quote him, not all the time, but reasonably often. Like when I say something is make-believe, like elves, gremlins, and Eskimos. Ooh, and I have a genuinely deep and abiding fear of sock puppets. So yes, when I think about it, I really do like Homer Simpson.'

'Ah, Minxy,' he says, shaking his head and looking into my

eyes. I don't know what he means by this, or why he asked me about Homer Simpson, and I don't care. I feel so at ease with him right now that it would be the most natural thing in the world to lean forward, rest my head on his chest and close my eyes. A thought pops into my head, so clearly and loudly, that I have to check for a second that I didn't say it aloud. *I just adore you.*

'So tell me about your dinner,' I ask. Yes. Small talk. Small talk to break the tension.

'Well,' he says. 'The most interesting conversation was about Mo-vember. Do you know it? Guys are sponsored to grow moustaches for the whole of November and the proceeds go to a prostate cancer charity . . .'

'Eddie and Mitch did it last year. Disaster for both of them,' I nod. 'I'm hoping to get a female-equivalent charity going. I want to call it Pit-tember.'

Jake laughs quite hard at this. I like making him laugh.

'Tell me about the last time you had your heart broken,' he says, taking a sip of his drink.

I arch an eyebrow. He likes the random questions, this guy. The random personal questions, too. But I shouldn't show him my soft white emotional underbelly. He only gets to see the shiny protective funny tortoise shell. That's how flirting works. (Not that I am flirting. Am I?) 'Uh . . . it wasn't really a heartbreak, it was nothing, really . . . about nine months ago I was seeing a guy, and he wasn't very nice anyway, and we were at a party, and I was a librarian, and I caught him cheating on me with a Pink Lady.'

He looks confused.

'You know, from *Grease.*'

He still looks confused.

'The musical.'

'Ahhh, from *GREASE*!' he exclaims. 'I thought you meant the Pink Lady apples, and then . . . it became very . . . weird in my head. Of course. Why were you a librarian?'

'It was a "Come As Your Childhood Ambition" theme party. You know: vets, pilots, ballet dancers . . . I really did always want to be a librarian.'

'You're actually just a big dork, aren't you?' he says.

'A big *sexy* dork,' I correct him, taking a sip of my drink. 'And that's MISS Big Sexy Dork to you.' (Oh, hush. I know it's obvious flirting. It just came out.)

'Cocky. So cocky,' he says, shaking his head.

I'm not sure what to say to this. Cocky is certainly not how I'd describe myself.

'See? You're not even bothering to reply. Cocky. Fine, I'll talk. Even though you haven't asked me, I would have come as a dog. I thought I was a dog, actually, till I was five. I would only eat from a bowl on the floor next to our real dog, Scooby, and I wee-ed against trees whenever I could.'

'Good boy,' I say, smiling at him. 'Lucky your parents didn't have you neutered.'

'Very lucky,' he agrees.

There's a slight pause and we smile at each other.

'What is with you people and theme parties, anyway?' he says. 'Is it because you've run out of things to talk to each other about, or something?'

'Yes, that's entirely it. Sometimes we use cue cards for conversation topic prompts, too. It just saves so much effort.'

He grins. The last few minutes have been so warm, so easy, an odd combination of thrilling and comforting. I love this anxiety-free, satisfyingly silly conversation.

And then, like a slap, I'm hit by complete and utter fear.

It's so obvious we're going to kiss. Or he's going to ask me out. Or both. And this is just the trap I don't want to fall into. This is why I need a Dating Sabbatical and why I must strictly adhere to the Rules. He's too funny, too confident, he's got that sparkly charming handsome thing going on that defin-itely means that underneath it all is a bastardo and he'll just get tired of me and be mean and dump me and I have to go home.

'I have to go home,' I say.

He looks surprised for a second, then quickly assumes a look of nonchalance. 'No problem, Minxy. I'll come outside and get you a cab.'

'No!' I exclaim, a little too enthusiastically. 'No, I'll get Bloomie . . . I need to . . . to ask her something.' I put my trench on quickly, pretending not to see him trying to help. 'Well, I'll see you around.' I lean up and kiss him on both cheeks goodbye. He wasn't ready for this, and starts slightly before composing himself.

'Yep. See you.'

I walk away quickly, without looking back, grabbing Bloomie on the way out without pausing my stride.

'Put me in a cab,' I say.

'What's wrong, darling?' says Bloomie. 'You're so pale!'

'Jake – I can't – the Sabbatical – but there's something . . .' I take a deep breath and shake my head. A black cab pulls up, and Mitch jumps out and envelops me in a huge hug. He's pissed.

'You don't have to leave, now, darling, I'm here,' he says. 'The party can commence.'

I shake my head. 'Bloomie, say goodbye to everyone for me. Bitch, stay away from Eddie's sisters. I'll text you when I'm home safe. Pimlico, please!' I don't even wait for a response from Bloomie, Mitch or the driver. I just get in the cab, slam the door, and look straight ahead as he drives off. All I can think is that I have to get away. Get far far away.

When I'm finally home, I have slight trouble putting my key in the door. There are scratch marks above and below the keyhole from the many times I've had similar trouble before. Which I find funny and yet pathetic.

I run up the stairs and into the kitchen, put my lucky yellow clutch down and lean over the sink.

Thoughts are tumbling through my head, one after another, so fast I can hardly even think each before the next lands. I wish I hadn't met Jake. I wish I'd never met Rick either, or Posh Mark. I wish I hadn't kept going on dates time after time after time in that kneejerk-reaction way. I wish the bright shiny way I used to approach everything wasn't so dull and tarnished. I wish I didn't have to go to work and see Andy on Monday. I wish I wasn't so shit at everything. I wish none of this was happening. I wish I could block everything out.

Talk about spiralling. My breath is coming out in gasps, I feel all jumpy and weird and I can't calm down. My heart is racing and I can hear the sound of nothing roaring in my ears. Is this a panic attack? Is it? Is it? Oh fuck me, is it?

Breathe. Breathe. Breeaaaaaaaaathe.

I focus on inhaling and exhaling slowly, and shut my eyes. This seems to do the trick. It's not a panic attack. Fucking drama queen.

I fill up a pint glass with water and drink it slowly as I turn around to look at the kitchen. I've been living in this manky little flat for years and years, and my life hasn't changed at all.

Everyone else's life has moved on and up and I'm just here, treading vodka, doing the same things and making the same mistakes. Time after time after time. And you know, they're not all mistakes really, or choices, they're just passive reactions that keep me in this pathetic holding pattern. I can't move forward, or sideways, or anywhere. I can't imagine my future and I don't even know what I would want it to be like if I could.

And you know what else? I really do think I started out normal. Then somewhere along the way I got lost. I look back on the Rick period – and afterwards – and feel desperately sorry for that girl. And I look back at the Posh Mark period and feel unsurprised that I held him at arm's length. And let's not even start on Jonathan and Robbie and Brodie and Henry. Each of them dumped me. And I never saw it coming. After all that, wouldn't you feel the way

I do? I don't know if I'm incapable of having a relationship, or if this is just really, really, really, really fucking bad luck, but I do know one thing. I'm not doing it all again. I just can't.

I CAN'T.

I think this so loudly that I cause my fingers to involuntarily drop the glass and it shatters on the floor. How dramatic, I think, staring at it.

The Dating Sabbatical isn't a drunken vow anymore. It's serious. It's the only thing that can protect me from this vicious circle of dating blunders, it's the only thing that might help me save my sanity.

I'm going to obey all the Rules without fail. I am going to avoid going places or parties where I might see Jake. There's something between us, and it is just confusing and would obviously be disastrous if anything ever did happen, so I should simply block him out entirely. I can't trust myself not to fall into the same trap I always do. Instead, I will work my arse off, and nail this pitch. I will grab hold of the things I can control, figure out what I want, and make it happen.

I'm going to change my life.

Chapter Twelve

I wake up at 6 am on the three-month anniversary of my Dating Sabbatical, stretch and sigh, and smile at the ceiling. I don't think I've ever been happier.

In fact, I think as I lace my trainers to go for my morning jog, I didn't used to think it was possible to even be this happy. And it's all thanks to the Dating Sabbatical.

And you know what else? My life isn't that different: I'm in the same job and the same house and all that. But I've changed the way I live it. I've changed.

As I head out the door and start my favourite jogging route through Pimlico and over Chelsea Bridge to Battersea Park, I look up at the beautiful pinky-blue early morning sky and smile. Everything, to misquote *Sixteen Candles*, is platinum. Remember how I woke up on that first Saturday morning after Mitch's party with that happy clearness that came, it seemed, more or less directly from not thinking about dating? Well, that was just the beginning.

Not only am I not heartbroken or obsessing over some idiot guy, but everything else is so easy. I've been working hard, and – bizarrely – loving it. The fortnightly meetings with the Germans have gone really well and I think we're going to win the account. Coop is thrilled with me. Andy, the evil head designer, has more or less stayed out of my way. I'm not going out as much (partly as half the time I was only going out to meet guys anyway, and partly because I've been working late quite a lot) so I'm drinking less and spending less, which makes using my brain-abacus much easier. When I do go out, I've had awesome nights that don't end in pulling or tears. I've also spent a few really relaxing weekends at home with Mum and Dad, which is a first. I never used to go home on weekends in case I missed out on, you know, boys.

What else? Gosh, everything. I run a couple of mornings a week, as it's easy to get up at 6 am when you haven't had anything to drink the night before, and it's a euphoric way to start the day. Other mornings I write for a couple of hours before work – nothing big, but little things that make me happy. I've read more books than I have in years, and I've even started to read the papers. You know, the boring, I mean the financial bits. (I often have to call Bloomie to get an explanation about something, but that's OK. Baby steps, you know?) The Dating Sabbatical isn't a magic recipe for success in every area of life – I tried to cook a roast one night for Bloomie, Eugene and Mitch, and the resulting charred mess led Mitch to loudly beg me to adopt a Cooking Sabbatical. But on the whole, it seems like all I had to do was obey the Rules and my life seemed to sort itself out. I'm pure, cleansed, totally detoxed from dating.

In other words, I'm a lean, mean, date-free machine.

I'd say I feel like myself again – like myself from pre-Rick and every other break-up – but really, I'm better than the old myself. I'm the best myself I've ever been. I fucking love it.

I can't actually believe it took me six break-ups to think of it. I've been so smug about the Sabbatical, actually, and so convinced I've discovered the secret to a satisfying, productive, stress-free life, that a few weeks ago, I rang my mother to tell her about it. Her reaction makes me laugh even now, prompting some other joggers going past me over Chelsea Bridge to give me funny looks. I poke my tongue out at them.

'Oh . . . darling,' she said, her voice breaking. 'I wondered why you'd spent so much time with us recently. You've become cynical . . . just like that nasty redhead with the bad table manners in *Sex on the City*.'

'*Sex AND the City*, Mother. And I have not. And I only spent two weekends with you! Like, seriously . . .'

'You should be out having fun at your age! That Mark sounded so nice. If you don't want to go with him, then why can't you just be like me and my friends when we were young? Play the field, baby. Play. The. Field.'

'I know it's not really a viable long-term plan, Maman,' I said, wondering at the same time if I really do think that, given how well it seems to be working out for me at the moment. 'It's just something I'm doing for now.'

'For how long?'

'For the moment. Can I please talk to Dad?'

My father, of course, could not be more thrilled that his only child, his little girl is not dating men.

'I think it's a wonderful game plan, Sassy Sausage,' he said. 'It gives you time to consider your options and reformulate your strategy. There's no rush. No rush at all.'

Please don't tell anyone he calls me Sassy Sausage.

My friends are also accustomed to the idea of the Dating Sabbatical. At Fraser's birthday party a few weeks ago, no one even bothered to tease me. (Ant, actually, ignored me for most of the night, which was wonderful.) Bloomie, who is still dating The Dork and glowing with happiness despite work-induced exhaustion, has been telling people in her office about it, and two of her colleagues claim to have started Dating Sabbaticals (results pending). Anna, my flatmate, tried it, but then got back together with was-married-now-officially-separated Don three weeks later. (So perhaps it worked.) Mitch loudly announced his own Dating Sabbatical in a bar one night, largely as he thought it would attract women who'd see him as a challenge, but after six attempted pick-ups in a row ended with the girl walking away as soon as he mentioned the damn thing, he pronounced it a 'ridiculous fucking idea' and gave it up.

Funny, as it has the opposite effect on men. And I'm not advertising the fact that I'm on a Dating Sabbatical, either, because as Rule 5 tells us, that would be seen as a challenge and just intrigue them. But I must be giving off some come-hither-fuck-off aura that men find irresistible, as I keep being asked out. It's bizarre. When it happened three times in the first four days of the Dating Sabbatical, I put it down to coincidence. But after three months, it's absurd.

I've been chatted up and asked out on each of the few nights I've been out (one guy followed me to the bathroom to ask for my number, for Pete's sake), in the tube (a hotbed of sexual tension, have you ever noticed?), in my morning coffee place (which is annoying, as I've since seen the same dude in there twice, so I've started having coffee at home instead, and you know how I feel about that coffee place – that is how far I'll go to maintain Dating Sabbatical integrity) and even in Pimlico Sainsbury's (over the banana stand, which according to Bloomie is 'always the way'). It's actually kind of annoying.

And you know, I haven't got any better looking (dash it). And I'm not any funnier than I used to be (double dash it).

So I can only conclude that the reason I'm being asked out like this is that somehow, they can tell I'm not interested, and want what they can't have. The less I want men, the more they want me. It's playing hard to get on a whole new level.

But God, life is so much easier than before. Being on a Dating Sabbatical isn't just second nature now, it's my only nature. And also, I can't lie. I don't want to date any of them. None of them interest me even slightly. There's been the odd cute one – like that American, the first night, or even Lukas, the hot German at work, or smartarsey Jake – but I don't have to think, like I used to, 'Habla bastardo?', as it's a non-issue.

Sometimes I wonder if I would break the Dating Sabbatical

if I met someone I really, really liked. Then I remember that it would have ended the same anyway. It would have gone sour, he'd be mean, something bad would have happened and then I really would be one step closer to being the cynical redhead with the bad table manners on *Sex and the City*.

I know what you're about to ask. I haven't seen Jake. I thought I saw him, once, in a restaurant when I was having a Sunday lunch with my mum and dad, but it was just the back of another tall guy with nice big shoulders. And another time, I thought I saw him at the far end of the tube carriage I was in. But he got off before I could see properly. And I don't think he's been around much anyway. No one has really mentioned him. And I haven't asked.

Not that it matters anyway.

And now, it's Wednesday, and exactly three months since Posh Mark dumped me and the Dating Sabbatical was born. It's an important day, too. We're meeting the German clients at 11 am for the final presentation – we're unveiling our final choice for the name and strapline, and the logo and how we want to position them in the market. (Oops, there I go. Talking about work again.) I can't wait.

And tonight I'm meeting Bloomie and Kate for dinner. I've been working so hard that I haven't seen them properly in over a week, in fact, since the weekend before last when we had a reunion of all our university girlfriends. (Great night: we went to a club night called Guilty Pleasures where they play the best worst songs of the past 20 years; naturally the night included much drunken debauched behaviour. I was debauchery-free, by the way: I simply demonstrated my best 80s dance moves, showed off that I know all the words to Dolly Parton's '9 to 5', rejected three would-be suitors and was tucked up alone in bed by a perfectly decent 3 am.)

Ah, yes, I forgot to tell you about Kate. She left Tray, you probably won't be particularly surprised to hear, just a few weeks after our shopping trip. She moved in with Bloomie, and has been almost unbelievably fine about it all. (Another reason I've been going out a bit less, actually – there've been a few quiet catch-up dinners over at their place instead.) I haven't seen Kate this happy in years. She thinks she mourned the demise of the relationship before it had stopped ticking, as she'd been crying and worrying constantly for months. She says she's only cried once since she moved out – when she had to go back to the house they shared to pick up her things – but calmed herself by repeating 'Just because we're nice people doesn't mean we have to be together. I don't want him. This is the right decision. This had to happen.' Talk about stable. At least, she seems stable, but then again, she's a controlled, private sort of person. She could be a basket case and we wouldn't have a clue about it unless she wanted us to.

I spend most of my jog thinking about the day ahead of me, get home at 7.15 am and head upstairs to shower and change. God, I love the almost-summertime of early June. It's better than real summer, when you're always a bit panicked about not making the most of every moment of sunshine as it's probably going to disappear for six months at any moment.

Thinking about work pushes all sartorial planning out of my head, as it keeps doing recently, and I find myself – post the usual shampoo/scrub/shave routine – standing in front of my wardrobe, utterly unable to think of an outfit. Fucking hell, I can't believe this keeps happening to me. Me, of all people. It's like a Casanova becoming impotent, I muse. Right. What do I want to wear today?

Nothing distracting, nothing fussy, nothing silly. Something practical.

Wow, did I just think that? What the hell is wrong with me? Get inspired, damn it! Practicality is the enemy of all that is good and decent in the world.

Fine. Katharine Hepburn Having Lunch. A pair of navy

high-waisted wide-legged trousers and a pale buttery yellow short-sleeved sweater, tucked in. Hair back in a low chignon. Red ballet flats for a bit of pop. Make-up minimal, with some good ol' MAC Satin Taupe eyeshadow just for shits and giggles. Eyebrows are – I smile at them and resist the urge to blow a kiss – adorably perfect. OK, now I'm ready.

I glance over at my clock radio. It's 7.18 am, which is pretty damn early, but I'd like to get to work as soon as possible so that I can run over everything before everyone else gets in. I need to check the boardroom, double-check the presentation and go through who's saying what. We're having a practice run-through at 9.30 am, so there's time to fix anything that needs fixing before the Germans arrive at 11. As well as managing the creative work, I'm pretty much running these meetings when it comes to presenting the creative side of things. Cooper said he wants to sell the agency as a place full of creative leaders, not just an ad factory that lives and dies by him. Shit! I also have to make sure that Amanda The Office Manager makes tea and coffee. I flip open the little notepad I've been carrying around the past few weeks and write this down, which I know is anal and Kate-esque of me, but the second time I forgot something important for work I could really have killed myself, so getting a little notepad seemed easier than you know, buying a gun. Ooh, and I'll pick up some decent biscuits on the way, too. Leaving biscuits up to Amanda The Office Manager backfired two weeks ago, and I'm not making that mistake again. Rich fucking Tea indeed.

I look at myself in the mirror again quickly. Yep, enough preening. Let's go.

I look around for my lucky yellow clutch. It clashes with the buttery yellow top, I fear – the clutch is a bright yellow – but I can't not wear it today. Call me superstitious, but after a year of really not being lucky at all, this clutch is finally living up to its appellation.

As I stride out the front door – there's nothing like striding in high-waisted trousers, have you ever noticed? – I do a skippy-bunny-hop and smile up at the sky. Wish me luck today.

Chapter Thirteen

The office is completely empty when I get in, which gives me blissful silent preparation time. The two final creative routes we've got are (I think, I hope) good, and the boards (onto which we've pasted our branding and launch ideas) look excellent. The weekly work-in-progress 'tissue' (ew) meetings have gone really well, even though they've only been with ol'-blue-eyes Lukas, the UK MD. He looks over what we're doing and says what he thinks, but he's so new to the Blumenstrauße business too, so he probably has about the same amount of insight as we do. But today is different. The two most senior guys, Stefan and Felix, arrive this morning from Germany. I met them briefly about six weeks ago when they came over for a few meetings about the strategy plan, but this is the first time I'll be speaking to them at length. Hopefully it won't be the last.

I read over my presentation notes and thoroughly proof the boards one last time and look at my watch. It's 8.36 am. The office is still empty. I send a quick email to Amanda The Office Manager to remind her about coffee for the Germans, and check my notebook. Yep, looks like I've done everything. And there's still over two hours till they all get here. I can relax. I take a deep breath and exhale slowly. Zen. Zenny zen.

'Hey. I'm here to see if you need any help before the meeting.'

It's Danny, one of Andy's crony-ish art directors. He's been working pretty hard on this pitch, but all the same, he's never

121

been in the office before 10 am, ever. I'm staggered. He even – I look him up and down quickly – has cleanish jeans and a long-sleeved shirt on.

'Oh, wonderful. Yes, please,' I say, thinking quickly about what he can do. 'You could go over the branding presentation and check it, and if you have any time after that, more example imagery would be great for us to stuff into the leave-behind.'

'No probs,' he says.

For the next 45 minutes we work together in silence, with just the tinny strains of Ladyhawke coming from his iPod head-phones. The rest of the office starts trickling in – first the account managers, then the creatives. Everyone's a bit earlier than usual, probably as they know it's such an important day for the agency.

At 9.30 am we do a quick run-through with just the team who's doing the pitch. Me, Charlotte the account manager, Scott the account director and Cooper. We all know who's talking, who's introducing who, and who's sitting where. Scott is good at this shit. He was trained at Ogilvy, and as a result has that glossy sheen that rubs off nicely on the rest of us. Charlotte's a bit gushy, Cooper adds a stern gravitas and I – I wonder what I bring to the table? I don't know. Anyway. It goes well, I think, I don't forget anything in my presentation. Charlotte and Scott agree to make some last-minute tweaks to their part of the pitch document, and I go back to my desk and practise deep breathing. One hour and 15 minutes till all the work we've done for the past three months is rated yay or nay. I'm not dreading it. But I'm not exactly frothing with excitement either. I just want it over and done with now.

The last person in, at 9.50 am, is Andy. He ignores everyone, as ever, and walks over to his desk to noisily dump his stuff. He looks over at Danny's computer and, seeing – I assume – the Blumenstrauße work on the screen, makes a 'humph!' sound through his nose and frowny-smirks. I narrow my eyes. That

122

little trousersnake had better stay out of my way today. If he doesn't, I'll . . . OK, I'll probably just try to ignore him.

Now is the time to admit that since the little scuffle on the day Coop told me to talk to everyone about the pitch, I have only been – how can I put this – quasi-assertive with the whole Andy situation. You don't start loving confrontation just because you're on a Dating Sabbatical, you know. So I've kept my head down and stayed out of his way, and he's stayed out of my way. (If you call swaggering around the office being loud and obnoxious and talking jovially to everyone except me 'staying out of my way'.) When we couldn't avoid each other, I stood up for myself and my ideas (which is an improvement! Right?) and then, you know, ran away.

I am really enjoying work, despite Andy. Everyone else in the office has been positive about and dedicated to the pitch work. And they're all smiling quite a lot, which must be a good sign. Oh, and I've noticed something else, too: the junior creatives have been showing me their ideas for approval and feedback, or asking me advice when they're stuck on jobs for all our different clients. *Me*. Not Andy. A couple of times, Andy has come over and loudly contradicted something I've suggested, and they've followed my advice anyway. These are all small, but very satisfying, wins.

I look back to my work for a few minutes, but look straight back up when I hear Andy saying 'Knock knock, mate!' loudly at the side of Coop's Chinese screens.

'Enter,' he calls back.

'Just me, mate . . .' says Andy, walking around the screens.

I wonder what he's up to. This is the problem with small offices, you know. You're completely aware of what everyone else is doing at all times.

Ben, the second of Andy's art directors, walks over to my desk. 'Need any more help?'

'Yes,' I say, standing up. 'Please take the boards through to the meeting room. We're going to set up soon.'

123

'Righto,' he says.

I look at my computer clock again quickly – one hour to go exactly – and walk through to the account management room to ask Charlotte and Scott a quick question about the introductions. I'm heading back to the creative department when I hear someone shouting 'OH FUCK!' from the meeting room. I run in.

Ben has spilled a large silver Thermos of coffee all over the boards. The ones with all our beautiful ideas on.

'I thought it was empty! I knocked it over!' he's shouting. 'Fuck!'

Ben is brushing the coffee off the top board and basically spreading it around even more.

'Don't panic,' I say. 'And stop doing that.'

I quickly separate the boards and survey the damage. The bottom three are OK, with minimal stains at the very edge. The top three are dreadful, with coffee completely covering one and seeping badly into the sides of the other two. Fuckety fuck. It takes an age to print this much in colour on our shitty printer, and then we'll have to laminate and re-stick them to the boards. I look at the clock on the wall. We have 52 minutes.

'Get tissues, Laura, Charlotte and Amanda, now,' I say, standing the three boards that can be saved against the wall to dry. Ben leaves the room at a sprint, shouting on the way, and is back in about ten seconds with the tissues. He looks like he's almost in tears, which I guess means he didn't sabotage the boards on purpose.

'I'm so sorry . . .' he says, as Laura and Amanda The Office Manager scurry in.

'Don't worry about it. Shit happens,' I say briskly mopping up what I can. 'Laura, I want you and Ben to start printing these three again immediately. Do you know where they are saved on the server? Check that it's the right version, Danny will know if you're not sure. Make sure you're doing it on the right paper and then stick them on the boards again. I think we're nearly out of the adhesive backing, so Ben, please fetch some more from the storeroom. Charlotte, tell everyone that they cannot send anything to print for the next hour and send an email to the entire office to stay out of the printing studio, too. Amanda, get kitchen towels, cleaning spray and sponges. And in future, please wait to put coffee and tea on the table until the clients get here. It would have been cold anyway, and mistakes like this happen.'

The three of them, nodding like little taxi-dashboard-dogs, practically sprint out of the room. Amanda The Office Manager is back almost immediately, and, though I can tell she's sulking at me slightly for telling her off, we quickly clean and scrub the spilled coffee. I thank Amanda and ask her to fix hot coffee, this time for exactly 10.55 am, and to use the good cafetiere, not the Thermos. As I'm heading back into the creative room, I run into Cooper and Andy.

'Just the person I'm after,' says Cooper. I glance quickly from him to Andy. Andy isn't looking at me, but he's holding a bunch of black and white scamps on small boards.

'Andy has some ideas for Blumenstrauße advertising,' he says. 'He wants to present them today, throw them into the mix. It's your call.'

'You worked on the pitch . . . on your own?' I ask. I'm astounded. This is completely out of the ordinary. And it's a massive vote of distrust against me as lead creative on the pitch.

'I was telling Coop how I've been having trouble sleeping,' Andy says, looking at me with mild disdain. 'I figured I'd put my insomnia to good use. So the past two nights I've been working up some ideas. And you know, I figured every little helps, as Tesco says.'

I can feel them both looking at me, judging my reaction. Aside from fury – how dare he elbow his way in at the last minute? – I'm also stunned that Cooper is putting me in charge of making the decision about putting Andy's work in my pitch. It must be a test. I have to be impartial. I'd hate us to lose the pitch and then find out that Andy's ideas could have saved us.

'Let's take a look,' I say. 'A good idea is a good idea, no matter where it comes from, though it's a shame you didn't work with the rest of us, it would have been great to have had your help . . .'

'Someone had to look after all our other clients,' he calls over his shoulder, barging past me through to the meeting room again. That is so unfair. I've worked on all our other clients' stuff, too. Cooper holds the door open and looks at me quizzically, trying to read my reaction. I assess my outward composure, and give myself a pass. I am professional. Cooper trusts me.

'Let's take a look!' I say brightly, walking through to the meeting room.

'Here's what I was thinkin',' says Andy to Cooper, laying out his boards on the table. I glance over them quickly, but my head is spinning and I'm having trouble taking it in. It suddenly occurs to me that the past few months of hard work could be ditched for a two-night effort from Andy. That would suck. His ideas might be good. He's a lot more experienced than me. Shit.

'I took a look at Charlotte's strategy on the server last night, and I've kept the name "Bliss" that you lot came up with, so this fits that with a few minimal tweaks. Here's my basic insight: toiletries are for girls. So I say, let's embrace that. Forget that boring PC shit. Girls make buying decisions, girls care about what shampoo their boyfriend is using. Men couldn't give a fuck. All they want is, you know, sex. And all girls want is for men to want them.'

So far, so pseudo-simplistic-slash-empowering-slash-sexist. 'Girls' versus 'men'. Grrr.

'I was thinking, let's be a bit cheeky. Let's make this brand about the pleasure of toiletries. Sex appeal. The body.'

My gaze falls back on the boards as he reads his first board out loud.

'"Bliss. For her pleasure . . . And yours."'

My eyes finally focus on the board. It's a black and white drawing of a woman's body: in shadow, arched in ecstasy, enormous breasts thrust to the ceiling, as she lies in what appears to be a bubble bath. Across it he's written his strapline, and added a secondary line 'Show me the bubbles.'

I look at the second board. It's another woman's body, this time in the shower, both arms pressed against the wall, again, apparently in ecstasy. The same main line, and then 'Show me the clean.'

I look at the third board. It's a woman in a bathrobe, one shoulder sexily revealed, shaving her legs. 'Show me the smooth.' I look quickly at the rest. They're all the same shit. The logo is a single line showing the upper silhouette of a woman lying on her back, breasts thrust skywards. The line ends in a little flower head. And again 'For her pleasure . . . And yours.' I look over at Coop. He's looking at me, his face a blank mask.

'What do you think?' I ask Cooper.

'What do YOU think?' he replies.

I clear my throat and start talking as crisply as I can, so as not to stammer. 'Well, let's see. I'm . . . Uh, what exactly are we saying here with the main line, "For her pleasure . . . And yours" . . . that Bliss products will please a woman sexually, so it'll save a man the bother?'

'Sure, whatever. The point is, it's sexy,' says Andy. 'It's tongue-in-cheek. Let's have fun with it. I think we should rename the body cream Funderwear.'

('Funderwear' is the name that Andy wanted to use for a bra pitch he led about a year ago. His 'idea' was ordinary women doing their ordinary jobs, in their underwear. 'Like a police-woman conducting traffic – but in a bra and knicks!' Ah, the objectification of women. How I love it. We lost the pitch. Obviously. Cooper hasn't really involved Andy in pitches since then, now I come to think of it.)

'That's not tongue-in-cheek, really, is it? It's just . . . um, I think it objectifies women and it's sexist.'

'Just because it's a woman's body, it's sexist? Come on . . .' Andy rolls his eyes. I don't think he knows what objectifies means.

'No, it objectifies women by implying that we're sexual objects even when we're just having a bath; it's sexist because we're selling women's toiletries to women, but the copy is talking to the man. Why is he "you", and she's "her"? Can women not buy their own toiletries?' I'm talking to Andy, but staring at the boards, as it's too hard to say this stuff to his face. 'And the lines . . . I mean, I just don't . . . the lines are messy. Who is saying show me? The woman? Or are we saying it to her, so she reveals her body to us? I'm all for a bit of nudity, but only when it's done in a fresh or funny way . . .'

'Don't tow out your hairy old feminism,' groans Andy. 'It's sexy and witty. And it's aspirational.'

Oh my God, I loathe it when people start talking about feminism like it means death to all men, but I'm not going to win that argument against idiots like Andy. And what does he mean, aspirational? What am I meant to aspire to? Lying tits-akimbo in the bath? I look at Andy quickly and look back at the boards. 'What, exactly, is sexy or witty or aspirational about these? That she's having an orgasm or that she's built like a porn star?'

'Both. Everything. Look, it's advertising 101: it's telling a woman that she'd have a man after her, thanks to these products. You can imagine how that would feel, can't you, sweetheart?' I can feel Andy looking at me in disgust.

I take a deep breath. I hate being called sweetheart by fuck-wits. I must not be emotional about this. I look at Coop again, but he's still staring at the boards, his face utterly blank. I really think these are terrible ideas, but if I get angry I'll cry, and if I let him or Cooper see how much this angers me – not just the casual sexism of the ads, or the shit idea, but also Andy coming

128

in at the eleventh hour and assuming he'll be able to take over – then I'll lose. And I have to win. It is time for me to win.

'The lines don't work, Andy—'

'So maybe the "show me" lines need work,' Andy interrupts. 'It's the idea that counts.'

'There is no idea here. Andy, we are talking to women and they won't respond to this . . . this soft porn.'

'You may not want it to work, but it will. Sex sells. Look it up.'

Don't lose your cool. I look him straight in the eye and keep my gaze there. (Wow, it's not that hard after all.)

'We're talking to women, not men. Women aren't stupid, Andy. Look at the Dove "Real Women" ads from a few years ago. Sales went up, like, 700%. It was an attractive packaging of the truth, it was warm and friendly . . . it wasn't cold, glossy, obvious lies. Women won't respond to this. You can't patronise them with this "aspirational" shit. It's *Playboy* with a shampoo bottle in the corner.'

'Calm down, sweetheart,' laughs Andy. 'It's a bit risqué but . . . that'll get us the press. Remember Wonderbra "Hello Boys"? Remember "FCUK me"?'

I take a deep breath. It's time to get it all out.

'Yes, "Hello Boys" was fresh and naughty, but it was also a generation ago. And this *isn't* fresh or naughty or relevant . . . Thank you for putting so much time in on this pitch, Andy, but these ads simply won't work.' I see that he's about to argue, but I hold his gaze and continue, trying to sound as neutral as I can. 'To be honest, they're also really derivative. The idea of orgasm through toiletries is a rip-off of the old Herbal Essences ads. The ones where the woman is moaning and shrieking in the shower.' I see Cooper nodding out of the corner of my eye, and I take a deep breath and keep going. 'That started as a *When Harry Met Sally* thing. Hilarious, yes, but that was 20 years ago. Secondly, the "show me the . . ." line is clearly a Jerry McGuire thing, which is also over ten years ago. It's not something people say anymore.'

'It could be, can't you see?' Andy is raising his voice slightly. 'Look, sweetheart, perhaps you just don't have the experience to go out on a limb like this . . .'

'It's not going out on a limb. I think, um, that the whole premise is kind of boring and outdated.' Why the fuck isn't Cooper talking? Is this a test? 'Andy, the clients are due here in 18 minutes. We don't have time for this, even if it was the perfect route which we somehow missed during the 14-hour days we've been working for the past few months. We have two routes that we're very happy with, and that Lukas – who is the MD, after all – thinks the head guys will love. Thank you for your help, but we can't use these ideas.'

There's a long, long pause. I cannot believe how tense it is in here. I'm sweating slightly.

'Right,' says Andy, standing up and pulling his boards together roughly. 'Good luck in your meeting.'

'Thanks, Andy,' says Cooper, standing up. 'Appreciate all your hard work on this. We'll see how we go this morning and get back to you.' Fuck, he really is testing me. If my ideas fail, Andy's are in. My stomach lurches with nerves. Mantra, mantra where is my mantra. I haven't needed it in months, now that I think about it, but by God, I need it now. As we walk out of the room, Andy holds open the door for Cooper, and then lets it slam in my face.

'Wouldn't want to be sexist,' he says snarkily.

'Thanks,' I beam back.

I want to kill him.

I walk straight to the printing studio area, where Laura, Ben and Danny are smoothing the last airbumps out of the replacement boards. Don't think about Andy. Think about all the other fucking crises facing this pitch.

'How's it looking?' I say.

'Good,' says Danny. He looks seriously relieved. I check over the boards quickly. I see that the first two are fine, but the third . . .

'This isn't the latest version,' I say. 'We changed that line on Monday.'

'FUCK!' says Danny.

'We have 15 minutes. Fix it,' I say. He runs to his computer to find and print the correct board.

'I'm so so so sorry!' exclaims Laura, turning to me with a panicked look on her face.

'Laura, calm down. It will be fine. Take them through to the meeting room. I'll be there in a few minutes.'

I walk to Danny's desk and look over his shoulder till he finds the right board, then walk back to my desk and stare at my presentation notes. The words are blurry, and the furore of the past 15 minutes is playing in my head. Was I clear enough? Does Coop think I'm wrong? I think . . . I think it went well, actually. I said what I thought and I didn't stammer. My head is spinning. Deep breaths. Posture and confidence and poise and breathing and – ooh, a new email.

It's from Cooper:

Well done. Couldn't have put it better myself. Good luck this morning. Let's show them what we're made of.

My chest leaps in happiness. He does believe in me. I should have trusted myself. (I wonder why he didn't tell Andy all that himself? Never mind, there's no point in worrying about that now . . .)

Danny runs over with the final board, showing it to me anxiously. I look over it quickly. It's perfect.

'Well done,' I say. 'Thank you, you're brilliant.'

He beams. Holding the final board, I leap up and stride around to Coop's desk.

'Ready to go?' I say, giving him a huge smile.

He looks up and winks, and makes a 'shh' gesture with his

131

finger to his lips. He means Andy can hear everything we say. He clears his throat and says in a businesslike voice: 'Ready. See you in there.'

As I walk through the office towards the meeting room again, Laura calls out 'GOOD LUCK!' and starts clapping excitedly. Suddenly, Danny and Ben start clapping and calling 'Good luck!' too, and even sulky Amanda The Office Manager (who's in the kitchen making the coffee and tea for the meeting ever so slightly late) joins in, and even the two account execs gossiping in the printing studio peer out and start cheering. I look behind me quickly. Cooper is still in his little quasi-office. They're cheering me.

Gosh, how delightful. I can't stop smiling.

'Thanks, everyone . . .' I say. 'But save that until we win the account!'

'Couldn't have put it better myself,' says Andy to no one in particular.

'Thank you, Andy!' I smile sweetly and walk through to the meeting room. Four minutes to go. Let's do it.

Chapter Fourteen

Stride, stride, stride, stride, stride, skippy-bunny-hop, stride.

That went well. No, that was . . . BRILLIANT! I skippy-run the last few steps up the Fulham Road and into Sophie's Steakhouse, where I'm meeting Bloomsicle and Katiepie.

An exhilarated feeling has been pounding through my chest since the meeting ended. The whole pitch is a blur now – but the smiles and handshakes at the end are on repeat in my head. Cooper and Lukas both gave me secret high-fives when Stefan and Felix had left the room at 1 pm, and the next few hours flew by as I had so much to catch up on for our other clients. There's no news from the Germans yet, but Cooper went to lunch with Lukas, Felix and Stefan and they didn't come back, which must be a good sign . . .

I suddenly find myself gazing at the bar and realise I've been staring into space and smiling in a slightly mad way for about a minute.

'HELLOOOO!' shout two voices to the left of me. I turn around quickly. It's Bloomie and Kate, sitting at our usual little table in the bar area.

'Vagueness! Come ON, darling, chop chop!' exclaims Bloomie.

'Sorry! I . . .' I scurry over and sit down. 'Sorry . . . I'm a bit . . . giddy. Good day at work.'

'That pitchy thing?' says Kate, leaning over to kiss my cheek. I nod.

133

'Well, rah to you, darling, this is a double celebration then!' exclaims Bloomie.

I look at the table and see that she's got three shots of vodka on the table.

'What's this?'

'Happy end of Dating Sabbatical!' exclaims Bloomie. Kate cheers and whoops. Damn, she's gregarious recently. I look over and notice she's wearing a hot pink corsage on her dark grey accountant's suit.

I start to laugh. 'Happy END of Dating Sabbatical?' Shit. I don't want it to end. I really don't.

'Sass! Darling! We're just happy to see you happy!' exclaims Bloomie, grinning. 'Now, don't worry, I have prepared a speech on your behalf. I am going to read through the Rules, and we shall see if you have obeyed them all.' She clears her throat and cocks an eyebrow at Kate and I. 'Ready?'

'I've got the Rules in my clutch,' I say. They're pretty much ingrained on my brain, but I carry them around anyway. 'Want to read my copy?'

'I'm all good. Now then. The Dating Sabbatical Rules. Rule 1. No accepting dates. Check. Rule 2. No asking men out on dates. Check.'

'I never understood why that rule was in there,' I say thoughtfully, accepting my vodka and soda from the waiter. 'I mean, as if.'

'Ahem! Rule 3. Obvious flirting is not allowed. Are we checking that, Katiepie?'

Kate makes a 'tis a pity' face. 'I saw her behaviour that night of Mitch's, with He-Whom-She-Will-Not-Mention.' I frown. What does she mean? Jake? I was so well behaved at the cocktail party! And I've done everything I can to avoid seeing him again, too. I did wonder if he'd be at Fraser's party last month, but he wasn't, and – oh, pay attention. 'But I think we can overlook it for the time being.'

Bloomie nods. 'Agreed. Rule 4. Avoid talking about the Sabbatical. Check. Rule 5. Talking about the Sabbatical is permitted only in response to being asked out on a date. Check. Rule 6. No accidental dating. Check, although I had my doubts that night in Montgomery Place.'

'I didn't know Jake would turn up!' I protest. Oops. I have been trying not to mention him. I decided, you see, that talking about Jake – the man who, after all, threatened the success of the Sabbatical when it was only four days old – would encourage me to think about him as a potential love/lust interest, which is against the spirit of the Dating Sabbatical and could jeopardise my happiness. (See how good I've been for the past three months?)

'Hush darling. Rule 7. No new man friends. Check again. She's doing well, isn't she, Katie?'

'That's our girl!' grins Katie. This is the most exuberant I've seen her since she left Tray. I wonder if they've been tucking into vodka shots without me.

'Rule 8, kissing is forbidden, doesn't matter, hasn't even come close to meeting a male model slash comic genius . . .'

'Ah, the ol' male model slash comic genius caveat,' I nod. 'They have them in pre-nups now, right?'

'Rule 9, no visitors in the ladygarden—'

'I should think not!' I say primly.

Bloomie continues as though I hadn't spoken. '. . . Check, that thing must be a forest by now, and finally, Rule 10, no bastardos. Check.'

Kate cheers. I smile at them both. 'My sweet friends, I couldn't have done it without you. And the ladygarden remains a neatly trimmed topiary hedge. One needs to have standards, if only for oneself.'

We raise our shot glasses and toast the Dating Sabbatical and ladygarden standards, and tip the vodka back down our throats.

'So, now you're over Posh Mark. Time to start dating again! Welcome back to real life!' says Bloomie.

Posh Mark? Oh, him. 'It wasn't about getting over some break-up, Bloomie,' I say, stirring my drink thoughtfully. 'It was about choosing to be alone rather than be in a shit relationship that would go wrong anyway.' I look up, and see them exchanging glances. 'And now, it's about channelling my energy into my life, not just my lovelife. Reclaiming the power of singledom.' I flash the girls a two-fingered peace-sign, though I'm not sure just how much I'm joking.

Kate laughs, and Bloomie smirks and rolls her eyes. 'Seriously, darling . . . there is such a thing as taking it too far. And choosing celibacy for the rest of your life is probably the definition of taking it too far.'

'I'm not choosing celibacy,' I protest, though this isn't the first time the idea has occurred to me. I do miss sex. And I do want to have sex again. Perhaps I'll have to do the one-night-stand thing. Sorry, I digress. 'That's just a side-effect of the Dating Sabbatical. And of course I can go without sex. I mean, look at the nuns.'

'Those nuns and their Dating Sabbaticals, huh?' says Bloomie.

'They're crazy for them,' I say. 'That's why they're always singing.'

'Don't you miss talking to guys? You used to be so good at it,' says Kate wistfully.

'That night of the reunion at Koko – the others couldn't believe the difference in you,' says Bloomie. 'Rach asked if you were a lesbian or something.'

'Oh, for fuck's sake,' I say. 'Rach spent all night trying to pick up that dude in the grey blazer, who looked like a complete arse to me, by the way . . . and then when she didn't, she got in a really bad mood and just went home. Did she even have any fun?'

'We're not saying be like her . . .' says Kate.

'But . . . there's a balance,' says Bloomie, 'and now that the Sabbatical is over, you can find it.'

I clear my throat. 'No. I'm extending it indefinitely. It's really working for me.'

'You can't do that, darling,' says Bloomie. 'It was only ever for three months. I didn't make up the Rules. Oh wait, yes I did . . .'

'No!' I exclaim with a vehemence that surprises me. Bloomie and Kate both look shocked. 'No . . . I don't want to give it up yet. I like my life now . . . I'm finding it easier to concentrate on, you know, everything else.'

'Isn't that what they say about all-girls' schools?' asks Kate. 'That girls concentrate more and get better results, because there are no boys around to distract them? But boys thrive in co-ed schools, because they're calmer and try harder to succeed when girls are around.'

'See?' I say, looking at Kate delightedly. 'It's biological!'

'It's biological for 15-year-olds. Not 28-year-olds. At some point, darling, you're going to have to declare it over,' says Bloomie. 'Sabbaticals, by their very nature, cannot last forever.'

I shake my head. I am not dropping the Sabbatical. I do not want to go back to the old me, to the dating-dumping-desperado. There is nothing they can do to make me change my mind. 'Let's talk about something else. How are you, Katie, darling? How's single life this week?'

'Good,' she says thoughtfully. 'Weird. And a bit scary. But good. I saw Tray last night . . .'

'How was it?' I ask.

'Good,' she says again, chewing her lip. It's a classic Kate conversation-evasion technique. Then she suddenly blurts out: 'He wants to get back together and I said no straightaway . . . He looked so upset. Now I feel sick when I think about him. He's miserable and it's all my fault.'

'It's not your fault!' say Bloomie and I in indignant unison.

Kate shakes her head. 'If it was the other way around, you'd be calling him a fucking bastardo cockmonkey right now and you know it.'

There's not much we can say to this. It's kind of true.

'But you weren't happy . . .' I say.

'It was the brave thing to do,' adds Bloomie.

Kate is tearing her napkin into perfect tiny squares. 'I couldn't sleep last night because I was so upset about it.' She looks over her shoulder quickly to make sure no one's around, and whispers, 'I was thinking about getting a vibrator. That would help me sleep.'

I laugh so hard at this that I start choking. It was the last thing I would ever expect her to say. Bloomie and I talk about sex, but Kate never does.

'They're fabulous!' exclaims Bloomie.

'They're hell,' I say. 'Noisy and gross. Mine did nothing for me. There was nothing Rampant about it at all.'

'Sass, you must have been using it wrong. I LOVE mine,' says Bloomie. 'Both of them . . . I have two I can choose from according to what mood I'm in,' she adds defensively, as Kate and I crack up. Two vibrators? Yikes.

Kate turns to me. 'Why do you hate it?'

I shrug. 'I was so excited about getting it and then it was just so loud and cumbersome and . . . neon. It just lay in my sock drawer for ages. I called it The Sleeping Giant.'

Bloomie and Kate fall about laughing. Bloomie knows about The Sleeping Giant, but I've never talked to Kate about it. I thought she'd be shocked.

'Well, maybe I won't get one. But I can't stop thinking about . . .' she lowers her voice and whispers 'sex.'

'Perhaps it's because you're not having it anymore?' I suggest helpfully.

'I wasn't having it before!' exclaims Kate. 'I wasn't interested at all, I was starting to think something was wrong with me. But now it's all I think about . . .'

'I was obsessed with sex after Richie and I broke up,' says Bloomie. He was her long-term relationship from university to about 25. 'But I never feel like it after I've been dumped.'

'It's a libido-killer,' I agree.

'I think The Dork thinks I must be a nympho,' says Bloomie thoughtfully.

'How sweet,' I say, as Kate gets the giggles. 'It must be love.'

'It is,' grins Bloomie.

'And marriage?' says Kate hopefully.

'Yeah, and having kids and moving to Surrey,' I scoff. As if. Marriage is something other people do. Older people. Grown-ups.

Bloomie clears her throat nervously. 'Actually, we've talked about it.'

I'm stunned. 'Seriously?'

'Yep,' she says, glancing at us both with an uncharacteristically insecure look on her face. 'Not the child and Surrey part, but I just . . . I, um, sort of know it's going to happen. It just feels right when I'm with him. It's not like we never argue or anything, we do, but I just . . . I love him.'

'I knew it!' crows Kate happily. 'Iknewitiknewitiknewit.'

I'm speechless. I knew she was in love with The Dork, and that things were going really well, but I still can't imagine Bloomie getting married. I can't imagine any of us getting married. It seems so . . . so final. Bloomie seems a little surprised by her admission, too, and goes all quiet and shy. We all look at each other for a few seconds, and Kate quickly changes the subject by asking me about work today.

'This Andy guy sounds hell, I'm glad you put him in his place,' says Bloomie after I tell them the highlights.

'Does winning the German thing mean free toiletries?' says Kate. 'Could be handy, if Bloomie and I get the sack . . .'

'You'll both be fine,' I say, slightly untruthfully. Actually, I read in the financial bit of last week's *Sunday Times* that Kate's company has issued a statement revising expected profits and the top management dudes have all volunteered to not get bonuses this year. Not a great sign, apparently. So I turn to Bloomie. 'Your bank just bought that other bank, right? So you must be doing OK.'

'Mmm, but there are two people for every job now, you know?' says Bloomie, her forehead creasing into an uber-frown. 'So that sort of means half of us will probably get the boot.'

Ooh, I never thought of that. That's not good.

The conversation quickly moves on to cover Kate's hot pink heels from asos.com ('I just thought, I am tired of wearing boring little LK Bennett heels at £139 a pop and I don't care if these are slutty and made of cardboard and plastic, they cost £25 and I LOVE them'), and gossip: Eddie and Mitch being friends again following a month-long froideur caused by Mitch pulling Eddie's sister Emma that night at Montgomery Place, and Fraser and Tory's on-again, off-again relationship.

Then we start discussing our plans for the weekend after next. We're all going to Eddie's parents' place for a weekend-long houseparty. 'Weekends in Oxfordshire are the new weekends in Ibiza!' he exclaimed at Fraser's birthday drinks a few weeks ago. I'm getting slightly tired of people trying to sell recession-friendly things as 'the new' something else. Mitch has been trying out 'Sex with me is the new one-on-one with a personal trainer', with limited success. Anyway, Eddie's party weekend will be good, old-fashioned fun. Eddie's folks have joined the twins in Spain, so the house is empty, and it's very large with loads of room for sleeping bags (although we, obviously, as first-tier friends, have already baggsed rooms).

Bloomie and Kate tell me that the plan is a quietly boozy Friday and a loudly boozy dinner party on Saturday, with lots of messing about in the countryside in between.

I'm just taking a sip of my vodka when Bloomie says quickly and with no pre-empt: 'Jake is coming.'

My sharp, shocked intake of breath is badly mistimed with my drinking. I inhale the vodka and immediately start choking. My eyes and nose are streaming, my chest convulses with violent hiccups and I dribble and spurt the remainder of the vodka in my mouth all over my chin, sweater and the table.

'Holy shit,' says Bloomie.

I look up with panicked eyes, trying to tell them this isn't an ordinary coughing fit, and Kate jumps up and starts banging on my back. After about ten seconds of this, though it feels like longer, all the vodka is out. I'm a wet, sticky mess, I can feel the eyeliner smearing all the way to my temples, and everyone in the bar is staring at me with a mix of panic and revulsion. I take a deep, shaky breath and bury my wet face in my wet hands. How. Fucking. Mortifying.

Jake is coming. Jake is coming.

What the hell is wrong with me?

Kate is handing me – what the? – pre-moistened scented tissues.

'You carry wipes in your bag?' I croak.

'Now is not the time to make fun of me,' she says, and starts wiping my hands and face. A bartender comes over to dry the table. Bloomie orders us three more drinks.

'Do you want to talk about Jake?' she asks with a sly smile.

'Nooo, nono,' I say, clearing the last of the vodka from my neck and patting the dribble on my thighs. 'That fluttery tummy thing I got when I met Jake was just a perverse subconscious reaction to my Sabbatical. And also, my body was thinking – erroneously! – that it could not do without sex and therefore felt desirous of the nearest man with the appropriate pheromones. It was lust, pure and simple.' I'm going to see Jake. Finally. But – oh shit, maybe I shouldn't go to Eddie's weekend party. But Eddie is my friend, damn it. Jake is just stupid Mitch's stupid cousin. I have invitational precedence. And I can handle it. It's been three whole months since I saw him. I'll be fine. I haven't broken any of the Dating Sabbatical Rules. I'm not about to start now. Get a grip, Sass, I tell myself.

'Let's order, then, shall we?' I say brightly.

As Bloomie turns around to get the attention of someone to order, I check my phone quickly. I've got a text from Laura.

Well done today! Everyone talking about it!

Oh, how lovely. I text back quickly.

Team effort – well done to everyone!

She replies:

I mean Andy! So glad someone took him on!

Oh my gosh. I've never got a text like that before. Well, nothing like today has ever happened to me before either, so that's no big surprise. And it's all because of the Dating Sabbatical. God bless it.

Chapter Fifteen

Three burgers later, the night is going well. The thought that I'll be seeing Jake next week is bouncing around my mind like an ADD child pre-Ritalin, so I've sat it on a naughty chair in the back of my brain. So far, it's stayed there pretty obediently, and let me get on with my evening. We're now talking animatedly about the joys of singledom (me and Kate) versus the delights of new love (Bloomie).

'Middle of the bed sleeping.' That's me.

'Perfect spooning all night.' That's Bloomie.

'Waking up and knowing no one is going to fart unless it's you,' says Kate, and Bloomie and I laugh. Especially at the way she lowers her voice daintily around the word 'fart'.

'Getting a kiss before you open your eyes.'

Blecch. Kate and I roll our eyes at each other.

I raise my finger. 'Not having to pack your bag twice a week to sleep at his place.'

Bloomie grins wickedly. 'Knowing he'll always, always stay at yours.'

Kate replies: 'Dressing up every day because you never know who you might meet.'

Bloomie raises an eyebrow. 'Dressing up every day to impress him . . . and getting compliments every time.'

I throw a chip at her.

'Reading in bed till whatever time you want,' I say. It's not a

143

great one, but I've never had a boyfriend who liked to read as much as I do.

'Lying in bed talking and laughing for hours.'

Bugger. Is there any way to beat lying in bed talking and laughing for hours?

'Going to bed coated in a facemask, hairmask and fake tan, and knowing no one will see you,' I say. Kate leans over and high-fives me.

'Sex.' Bloomie throws her trump card down. 'Crazy all-night sex, wake up with your face blistering from stubble-rash and going at it again sex, tapping him on the shoulder at 4-am because you can't sleep sex. Sex.'

We sit in silence for a few minutes. Again, the subject of sex rears its ugly, erm, head. What is there about being single that can possibly beat that?

'Knowing you're not about to get dumped,' I say. 'Not having that sick feeling waiting for him to ring. Not analysing every text and email. Not worrying that you've made the wrong judgement call on the wrong guy. Not becoming a crazy person over a cockmonkey.'

Kate and Bloomie are staring at me with slightly overwhelmed looks on their faces. I did deliver that speech with a little more vehemence than is called for, it's true. Bloomie is about to say something, when Kate gasps and hisses. 'Rick. Rick. Rick. Behind you. Behind you.'

I start, and the first thing I think is 'I can't see Rick now. I look like shit.' I haven't even bothered to check my make-up since the vodka-splutter-choke-fiasco. Bloomie is even faster than me: she's thrown her utterly enormous make-up bag in my lap and snaps: 'Bathroom. Now. Go. Go.' I get up from the table, without straightening my legs or raising my head, and scurry off to the bathroom, make-up bag nestled securely under my arm. Oh my God, Rick.

I know what you're thinking. And let me state, hand on heart, that of course I don't want him back, or like him, or have any secret feelings for him. I'm on a Dating Sabbatical, for a start, remember? And anyway, I promise I wouldn't take him even if he did want me back. If he ever crosses my mind these days – and he barely does – I just feel a genuine self-righteous anger that he could dare to treat me as badly as he did. I think about my poor little self being manipulated by him, and my clueless hope that things would get better and how the spotlight of his adoration would flick on and then off again, and feel like it happened to a different person. She didn't deserve to get treated like that. And she did not deserve to say I love you and not hear it back, or walk into a room to see him screwing a Pink Lady. I feel flushed with self-righteous anger.

But do I want to look as good as possible the first time I see him, post all that trauma? Holy motherfucking hell yes.

Bless the person who gave this bathroom decent lighting, and bless Bloomie for her alpha-high-maintenance tendencies: her make-up kit is comprehensive. Three minutes of brushing, blending, powdering, pencilling and glossing, and gazing back at me is me, but better. What would we do without make-up? I mean, seriously.

I point at myself in the mirror. Be confident. Be cold. Remember he is a bastard. Don't let him think he's had any effect on you. And remember you're on a Dating Sabbatical and far, far superior to all that rubbish.

I walk up the stairs to the restaurant to see that Rick is talking to Bloomie and Kate. He's wearing a rather nice dark blue suit. He wore a lot of dark blue when we were dating. He once told me it was because it brought out the hazel in his eyes, which struck me even at the time as an oddly vain thing for a man to say.

Oh holy fuck, it's really him.

Adieu, self-righteous anger. Bonjour, pure fear. Holy shit. I can't believe I'm about to talk to Rick.

The last time he spoke to me, I was not calm or in control. And the last thing he said to me was 'I don't love you and I don't want you.' After shagging, SHAGGING, a Pink Lady in front of me. Bastardocockmonkeyroosterprick. I hate him for doing that to me.

But I'm not going to make a scene. I am better than that. I am calm. Mantra, engage.

I reach our table. My heart is racing and I think my hands might be shaking, so I hold the make-up bag firmly behind my back. What will I say to him? I want to appear polite and remote and dignified. Yes. I am in control. Mantra, engage.

'Sass,' he says, eyes flicking up at me. 'I was just talking about you. How are you?'

I don't reply, but just smile. I hope my smile is not as watery as my insides. He leans forward and gives me a kiss on the cheek. His face is very warm. My hands are still shaking, and I think my smile is twitching on one side.

'I thought you were talking about you?' says Bloomie sweetly. I try to take a deep breath, to calm myself down as surreptitiously as possible.

'Was I?' he says, but I don't think he heard her. He's gazing at me with a curious look on his face. 'You look great, Sass,' he says, running his eyes over me. Somehow, through my yogic breathing, I find the courage to look back and appraise him properly for the first time in almost a year.

He's not that tall, certainly not tall enough for me to wear three-inch heels with, medium-brown hair, with the aforementioned hazel eyes. His eyelashes are too straight, too pale and kind of droopy. I can see nose-hairs escaping his flaring nostrils. His skin looks dry. He should use a better moisturiser.

I find myself smiling at him. This is interesting. I don't find him attractive. At all.

'How are you?' I say.

'I'm fantastic. But you knew that,' he raises an eyebrow at me

146

and curls his lip in what is probably intended to be a sexy snarl. He has a long, long eyebrow hair that is curling over his eye.

I can't handle this, I need to get away. I turn to Bloomie and Kate. 'Can I get anyone a drink? I'm going to the bar.'

They both raise their hand like they're eight years old and trying to be picked for a sports team.

'I'll come with you,' says Rick. Shit. 'Or we could wait here for table service. You know how much I prefer people doing things for me.' He grins, clearly expecting us to fall about laughing. Was that the kind of thing I used to giggle helplessly at, or did he used to be funnier? And why is he acting like we're friends or something? Does he not remember the I-don't-love-you? The Pink Lady?

'Yuh, but the bar is quicker,' I nod.

'Alright then,' he says. We walk to the bar. How the hell did this happen? Why am I alone with him?

'You really look fantastic,' he says.

'Thanks,' I say. Maybe he really doesn't remember the Pink Lady night. He grins. Quite an attractive grin, it's true. He doesn't seem to want to ask me anything, so – dignified, polite moi – I say 'How are you?' and he starts talking.

I am half-listening and half-panicking, but I know when to laugh at what he's saying and when to say 'Really?!' in an amazed / impressed voice. I concentrate on stopping my hands from shaking and meeting his eyes without flinching.

When I finally pay for our drinks (he never was very generous, I must say, though he earns about five times my salary), he says, 'I think I'll come and sit with you girls for a bit. I'm meeting Skipper here' – I have no idea who Skipper is, but he either thinks I do or doesn't care that I don't – 'but it's really great to chew the fat like this.'

I turn around and look him straight in the eye. I can't take him coming over and sitting with us. Pulling together all the determination and strength that my Dating Sabbatical has given me, I take a deep breath and smile at him. 'That would be lovely, Rick,' I say. 'But we're kind of on a no-men night.'

He looks taken aback. Oh hell, he probably thinks I'm – hang on, why am I wondering what he thinks? Take charge! 'I hope I don't sound terribly rude. You understand. Really nice to see you, though, Rick.' I lean forward and kiss him on the cheek. 'Take care.'

He doesn't say a word as I pick up our drinks and walk back to the table. I am so fucking calm and in control. High-fives to me!

'What happened there?!' hisses Bloomie. 'The stupid fuckwit is still staring at you. I've never seen him look like that. He is speechless. He is without speech.'

'What a cockmonkey . . .' I say, half to myself. I look up and see Bloomie and Kate gazing at me. 'Did you actually ever like him when I was dating him?' I ask quietly. My heart is still pounding. Not from love, I am sure. Just from the shock of seeing him. 'I mean, I know you don't now, but before he . . . you know. Pink Ladied.'

Bloomie and Kate make a hummmmm sound and look at each other.

'Well, let's see,' says Bloomie. 'He's a real alpha, and I think when he turned the attention away from himself and focused on you, it was hugely . . . um, seductive. But, no. He's a dick.'

I nod.

'It helped that he never came out with us, so I never had to really see him . . .' She looks at me and sighs. 'He wasn't even that nice to you. Even before the Pink Lady night. What more do you want to hear, darling? After the I-love-you thing, and after that party . . . I wanted to kill him for hurting you.'

I nod. I hate hearing this, as it makes me feel like such a damn fool, but it's probably good for me. And it's nothing I couldn't have guessed from things she's said about him in the past. I look over to Kate for her verdict.

148

'Obviously, I hate his guts for what he did, too . . . But he can be very charming,' says Kate carefully. 'And I think you had a very . . . humanising effect on him.'

We all start to laugh. Humanising? At that exact second, Rick walks past to greet the guy who must be Skipper, completely ignoring our table. We laugh harder. He flinches slightly. Is it bad to say that makes me feel kind of happy?

'Did you like Posh Mark?' I ask. I'm not particularly interested in the answer, but I do kind of wonder. Bloomie pretends to fall asleep and starts snoring loudly and Kate gets the giggles again. 'Fine, he was a bit boring,' I say. 'But his body . . .'

Thank goodness for my Dating Sabbatical, I think, as I see Rick calling the waitress over to order. I never have to go through something like that again. Calm down, jumpy insides. I turn to the girls, but find myself unable to think of anything else to say whilst Rick is in the same room. I have to get out of here.

'Well, stick a fork in me,' I say. 'It's 10 o'clock. I'm done.'

'Quick fag?' says Kate, who's been embracing smoking extremely enthusiastically lately.

We get the bill and, ignoring Skipper and Rick completely, head outside with our drinks. I can't believe he wanted to come and sit with us. Cheating, horrible prat.

'Two guys, only two tonight,' says Bloomie, taking out her cigarettes and handing us each one.

'Huh?' I say.

'Only two guys in the bar were looking at you. It's usually more, recently. Only about one in seven actually comes over to talk to you, mind you.'

I grin as Bloomie lights my cigarette. 'Really? I didn't even notice any guys in there. Apart from fuckfeatures, of course.'

'Actually, I was the one who noticed Rick,' says Kate. 'You never would have.'

I exhale thoughtfully. It's true. I could not tell you if there were any men in the bar tonight: good-looking, ugly, young, old, short, fat . . . I just wasn't aware of them. At all.'

'You, of all people, not noticing the guys . . .' Bloomie shakes her head. 'And I've never seen you get so much attention.'

'They must have a sixth sense for what they can't have.' Realising this sounds arrogant when I really don't mean it to, I quickly add: 'Anyway, if I did notice one of them, the best case scenario is that he'd date me and then dump me. That was proved six times in a row. I'm not on a Dating Sabbatical as a social experiment. It's genuine self-preservation.' I exhale and make a half-arsed attempt at smoke rings.

'What would you say if someone asked you out?' says Kate. 'Nice smoke rings.'

'Thanks. Actually, I try to deflect any chat-ups now before they get to the being-asked-out stage as it's so, you know, tedious . . .' Bloomie is frowning quizzically at me. I wonder if she can tell how shaken I am about seeing Rick. I don't want her to know; after everything they've said about him, they'll think I'm cuckoo. As I probably am. Time to deflect. 'Do you want to hear the standard reactions to me mentioning the Dating Sabbatical?'

'Yes please,' says Kate.

I start listing them on my fingers in a monosyllabic voice. 'Are you gay. Did some guy really burn you. How arrogant you must be to think you need a Sabbatical to not be asked out. A drink is not a date. How about just sex then.'

Bloomie and Kate are laughing now.

'Dudes, it's so boring. And I'm never even tempted.'

Kate is toying with her straw. 'Was anyone looking at me in there?' she says, making a sad pouty face which is probably only half in jest.

'I'm sure they were . . .' says Bloomie. 'But it's different. You probably still have an "I'm-taken" vibe going on.'

'No! How do I get rid of that?' Kate pauses, and flinches. 'Oh God, a Tray-related guilt feeling . . . it's gone now.'

'Try a Sabbatical,' I suggest. 'It's like catnip, apparently.'

'I can't do that before I've even had a date. What else is there?'

'Flirt,' Bloomie and I say in unison.

'But I'm not talking to them,' says Kate.

Bloomie rolls her eyes. 'It's the pre-conversation flirt, darling.'

'Huh?' says Kate.

'You know . . .' I say. 'Make eye contact once, twice if you want to be quite clear, then go to the bar within 15 minutes, and he will follow you if he fancies you. Guaranteed.'

'It's like a mating dance,' nods Bloomie.

'Really?' Kate looks deeply confused. 'Then what happens? He asks you out?'

'No!' we say in unison again.

'Then you look around at the bar and can either ignore him completely – this works well if he's very good-looking, as it'll intrigue him – or, if he's more normal-looking, smile at him—'

'Lips closed! Make it a little smile! Not a big grin!' interrupts Bloomie.

'And turn back to the bar. Either way he'll say something off-the-cuff, like comment on what you're ordering, or how long it takes to get a drink . . .'

'And you arch an eyebrow and smile and say something like – well, that depends on what he's said. But you say something witty.'

'Yeah, something witty.'

Kate shakes her head. 'Did I ever know all this stuff?'

'I'm not sure,' I say. 'This took several years to perfect, and during that time you were shacked up in pre-marital bliss.'

'I missed out on all that rejection and heartbreak and bastardos . . .' says Kate sadly. 'OK, I'll try it. One day.'

'Mkay,' I say. 'On that note, I'm off. That Rick thing was . . . too much.'

I kiss them both goodbye, pick up my lucky yellow clutch, and turn around to walk towards the street to hail a cab. I need to go home and think about the Rick encounter, and the fact that I'm going to see Jake in less than three weeks. Actually, no I don't. I'm on a Dating Sabbatical, I remind myself.

Two guys standing on the pavement are looking at me, and one raises his hand to wave me over. Moderately good-looking, very bad shirt.

'Oh, for God's sake,' I think. Why now? When I'm not dating? Where were they six months ago?

Chapter Sixteen

Shampoo, condition, brush teeth, scrub with exfoliating gloves and body wash, shave armpits and legs. It's the morning after the Sophie's Steakhouse night with Rick, and it's sunny and almost warm. I'm still slightly flushed from my morning run, so I stand be-knickered in front of my wardrobe and wait for sartorial inspiration to strike.

Five entire minutes later, cursing this new sartorially-challenged side of myself, I pull on a white vest top, a little black pinafore dress and some flat black sandals. I decide to call it St Germain Schoolgirl and add a long, skinny, stripy cotton scarf. Hair: extreme side parting, low chignon. Make-up: yes please. Winehouse-lite eyeliner, pale pink blush. Brows being almost suspiciously obedient. I step back and survey the results. It took a little longer than I'd like, but Inner Self and Outer Self are linking arms and skipping happily down the street together.

Today is going to be pretty easy at work, but I'd like to get in early anyway. The chaos of yesterday, with the print/coffee fubar and evil Andy and then the pitch, was kind of exhausting, and I want some peace and quiet to tidy my desk and regroup.

The thought that Jake will be at Eddie's the weekend after next floats into my head. I let it stay for a moment, then watch it float away again. Does he think I'm weird for running away that night at Montgomery Place? Why is it that I think of him every day, even though I haven't seen him in three months?

Doesn't matter. Can't think about him, I'm on a Sabbatical. Lalalaaa. Hello calmness, my old friend.

Calmness is quickly kicked in the head by Rick, waiting impatiently in the wings. Running into him last night was deeply unsettling. I still can't figure out how I feel about it. I felt disinterested when I was talking to him, I thought he looked kind of unattractive and I still loathe him for being such an utter bastardo cockmonkey. So why have I run over every second of seeing him so many times?

In fact, I may as well be totally honest with you. Lying in bed last night, I indulged in a very anti-Sabbatical fantasy whereby Rick turned up on my doorstep and told me I was the most beautiful, wonderful person he'd ever met, and that he'd made the biggest mistake of his short, stupid life. He added that he was a self-centred, arrogant pig. My reaction to this was not actually in the fantasy, though obviously I looked at him disdainfully as he was talking. And I was wearing something fabulous. I rewound and replayed said imaginary scenario more times than I'd like to admit. That probably wasn't a very Sabbatical-compliant thing to do. And the Sabbatical isn't over, despite everything Bloomie and Kate said. It really isn't.

I look in the mirror, make an angry face and point at myself. Stop this Jake-Rick-Jake-Rick thing, and I mean now. Stop thinking about these bastardos, goddamnit. It is pathetic. You are still on a Dating Sabbatical. You are happier than you've ever been before. Get a grip.

I love telling myself off. Especially when I don't talk back.

I skippy-bunny-hop down the stairs, noting on the way that Anna is AWOL again, which must be good for the relationship with Ron or Don or whatever his name is, not to mention good for me. I do love a flat empty of flatmates. It's such a lovely day that I walk to work, through St James's Park and the beautiful June sunshine. This clears and stills my busy mind, and I get to work feeling calm and centred. I have quite a bit to do for various

154

clients, so the morning passes relatively fast. I wonder when we're going to hear from the Germans about yesterday's pitch. Everyone else seems to think I must have the inside track, as they keep asking me what's happening.

When Coop storms into the office at about 11 am, the entire office falls silent and snaps to attention, but he just marches straight over to his screened area with his mobile at his ear, barking 'Yes. Yes. Yes. Yes.' I sigh, and turn back to my computer.

It's weird how depressing it is not to have the pressure of the pitch on, now that I'm used to it. And, annoyingly, there's not much else to distract me from thinking about things I'm not meant to think about. Like seeing Rick last night and Jake next weekend. I've banned myself from online shopping till the end of the month, and it's all quiet on emails, too. (At some point in my mid-20s my friends and I stopped sending emails every few minutes. So different from when we were in our first jobs. Sample email: 'I'm hungry. What should I eat?' I specifically remember having an I-spy game over email with people in offices in London Bridge, Liverpool Street, Mayfair and Park Royal – ie, the opposite sides of London.)

Coop calls me over mid-afternoon.

'Wordgirl. German dinner at my house tonight,' he says, shuffling through his utter tip of a desk. 'Coming?'

'Huh?' I say.

He hates spelling things out. 'The Germans. Are coming. To dinner. At my house. Tonight.'

'Why?'

Cooper sighs. 'It started as a one-on-one catch-up dinner with Stefan and I, but then we scheduled the rest of the pitch for yesterday, so I had to ask Felix, and then I couldn't not ask Lukas, and so now we've also got Marlena and her sister and you.' He pulls out his mobile and checks a text. 'Wait, Marlena's sister can't come. She's on an emergency yoga retreat. What a freaking nutcase. Anyway, I'd like you to come. I hope they might tell us if we've won the account.'

After work I shoot home to shower quickly and change into client-courting-but-not-in-that-way clothes. I pull out an extremely demure spotted tea dress, like the one Vivian (mah name is Vivian) wears to the polo in *Pretty Woman*. Only it's in navy, not brown. And, um, the dots are smaller. (OK, it's nothing like it. But that was why I bought it originally. Shush.)

Red shoes, hair down and parted on one side and held back with a clip, trenchcoat – perfect. Workchic. My clothes powers are, perhaps, returning. I hop in a cab to the public transport no-man's-land of Battersea (speak not to me of buses and mainline trains, I beg you, this is work-related and I can expense the fare, do I need any other excuse?), and am greeted at the door of Coop's terrace by Marlena in an I-picked-this-up-in-Ibiza-years-ago white dress. She's all long smooth arms and collarbones and cheekbones, and long shiny chocolate-brown hair.

'Ah, Sass. Lovely to see you,' she smiles. Perfect, perfect teeth. No make-up – which I knew would happen and therefore wore minimal make-up myself, or rather, wore quite a bit but only to give myself a very natural look.

I try not to be jealous of other women, I really do. It's such a negative, pointless emotion. But I do love the effortless perfection of her, and wish I could be just a tiny bit like that. I feel like a child's dress-up doll in comparison.

Sigh. Never mind. I am a dress-up doll.

We walk through to the living room, which has a high ceiling and long, plump white sofas. Coop's in the corner, rearranging his choice of LPs for the evening.

'Can I help you with dinner, Marlena?' I ask, accepting a glass of champagne.

'No.' She waves a hand as she leaves the room. 'I have bought some of those easy meals from M und S. I hate to cook. It's not organic, but I thought, let's be vild!'

'Why not?' I nod, wondering why Cooper suggested dinner in the first place.

'I thought it would be a nice personal touch for them to come to my place,' he says, as if reading my thoughts. 'I'm regretting it now, yes.'

'What are those things?' I say, looking over at his records. 'Laser discs?'

'Very funny,' he says, without looking up.

'Can I do anything to help? When are the Germans coming?'

'No. Now.'

He's nervous. I shrug, and start looking around the room. I glance over a few photos of the younger even more beautiful Marlena in bikinis, shots of the two of them on holiday, and then come to a few of Coop on his own, when he was in his band in the 80s. He has a serious feathered mullet in some, is wearing rather a lot of make-up in others – God bless New Wave – and in every photo is doing the textbook definition of making love to the camera with his eyes.

'You were quite the little stud, weren't you?' I ask.

He glances up. 'I was extremely successful with women, if that's what you're asking.'

'I imagine you were quite the bastardo to some of them.'

'If I was, it's because they were the wrong ones for me,' he shrugs.

I'm not sure what to say to this. It goes against my whole some-men-are-bastardos-no-matter-what theory.

'But that goes against my some-men-are-bastardos-no-matter-what theory,' I say, taking a sip of my champagne. It always makes me feel quite heady straightaway. Woo.

'You're such a cliché,' he grins, looking up at me.

'Seriously. And the reason I'm on a Dating Sabbatical – not that you'd know since you haven't asked me about it, though I've dropped loads of hints – is that I can't tell the bastardos from the nice guys, and I kept getting dumped or making mistakes, and you know, all of that.'

157

Coop finally puts The Cure on and stands up. 'It's not meant to be that hard.'

I hate it when people say that. 'Well, it is.'

He smiles at me and shakes his head. 'You'll meet someone you prefer to everyone else in the world. If he's being a bastardo, you'll just . . . call his bluff. And he'll call yours when you're playing up. You'll love it. You'll figure it all out when you're a grown-up.'

When I'm a grown-up? Ouch. I'm starting to feel pretty damn immature lately, what with Bloomie talking about marriage when I can't plan more than two weeks in advance. Then again, I'm nailing things at work. I've made the very grown-up decision to press the pause button on my lovelife. And I read the financial pages now. That's mature of me, isn't it? Fuck, yeah.

I'm about to ask more questions when the doorbell rings.

I hear happy German voices, and in a couple of minutes everyone comes into the living room and Cooper introduces them to Marlena. Stefan, the global director of marketing, is tall and blond and a bit intimidating, though he and Coop are pretty close, Felix the global CEO is slightly – OK, very – rotund and balding. Lukas, future managing director of the UK arm, is his usual chiselled, blue-eyed self, but there's something different about him tonight. I stare at him for a second before realising: he's shorn off his Euro-locks. The improvement is dramatic. He's also wearing an exceptionally nice shirt and jacket, and some rather cool scruffy jeans.

Wow, the champagne has certainly kicked in.

'Before we wait any longer, I would like to give a little speech,' says Felix happily, as Coop hands around glasses of champagne.

'After today's meeting, it became very obvious what the next step was,' he smiles. I glance over at Coop, who's staring at his face like a man possessed. 'We are very happy to announce that we would like to work with Cooper Advertising for our launch in the UK.'

Cooper lets out a cheer, and everyone starts talking at once. I clap my hands with delight, then notice myself doing it and put them down. I look over and see Lukas grinning at me.

We toast to the future of the company, and start discussing plans for the launch. Then Marlena interjects with some questions for Felix about Frankfurt, where they're both from, and Lukas and I start chatting. He's flathunting at the moment, and says he's thinking about Marylebone or Belsize Park.

'I hear rents have dropped, I should be able to get something quite nice,' he adds.

'That's a great idea, they're both really lovely areas,' I say.

'Maybe you could show me around, once I move here,' he says. 'I'd love to get to know London better. Maybe go to Borough Market, walk in Hyde Park, explore the bars in Chelsea . . .'

I'm nodding amiably as he says all this, then . . . wait a minute. Does he mean we should go out . . . as a date? That's Rule 1! Or would it be just as friends? But wait, that's Rule 7! Out of the corner of my eye, I suddenly notice Stefan and Felix laughing.

'That's a good idea. London has probably changed so much in the three years since you last lived here,' says Stefan.

I turn to Lukas, shocked. 'You lived here before?'

He doesn't even look embarrassed, just grins at me. 'Yes . . . but it never hurts to have a refresher course.'

I'm speechless, and the subject changes to the economy. Did he fib about not knowing London, just to ask me out? No, he's just lonely. That must be it.

Felix starts telling a long story about a friend of his who has gone bankrupt in Germany. I've drunk two glasses of champagne and am feeling slightly tipsy, but follow as best I can, till the story is over.

'Please excuse me whilst I pop outside for a cigarette?' I say politely.

'I'll join you,' says Lukas. Great.

We open the French doors leading to the garden and step

outside. Coop's back garden is surprisingly big and pretty: it's very green and quiet, and Marlena has planted lots of white wild flowers and put up fairy lights everywhere. I sit on a wooden table, resting my legs on one of the chairs.

Lukas lights my cigarette without speaking, and for a few seconds we sit in silence. I remember my job is to entertain the clients, and launch into my client-safe small talk.

'Well! Isn't that great news? I'm really excited about working on Blumenstrauße,' I say. Mmm, I love saying that name.

He looks up at me quickly, and I notice again how very clear and blue his eyes are. 'I am looking forward to working with you,' he nods.

'Yes, I think it's a very . . . uh . . . interesting opportunity . . .' I continue brightly, taking a sip of my champagne.

'Look, I am sorry I pretended I'd never lived here before,' says Lukas. 'It was very bad of me.'

I look over at him and he's making a face of such genuine, heartfelt contrition that I start to laugh. 'Cheeky, perhaps, if not truly bad . . . How long did you live here for?'

'Four years.'

'Four years!' I'm still laughing. 'Haven't you got better things to do now you're back than hang around with me?'

'Not really,' he says, smiling. He's very smooth. Smooth shaven, smooth jawed, smooth mover. We're almost flirting now. (Rule 3, my old nemesis. We meet again.) Time to move the conversation back to small-talk territory.

'Are you sad about leaving Berlin? I love Berlin. It's such an incredible city.'

'Ah, Sass, I am tired of Berlin,' he says, ashing his cigarette. He pronounces 'Sass' in a very clipped way. 'I'm ready for a change, I just broke up with my girlfriend, and you know . . . it is time to meet new people.'

I contemplate telling him about my Dating Sabbatical, but decide that it'd be better to not talk about dating. I don't mind seeing that he's nursing relationship wounds – in fact, it kind of makes me like him a bit more – but I'm damned if he'll discover that I am, too.

'Do you have many friends left in London from when you lived here before?' I ask.

'Well, lots have moved, of course, it's a big city and I was friends with lots of French and Germans. I do still have two very good friends here . . . thank goodness,' he adds. 'It's hard to move somewhere with no network at all.'

'Oh, I know,' I say, and take a sip of my drink. 'I call my first year in London "The Lost Year".'

He starts to laugh. 'That's like my first year here! I was 24, God, it was so difficult . . .'

We start telling loneliness stories about being fresh to London and diabolical Saturday nights spent in the West End before you realise that no one goes into the West End on a weekend. Ever.

'I would rather slash my wrists than spend a Saturday night in Covent Garden,' I say cheerfully. Lukas agrees. He's likeably easy-going. I can forgive him for almost tricking me into a date.

We finish our cigarettes and walk back inside to discover Cooper and Stefan talking animatedly about their rock days – Stefan is also an ex-musician – and Felix and Marlena are sitting on the floor together chatting away in German.

Coop starts telling wild stories about tours and fights and groupies and drugs, and for each story he tells, Stefan has a Teutonic one to match it. Soon Lukas and I are in fits of laughter, Cooper's gone mildly cross-eyed with drink, and Stefan's face is bright, bright red. He looks at himself in the mirror over the fireplace and shakes his head sadly.

'This is the reason I took so many drugs in the 90s,' he says mournfully. He pronounces it 'druks'. 'Drinking is so bad for me. Look at my tomato-head.'

Felix stands up. 'Cooper, I have been talking to your lovely wife, and drinking this lovely champagne, and we have decided that since she hates to cook and, since we are celebrating, we are going to go out to eat,' he smiles.

'WOOOOOO!' cheers Marlena. I have never heard her say anything so loud.

'I am booking a table at Nobu Berkeley,' says Felix. 'So Cooper, you must call a cab, and that is that.'

This is quite possibly the first time anyone has ever bossed Cooper around. He takes it awfully well: he's already got his phone out and is dialling his local taxi company. Marlena announces she's going to start smoking again tonight, and I head outside again with her. God, I love smoking and drinking champagne.

'Lukas, he likes you,' she says, inhaling awkwardly and exhaling almost straightaway.

'Meh,' I say. I feel a bit light-headed and try to count how much I've had to drink. No more till we get to Nobu. Ooh, Nobu. How pre-recession of us. 'I'm not really interested.'

'He is a good man,' she says, clutching my arm and looking into my eyes meaningfully. 'Felix has been telling me about him. He has just come out of a terrible time with his girlfriend . . . she was not a good person.' I nod, feeling mildly scared of her intensity. How much has she had to drink?

Her eyes are slightly unfocused, and she starts talking about what a good person Felix is, and then what a good person Stefan is. Clearly, everyone is a good person when Marlena's had half a bottle of champagne and four vodkas.

Soon, the minicabs arrive. Marlena, Felix and I are in one, and Coop, Lukas and Stefan in the other.

I check my phone as we walk out the door, and see I have two missed calls. From Rick. At 7.59 pm, and again at 8.43 pm. No message. My hearts skips a beat when I see his name on my phone. I can't help it, it's Pavlovian. It's an egg-white-based dessert.

The other two are already in the back of the cab, so I sit in

162

the front, feeling slightly tipsy and wondering why the sweet hell Rick would be calling me. We've just reached Chelsea Bridge when my phone rings.

It's Rick.

I let it ring four times, and decide there's no harm in finding out what he wants: Felix and Marlena are talking in German and won't be able to hear me over the Turkish pop on the radio.

'Hello?' I also decide it's a good idea to pretend I've deleted his number and have no idea who is calling.

'Ah, finally!'

'Uh, hello . . .? Who is this?' I try to sound detached, busy and uninterested, whilst secretly grinning to myself like a maniac. A tipsy maniac.

'It's me. It's Rick.'

'Rick! Oh, gosh, sorry, I didn't recognise your voice.'

Pause. I could say what's up, but why bother? Make him work for it.

'So . . . how are you? What are you up to tonight?' he says. What's with the small talk? He never called to ask me how I was when we were actually bloody going out.

'Ace,' I say breezily. 'Although I'm actually just off to a work dinner so I can't chat . . .'

'Anywhere nice?' he says jovially. Why is he being so nice like this? He sounds weird.

'Nobu, actually. The Berkeley Square one . . .'

'Oh, nice. Say hi to Nick behind the bar for me.' What a pretentious thing to say. And he sounds surprised I'd get to go somewhere nice for my job, which he always dismissed with an indulgent smile.

'Will do.'

Long pause.

'Well, I really shouldn't stay on the phone, Rick, I'm neglecting people . . .'

'Yeah, yeah, I just rang . . . basically, I rang to say that you and I should have dinner.'

Suddenly, I feel very detached. 'Really.'

'Yes. We should have dinner, together, tomorrow night. Seeing you last night . . . I have a lot of things I want to say to you. So I've booked a table at the Oak for 9 pm. You can meet me there.'

Of course he booked the Oak. It's about two streets from his house, the lazy bastardo. I don't know what to say.

Naturally, 'no fuck off' springs to mind, but it's so oddly rewarding to have him ask me out like this when I pictured him calling so many times the week after the Pink Lady. The Pink Lady! Fucking hell! Perhaps he wants to apologise. Perhaps he's desperately in love with me and I can reject him this time. That would be good. My mind flutters around like this for a few seconds till I realise I should speak.

'I don't know . . .' I say. I know I should say no. Pull yourself together, woman. 'I can't . . .'

'A drink then?' he says. 'I need to talk to you. Come on, please? Do you want me to beg? I will . . .'

I shouldn't I shouldn't I shouldn't. I think back to Rule 1. The most important Rule of all. No accepting dates.

'Come on,' he says, mildly impatiently. 'Please? I have something to say.'

'OK . . .' I say. 'But not a date. A drink. Just a drink.'

It's not a date when I've already dated him, is it? I think back to the Rules again. Nothing about not seeing ex-boyfriends in there. Nothing at all. Lalalaaa.

'Great,' he says.

'Chelsea, though,' I say. I seem to spend my life travelling up to Notting Hill and I'm damn well not doing it to see him. 'I'll meet you at the Botanist at 8 pm.' Ooh, I'm taking charge. This is a change.

'It's a date!' he says.

'It's a drink,' I correct him quickly. My champagne buzz has

164

been replaced by a mildly guilty feeling that I oughtn't to be agreeing to this. I ignore it and hang up without saying goodbye. I'll go along, see what he has to say, and leave. That's fine. Totally fine. I am still in control of this situation. I am still on a Dating Sabbatical.

When we get to Nobu Berkeley, the other three are already sitting at the table, and have ordered six matsuhisa martinis. Vodka, sake and ginger. Freaking delicious. I sit down and drink about a third of mine in one gulp.

'When I can't pronounce it anymore, stop me drinking,' I say to no one in particular. Lukas grins at me.

I'm sitting between Felix and Lukas. We're a very loud table. Felix calls over a waiter. 'Bring us hot miso chips, spicy tuna maki, the sweet potato tempura, oh, and toro tartar to start, and we'll have six more of these,' he says, tapping his martini glass. He looks around to the group. 'They're my favourites,' he says apologetically. He has favourites at Nobu?

To distract myself from thinking about the fact that I've just agreed to go out with – sorry, meet for a very quick drink so it almost doesn't count – Rick again, I start looking around the restaurant. I can see some people who I think might be C-list celebs but, as ever in London, it's the under-the-radar beautiful people who automatically command all the attention. They could be from England, France, New York, Russia, Brazil, or Dubai (or all of the above), look exceptionally well rested and well dressed, and chat to each other at the bar and across tables. Such assurance, such casual perfection. I wonder if they have mantras. Somehow, I don't think so. Suddenly my eye is caught by a middle-aged guy waving at me from two tables down. I stare at him. He's in a grey suit and is sitting at a table with a blonde woman drinking sake. He keeps waving, and I stare more. Suddenly, it clicks.

It's Smart Henry. Serious coin Smart Henry. And he's beckoning me over to his table.

'That guy is waving at you,' points out Lukas.

'I know, I know,' I say. Shit, I guess I'll have to go over.

Smart Henry jumps up when I arrive over. He's looking kind of bloated and pudgy, despite the slick suit, and much older than his 34 years. Where's his nice old tweed jacket? I think sadly. He seems thrilled to see me, and gives me a big hug hello.

'SARAH!' he exclaims. 'You look FANTASTIC!'

'Thanks,' I reply, slightly overwhelmed. 'How are you?'

'SUPER! How are YOU?' he says. Wow, he was never this enthusiastic about anything before.

'Super!' I say, peering at his face in slight shock. He's so fat and bankery, what happened to the skinny, laconic indie writer who I cried and cried over? 'How are you, I mean, how's Harvard?'

'Off the HOOK!' Smart Henry says, and introduces me to his date. Her name is Kristina, she's some kind of Scandahoovian. Fake boobs, fake blue contact lenses, that funny pinched-temple, pulled-eyebrow lift like Kylie and the blonde one from Girls Aloud have. But she has a very sweet smile.

'You look great!' he exclaims. His voice has become oddly transatlantic. 'What are you up to these days? How's PR?'

'Uh, I'm still in advertising,' I say. 'And you?'

'I just finished my MBA, you know, so I'm back here with Kristina on the way to Zurich. I'll be working there from July for a major European VC.'

'The finance world must be tough right now,' I say. What the fuck is a VC?

'A pretty girl like you doesn't need to worry about that,' he says, smiling down at me in what – now that he's fat and middle-aged looking – can only be described as patronisingly benevolent. Is that the kind of thing I used to think was ironic and amusing? He only broke up with me two years ago, has he changed that much? Or have I? No, I'm still me. It must be him.

'I'd better get back to my . . . my table,' I say, smiling at them

166

both. Kristina's face looks like it might hurt to smile. 'Nice to see you again.'

Smart Henry gives me his card – of course – and I walk back to our table, wondering how the devil I was ever in a relationship with that shallow oaf. I sit down and see Lukas peering at me questioningly, and, raising my glass, grin at him and drink it all. Holy crap, Smart motherfucking Henry. Smart Henry is a wanker with a plastic girlfriend. Rick asked me out and I shall reject him in person tomorrow night. High-fives all round.

'So,' I say conversationally, feeling the alcohol hit my bloodstream. 'When did you break up with your girlfriend?'

Lukas raises his eyebrows in surprise, finishes his matsuhisa martini with a masculine flourish, and grins back. 'Two months ago,' he says. He pronounces it 'muns'. He shrugs, and flicks his eyes up to meet mine. 'She left me, actually. For my friend.'

'Shut the front door!' I say. 'No way. How long had you been with her?'

He is a bit perplexed at the front-door thing, but keeps talking. 'A bit less than five years,' he says, then takes a deep breath. 'They had been having an affair behind my back.'

'Fucking bastardos,' I say, wondering a second too late if it's appropriate to speak like that to a new client.

'Fucking bastardos indeed,' he agrees calmly. 'So, I will move to London. Start again. Meet someone else. Trust in destiny.'

'Wow,' I say, surprised he's so positive, after all of that.

'And you? You have some fucking bastardo in your past, I think?' he asks with a smile.

I nod back and give a half smile. 'Yup.' And I'm meeting him tomorrow night. Because I am thtoopid.

The food starts arriving, and we get lost in an orgy of tasting and sharing. Felix orders the next lot of dishes – beef kushiyaki, spicy sour shrimp, butter crab and of course, black cod in miso.

As we eat, Stefan and Coop get stuck in a conversation about music, and Felix is talking to Marlena about his kids. Lukas and

I start talking about travelling. It turns out we both went to Venice the same summer about ten years ago and searched desperately for an apparently non-existent Venetian nightlife. It's a fun, easy conversation, and the rest of the meal passes quickly.

By the time we've finished dinner, it's almost 11 pm. I've been trying to sober up and failing, so I'm now concentrating on being quiet. I look over and see that Smart Henry and plastic Kristina have left. Thank hell.

We head downstairs, where the bar is packed with people drinking and talking.

As we walk out past a bunch of loud, moderately drunk guys in suits, my eye is caught by one of them. Tall, broad shoulders, dark hair.

He's got his back to me, but I'm sure it's him.

We walk straight past, and all the way down to the door, and I can't help turning around to stare at the back of his head, just as he turns his head to greet someone. Should I go and say hi?

It's not Jake. The guy has a monobrow, for God's sake.

Disappointment floods through me. I'm such a fool.

I turn back to the door, which Lukas is holding open for me, and walk out into the night. Outside it's an orgy of handshakes and kisses goodbye. I'm dying to turn back to look at the guy inside and make absolutely sure it's not Jake. But I know it wasn't. I was – what's that term? Projecting.

I wish, I wish it had been Jake. Why am I meeting Rick? What do I have to prove? Why can't I just walk away? Argh. I smack myself in the forehead, getting a strange look from Stefan in the process, and quickly pretend I'm fixing my hair.

After much 'no, you first' protestations, Felix and Stefan get the first cab, and Marlena turns to me, Cooper and Lukas.

'Let's go to MAHIKI!' she shouts, and makes a 'rock out' gesture with her hands. Wow, she's hammered.

'I'd love to,' says Lukas.

'I'll come too,' I say, almost without thinking.

'No, we're going home,' says Cooper firmly, putting his arm around Marlena's waist and manoeuvring her towards the next cab.

Lukas turns to me.

'Looks like it's you and me,' he says.

'Looks like it,' I nod. Whoops. Shit. I'm breaking Rule 6: Accidental dating! I'm too tipsy to think of how to get out of it. Oh, well. As we start walking towards Mahiki, Lukas automatically moves around me to walk on the outside edge of the pavement. Very nice manners.

'Have you been before?' he asks.

I shake my head. 'It's not really my bag. I'm a drinker and a talker. I'm not so much of a dancer.'

'It's good for drinking and talking too,' he says and, ten minutes later, we're inside Mahiki, and I'm sitting on some kind of large bamboo-y Tiki-type chair, with an enormous drink in my hand.

'What am I drinking?' I shout, over the music.

'A Honolulu Honey,' Lukas shouts back. It sounds so funny in his accent that I find myself laughing. He leans in towards me, pulling his chair right forward so we can talk closer.

'Will you go for dinner with me, when I move here?' he asks. 'I'm not tricking you. I'm just asking you.'

'Umm . . .' I say. Oh God. I look Lukas right in his perfectly blue eyes, and decide to just tell him the truth. It is permitted in Rule 5, after all. 'Look, I'm on a Dating Sabbatical,' I say, and he nods and leans closer.

'OK. Tell me more.'

So with his ear so close to my face that I can smell his after-shave, I explain the whole Dating Sabbatical premise. He takes it all in, nodding seriously. After a minute or so, when I'm starting to gabble: 'I'm not . . . cynical, or um, damaged, I just don't want anything romantic in my life for awhile, um . . .'

169

'So when is it over?' he asks, leaning back. 'Your Dating Sabbatical. When is it over?'

'I don't know,' I say. 'Maybe never. It's awfully easy.'

'I think,' he says, leaning in to me again, 'that it should be over when you meet someone you want to talk to much more. Someone interesting. Someone who is not . . . a fucking bastardo.'

I laugh. 'Probably.'

'That is me. I am a nice guy. And I think you are amazing.'

What?

'What?' I say.

He leans right in to me, so close that I can feel his warm breath on my ear. 'I think you are lovely. Confident . . . strong . . . easy to talk to . . . I want to spend more time with you.'

He does? I am? He doesn't know me. I'm only confident in select areas of life and I'm definitely not strong, I can barely get out of bed most mornings. Actually, that's not entirely true anymore.

'You make me smile, I think you are lovely, we get along well . . . It is not a big deal. Your Dating Sabbatical can finish . . .'

It does seem very, very straightforward when he puts it like that. He is easy to talk to. We do get along well. He's probably not a bastardo, given his ex-girlfriend sounds like one. And he asked me out, so why not say yes?

Because that's what I always do, I fancy people because they fancy me. And I can't break the Dating Sabbatical. Not when I'm so in control of everything in my life, for the first time ever.

I'm pondering these thoughts, and feeling the temptation recede, when he suddenly shifts his head two inches and we're kissing. I'm so surprised that I don't even kiss him back for a few moments, and then instinct kicks in and for about 30 seconds I just enjoy the sensation of kissing someone after three long months of no kisses at all. They're slow, thoughtful kisses: his lips are a little colder than I would have expected, and his tongue is a little more aggressive than I'd like, but well, unless there's a serious technique failure, kissing is almost always fun. Don't you think?

Then suddenly, Jake pops into my head. Not the Sabbatical, though I'm breaking Rule 8 with wanton abandon, not the fact that Lukas is the MD of the company who just hired my advertising agency. Just Jake. And I pull back so fast that Lukas hangs in the air for a moment with his eyes closed and his lips puckered.

I search desperately for an excuse. The Dating Sabbatical isn't going to cut it a second time, I fear. 'You're our new client. It's totally unethical.' Jackpot.

'Pfft . . . that means nothing,' says Lukas. 'Everyone meets at work.'

I shake my head. 'No. No, it's not a good idea. I'm going to . . . go home now.'

As we stand up, Lukas reaches out to take my hand, and I deliberately fiddle with my lucky yellow clutch so as to avoid it. What a bad idea. Oh fuck, I kissed a client. I'm so preoccupied with these thoughts that I barely talk as we exit Mahiki, and I see a black cab outside. That little yellow light that shows it's free is the best sight sometimes.

'Thanks for a great night, Lukas,' I say.

'I hope . . . you are OK?' he says. 'I'm going back to Germany tomorrow, so I won't see you for a fortnight . . . I hope you won't be angry with me?'

'Not at all,' I say. 'Don't worry about it.'

'Can I have your number?'

I pretend not to hear, and lean forward to give him a quick kiss on the cheek. As I get in the cab, Lukas tries to give me a special look. I pretend not to see it and close the door. 'Pimlico, please.'

If I'd met Lukas at any point in the past eight years, I'd have jumped at the chance to go out with him. I'd be snogging him furiously in Mahiki right now, and being as flirty and funny as

171

I could, with no thought for the consequences. The Dating Sabbatical really has changed me. I've decided to ignore the fact that it was Jake I thought of, not the Sabbatical. The point is, I stopped kissing him.

I feel proud of myself for a second, till I remember about the drink with Rick tomorrow night. Oh doublefuck, the drink with Rick.

Twenty-five minutes later I'm showered, pyjama-ed and in bed. The room is rocking ever so slightly.

How can I have added another ball to my endless thought-juggle? I wonder as my head hits the pillow. Lukas-Rick-Jake. Jake-Rick-Lukas.

Suddenly, it hits me that I can just cancel the drink with Rick tomorrow night. And I will have the upper hand, because he asked me out and I said no. Yes. I will cancel it. No Lukas. No Rick. Easy.

Chapter Seventeen

You know that you're probably doing something naughty, even if you're pretending you're not, when you keep it from your best friends. I don't tell them that I agreed to go on a date with Rick.

For a drink, I mean. It doesn't matter, I reason, since I'm going to cancel. Yep. Cancel. I send him an email mid-morning on Friday:

Rick. I'm so sorry, I can't make it tonight after all. I'll explain another time.

Abrupt, distant, vague, polite. Perfect.

I get an out-of-office response back 20 minutes later. He's not at work all day, with no access to email. He's the only lawyer I know who doesn't carry a BlackBerry.

I text him instead:

Can't make tonight – something has come up. Sorry.

No reply. Good, there's that dealt with then. I mentally high-five myself, and look around the office quickly. It's very quiet again this morning, everyone is catching up on work we put on hold during the pitch, but there's a happy, slightly euphoric buzz about the place. Cooper hasn't come in, and texted me at 9 am to tell me to round up the troops and tell everyone the good news. My God, it felt good doing that. I singled everyone out and thanked them for their individual contributions. Everyone worked so hard, and they deserve the praise and recognition. (Andy spent the whole time sending, or pretending to send, texts.)

I haven't heard anything from Lukas, by the way. A minute after waking up this morning I remembered kissing him, and immediately had a stomach-lurch of nausea which was, I swear, more cringe than matsuhisa martini. Apart from that, he's barely crossed my mind. I'm quite good at ignoring things I don't want to think about, you won't be surprised to hear. He's gone for two weeks now, anyway.

So now I'm writing pseudo-70s e-card copy for a boiler company, which is traditionally something people only buy when the old one carks it – ie, a 'distress purchase'. The idea is that if the e-card is funny enough, people will send it on to their friends, thus helping our client reach more potential customers. The 70s thing is so that people realise how out-of-date their boiler is. Supposedly.

We've got some amusing photos of Burt Reynolds-alikes in camel-coloured Dacron flared suits staring lovingly at the camera, so all I have to do is come up with the line, and leave a space for people to type the name of the person they're sending it to.

[name], you remind me of a shag carpet. Soft, warm and hairy in all the right places.

[name], would you like to come out for a drink with me? Just sit quietly in my car and I'll be out when the pub shuts.

Hmm, moderately funny. I'm really not sure how well this whole strategy is going to work. I didn't come up with it originally. It was Andy and Danny, when I was working on the German stuff, so it's the first time I've really seen the brief.

Cooper and Andy are out all afternoon seeing another client, so I write an email about my concerns to them both. I choose my words carefully: I don't want to sound rude, but I want to be quite clear and confident. Gosh, it's quite satisfying being more involved in this sort of thing. A few months ago, I'd have shut up and just written the lines.

Suddenly, my phone beeps. A reply from Rick.

Don't be silly – push your other thing back. It's only half an hour.

How irritating. There is a difference between being bossed around charmingly, which I love, and just being told what to fucking do, which I hate.

I can't. Sorry.

He replies.

Please – I need to talk to you.

Annoyingly intriguing, and he did say please . . . maybe he really IS in love with me. That would be interesting. Not that I love him back. At all. I'm not even interested.

But it would be lovely for me to be the one to reject him. Maybe he is not a bad person deep down underneath it all. No, he's not, I mean, yes he is, he's a bastardo and he wasn't even nice to me when we were dating, before Pink Ladygate. God, my head is exhausting me.

You know what, I'll just meet him and leave halfway through the drink. That's totally fine. It hardly even counts.

An email in my inbox from an unfamiliar name distracts me from my self-centred reverie. From Eugene Durand, sent to me and Katie. Who the – oh. The Dork.

Hey there . . . Sorry to bother you . . . Just wondering if you know if Bloomie is OK . . . I haven't heard from her since Wednesday night . . . Thanks . . . Eugene.

I think for a second. That was the Sophie's Steakhouse night. I haven't heard from her either. I take out my mobile and call Bloomie's work line and then her mobile. It rings out both times. An email from Kate arrives, just for me.

Have you heard from B? She's not replying to my emails or texts, and if she slept at home last night, I didn't see or hear her. What should we do? The Dork is worried.

Gosh, perhaps Bloomie is having an affair. But she said she was going to marry The Dork, so that can't be right. I ring her work number again, this time hiding my mobile phone number – stalkerphone! – and at the sixth ring, she answers.

'Susan Bloomingdale.'

'Blooms, it's me . . .'

'What's up?'

'We were just wondering if you're OK, we haven't heard from you, Eugene is worried, Kate says you didn't come home last night . . .'

'I'm working. I have a job, in case you haven't noticed.'

She hangs up. Fucking hell, she's a cranky bitch sometimes. I ring Kate.

'I stalkerphoned her, she says she's just working.'

'I've never seen anyone work like she does. Apart from seeing us on Wednesday, and Eugene on Sunday, she's worked at least 17 hours a day, every day for the last two weeks.'

'Fucking hell. That's ridiculous.'

'At least she has work to do,' says Kate in a whisper. 'I've got almost nothing to do. I was about to suggest a game of i-spy over email.'

'Ha. I have to go, Katiepoo. I'll email The Dork.'

I hang up from Kate and compose a quick mail to Eugene.

She's just working! Try dropping her an email . . .

Eugene:

After the three I've already sent? . . . Oh well, I'm glad she's not dead. Thanks.

Wow, that's awfully dark humour there. He's obviously rather pissed off. Bloomie has always been a work-focused little bunny, but it has taken on a new level of madness in the last year. She's so focused on it, I realise, that it's starting to throw everything else out of kilter. Like me and dating, in the olden days. Maybe she needs a Work Sabbatical.

My thoughts turn back to tonight. Fuck, Rick. I'll just have two sips of my drink, hear what he has to say, and leave. Perfect.

On the way home after work, I get a text from Bloomie. She apologises for being rude on the phone earlier and says she and Kate are having a pizza and poker night at their house with Eugene and Eddie. I reply that I'll be along a bit later. It would be too hard to explain now why I am going for one sip of a drink with Rick tonight.

In fact, I won't imbibe at all. I'll just wave the drink near my face, hear what he has to say and leave.

Quick shower, yada yada, washed hair this morning so I just tease it into a bouffant chignon thing, deodorant, perfume. No perfume. Oh, go on, perfume. Does that send the wrong impression? No. It just shows standards. Oh, it's Le Dix by Balenciaga, since you ask, and it took me years and years to discover it. Each previous perfume, predictably, reminds me of a boyfriend or period of time. My mum gives me a new perfume every birthday, and you know, it always seems to coincide with a life change. Anaïs Anaïs is school, Lou Lou is most of university. Arty Jonathan is Gucci Rush. Rugger Robbie is Chanel No. 19. Clapham Brodie is Allure. Smart Henry is L'Instant de Guerlain. Rick is Shalimar, and I don't know what I was thinking wearing that at all. When I smell it now, I feel sick. I suppose Le Dix should remind me of Posh Mark but I'm afraid it just reminds me of me now, not him. Now, where was I?

Ah yes . . . what the sweet hell to wear. I want to look kind of hot, obviously, but not like I've made an effort, ie, I shall be fully-but-sexily covered up. And tall, since he is not that tall. Ha. Three-inch tan platform heels. White kickflare jeans that more than cover my heels so I look like a giant. White vest top. Red belt. Another white vest top over the top because they're cheap and cheap things look better layered, I think/hope. White wrappy jacket thing. Hair down. Yes. I christen thee Virginal Jetsetter. I glance at my watch. It's 6.05 pm. We're not meeting for another two hours. Sigh. I want to get this over and done with.

I re-examine my make-up and add some winged eyeliner and taupe eyeshadow. Mew.

I am not good at killing time. And living in a city like in London, I don't usually have to. I just whirl from one spot to the next. I contemplate writing something – my little stories are coming along rather nicely – but I can't right now. So instead, I tidy my room, try on three pairs of alternate shoes, and head down to the kitchen. On the way, I run into Anna, who is heading towards the front door with a huge overnight bag slung across her back.

'Anna!' I say. 'Hello.'

'Oh, oh, hi,' she says, turning back into the hallway and dropping the bag slightly dramatically. I look closely at her and see that her eyes are badly swollen and pink. Newborn puppy syndrome.

'Um . . . off anywhere nice?' I ask. Which was obviously a stupid thing to say, but so is 'are you alright?' to someone whose face looks like a cyst.

'I'm going to Edinburgh, home to Mum,' she says, searching her cardigan sleeves for a tissue. About seven fall out onto the floor. 'Don left me. Again.'

'Oh God, I'm sorry . . .' I say. I try to remember the last time we ran into each other, when she was happy. Last week? 'Well, I'm sure his marriage is . . . you know, very, um . . . complicated and that's kind of understandable . . .'

'He's not back with her!' she exclaims. 'SHE left HIM for someone else. I didn't know, because he never told me any details. When I thought he was back with her I was wrong . . . he'd told me he needed space, so it was a pretty natural assumption. Space!' she adds, spitting out the word like a chewed cuticle.

'Fucking bastardo,' I say.

'I know! I thought the Dating Sabbatical was the trick, to get him back, you know? I really thought it was.' She looks at me, slightly wild-eyed. 'I didn't return his calls, didn't read his emails, and then he turned up at work one night, and then everything was so good for a whole month!' She pauses dramatically.

'And then I asked him about his divorce and where we were going as a couple, and he left me again.' She starts crying hysterically. 'I make the wrong decision every time! I'm like a water-stick thing for the wrong decision!'

'Divining rod?' I suggest. Her sobs get louder. 'Oh, Anna, don't, um, upset yourself . . .' I add, a bit pointlessly. 'Just have some perspective, things will be OK . . .'

'I have to go home,' she says, her voice rising into a slight wail. 'I can't take my life anymore. I just cannot take it.' She leans over to pick up her overnight bag. 'The only good thing about all of this is that I've lost a stone.' She stands up and smiles at me triumphantly. 'How great is that!?'

'Great!' I say.

'OK, well, see ya!' She slams the door after her.

Wow. I think this last dumping may have made Anna actually insane. That would have happened to me. That could still happen to me. It's so easy to think you're making the right choices, when you're doing everything wrong . . . Oh God, oh God, I think I'm doing everything wrong.

I open the fridge and think about eating something to calm me down. I spent quite possibly my entire teenage years standing in front of the fridge when I was bored, thinking about eating something and hoping that at any moment some cold, chewy brownies or leftover sticky honey chicken drumsticks would magically appear. Because my mother was in charge of that fridge, such magical things sometimes really did happen.

As always, however, my shelf in this fridge is filled with Laughing Cow Extra Light, organic peanut butter, and a bottle of Japanese rice vinegar from a rather unsuccessful sushi-making dinner party I had last year. There's bread in the freezer (no point in buying a fresh loaf when you only eat a few pieces a week), but I can't be bothered to toast it. I don't even own any milk to make myself a coffee.

179

This is not a grown-up's fridge, I think to myself. At some point in my life, I'd like to have real food in a real fridge.

I close the fridge door and stare out the kitchen window for awhile. Behind our house is a lovely little cobblestone mews. All the little mews houses are different pastel colours, like sugared almonds in a row, with Porsches and Range Rovers lined up outside.

Sometimes, very very early in the morning, I see the husbands that live in the mews houses leaving for work. At 9 am the nannies take the toddlers for a walk. At about 10 am the wives' personal trainers arrive. And then at about 1 pm the now immaculately-dressed-and-coiffed wives head out for lunch, sometimes with immaculately-dressed-and-coiffed toddlers in tow, sometimes not.

And these people aren't even the real rich in London, you know, yet it's still a life I just can't imagine ever having – and it's not like I'm a pauper by normal standards, either. It's just London. There is so much money in London that to compare yourself to it becomes simply ridiculous. I'll never earn enough to buy a house in London. Some of my friends will buy houses, and some like Bloomie already have, but I'll probably be renting forever. My mortgage would be two-thirds of my monthly salary, not including bills and furniture and all the rest. I did the maths (well, Kate did it for me), and it gave me financial nausea. No wonder I haven't grown up. The economy won't allow me to.

Do you know, I haven't had a pay rise in all the time I've worked for Coop? I've never asked for one, and one's never been offered. I'm going to have to do something about that.

God, this shit is depressing.

I turn around and, almost without intending to do it, take a tumbler out of the cupboard above the sink, throw in some ice and add three fingers of vodka. I would add a mixer, but we don't have any. I look around the kitchen to see if we have any lemons, but we don't have them either. Just a stack of my unopened bank statements on the breadbin, as usual.

I head out to the living room, grab a fag and a lighter from my bag on the table, walk back to the kitchen to lean out the kitchen window and light my cigarette. Thank fuck I am sticking to the Dating Sabbatical. Without it, I would be like Anna. Well, perhaps not as insane. But possibly not far off. A few more years of bad dates and Ricks and . . .

Oh God, the Sabbatical, and Rick. Rick, Rick in . . . I look at my watch . . . one hour and 20 minutes.

Leaning out the kitchen window, I can see right into the living room of a guy watching some kind of reality show on a massive flatscreen TV. It's one of those *Pop Idol* shows. I'm not that devoted to them, mostly as I have never been organised enough to remember when they are on, and I think it might be Saturday night and that's always been devoted to dating or drinking. But whenever I do find myself watching them, I'm almost guaranteed to cry at least once, usually twice. Seeing people hope for the best, and lose is, of course, a bit sad. But seeing people hope for the best, and then win – oh God, dude, it just destroys me. Even thinking about it makes me a bit teary.

I finish my cigarette, pour myself another three fingers of vodka and light another fag. Why did I go out with Rick for so long when he was being such a bastardo? Why did I keep trying to make him as crazy about me as he had seemed in the first few weeks? Will he explain why he shagged a Pink Lady in front of me? Does he want me back? It's too late. I don't love him anymore. If I ever did, if that was love, whatever that was. Urgh.

Why am I navel-gazing this much when I'm meant to be just breezing through life on my Dating Sabbatical?

I take out my phone and consider calling Bloomie and Kate. Shit, I can't. They don't know I'm about to see Rick. I feel duplicitous not telling them. But then again, what am I meant to do, report every thought and plan that I have, every second that I have them?

I look at my watch. 6.45 pm. Argh. Ages to go. I take out my phone and call Mum. She'll be at home now thinking about what to have for dinner and whether she and Dad should just go out instead.

'Hello?' she says, after the phone has rung about ten times and I'm about to hang up.

'MummAY!' I say, using the pet name I have for her, which is basically just a baby way of saying Mummy. When I am home I sometimes lie in bed and shout it till she comes in to kiss me goodnight. This is, I know, immature of me. I wonder if I stopped doing it, would I start thinking about growing up and getting married?

'Oh, little darling, hello!'

'Ça va, Maman? What are you up to?'

'I was just thinking about dinner and whether Dad and I should just go out instead.'

'Definitely go out. Life is too short to stuff a mushroom, girlfriend,' I say, taking a slug of vodka. One university holiday, Mum and I started reading her old feminist literature to each other. It is damn funny stuff. (Important. Important and funny.) 'How was bridge today?'

'Ah . . . it was good,' she says. I can hear her settling into the couch and cradling the phone in her ear. 'I was doing very well for the first hour, and then I was playing with Frances, you know, from yoga, and she and I always enjoy playing together, but the other two were taking it terribly seriously, and then Frances forgot what she was playing, and then I couldn't remember either, and we laughed till Frances almost fell off her chair. It didn't go down very well at all . . . They're so uptight there.'

I laugh at the idea of Mum and Frances in hysterics in a bridge game. They recently outlawed alcohol at her bridge games – I think Mum and Frances may have had something to do with it.

'What's news with you, my little darling?' she says.

'Oh . . . Mummay,' I sigh, leaning my head against the kitchen

182

window and gazing at the mews. 'Well, work is ace. Really ace. And, um. I'm about to go and see this guy Rick for a drink.'

'Rick? The one who cheated on you?'

Damn, I forgot I'd told her about it. 'Uh . . . yes.'

'Oh, darling, why? Why on earth. Would you do that.' My mother likes to cut her sentences up sometimes for dramatic emphasis.

'Um . . . because he asked me?'

'He doesn't deserve it! He is not. Good enough. For you.'

'Well . . . I've agreed to it now . . .'

'Move on! Kick him to the curb, honey! Kick him. To. The. Curb.' Sigh. She also watched too much of Ricki Lake's TV programme years ago and now uses the phrases she picked up with joy and abandon.

'But . . . Shouldn't I even see what he wants?'

'No. Absolutely. Not.'

'But . . . it's rude to cancel now.'

'For someone so smart, my little darling, you are very silly . . . I mean with your love Sabbatical, and before that it was your no bastardos thing, and now you're seeing Rick who is the worst of the whole lot . . .'

God, when she puts it like that, I really sound like a mess. I make a pathetic mewing sound into the phone to make her laugh.

'What do you want? Do you want him to turn around and say that he's sorry and he's in love with you?'

Yes. 'No.'

'Then why did you agree to see him?'

'He was quite . . . persuasive.'

'Don't allow yourself to be dominated by a stronger personality. And don't just go out with someone you can dominate, either.'

Ouch. That would mean Rick and then Posh Mark. Now I sound like a fucking basket case.

'I remember when you were a little girl, you were such a happy little thing, but if someone at school didn't like you, you thought it was your job to try even harder to win them over.'

'I'm not like that anymore,' I say stoutly, realising that actually, perhaps I am. 'Well, anyway, it's a female trait. We're pleasers. Society teaches to be pretty and pliant. The feminine mystique.' The vodka seems to be kicking in.

'Rubbish. The feminine mystique is about women only finding identity and meaning through their husband and children. Betty Friedan! And I certainly did not bring you up to be pretty and pliant! I subverted the gender assumption! I even gave you trucks to play with.'

'And I called them Ursula and Grace and put dresses on them and had a tea party.'

'Yes, you did,' she laughs at the memory.

'Um . . . OK . . . well what should I do?'

'You're 28 years old!' she says briskly. 'You decide! You're perfectly. Capable. Of making your own decisions.'

'I don't feel like I am,' I say. Right now I feel rather pathetic, actually. I want to lie on the couch with my head on her shoulder and watch *Calamity Jane*, our favourite family holiday film.

'You can't keep on like this forever, you know. Just clothes and going out and having fun. We're still in a recession, you know. I hope you're saving money . . .'

'Oh, Mum . . .' I don't want to lie on the couch with my head on her shoulder if she's going to lecture me, obviously.

'I'm serious. Bloomie and Kate seem to have themselves sorted.'

Now wait a minute.

'That's not true, Mum. I'm doing so well at work, and on the Sabbatical, and Bloomie has to work a million hours a week, and her boyfriend doesn't know where she even is half the time, and Kate's company is going under, and she left Tray. None of us are sorted.'

'Well . . .' she says, grudgingly. 'Well, it does sound like you're

184

enjoying life more, anyway. Now . . . back to this "Rick". Why are you seeing him tonight?'

I don't say anything.

'If you didn't have this "Sabbatical", what kind of boyfriend would you want? Would it really be him?'

'Umm . . .' I think hard. Deep down, I know what I want, really, and I know it's not Rick. 'I just want someone I feel a . . . I don't know . . . a click with. Someone who's funny and quick, someone who makes me laugh and who I make laugh . . . And who underneath all the banter is kind and surprising and interesting . . .' It feels a bit ridiculous to be making a shopping list like this. And impossible. Underneath, any man who fulfils all these criteria would be a bastardo. 'The problem is, Mum, that I always, always choose the wrong guy. No matter what.'

'Well, since you're seeing this "Rick" tonight, that's clearly true,' she says tartly. 'Tell me, does "Rick" make you laugh?' She pronounces his name exaggeratedly, as though it's actually a pseudonym.

'I don't remember.' I really can't think about it right now. I was focused entirely on making him like me. Because when he did, it felt really good, and no one had ever made me feel like that before.

'Can't you just go out and meet someone new who makes you laugh and you find attractive and so on?'

Suddenly, I think about Jake. Lovely, funny, warm, sexy-as-fuck Jake.

'It's not that easy, Mutti . . . and I just feel like everything always goes bad anyway.'

'Oh, God. Don't be so defeatist, darling. Change the paradigm!' This is something else she says sometimes, though I don't know for the life of me where it came from. Or what it means. 'Just . . . be yourself! And be positive! Everything happens for a reason!'

'Thanks, Maman,' I sigh. 'OK. I'll do some thinking.'

'Oh, Dad's just come in. I love you. Are you going to be OK?'

'Of course I will! I'll call you tomorrow. I love you too. Thanks, Mum. Can I have a chat to Daddy?'

There's a long pause and some talking in the background, and I'm thinking they've forgotten about me when Dad holds the phone up to his ear.

'Well, we can just eat there. Darling?'

'Hi, Daddy!'

'Hello, darling. You sound chirpy. How are you?'

'Good.' I tell him about dinner last night at Nobu. Dad's a bit of a foodie.

'Sounds very good,' he says. 'Now, tell me the latest with your game plan.'

'Um, I think I'm on half-time, actually, Daddy. I'm not sure how it's working, though it's been pretty straightforward so far, the opposition hasn't been up to much.'

'Right, right,' he says. I can tell he's grinning. 'Well, they'll have considered which moves worked in the first half and which didn't. So just be on your toes. Remember, it's a game of two halves.'

'OK, Papa,' I say, taking another slug of vodka. 'I'll keep you posted on the results.'

'Well, consider this your chance to take a time-out, too . . . and think about what you want to achieve next. And remember that the best indicator of future performance is past performance.'

'OK.' I feel overwhelmed with parental advice and feminist sayings and sporting metaphors now.

'Well, it's whisky time here. Give us a call on Sunday? Love you, darling.'

'Love you, too, Daddy.'

'Call. Him. And. Cancel!' I can hear Mum shouting from the other side of the room as Dad hangs up.

I pour myself another three fingers of vodka and light another fag.

I know they're right. For a minute I feel very sorry for myself, then annoyed at myself for being so pathetically self-pitying, then mildly amused that I'm going through all of this angst at all as I feel like Bridget fucking Jones (though I do, obviously, love her), then sorry for myself again. Vodka is so easy to drink.

I finish my drink, pour another, smoke two more cigarettes, and give myself a quick peptalk that centres on: it's not breaking the Sabbatical, I don't want him back anyway so it's not a date, I am in control, be positive, everything happens for a reason, maybe he'll apologise and somehow I'll feel better about that horrible, horrible night at the Pink Lady party. It's not the most imaginative of peptalks, but it works. Kind of.

Then it's 20 to eight, and time to head to the Botanist.

Chapter Eighteen

When I walk into the Botanist, I can't see Rick anywhere. He's late. That's just great. It's packed, as usual, but I eventually squeeze myself to the bar, order two gin and tonics, because it would be a waste of time to get him to go to the bar and line up all over again when he gets here, and head outside for a fag.

After one fag and my gin and tonic, he still hasn't turned up. I look at my phone. It's quarter past eight. I don't even like gin and tonic that much, I think. Why did I order it? Because Rick always drinks it, came the answer right back. You stupid woman.

I start drinking Rick's gin and tonic and light another fag. I love looking at the posh types that hang out at the Botanist. I wonder where they used to go when this place was a shitty little pub. It was refurbished a few years ago and is now a busy, buzzy bar and restaurant. It's the only place worth going around Sloane Square, really. The Oriel is Eurotrashtic, and the Chelsea Brasserie has amazing food but suffers from the taint of being a hotel restaurant, and up towards Belgravia is the cosy, mildly shabby Antelope pub, which comes into its own in dark freezing winter, when all anyone wants in life is to drink red wine in front of a crackling fire.

I entertain myself by gazing at the crowds of 30-something, terribly successful-looking people who are all standing around outside the Botanist smoking and basking in each other's glossy perfection. The huge, knee-to-ceiling open windows along the length of the bar mean people are very happy to stand outside for hours, passing drinks back and forth with friends inside. I'm standing at the eastern side of the crowd, so as to have a better vantage point for when fuckfeatures, I mean Rick, arrives.

I'm just admiring one girl talking very loudly and proudly about her friends Fenella and Tarquin's plans for Cowes Week when I see, out of the corner of my eye, Annabel Pashmina Face getting out of a black cab. I immediately spin around and face the other way, even though there's nothing much to look at behind me. Posh Mark's agenda-loaded best friend is the last person I want to see. Then, overcome by curiosity, I peek over my left shoulder, using my hair as a veil. She's got her raspberry pash on today, which must mean she's in a good mood, and then—

Holy shit, there's Posh Mark, running across the road from the Square, shouting 'Belly!' Is that some kind of secret nickname? I don't have time to wonder, as I realise that Pashmina Face has stopped still and is waving joyfully at him. They're going to be hugging hello in that long-lost-dancey-way they always do, about three yards from me!

I quickly crabwalk four steps, until I hit the wall of the Botanist and shift to the left slightly. I'm now cowering behind a couple of stick-thin Botoxed lovelies in Temperley and Issa who look at me – fag and gin in hand, yellow clutch shoved under my armpit – like I'm wearing H&M. Which I am.

Posh Mark and Pashmina Face dancey-hug for a minute or so, and then link arms and start walking up Cliveden Place towards Belgravia. They're heading for the Antelope, I think furiously. I showed him that pub way back in January.

Then, in a split second, as they reach the far pavement, Posh Mark grabs her hand and stops her, and they stop for a tender little snog.

I gasp. I knew she liked him! Fucking brilliant! I smile broadly. He deserves someone to adore him. They'll get married and have lots of thick, posh babies and live happily ever after.

189

There's a tap on my shoulder.

It's Rick. Twenty-five minutes late. Fuck, I'd forgotten about him.

'Afraid I started on your drink,' I say, instead of saying hello. Oh dear. I'm tipsy. He leans in to kiss me on the cheek. His breath is sour, barely masked with a recently-discarded Spearmint Extra. I'm towering over him in my heels, I notice. Hah.

'No problem,' he says. 'Sorry I'm late. I had a drink with Morse and McKinley and we ran over.'

Who the sweet hell are Morse and McKinley? Why does he assume everyone knows everyone he's talking about?

'Glad you could meet me,' he says, as a group gets up to leave the little table behind us. 'Grab this table and I'll get us a bottle of wine.'

It seems a bit odd to say I only intended to stay for half a drink when I'm already one and a half down (and three – or was it four? – pretty stiff vodkas at home), so I nod and sit down, almost knocking over the table with my knees in the process. Shit, I shouldn't have made those gins doubles. Tipsywoo. I slump back in the chair and light a fag. Posh Mark and Pashmina Face! I start giggling to myself, then stop as the Temperley woman whispers something to the Issa woman, and they both turn to glare at me. Bitches.

I curl my upper lip and make a snarly bear face at them, just as Rick returns with a bottle of white wine and two glasses. I've resolved to sip my next drink slowly. This much alcohol tends to make me loquacious and exuberant. I must remember that I am not here to charm and flirt and sparkle. I am here to hear what he has to say.

And it's a lot. Yet nothing at all.

Over the next 15 minutes, he regales me with stories about how incredible his flat is, how well his cases are going, how he thought of brilliant law-genius solutions that no one else could think of, how amazing his new car is, and how wild his trip to Ibiza will be next weekend.

And you know what else? Whilst he's spouting all this rubbish, he's not even looking at me. He's looking at the wall behind me, the women standing around us, the cars going past, and then the women standing around us some more.

In short, he's the worst date-not-that-this-is-a-date I think I've ever had. He hasn't even asked me one question about myself. He's simply monologuing.

Was he always this self-involved? Did he ever make me laugh? Why did I like being with him so much? Didn't he say he wanted to say something in particular to me? Should I ask? I really can't be arsed. I take another sip – OK, it's a slug, oops – of my wine, sit back in my chair and gaze at him through slightly narrowed eyes.

What an absolute prat.

I start observing him in a detached way, taking long sips of wine. (Oops again.) His hair looks a bit dirty at the roots and, like at Sophie's Steakhouse the other night, I notice his eyelashes are pale and droopy. That one single long eyebrow hair is still curling right around. I wonder how long the eyebrow hair would be if I pulled it straight and if he'd squeal like a little girl if I pulled it out right here, right now.

After a bit more gazing and slurping, I can just remember what I found attractive/enticing about him before – the unswerving self-confidence, the arrogant humour. But now I can finally see that he really is an idiot. Not even an idiot bastardo, mind you, but just a rude, self-involved, superficial idiot. What a waste of time. Dating him, thinking about him, crying over him, and most of all, what a waste of a good Friday night being here with him.

I never loved him. How could I have ever, ever thought I did?

By now I don't care why he asked me here. I just want to leave. My mother is right. He is not good enough for me. I am sitting forward in my chair and pouring myself another glass of wine, trying to figure out how to interrupt him, when he finishes a story about how his crowd knows all the best dealers in Monaco – 'and I don't mean blackjack' – puts his hand on my knee and says: 'Thanks for taking all that party stuff so well, by the way.'

I snap to attention. 'Sorry?'

'You know, the party, and all that . . . thanks. I needed some time off. It was getting too intense. But you know, seeing you the other night . . . you look great. I miss you. Now, I was thinking we could just . . . pick up where we left off . . .' He leans in to me, as if to kiss me, at the same second that I move my leg so his hand falls off my knee and lean back sharply.

'I beg your fucking pardon?'

'What?'

'Why?' I say.

'"Why?"' he repeats incredulously.

'Yes. Why should I? . . . No, actually, why *would* I ever go out with you again, Rick?'

He doesn't say anything, just looks at me with his stupid long curly eyebrow hair brushing his stupid droopy pale eyelashes. My drunken detachment is completely gone; in fact, I am bursting with self-righteous rage. What did he expect, to come here and we would go back to the way things were – which was pretty damn horrible anyway? After I told him I loved him and he responded by cheating on me, *in front of me*?

I sit up straight in my chair, trying hard to get every thought in my head in the right order to come out without stammering or garbling. It's going to be difficult with the vodka and gin and wine sloshing around. I take a deep breath.

'N-n-no. Rick. No way . . . You've never, you've never even apologised for t-treating me like that, you never said sorry I shagged a Pink Lady in front of you, sorry I was a selfish, horrible boyfriend and chased and chased you until I got you and then only called you on Sunday nights for sex and, and, and then discarded you without a thought . . .'

He's staring at me in open-mouthed shock. 'What? Sass, I—'

I am inflamed with anger. My face is burning and my voice is shouty, yet shaking.

'You never called me after that party, you never tried to do anything to make me feel better like s-s-say sorry or, even ad-admit that you behaved badly. And you did, you did behave badly . . .'

Rick rolls his eyes and backs his chair away from the table as if to get up, so I stand up, right in front of him.

'I thought you might apologise for everything tonight, but you know what? I don't care. I DON'T CARE. I don't want you, I don't even like you. At all. You're . . .' My heart is hammering in my chest, and all the insults I have been hurling around my head have left my booze-befuddled brain, and all I'm left with is to hiss at him, like a cross between my mother and Marlena: '. . . You are. Not a good person. You are just. Not. A good person.'

'Whatever, sweetheart,' he shrugs, and stands up, picking up his blazer from the chair behind him. 'What the fuck did you think you were coming here for?'

'I have no idea,' I say, knowing as I say it that it's not true, and I was secretly hoping he'd crawl back, and I'd get to reject him, and feel great about myself. Instead of the debonair, killingly charismatic man I was hoping for, however, there's this shallow, horrible, black hole of a man who assumed I'd do exactly as he expected, probably because I did before.

Not this time.

I take a deep breath. 'You know what, Rick? You can just . . . you can go to hell.'

He glances at me as he straightens his collar out, and makes a brushing-away motion with his hand at me. 'Whatever. Screw you, too.'

I can't help it.

In one smooth move, I reach down to the table, pick up my full glass of wine, and throw it in his face. Then I pick up his glass of wine and throw it in his face too.

All the glamorous people standing around us gasp and back away. Temperley and Issa clutch each other's arms in alarm. Rick wipes the excess wine off his face and looks at me through his fingers. I see real fury in his eyes and, for a second, I am actually scared.

So I sprint three steps to the road, hail a black cab that's fortuitously going past right that second, get in and slam the door.

'Westbourne Grove, please,' I say, my voice still shaking slightly. Time to see Bloomie and Kate and get far away from this horrible situation.

As we drive around Sloane Square in the fading early summer light, I peek over the back of the cab and see Rick striding off in the direction of Belgravia, with a few of the people outside the Botanist staring after him. The rest have just gone back to their conversations, as any crowd in any bar in the world will do after witnessing a girl throw a drink in a guy's face.

Then, as we wait at the lights and I look back over Sloane Street at the crowd outside the bar again, I see one tall figure staring over at my cab.

The figure is standing outside the Botanist, at the very other side to where we were sitting, with two men who are laughing uproariously at something. He seems completely transfixed by the progression of my black cab around the Square. He's close enough that I think I know who it is, but I can't be completely sure, partly as my vision is slightly doubled.

As we swing back around towards the Botanist and then up Sloane Avenue towards Knightsbridge, I get a better look at him. He's tall, brown-haired, wearing a dark grey suit, and still staring straight at my cab. At me.

It's him. It's Jake.

Chapter Nineteen

In the cab, driving up Sloane Street, I try to collect myself.

You know, I really wasn't built for confrontation. I can't help crying when I'm angry. I think it's just because there's an overflow of emotion and it backs up into the 'weep' area of my head. And though I managed to keep it all in when I was saying those things to Rick, the tears are now escaping from the corners of my eyes.

I try to control my breath, which is coming out in lopsided gasps.

Calm. Caaaaaalm.

Oh God, that was awful. I feel dirty just from seeing Rick. What the fuck is my problem? The Dating Sabbatical was meant to protect me from shit like that, and instead, it practically led me straight into the arms of the King O' Shits.

Ew. I can't believe I was ever actually really and truly in his arms.

My breathing regulation attempts are failing. As we cross over Knightsbridge and start driving alongside Hyde Park, I start to feel like I'm hyperventilating. I put my head between my legs and try to inhale and exhale as slowly as possible. The cab stops quickly at some red lights, and I, predictably, am jerked forward sharply, bang my head against the opposite seat and land in a heap on the floor of the car.

'Ow,' I say. It's surprisingly comfortable down here.

'You alright, love?' calls the driver.

'Fine!' I call back. 'Totally fine.' At least the fall stopped the tears.

I clamber back up and lie down across the seats. My head needs a rest. Never mind that a million people have sat here with farty bottoms. Right now the back seat of this cab is a place of rest and respite. I rest my head on my lucky yellow clutch and close my eyes. My mind is whirring, and I think the wine just hit my nervous system.

Next thing I know, we've lurched to a halt and I've almost fallen off the seat again.

'Chepstow Villas, my love!' exclaims the driver. I sit up in a rush. I must have fallen asleep slash passed out.

'Sorry! Gosh! That was quick!' I say in a high-pitched voice, and pay the fare. Bloomie's house is just across the road, so I walk over – slightly unsteadily, I notice, damn heels – and ring on the doorbell. It seems to take Bloomie ages to answer the door, so I lean against it and rest my eyes for a minute.

'Oh holy fuck, darling, what happened to you?' She must have opened the door. I didn't hear her do that.

'Had a drink. With fuckwit. Rick.' Suddenly, full sentences seem terribly hard. The wine, vodka and gin are having a meet-and-mingle party in my body. And not getting on.

'You fucking WHAT?' she exclaims. 'What the fuck were you thinking?'

'Don't tell me off,' I say, leaning into the door. I can hear myself slurring. I think the gin and the wine are having a fistfight. 'I learned my lesson. Was very bad. I threw a drink on him.'

'You threw a drink on Rick?'

'At his face.' Somehow, I'm now up the stairs and in the living room, and can see Kate, Eugene and Eddie all sitting at the dining room table with cards in front of them. They're all staring at me. I hate being this person. I'm never this person. Well, not since the weeks after I left Rick. Then I was this person a lot.

'Hello everyone . . . Shit . . . I got drunk by mistake. I'm . . .

196

God, guys, I'm sorry, I didn't mean this to happen . . .' I lean against the couch for support. I can't focus on anything.

'You're a mess,' Bloomie says. 'I can't believe you're doing this again.'

'It was so awful. No more. He's not a good person.' I try to smack myself on my forehead but miss and nearly fall over.

'I'm putting you to bed. And we're talking about this in the morning. Enough is enough.'

'I'm so sorry . . .' I whisper. Somehow we are now in the bathroom and Kate is cleaning my face. I feel seasick. I want to get all this alcohol out of my body. Now.

'Oh, Katie . . . I think I'm . . . I don't feel well . . .'

In what feels like one swift manoeuvre, though really, who can say, my head is over the toilet. In between my – almost entirely liquid – vomit, I keep gasping out my apologies.

'Amsosorry . . .'

'That's OK, honey . . .' she says, rubbing my back. 'Better out than in.'

'Amsosorry . . .'

I hear Bloomie's voice in the doorway. 'Oh, fucking hell.'

And now we're in Kate's bedroom and she and Bloomie are putting me in PJs and into bed.

'Sass, stay on THIS SIDE,' Kate orders me. 'Do not even TRY to cuddle me later.'

'You won't even know I'm here!' I exclaim, one eye closed so I can see her face without it bending into double. 'I'm so quiet . . . I'm quiet as a mouse. As a mouse!' I close both eyes. Relief immediately overwhelms me.

'She better have a good fucking explanation for seeing him again,' I hear Bloomie say as they walk out of the room.

'Oh, leave her alone,' says Kate. 'You know how much he messed with her head.'

'After the week I have had, I just don't need her turning up here like some idiot in fresher's week.'

'Bloomie, come on. For God's sake. Give her a break.'

'I saw Jake,' I whisper as they're closing the door. But they don't respond. God, I'm so very, very tired. I open one eye again. The room is spinning. I think that tumble in the taxi may have given me a concussion as surely, the room should not be spinning this much just from half a bottle of vodka, two gins and two glasses of wine. I close my eyes again and surrender to drunken sleep. My last conscious thought as I close my eyes is that this is why the Dating Sabbatical exists. When I try to live my life without it, I crash and burn.

Chapter Twenty

I wake up the next morning to the beepbeep of a text message. I open one eye and look over at the pink-curtained windows in Kate's room, and with a jolt remember everything that happened last night. Oholyfuck.

I close my eyes again and go through the events in my head. Accidentally took Dutch courage one step too far. Accidentally met up with Rick for longer than the two minutes it should have taken for me to wave a drink in front of my face and leave. Accidentally lost my temper and threw a drink at him. Accidentally turned up on Bloomie's doorstep, absolutely hammered, threw up and was put straight to bed.

As my science teacher Mr Campbell would have said, what do we learn from this? We learn that the Dating Sabbatical is back the fuck on, that's what.

I try to talk myself into doing my happy stretchy thing, but it won't come. I feel paralysed by an extremely parched throat and the sick feeling that I messed up. Again. I don't want to deal with it. I take a deep sigh and roll over to face Kate.

She's crying silently. Eyes closed, perfectly still, tears just running down the sides of her face and into the pillow. One hand is clasping her phone on her tummy.

'Katie . . . oh, darling, are you OK? Did something happen?'

She looks over at me and nods, and clears her throat to talk.

'Just a text . . . from Tray. He's so sad . . . and it's all my fault . . .
I want him to be happy. I really, really do.'

Oh God, poor darling Kate. I sit up in bed, reach over to the
box of tissues she has on her bedside table and hand her one.

'I know, I know I did the right thing, I know it.'

I nod.

'But sometimes I feel so . . . sad . . .' Her voice goes all wavery
and high on 'sad' and she starts crying silently again.

I take one of her hands and start stroking it, and after a few
minutes say (aiming my words downwards, as my breath must
smell like a dead homeless person): 'Darling . . . you won't feel
sad forever. I know it.'

'But it hurts so much . . . And I would have been . . . fine . . .
with him. But I just didn't want that life. I didn't want him.'

She starts crying again, and I reach over her for another tissue
and hand it to her.

'Does breaking up with someone always feel this bad?'

'I don't know,' I say honestly. 'I've never done it.'

Kate looks at me for a second and, seeing I'm grinning, starts
laughing through her tears. Spit and snot fly everywhere.

'Dude!' I say, grabbing more tissues and mopping her face.
'Gross.'

'You know what?' she continues, in a more normal, non-teary
voice. 'I don't even feel single. I can't imagine going on a date
with someone, even though all I've done for months is fancied
every half-decent man I see.'

'That sounds . . . healthy?' I say. 'It's a sign that you're moving
on, when you find other men attractive.'

'You should see me on the tube. I look up at every stop in
case someone hot gets on.'

I start laughing. 'And what do you do then, start licking the
pole?'

We both giggle for a few seconds and then take a deep, deep
sigh in tandem, which makes us giggle even more.

'You broke up what, seven weeks ago now? It's probably time for you to get back in the saddle again.'

'Maybe,' she says. 'Are you OK?'

I nod. 'I'm sorry I turned up here like that.'

'That's OK. I can't believe you saw Rick, what happened? . . . No, wait. Let's wait till Bloomie is here for the gory details.'

'Can't wait,' I sigh. I vaguely remember Bloomie was pretty angry last night. I usually try to avoid any angry Bloomie situations, but I don't know how I'll get out of this one.

'She's just worried about you,' says Kate, reading my mind. 'Oooh. How about pancakes?'

We head out to their little kitchen. We're trying to be quiet, as Bloomie and Eugene are still in bed, but after a few dropped saucepans, and stifled giggling fits, as well as the gurgling burps of the Nespresso machine, Bloomie pads into the room in her flannel PJs and Big Bird slippers.

'Morning, angel,' I say. 'Before you say anything, I'm sorry I was such a social hand grenade last night. I've learned my lesson.'

She leans against the doorway, rubbing her eyes and frowning at me. 'Seriously, darling. I cannot handle you getting smashed every time you go out, and turning up on my doorstep crying.'

'I won't!' I say defensively. 'I haven't done that in months and months!' Since the post-Rick period.

'What were you even thinking, seeing that fuckwit? I mean . . . for fuck's sake, that was wrong and you know it.'

'I keep TRYING to do the right thing, Bloomie,' I say, raising my voice slightly. 'My entire fucking life is built around that, actually.' It's not her job to tell me off. It's her job to be my friend.

'How can seeing Rick again be the right thing? God, never mind . . . it's so pathetic, that's all . . . Sort yourself out.' Wow. Harsh.

'Pathetic?' I say, raising my voice. 'I don't have to ask your permission before I do things, you know. And you're not perfect.

201

Your boyfriend had to contact Kate and I to find out if you were even alive yesterday. And by the way, when I rang you, you were fucking rude.'

'I have a real job. I can't always chat,' says Bloomie.

'I have a real job too, Susan. What the hell is that supposed to mean?' I'm angry now, and my usual anger-tears are nowhere to be seen. How odd.

'Nothing,' cries Bloomie. 'I didn't mean . . .'

'Like fuck you didn't. Christ, that's a horrible thing to say.'

There's a pause as we stare at each other furiously. Kate is stirring the pancake batter silently, peering into it like it's the most interesting thing in the world.

'I'm sorry,' says Bloomie, dropping her voice and her eyes. 'I'm sorry, I didn't mean that. I get upset when you're like that . . . I hate you being miserable.'

I sigh. 'Everything has changed over the last few months, Bloomie. OK, I fucked up last night, but like . . . I'm trying. And you can't get pissed off at me for living the way I want to. It's my life, not yours.'

'I know. But . . . can't you remember after Rick last time, the utter disaster area you were afterwards?'

I pause. I don't remember that period very well, actually. I try not to think about it.

'Blooms, thank you for looking after me after . . . after Rick. I mean it, thank you. And last night . . . Look, I know it was a stupid move, and I knew it even as I was doing it, but I couldn't stop myself. He rang on Thursday and said he had something to say in person, and I was intrigued and I wanted him to say sorry for the Pink Lady and that he made the biggest mistake of his life, or something . . . And I know what that sounds like, but I really couldn't stop myself.'

'I can understand that,' says Kate supportively.

'I am sorry I turned up here last night. I didn't mean to get that drunk,' I say. 'I was feeling odd and introspective and I drank

202

half a bottle of vodka, and then gin, and then wine, and then Rick was just so ah-paw-leng . . . and then I threw a drink on him.'

'WHAT!' says Bloomie, shaken out of her disapproving stance. 'You mumbled something about that last night but I thought it was wishful-drinking talk. Tell us everything.'

'Alright,' I sigh. For the next ten minutes, as we fry the pancakes, discarding the first one as a sacrifice to the pancake gods (it never turns out right), and pile them up on three plates with, according to individual tastes, lemon and sugar, Nutella, or English mustard and ham (guess who that is), and flop down together on the couch, I relate everything that happened last night.

As I tell the story, they interrupt at various points – 'You bought him a gin and tonic even though he was already late? AND HE was the one who asked YOU out for a drink . . . No wonder he thinks you're a chump,' (Bloomie, of course) and 'I wish I had seen his face when you threw the wine at him!' (a gleeful Kate) and finally 'Are you sure it was Jake?' (both at once).

'Yes,' I say. 'Definitely Jake. It's the last thing I can clearly remember, actually. God, that guy has some kind of homing beacon for me or something.'

'Is that what you kids are calling it these days?' says Bloomie.

'Are you admitting that you like him?' asks Kate excitedly.

I frown and shake my head. I don't know what to say, so I just take a big bite of my lemony pancake instead.

'Well done, anyway, Sassafras darling. I wish you'd decked him,' says Bloomie. There's still a slight froideur between us, but it'll be OK soon. 'Though I still don't see why you accepted a date – OK, OK, a drink – with him in the first place.'

I shrug. 'Well, that's because you're you and I'm me . . . you don't have to understand. You just have to, you know, adore me anyway.'

'Oh, darling, I do!' says Bloomie, reaching out for a hug. Ahh.

Now there's the Bloomie I know and love. That tough ol' alpha is marshmallow inside. 'I'm sorry I was a bitch on the phone yesterday. And I'm sorry I said that about your job,' she mumbles into my hair. 'Please forgive me. I've had a horrible, horrible week, but I know it's no excuse.'

'Do you want to talk about it?' I ask.

'Nah,' she says, pulling back. 'No point, it's over now. You smell ever so slightly of vom, by the way.'

'Actually, that's my new shampoo. Hint Of Bile. Anyway, guys, the last thing I'll say about it is that, clearly, I genuinely do have instinctively kamikaze dating instincts, and the only way to survive is to romantically quarantine myself, which is why the Dating Sabbatical is being extended-o-fuck-me!' I interrupt myself. 'I saw Posh Mark last night! I completely forgot!' I quickly tell them all about Posh Mark and Annabel Pashmina Face kissing on the street.

'How do you know she always liked him?' asks Bloomie.

'She used to practically frot his leg whenever she saw him,' I say.

'What does frotting mean?' says Kate.

'Dry humping, darling,' I reply.

Kate snorts with laughter. Bloomie hands me over the last of her Nutella pancake. I know it's a peace offering, so I grin at her as I take it.

'Since I'm – thank you – telling all, you should know I kind of broke Dating Sabbatical Rule 8 with a client,' I say. 'The kissing one,' I add, as I see them both looking confused.

'WHAT?!' they say in unison. I haven't been the source of this much drama in . . . well, a few months, anyway.

I tell the Lukas story quickly, finishing with, 'So you know, the Dating Sabbatical exists for a reason. I'm clearly utterly incapable of making the right decision, ever. This is why I'm detoxing from dating. I can feel the filthy dating toxins seeping from my body.'

'That's not dating, darling. That's booze,' says Bloomie helpfully.

'Nice,' comments Kate.

'I'm not surprised you jumped the hot German,' says Bloomie. 'Don't you miss sex?'

'Yes. I do,' I say, in a faux-snappy voice. 'I miss snogging and sex and cuddling. In that order. But not enough to make me want to date again.'

'A few more months of celibacy and the Dating Sabbatical would call itself off, I think,' says Bloomie. I shoot her a death stare and she winks back.

'Does that mean you won't come and meet men with me tonight?' says Kate. 'I need you to teach me the ways of pulling and dating . . .'

'No!' I exclaim. It's a gut reaction that surprises us all slightly, 'I mean . . . maybe. But like, look at what happened last night. I need to stay away from situations involving, you know, guys. And men.'

'Oh, guys *and* men,' nods Bloomie. 'Both kinds.'

Kate makes a pouty-kitten face. I feel bad. She has only been single for a few weeks. I really should be her wingwoman.

'OK, maybe I will . . .' I say. 'But only as a tutor. I shall not engage in flirtations myself.'

'Yay!' cheers Kate.

'Hey,' says Bloomie. 'You broke a Rule. Doesn't that mean the Dating Sabbatical is null and void? And why didn't you just hang on and break it with Jake?'

I choke on my coffee. 'I . . . have nothing to say about Jake. It was just weird seeing him, that's all. And Lukas kissed me. Not the other way around. The Dating Sabbatical holds,' I say with an easiness I don't feel.

'If you say so,' Bloomie says, and grins at me. 'Six sleeps to Eddie's weekend party . . .' Dash it. My poker face sucks. And I wish I'd never told her I still count things in sleeps. I vow not to mention Jake again, no matter how much he pops into my thoughts. (I wonder whether he saw me throw the drink on Rick? Oh God stop thinking about it. He is just another bastardo cockmonkey and I am on a Dating Sabbatical.)

As I am musing thusly, Kate's phone beepbeeps.

'Noooooooooooo,' she says, and makes a grand show of squinting through one eye and opening the text with a look of great trepidation, as though the phone might explode.

'Oh, it's just Immie,' she says with relief. 'She's going shopping on Portobello with Tom later! Goody gumdrops. I'm going to go meet them.'

'Can I come with?' I say, choosing to ignore the 'goody gumdrops'. Immie is Imogen, Kate's sister, and Tom is her baby.

'Yarse,' Kate says, swinging her legs off the side of the couch and landing on the ground with a crashthud. 'But you have to shower first. Dating toxins are evaporating from your skin like steam o'er a wintry morning lake.'

'Oh! That's so pretty,' I say and start to giggle. Kate in a silly mood is one of my favourite things. I'm glad she got over her little teary-burp this morning. It's been years since she's been this relaxed.

'I would love to join you, my darlings,' says Bloomie. 'But I have to go to work.' She checks her watch. Who wears a watch with pyjamas, I ask you? In fact, who wears a watch? 'The Dork is still snoozing . . . I won't wake him. I'll just jump in the shower and go.'

She pads her Big Bird slippers back to her bedroom, wiggling her bottom with each step, and Kate and I make whistling, catcalling sounds after her.

'Shake your tailfeather, toots!' shouts Kate.

'I hate to see you leave, baby . . . but I LOVE to watch you walk away!' I shout.

Then we quickly wash up the pancake stuff, shower and dress.

Kate, being Kate, has a spare, brand-new toothbrush for me. In fact, she's got four. And six spare rolls of cotton wool pads, three spare toothpaste tubes, and three bottles each of shampoo, conditioner and shower gel.

'Is there going to be a war?' I ask, coming out of the bathroom holding four of the cotton wool rolls. 'Is Boots going into liquidation? Do you know something I don't?'

'Don't start with me,' says Kate, turning off her hairdryer and holding up a hand. 'I don't like running out of things.'

'Can I use your make-up, darling?' I say.

'If you do mine, you can,' she says. Ah, the ancient ritual of grooming one's friends. 'Give me the full Dolly, please,' she adds, sitting on the bed, face perfectly still and looking up to the ceiling.

I start dabbing on concealer and highlighter. 'It could look pretty if . . . no. Prettier your way . . .' I say. I love that quote from *Dirty Dancing*. Does the sister even know what a bitch she's being when she says that?

Ten minutes later, we both look fresh and radiant and ready to hit Portobello.

I'm the same size shoe as Bloomie (jolly big) so throw on one of her many pairs of beaten-up Converses from the little cupboard next to the front door on our way out. Just as we're closing the front door, I hear a yell from the direction of the bedrooms. A second later, Eugene shuffles out in socks, boxers and a work shirt.

'*Risky Business!*' I say.

'Huh?' he says. 'Where's Bloomie, guys?'

'She went to work,' says Kate. 'She didn't want to wake y—'

'She went to fucking work?!' he exclaims, then gets control of himself. 'OK, thanks. I'll . . . get going myself.'

'OK . . .' chorus Kate and I in unison.

Eugene turns away and walks back to the bedroom. I see him shake his head slightly as he closes the door.

'The other night I heard them talking,' says Kate as we step onto the road. 'He was saying something about work to live, don't live to work . . .'

'Oh, dear. That's not good,' I say.

'Mmm,' says Kate. 'But they do seem to get on so well, you know . . .?' We walk in silence for a few seconds.

'As my dad says, no one sees the game like the players . . . Who won poker last night, anyway?' I ask.

'Eddie,' Kate says. 'He was in an unusually good mood.'

'Is Maeve coming over from Geneva for his houseparty next weekend?' I ask.

'He said she has to work,' shrugs Kate.

It's so sunny and lovely this morning that I suddenly feel joyously happy, so I grab Kate's hand and make her skip with me towards Portobello Road. No one on the street even looks at us; they're all nonchalant, groovy Notting Hill types more interested in heading to Portobello market, home from Portobello, or just getting away from the touristy nightmare that Saturdays on Portobello have become.

'Immie's meeting us in the Electric,' says Kate.

The Electric Brasserie is on my no-go list. I went there with Rick quite a lot. I suddenly realise that I don't give a shit. If I see him, perhaps I'll throw another drink on him. Ha. I can't believe I saw him last night. I am such a cockmonkey sometimes. I could seriously have jeopardised my Dating Sabbatical happiness. Never again.

Chapter Twenty-One

When we get into the Electric, Immie is already there. Tom, who has just turned one, is laughing at her from his Buggetyboo prammy thing (I forget the name but you know what I mean) (hey, I'm not a mother).

She jumps up as we come over and we all kiss hello. I love Immie. She got married three years ago, to a lovely guy called Michael. They live in Maida Vale, where apparently you have a decent chance of making new best friends every day just by taking your baby for a walk (roll?), as there are loads of other young mummies taking their babies for walks (rolls?), too.

'How are you, sweetie?' Immie asks, leaning over to touch Katie's hand. She looks just like Katie, all perky brunette prettiness, only about a foot taller. 'You sleeping OK?'

'Well, I had company last night,' Kate says meaningfully, arching an eyebrow.

'You little hussy,' says Immie, grinning excitedly. 'Tell me everything.'

Kate looks over at me. Immie follows her glance with a confused look.

'It was me,' I say. 'I'm a drunk,' I add, by way of explanation.

Immie laughs. 'Did Katie take advantage of you again?'

'Yes, it was ghastly . . . Oh, Immie, can I please hold him?' I love babies. (Hey. I said I'm not a mother. I didn't say I'm not motherly.) He's all milky and warm and soft and pudgy, with a huge naughty gummy smile like a little elf. 'Mmmm. Baby love.' I look up at Immie and grin. 'He's perfect. My ovaries are yearning.'

She smiles. 'Yeah, he's pretty cool. But you know I read this thing in *Eat, Pray, Love* – have you read it? You totally should, it's by Elizabeth Gilbert – that having a baby is like getting a tattoo on your face. You have to be pretty damn sure it's what you want, because there's no going back.'

We all laugh. Tom squeals delightedly and piercingly into my ear, carried away with the excitement of having three women around gazing at him adoringly. Future bastardo in the making, doubtless.

My ears are ringing. 'Ouch . . . I need more coffee, I think. And food.'

'Sausage sandwich,' says Kate.

'I'll have poached eggs,' says Immie.

'Um . . . just toast for me, I think,' I say. 'And, ooh, and bacon.'

After ordering our food and coffees (I'm tempted to order two coffees for myself, right now, just to save time), we start talking about Kate and Tray. Kate stayed with her the week between breaking up with Tray and moving in with Bloomie, so Immie is well versed in all the details, but we discuss it all anyway, and how it was the right decision.

'I knew something was not right between you guys at Christmas,' says Immie. 'I knew it, but I couldn't say anything. And Michael knew, too.'

'Did Michael like Tray?' asks Kate suddenly.

'Uh, yes, of course he did,' says Immie, about half a beat too late. 'I mean, he didn't really know him, Katie. He was . . . hard to get to know.'

'Mmm . . .' Kate says, and frowns into the distance for a few seconds. 'Let's talk about something else.'

'Want me to put my psychologist's hat on?' asks Immie. That was her job before she had Tom. She says she'll go back to it in a few years. Michael works in the City, doing something mysterious and deeply stressful involving words like equity and capital.

'Not for me . . . Baby, please!' says Katie, taking Tom and covering his face in kisses.

'You can analyse me, if you want,' I say. 'I'm a mess right now.'

'Faaaabulous,' says Immie. 'Let me just pretend to smoke as I analyse you – I always find it helps . . . Just like the good ol' days . . .' She purses her lips and flicks up her wrist, holding a pretend cigarette between two fingers like a *Vogue* model in the 50s.

'Fab prop,' I say. 'OK, so basically . . . I keep making the wrong decisions about, um, guys. They ask me out, I say yes, and then we're dating, and then I get dumped.'

'I pointed out that she's reactive!' says Kate proudly. 'I thought of you when I said it, Immie. Oh Tom, stop that . . .' The baby is starting to pull her hair and wail. (And voilà, my ovarian baby-yearn is gone.)

'Just put him down if you want to, darling. He's tired,' says Immie, then turns to me sharply and flicks her wrist up again. 'What kind of men have you been going for, then?'

'Uh . . . The ones that ask me out?'

'Mmmhmm . . . Anything else?'

'Um, OK, well, seriously . . . I think I tend to go out with guys who are perfect in one way. Like they're either funny, or smart, or kind, or get on with my friends . . . They never had everything and I never felt that connection with them. And they kept dumping me, every single time.'

Through all this, Immie is nodding and making 'mmm' sounds through her pursed lips.

'And then there was a particularly nasty guy called Rick. I was mad about him, mad being the operative word. Though I'd say I'm definitely over him now . . .'

Kate grins broadly.

'Right, right . . .' says Immie thoughtfully, in a deep therapy-speak

211

voice. 'Lost your head over a bastard. Well, let's start with the need for external validation . . .'

I look over at her in alarm. I hope she's not actually going to analyse me.

She winks at me. Phew, she's not. She takes a deep breath and continues in her deep therapy voice, waving her imaginary cigarette around to emphasise her points.

'Now, in schema-focused therapy, we learn that if one has certain core beliefs surrounding one's worth and ability to maintain relationships, commitment-phobic scoundrels will appeal and that we should try to resist them because they are simply triggering old-but-comfy dysfunctional beliefs.'

'Wow,' says Kate. 'You're saying she likes bastards because she secretly thinks she deserves them?'

Immie pretends to ash her cigarette. 'Let's ask her, shall we?' They both turn to me.

'No, I don't,' I say. 'I don't think I deserve them, I don't have low self-esteem . . . OK, I did after Rick a bit, but lately I feel kind of happy with myself again. I do think I deserve someone, um, amazing. But I don't think I'd know how to recognise an amazing guy if I tripped over him in the street. Maybe I just like scoundrels because they're wittier and more exciting . . .'

'Yeah, there's the rub, bastards are usually funnier than nice guys,' Immie nods. 'Can't deny it.'

'I'm not even sure they were all bastardos, you know, not all of them,' I say thoughtfully. 'They just didn't want to go out with me. Should that be enough to brand a guy a bastardo for life?'

We sit in silence for a few seconds, thinking. It's the first time that idea has ever occurred to me.

Immie clears her throat. 'Well, maybe you should get to know them better before you date them anyway. So, bastard or not, you know there's a something real underneath the banter.'

'Actually, I've put myself on a Dating Sabbatical, Ims. No more

212

dates. I can't trust myself to make the right decisions. So I'm not making any at all.'

Immie starts to laugh. 'A Dating Sabbatical? Try having a baby, there's a Dating Sabbatical . . . God, I'd love to go back to the days of dating and going out every weekend . . . it was so much fun, looking back. So easy.'

'Easy!' says Kate.

'Yes, Katie, easy . . .' Immie says. 'Look, I'm not being a know-it-all but . . . you guys should just, you know, enjoy yourselves and stop worrying. Because it won't last forever. I wish I'd enjoyed it more . . . I love being a mother, I do, but there's no going back.'

'Promise?' I say.

She shakes her head and laughs again. Our food arrives, and we stop talking for a few minutes and focus on eating. Then Immie heads off to meet Michael and Kate announces that she wants to find a coat, so we spend a few hours wandering the stalls along Portobello. I don't buy anything, though I am sorely tempted by an old army coat from the vintage military stall.

'You are too old to get away with that,' says Kate firmly.

'But . . . but it's so cool! It's German! It's East German!'

'You are too old to get away with a holey, shapeless, musty-smelling vintage East German army coat.'

I pout and put the coat back, and we move on.

'I guess you're right. We are pretty old,' I say thoughtfully.

'It's only two weeks till your birthday!' exclaims Kate. 'I'd forgotten. Do you want to have a party?'

'Nooo,' I say. 'No. Not this year.'

We walk in silence for a few seconds.

'How are you feeling about Tray, Katiepoo?' I ask, to change the subject.

'Fine, fine,' says Kate dismissively. The privacy shutters are up. 'Let's not talk about him, darling. There's no point.'

We keep walking, looking in shop windows, and get a cupcake each to munch as we walk.

'I think my company is going to give me the sack,' says Kate, apropos nothing.

'I'm sure they won't,' I reply, though I'm sure of no such thing.

'I wonder how much they'd pay me. I've been there for . . . six years. So that's . . .' Kate starts calculating in her head. I take a quick look at my brain-abacus. Nope, I have no idea.

'Oh, never mind,' she sighs. 'It's not worth worrying about.'

'It's really not,' I agree. 'It probably won't happen, and focusing on potential negative outcomes never helps.'

Kate raises an eyebrow. 'Says you. On the Dating Sabbatical. Because you focus exclusively on negative outcomes.'

I think I'll ignore that. 'Have you had a pay rise in the past few years?' I ask her.

'Yeah,' she says. 'Of course I have. Once I got through my accountancy exams, and then at most performance reviews . . . and I get a bonus, though I didn't last year . . . why?'

'I've never had one,' I say. 'Never. I've been on the same salary since I left university.'

'That's a joke,' says Kate. We walk in silence for a few seconds, and she adds, 'I'm not kidding. That's terrible. You have to do something about that.'

'I know,' I say thoughtfully. 'I've been thinking about it since the pitch. I mean, they wouldn't have won that without me. They really wouldn't have . . . I'm being paid like a graduate copywriter and treated like a senior creative.'

'So talk to Cooper. Make a list of points that demonstrate how you've proved your worth, and do some research to find out how much you could be paid at other agencies,' says Kate. She's in her element now, listing my must-dos on her fingers. 'Try to think of what he'll say, and have an answer for each point. And have a number in mind. Frankly, since you've never had a pay rise at all, I'd ask for a lot.'

'Alright,' I say. 'I'll ask for 40% . . . I just have to figure out what 40% of my salary is.' I pretend to count on my fingers and we both start giggling.

'Let's go home and veg out,' says Kate, and we meander back to Chepstow Villas. I should go home to Pimlico, but it's hard to muster the energy to get a tube or bus all the way to Pimlico and then walk all the way to my house and all the way up my stairs for no real reason. So we walk slowly back through Notting Hill to Kate's house. It's a typical London day in May: sunnyish, and just windy enough to be annoying.

Back at Kate and Bloomie's, we stretch out across the couch and watch *Mad Men* on DVD with popcorn and Smarties.

'I adore this show,' says Kate. 'I wish it was 1960.'

'Me too,' I say. 'We'd be married and have drinking problems by now. And children.'

'That would be so awesome.'

'I know.'

I feel very relaxed, but also have the vague feeling that surely, I should have something better to do with my Saturday after-noons than watch boxsets of DVDs. That I've seen before. Twice.

By about 6 pm we both have the twitchy-energised feeling you get from an afternoon of doing nothing. I fix us both a coffee and take mine out to the balcony with a cigarette.

'What shall we do now?' calls Kate, picking popcorn crumbs off her top and eating them one by one.

'You look like a monkey . . . I don't know.'

'The boys have been texting,' she says.

'I know. I bet they just send us exactly the same texts,' I say. 'Did you get that last one from Mitch? Read it out . . .'

Kate picks up her phone. 'It says . . . "Chicks",' she reads disdainfully. '"Fulham. Now. Rugby party. Dress nice."'

'Ha, just the same as me. Did he finish "Flaunt the legs"?'

'No, "Flaunt the boys",' she reads. 'What does that mean? Flaunt what boys? I've been wondering . . .' I raise an eyebrow at her and smirk, and comprehension slowly dawns on her face. 'Oh my God! He is such an arse.'

'I know. I can't face a rugby party, can you?' I say.

'My cousin is going out in Shoreditch,' says Kate, reading a text.

'Too many wankers,' I say.

'There are wankers everywhere,' says Kate.

'Yeah, but the ones in Shoreditch are really bad,' I say, thinking about Arty Jonathan and his mates.

'Fraser texted that he's going out in Soho if we'd like to join.'

'Soho? On a Saturday? Why would he do that?'

'Mona Horsearse is having birthday drinks in Clapham,' says Kate. That's a girl from university. With an arse like a horse.

'Clapham? Mona Horsearse? Are you on crack?'

'I know, I know. Can we go bar-hopping around here?'

'Oh, Katiepoo . . . do we have to go out?' With my luck, we'll run into Rick. Or worse, Jake. Since the night at Montgomery Place, I've avoided going out in Notting Hill in case I ran into him again. And I can't bear the idea of seeing him after he witnessed last night's public display of disaffection outside the Botanist.

'You promised!' she exclaimed. 'Please? Please. Please. PLEASE.' She jumps off the couch, skips over to the balcony and takes a drag of my cigarette whilst batting her eyelashes at me. 'I need to get out there. And I don't even know what "there" is.'

'Oh, OK . . . But only 'cos you slept with me last night and I'm hoping I might get into your bed again tonight. Shall I open a bottle of wine?'

Chapter Twenty-Two

By 9 pm we're standing at the bar at Beach Blanket Babylon. It's a great Notting Hill bar: good cocktails and quirky-opulent decor, sort of like Italian medieval royalty or something.

The problem tonight is that it's crowded. Aggressively, oppressively crowded. Kate and I finished our first drink 20 minutes ago, and the bartenders may well not see my hopefully outstretched hand and 'Serve Me Please' face for another 20 minutes at least. And while I'm trying to get served, I can't really talk to Kate, as if I take my eyes off the bartender nearest me for longer than two seconds, you can bet that's the two seconds he'll choose to flick his face in my direction and serve one of the other thirsty people near me.

I mean, this shit is stressful. And it's no wonder we used to bar-hop in threes, so while one of us is at the bar, the other two can at least talk to each other. Bloomie's having dinner with Eugene. Ah, the inevitable absence of a friend in love.

The bartender nearest me glances up at me and the four other expectant faces halo-ing my head.

'Next?'

'I'm next!' shouts an aggressive girl next to me. (She so wasn't.) 'Two mojitos, a margarita and a passion martini.' She turns to me and smiles triumphantly. She pronounced the 'J' in 'mojito'. I think she's a New Zealander. I smile sweetly back and turn my head towards Kate.

'Katie,' I say. 'Can we just, like, blow this off, and go somewhere else?'

'Totally,' she says, and we head for the door. 'I thought you'd tell her that's not how you pronounce mojito, at least,' says Kate as we walk down Ledbury Road.

'I think it's meaner to let her go on pronouncing it like that for the rest of her life, don't you?' I say.

I've borrowed more of Bloomie's clothes, by the way. She came home from work before heading out to dinner with Eugene, and we had a very girly trying-on-clothes session. (Oh, OK, since you asked, I'm wearing a short white dress with super-high brown ankleboots and an old, battered, brown leather jacket. I've christened myself Toasted Marshmallow. Kate is in her new favourite pink heels, an LBD and the white wrappy thing I wore to meet Rick last night. She wouldn't let me christen her outfit.)

'I love weekends away,' I say thoughtfully, as we walk towards Westbourne Grove. I haven't been home to Pimlico for over 24 hours. 'The weather up here in Notting Hill is fantastic. And the local people are so friendly.'

Kate giggles.

'Alright, darling, if we're going bar-hopping, we need a game plan,' I say. 'You want to . . . what? Talk to men? Get chatted up?'

'I'm happy talking to you all night, but it might be nice to, like, test my street value, I guess . . .' muses Kate thoughtfully. 'I want someone to ask me out, even if I don't fancy him.'

'OK, I'm your wingwoman,' I say. 'Let's try Westbourne House first.'

As we get to Westbourne House, I quickly case the outside and inside, as I did at BBB, to check for tall dark-haired Jake-types. A few false alarms and needless tummy-flips before I realise he's not here. (I wonder if it was him outside the Botanist? Never mind. Just cross your fingers we don't run into him.)

We get drinks pretty quickly and head over to near a pillar to pretend to chat to each other and actually case the joint.

'Anyone here?' I ask, out of the side of my mouth.

'Hmm . . .' Kate scans the room. 'No, no, maybe, no . . . maybe, no . . . yes. Oh yes . . . over there, in the black shirt . . . Your two o'clock. Maybe quarter past.'

I look towards my quarter-past-two-o'clock and see a good-looking guy in a black shirt standing with a few friends. I don't see anyone who looks like she might be his girlfriend. This is good.

'OK, now wait a minute or so, make eye contact with him, finish your drink and then go to the bar, like we talked about. You'll pass him on the way to the bar, so be really bold and flick your eyes up to make eye contact again as you walk past him. He'll definitely be looking at you.'

Kate nods obediently, and a few minutes later does just as I say. I see him staring at her as she passes him. He then quickly finishes his drink and walks up to stand next to her at the bar.

What an excellent student.

'Hey,' says a voice, and I look up. It's a blond guy in a deep V-necked T-shirt. I can see a smattering of really wispy blond chest hair. God, deep V-necked T-shirts are a ghastly trend for men.

'Hey,' I say back, in the least-friendly-without-being-rude way I can.

'I'm heading to the bar, can I buy you an island?'

I can't help but laugh at that. 'No, I'm all good. Thanks.'

'How about a drink, then?' He's got dimples when he smiles. I bet his mummy told him he was the most handsome boy in the world when he was little. I wonder if that's why he thinks he can still get away with lines like that.

'No, my friend is getting me one,' I say, looking away. Eye contact is all the encouragement some men need.

'Come on . . .' he says, trying out what must be his most charming smile. 'How about a shot? Have you ever had a flaming orgasm? I'd love to give you one.'

I sigh disappointedly, and look at him. 'Please go away.'

He's too stunned to say anything back, and shuffles away just as Kate races over. She's got a panicked look on her face. 'Outside. Now.'

We hurry outside and light cigarettes.

'It was going really well, I thought,' whispers Kate. 'Then you know, he asked what brought me out tonight, and I said it was my first night of being bar-hopping as a single woman, and then I felt so comfortable talking to him so I told him all about Tray, and how hard it is . . .'

'Oh, Jesus,' I say.

'What?' exclaims Kate. 'That was bad?'

'Never do that. Never mention exs. Or anything that's stressing you out. Now he thinks you're recently single and looking for a new boyfriend.'

'He does? Is that bad?' she says anxiously. 'It must be bad. He just said "well, have a good night", and walked away.'

'His loss,' I say. 'Don't worry about it. Let's finish our drinks and go somewhere else. This place sucks.' As I finish my drink, I think back to Jake asking me about when my heart was last broken. Why did I tell him the truth? That's so unlike me.

Twenty minutes later we're striding through the happy crowds standing around the Walmer Castle. We duck in to order two vodkas at the bar and head outside with them. The crowd at the Walmer is always fun: a mix of boozed-up types who went for lunch somewhere and accidentally kept going all day; loud, excited groups starting their Big Night Out and – last but not least – long-term Notting Hill eccentrics stubbornly sticking to their local pub come hell or high fashion.

We lean against the outside wall of the Walmer Castle and light two cigarettes.

'OK, how should I act, then? When a guy is chatting me up?' asks Kate.

'Assuming you want him to chat you up . . .? Well, the most

important thing, of course, is be yourself. But be happy. Be engaging. Be a tiny bit sarcastic and a little bit remote. Smile but don't laugh too much. Be warm, but not gushy. Don't share too much. Don't rush to fill a silence: let him think of something to say. Don't ever touch him or your hair/lips/neck: they're false flirting must-dos, and come under the heading of Being Too Obvious.' I'm listing everything on my fingers without really thinking about it, then it suddenly occurs to me that I don't have to do this stuff anymore. Thank fuck for that. 'When he finally asks you out, or asks for your number, don't look too thrilled. Just say "sure" and act like it's happened eight times that night. And most of all, don't waste your time. If he doesn't make enough effort, churn and burn.'

'I'm committing everything to memory using a mnemonic,' she nods. Typical. 'God, you're brutal. Churn and burn? How do you know this stuff?'

I think. 'Years of practice, I guess? I've been dumped six times but I must have had about 70 first dates by now, and many of them became second dates.' I think for a second. 'Very few got to three.'

'I've had like, two first dates, ever,' says Kate. 'I didn't know you had to play such a game.'

'A game?' It never occurred to me to think of it as a game. If it is, then I'm the biggest loser at it of all time. So Kate really shouldn't be making up mnemonics.

'What if someone does ask me out tonight? I've only been single a few weeks, is it too early to start a relationship?' she asks, her forehead creasing in stress.

'A lady waits at least a menstrual cycle before starting a new relationship,' I say. I'm joking about that, but Kate doesn't realise.

'This is so depressing! And stressful! And how will I know if he's a bastardo?' she asks. She looks very distressed. 'I know the obvious ones . . . like if they're rude to waiters or act bored when they're talking to you. What else is there?'

I sigh. 'Really, if I had a clue, I wouldn't be on a Dating Sabbatical.'

I stub out my cigarette, just as we're accosted by a young, good-looking guy.

'Ladies,' he says politely. He's Australian. 'I'm going to have to ask you to be careful over the next few minutes, as we are holding Notting Hill's inaugural speedskating competition. You don't want to get in the way. It's highly dangerous.' Hoighly daingerous.

'Gosh,' I say.

'What a privilege!' adds Kate, perking up considerably.

The Aussie guy peers closely at her. He's wearing long khaki shorts, a tight yellow T-shirt, Havaiana flipflops and reflective Oakley sunglasses perched on his head, so probably belongs in the drinking-since-lunch camp. But then again, he's an Australian man, and when in London Aussie men – even guys like this, who aren't 19-year-old backpackers, but are about 27 and probably work in the City – will take any excuse to dress in shorts and flipflops and show off their muscled legs. Not that I'm complaining.

'I speak sarcasm fluently, you should know,' the Australian guy says to Kate. 'It's like a second language to me. Or even . . . a first language.' I detect a very slight sway that means he's definitely an all-day-drinker.

'Rod!' shouts one of his friends. We all look over. There are about seven Aussie guys standing around and sitting on the nearest outside table looking at us, with two competitive-looking blondes in cool, pointless trilby hats watching protectively over them.

'Leave the chicks alone,' says another of his friends, a very tall and again, rather attractive Australian. 'You'll scare them off. This is a professional championship. We need hot spectators.'

'He thinks we're hot!' giggles Kate to me quietly.

I don't have time to answer, as two of the Australian men have suddenly lurched forward in perfect unison. Each is poised, perfectly still, and as one of the 'chicks' pretends to fire the starting pistol, they start swishing back and forward as if imaginary speedskating.

Now, if only I could draw a diagram for you . . . OK, picture this: lunge forward on your right leg. Stretch your left leg behind your right leg at a 45-degree angle. Your right arm is straight out behind you, your left arm is curled towards your body. Slowly swish your stretched left leg to the side and shift your weight on it, using your arms to balance you . . .

I'm confusing myself. Google 'speedskate' and watch it on YouTube or something. You'll know what I mean.

The Aussies are miming speedskating perfectly, swishing backward and forward over one or two metres of the pavement and glancing at each other competitively, as if neck-and-neck. Another of their friends is the commentator. Everyone around is cheering.

'This beats the shit out of imaginary rhythmic gymnastics,' I say to Kate.

The competition is in a dead heat now. Both men are skating faster and faster, faking extreme exhaustion, wiping pretend sweat off their brows and panting profusely. It's very exciting.

'Andnowwe'rereachingthefinalstretchandit'sneckandneck-forthesetwolongtimefriendsfirsttimecompetitorswhatwillthere-sultbe?' drones the pretend commentator. The two pretend speedskaters lurch forward with one final push to win, but one starts lagging half a metre behind, looking at his winning friend in anguish and fear. The cheering gets louder, and a few seconds later the commentator decides it's all over, and raises his voice to announce the finish: 'Andit'srosieladiesandgentlemenrosiehas-wonagainitlookslikethisguywasborntowinbetterlucknexttime-smithy.'

Rosie stands up and pretends to be exhausted, but thrilled with his victory, shaking both arms in the air in triumph. Smithy, the loser, is showing signs of being disappointed, but is putting a brave face on. He glances over at Kate and I, still cheering and

223

clapping madly. 'I'm always the underdog, you'd think I'd catch a break one of these days,' he says sadly.

'Better luck next time!' I say.

Kate turns to me worriedly. 'They must decide beforehand who is going to win. Surely?' She looks extremely confused.

'Yes, I think so . . .' I say. 'Since it's not actually a real competition. And there's no, like, ice rink.'

Smithy walks over, flashing a perfect Tom Cruise smile at us. He looks sporty in the way Australian men tend to, as though he played cricket and rugby in the sun every single day of his childhood. He probably did. 'Don't worry, ladies, Rosie has been king of this hill for years, but I'll knock him off eventually. It's the Winter Olympic dream.'

'Do you train very hard?' asks Kate sincerely.

'Is she for real?' he asks me.

'I'm going to the bar,' I say. 'Drink, Katie, and . . . Smithy, is it?'

'Yes please,' says Kate.

'I'm fine, thanks,' he says, flashing his Tom Cruise smile at me. 'I'll look after Kadey.'

I leave her outside to test her street value on Smithy. They're all pretty cute, though I haven't really been looking. The Dating Sabbatical lives on.

By the time I get back she's been pulled to sit at the outside table and is sitting happily between Smithy and Rosie. I stand at the end and light a cigarette as they chat. They're explaining the history of imaginary speedskating, which seems extremely long and convoluted.

'There was also imaginary luge, but we had to outlaw it. Too dangerous,' explains Smithy.

'People died,' adds Rosie.

'Wow,' says Kate, who seems to have the hang of this imaginary winter-sports thing now, and is being delightfully happy/engaging/ sarcastic/warm, as per my dating instructions. 'Well, I'm glad you're wearing protective gear.'

'Havaianas are officially sanctioned by the Winter Olympics Committee,' nods Rosie.

Rod comes over and puts his arm around me. He's a bit shorter than me in these heels, so I have no problem glancing around and down at him.

'Why, hello,' I say, vaguely disapprovingly. I don't want to be rude, but I don't want his arm around me, either.

'How you doing, sunshine?' he asks, leaning into me. He's slightly drunker now, and slurring.

Smithy looks up. 'Leave her alone, hot Rod.'

'She's alright! We're alright, aren't we?' he says to me.

I shoot Help Me eyes at Kate. She bounces out of her seat. 'Must dash! We have . . . um, friends to meet,' she says. Rod drops me and ambles happily over to the seat she just vacated.

Smithy hops out of his seat and comes to the end of the table to talk to us as we finish our drinks. 'Um, can I get your number, Kate? We're heading out to a club later, if you guys fancy it, or maybe we could, um . . . have a drink sometime?'

'Sure!' she says, looking utterly thrilled and then quickly assuming a look of nonchalance. He gets his phone out and she types in her number.

'Thanks,' he smiles.

'OK . . . well bye!' she says. We put our empty glasses on the table and walk off in the direction of Portobello Road.

'Street value . . . high. Very high,' I grin at her as soon as we're out of earshot of the pub. 'That was excellent.'

'That was so exciting!' she says excitedly. 'But God, what if he calls? What if we go out? What if it gets serious? I mean, he's going to want to go back to Australia eventually, right? Could I live in Australia? Oh, my God . . .'

'Maybe you should just not think about anything further than, like, having a drink with him,' I suggest.

'Yeah . . . yeah, you're right,' she says, nodding earnestly. Funny how when you're just out of a long-term relationship, you think

225

you're probably going to get back into one straightaway. The truth is very different.

'None of them were in the least interested in me, by the way,' I say. 'Perhaps my Dating Sabbatical mojo has gone.'

'No! Let's test it again. Montgomery Place? The bar at E&O? Ooh!' Kate says, looking excitedly at the bar we're approaching. 'Let's go in here!'

'The Lonsdale? Good idea,' I say. We step up onto the little wooden balcony area and into the Lonsdale, which is a très stylish bar, all 60s futuristic chic and clever, sexy lighting. It's packed with people our age drinking exuberantly.

As we push through the crowd to the bar, I do my casing-the-joint-for-Jake routine (we're safe), then we get our drinks pretty easily and stand at the edge of the bar, talking about the Australians.

'He's so funny and good looking,' says Kate happily. 'I hope he calls. You don't think he's a bastardo and would dump me, do you?'

'No, no,' I say, though I have no idea.

'Let's say I start dating him. How will I know if he's going to dump me?' asks Kate. 'It's been so long since I was single . . . I can't remember any of this stuff.'

This, I can answer. 'Well, you know, if he starts acting cold for no reason.'

'Like, doesn't reply to texts?' suggests Kate.

'Yes, but really, you shouldn't ever text him first anyway. You should only ever be texting him back. And never text him a question.'

'Why?'

I can't think why. It's just one of the things I do. I mean, don't do.

'And look for signs. Like if he starts cancelling things at the last minute, or takes phone calls in private. Or spends all his time with you texting other people. And if he's vague about his plans, or the future. Though you should never ask him about plans or his future, anyway. Or how he feels. Ever.'

Kate frowns at me. 'This is a Rick thing, isn't it?'

Yes.

'No,' I say.

'Yes, it is. This is all Rick. You trained yourself to not ask this stuff. That's why Posh Mark thought you were too reserved.'

'No,' I scoff.

'Yes, it is,' she says affectionately. 'You're a psychopath. I'm going to the bathroom. I want you to think about being a psychopath while I'm gone.'

Instead of thinking about being a psychopath, which is too depressing, I check my phone. There's a text from Bloomie. 'Fight with Eugene. Where are you guys?'

Shit. 'Lonsdale. Come meet us. You OK?' I text back.

She replies. 'Roosterprick.'

Eek. Kate gets back and we get another drink, and I show her Bloomie's text.

'Oh dear,' she says. 'I guess you have to have your first fight sometime . . .'

Hmm. I can't remember having a first fight with anyone. Every relationship I've had just chugged along till the whole thing went up in a fireball of rejection and misery. Surely, you should avoid arguments at all costs, as they mean something isn't right, right? It's dawning on me that this, on top of every other stupid and psychopathic dating rule/guideline/thought I have, may be the most stupid and psychopathic thing of all, when a guy walks up to us and says. 'Excuse me, but I believe there's a rule in this bar. You can't come in if you're not interested in dating.'

I look at him in disbelief. It's Mr America from Harlem bar. The cute, almost-certainly-a-cockmonkey American to whom I lost my Dating Sabbatical virginity. He's smiling so politely that I start laughing.

'Hi . . .' I say. 'I'm sorry, I never caught your name?'

'Rob,' he grins.

Kate and I introduce ourselves.

'So, you're stalking me now?' I sigh. 'Was I *that* funny and hot that night at Harlem?'

I'm feeling a bit pissed now, and wouldn't you know it, good old Rule 3 is going out the window. Hey ho.

'No,' he laughs. 'I live on Hereford Road. This is my local.'

'How ghastly for you,' I say, though it's not ghastly at all. You know, sometimes I just open my mouth and things come out that don't actually mean anything.

'It is, it is,' he grins. 'May I introduce you to my friends?'

His friends are a few metres away down the other end of the bar, and come over immediately. Pete and Nick. Both American jock-types, quite slick and very confident. Nick has a magnificent head of hair.

'You look like a Kennedy,' I say to him.

'Wow . . . uh, thanks,' he says, laughing. Kate is chatting happily away to Rob. It turns out the guys are all from New York and have been living in London for about a year.

'I love it here,' says Pete. 'But the bar measures are like, so small. That's my only problem. And the weather is shit. Apart from that, perfect city.'

I nod. 'Then again, the first time I went to New York, I had two vodkas and tried to start a conga line through Gramercy Tavern. So it goes both ways.'

'In some bars in Manhattan, two vodkas is about a gallon of vodka,' he grins proudly.

'You should print warnings on the glasses for unsuspecting Brits,' I suggest.

'Let's have a shot!' exclaims Nick excitedly, and buys everyone a tequila. The bar hits that 11 pm packed noisiness and we're all getting along very well. They're classic American expats: super-confident and polite, with, as previously noted, just enough American charm and attitude to somehow get away with saying

things like 'Lookin' awesome, by the way, ladies. Love the outfits.'
Aaaah-some. Rob's not as aggressive as I thought on the first night
I met him, either. He's kind of sweet. Perhaps not a cockmonkey
after all.

'Sorry about that thing, by the way,' he says to me. Kate's in
a passionate conversation with Pete and Nick about the global
cultural importance of *Saved By The Bell*.

'What thing?' I say.

'I was a bit of a dick outside Harlem that night,' he says, taking
a sip of his beer and casing the bar. 'I didn't mean to be . . . I have
rejection issues.' I think he's joking.

'Wow, how fun for you,' I say. 'I have dating issues.' He glances
at me and starts laughing.

'Well, honey, they have drugs for that now,' he says.

'Yeah, I believe it's called Rohypnol,' I say. He cracks up and
looks over to his buddies.

'Guys, did you hear that?' They all look up and over at us,
just as Bloomie bursts into the group. She's been crying, I can
tell, though she still looks pretty damn good.

'Bloomingdale!' I say, as Kate hands her the vodka we had
waiting for her.

'Thanks,' she says, composing herself and looking around at
the guys. 'Uh, hello. I'm Bloomie. Sorry for barging in . . . I've
just had a fight with my boyfriend. A big one.'

'No way,' says Rob. 'What, is he, like, an asshole?'

She starts laughing. 'No! I mean, yes . . . I mean, no. He thinks
I work too hard. That work means more to me than, you know,
he does.' She must be a bit drunk to be immediately confessing
all to strangers like this.

'You in finance?' asks Rob. What kind of a question is that?
Bloomie nods.

'Fucken' nightmare right now,' nods Rob.

'Exactly, right?' says Bloomie. 'You'd think he'd fucking well
understand. He said he can't be second best.'

'Oh, man. So, did you just like, run out?' asks Rob. Is it just me, or is Rob being awfully sensitive? I can't figure out if he cares, if he's hitting on her, or if it's just the way he is.

'Uh huh.' She takes a massive slug of vodka. 'We were only halfway through dessert.'

'I'm sure no one else saw,' says Kate supportively.

'Everyone saw. We were at Ziani's.'

'Oh, I love that place,' says Nick.

'Dude. Inappropriate,' says Rob, and looks at me with an 'Excuse My Friend' expression.

'Let's go outside for a cigarette,' I say to Kate and Bloomie. We leave the guys at the bar and head to the wooden smoking deck area out the front, and sit down next to the bouncer's snoozing dog.

'It'll be fine . . . he just wouldn't back down! And I wouldn't back down!' says Bloomie. She must be drunk to be repeating herself. 'What does that say about the future of our relationship . . . ? He needs to be on my side! I have a job! What is so bad about that?'

'Please don't shout, we have neighbours,' says the bouncer. Sure, because when you buy a house opposite a bar in one of London's most popular going-out areas, the last thing you expect is a little noise on a Saturday night.

'He just wants to see you more . . . That's a good thing,' Kate whispers.

'What does he want me to do, sit at home and knit?' she exclaims. 'I have a job!'

'He knows that!' I say. 'You can see his point of view, though, can't you . . . ?'

'I don't know . . .' she says and looks weepy again. 'He said he needed to know that I wouldn't always put work first, and I refused to say it, and said how dare he tell me what to do. And he said he wasn't telling, he was asking . . . And I just got up and walked out. And he hasn't even texted me.'

'Do you want to go home, honey?' says Kate.

'Yes,' she sighs. 'Yes please. I'm going to call him. I've really fucked up.'

I pop back inside to get our coats and say goodbye to the Americans. They've already started chatting up some other women at the bar, and don't seem particularly devastated by our absence.

'I know there's no point in asking for your number,' says Rob with a grin. 'So I'll just say . . . see you around.'

'Yeah, see you around,' I smile back. How nice he is, really. Perhaps not a bastardo after all. I head back outside, where a cab is waiting.

'Want to stay at ours again?' says Kate. 'You're more than welcome. I'm spending tomorrow with Immie, but you can hang out for as long as you want.'

'I should go home,' I say. 'My bedroom has forgotten what I look like.'

They put me in the cab and hail another behind it.

When I get home, I'm exhausted. I shuffle around my room, cleaning my face and teeth and putting on an old dark blue T-shirt and boxer shorts, the music from the Lonsdale still ringing lightly in my ears. As I get into bed, I sigh deeply. I didn't break any Rules. I bent the flirting rule, but only a little bit. And at least, I reflect, as I float off into sleep, I didn't run into Jake.

Chapter Twenty-Three

Sunday is all, all mine. And frankly, it's perfect. The first few weekends of the Sabbatical, I was a bit lost on Sundays, and contracted serious Sunday Blues (The Fear, The Demons, Meltdown Madness, call it what you will). But today I'm happy in my own company, and don't feel the need to fill my time with distractions. I don't feel like thinking about the Sabbatical, or Jake, or the ins and outs of dating. I don't even – gasp – feel like shopping.

It's sunny, so I put on my ancient, much-loved cutoff jeans shorts and Ol' Grey and walk to the local Italian café for a latte and a Parma ham ciabatta, and then pop in at the corner shop to get the papers. Just as I get home, it starts raining heavily. Hurrah. Now I can get back into bed without feeling guilty.

I decide to read both papers front to back – even the car and home bits, just to see if I can do it – and eat my breakfast in bed. Looks like Kate's company is in serious trouble. And Bloomie's is still going through some pretty massive changes. At about 11 am, I give her a quick call.

'Mushi mushi . . .'

'You OK, Bloomlaut darling?'

'Yes . . .' Bloomie says in a muffled tone. 'Hang on, darling, I'm just in bed . . .' After a few seconds later and a few door-closing sounds, she continues: 'I rang him when I got home, and asked him to come over, and we talked about it, and sort of . . . made up.'

'Great!' I say. That sounds positive.

'Mmm . . .' I can tell she's rubbing her eyes. It's something she does when she's stressed.

'Are you sure you're OK?' I ask. I'm not sure what to say. I can see Eugene's point of view about her putting work first, which is kind of weird. Whenever any of us has had a fight with a boyfriend before, we've universally called him a cockmonkey and despised him.

'I'm fine,' she says. 'I . . . It will be fine. I told him I love him, and that this is me, and he has to accept me as I am, and then he shook his head and smiled and we had sex . . .' She says all this in her usual ballsy way, then adds in a smaller voice, 'Do you think that was good?'

'Um,' I say. That really doesn't sound good at all. 'Well, you know, it wouldn't hurt to make him feel, um, like he's worth you changing your life for a bit . . .'

'I have changed my life for him. I'm in bed on a Sunday at practically midday when I should be at work.'

'No, you shouldn't,' I say flatly. 'It's Sunday. You should be in bed with your boyfriend.'

'Mmm . . .' she says. 'We have a really big thing on this week and I have so much to do, though . . .'

'Well, if it's really important, I'm sure he'll understand . . .' I say.

'Maybe,' she says. 'We're going to talk over breakfast today. I thought guys hated talking about this stuff, Christ, we seem to do it a lot . . . Anyway. Love you, darling. You OK?'

'Yeah, aces. Love you too,' I say. Nice to have the 'I love yous' after yesterday's kitchen-slanging-match.

The next few hours pass in a happy, lazy haze. It's raining outside, and I have absolutely no desire to go out. So I spend a delicious day with just myself for company. I don't think I've ever done this before: even when I was single in the past, I'd meet my friends for a late lunch or afternoon drinks (usually

233

somewhere lots of single men would be), or watch DVDs at someone's house, or you know, something.

Instead, I clean my room and do so many loads of washing that I find clothes at the bottom of the laundry basket that I realise have been there since I broke up with Rick. I read the weekend newspaper magazines and *Vanity Fair* in the bath for about an hour till my periodic refills of hot water run out. I finally open my bank statements (It's so easy! And no nasty surprises; my abacus isn't that far off) and start a new filing system – OK, start my first ever filing system. I research the best savings account to start putting money into (looks like they're all pretty bad). I play both my OK Go albums, back to back, very loudly, and sing along. I eat Tunnock's Tea Cakes in bed, looking at the ceiling, and think happily that isn't it lucky that (a) I have extremely nice feet and (b) it's nearly warm enough to ride my bike to work. I write a letter to my Romanian World Vision child (who is a girl but who I thought was a boy for months as she had a pudding-bowl haircut), and long, chirpy emails to our uni friends living in Hong Kong and Sydney. I call my parents and have a lovely long chat (with no I-told-you-so from Mother about the much-edited description of the Rick incident on Friday). I lie on the floor and stretch with some yoga poses I remember from back when I tried to be a yoga person and failed miserably. I write my Asking For A Raise checklist, and decide to call Kate later to see what she thinks. I read over the little urban fairytale things I've been writing on and off for the past few weeks, and change little bits here and there. I like my fairytales, I think happily. Then I write about my feet. Because I really do like them too.

I don't think about work, or Jake, or Lukas, or dating, or not dating. I just think about simple things that make me happy. At the end of the day, I am thoroughly cheerful and content from the inside out. It's such an utterly lovely feeling. The outside-in happiness from a successful clothes-shopping trip or a really good first kiss is, I reflect, also lovely and I'd never deny that, but this calm, inside-out cheering is just . . . bliss. And it's not just from not being unhappy about men and dating, but really, deep-down, just from me.

Inside-out happiness.

How lovely.

At about 9 pm I glance at my phone and see that I received a text message half an hour before. I must have been deep in thought not to have heard it.

It's from Mitch.

What the devil does 'minx' mean?

Ooh, fuck! I jump to attention. He must be with Jake. Jake must have referred to me as a minx! Is that good? I think that's good. I reply:

It means brilliant, intelligent, hilarious, natty dresser, surprisingly good at DIY, naturally stunning, etc.

Heh.

Five minutes later I get a reply from Mitch:

I'm sticking up for you here. Some people think you're a bit cocky.

Oooh. Jake is definitely talking about me to Mitch. He called me cocky that night at Montgomery Place. Which is probably a flirtatious way of calling me arrogant. (Moi?)

I reply, raising an eyebrow archly at my mobile phone, as if they can see me:

Thank goodness you know my true humble, charitable self and can correct their misinterpretation.

He replies:

Actually, I just told said people how much you used to blush. No one cocky could blush that often.

Damn! I feel the blood rush to my face again. Why would I blush when no one is even around, damn it? I thought I started to control that shit at university. I wonder what else Mitch is telling him. Please shut up Mitch, I think. I hope he's not telling Jake about the Dating Sabbatical. I hope Jake's not telling Mitch about seeing me outside the Botanist. I wonder where they are. Perhaps I could arrange for some kind of fire alarm to go off, so they have to stop talking and leave the building.

I feel exposed. I feel anxious. I feel nauseous. (Oh, no, I'm just a bit hungry. But I do feel exposed and anxious.) What do I reply?

There's a ball of nervous tension in my stomach, which is most unwelcome after my calm, content day of happy alone time. See? I think to myself. Even thinking about men interrupts my happiness. The wisdom of the Dating Sabbatical strikes again.

So I reply, as a way to end the conversation:

Well, you kids go have fun. See you next weekend.

Mitch replies:

With whips, chains and bells on, sweetheart.

Well, at least I know that is definitely Mitch, not Jake. It's one of his favourite sayings.

Chapter Twenty-Four

I am going to ask for a raise today.

I am.

It's Friday afternoon and yes, I've put it off all week. I've tried to measure Cooper's mood every day, and decided it's not quite amenable enough, and then decided to do it, and then he walks out to a meeting, or has a phone call, or I get peckish, or whatever. But enough is enough. It's Friday, we're going to Eddie's houseparty tonight, and just between you and me, I'm nervous about seeing Jake this weekend, so adding asking-for-a-raise nerves to that won't make a huge difference.

I also have a mild hangover from last night, which doesn't help. Bloomie and I had a catch-up dinner at an infamous bar-that-pretends-to-be-a-restaurant Nam Long Le Shaker, on the Old Brompton Road. It was great. We had a proper heart-to-heart talk, the kind we haven't had in months, maybe even years. She's always busy and distracted, and I was – let's be honest – a bit scatty and heartbroken. We have been approaching life from opposite directions. And after the post-Rick-vomit-fight on Saturday, we needed to properly make up. So over noodles, duck pancakes and Tiger beer, we did.

Bloomie told me more about her and Eugene, and how he thinks she's using work to hold him at arm's length. The fight isn't entirely resolved, but she's working through it.

'Apparently I have to . . .' she cleared her throat, as if the word was hard to get out, 'compromise.'

I don't think Bloomie has ever voluntarily compromised in her life.

She admitted she prefers work to men. Work has never let her down, and after almost as many bust relationships as me, that's understandably important. 'The thing is,' she said, 'Eugene could dump me tomorrow. There are no guarantees. But work is always work. Even when it's shit, it's work. I could lose my job, sure, but I'd get another one, and somehow it feels safer than . . .' She trailed off.

'I know exactly what you mean,' I said, wishing I could argue with her. But she's right. There are no guarantees with relationships. You just can't trust them. I hate that.

'He asked me the day after the Ziani's fight if I'd ever realised that things probably wouldn't work out with us if I didn't make an effort and that might mean working less and putting my job, if not second, then at least equal with him . . . And I hadn't. I thought I could just have it my way, which makes me sound like such a . . . a bastardo.' She takes a long sip of her drink. 'I hate being wrong.'

Eugene's emotional maturity is impressive, isn't it? He doesn't seem to have lost his temper about it, or given her an ultimatum, or told her she was being an idiot – three things which would have tipped her over the edge. He just brought the subject up and let her think about it.

He didn't even hold a grudge when she overreacted and stormed out of Ziani's, as I pointed out to Bloomie. That's pretty big of him to instantly overlook public humiliation.

'I know,' said Bloomie, looking a bit ashamed. 'I'm such a twat. He's so . . . not a twat.'

Things this week have been much better, apparently, as Bloomie has been out of work by 8 pm every night and available for emails and calls. I'm impressed and secretly surprised by this.

'What happened at work last week, anyway?' I ask.

She shrugs. 'It was just this deal that came in . . . I can't explain how hard everyone has to work when it happens – I only had two all-nighters, I got off pretty lightly. Anyway, it's fine now. This week has been positively boring in comparison. I've got nothing to do.'

'Did it turn out OK?'

'Yeah, we got there in the end . . . Let's not talk about work. What about you, darling?' she asked, letting out a teeny tiny Tiger burp, after we'd finished eating.

'What about me what?' I replied, letting out a teeny tiny Tiger burp of my own.

'The Dating Sabbatical,' she prompted. 'It's over and I think you should get back out there. I think you're ready.'

'"Get back out there"?' I repeated incredulously. She smiled and swigged her beer again. 'I've been thinking about this all week, and here's the thing. My life has genuinely changed since I started it.'

'Mmmm,' said Bloomie.

'At work, at home, with money, my writing, just . . . everything. It was only a small change, really, but it's had this crazy knock-on effect, and now I feel so balanced and really truly happy . . . Dating, and guys, and all that – it took up all my time and energy before. And I was never that happy, not really . . . not like I am now.' I'm tearing the label off my beer as I say all this.

'No argument there,' said Bloomie. 'But now it's taking up none of your time or energy. Apart from the Mahiki snog and Botanist blip, obviously . . . And that's not balanced either.'

'That's exactly what I mean. See? After snogging Lukas and fighting with Rick, I went straight back to being my old crazy drunk self. I hate being like that.'

'Dating and happiness are not mutually exclusive,' said Bloomie. 'It just takes the right guy. And every guy is the wrong guy until you meet the right one.'

Emboldened by the secrets-akimbo atmosphere of the evening, I decided to admit something I'd barely admitted to myself. 'I do . . . wonder if . . . I mean . . . Jake . . . is interesting . . . But . . .' I held a hand up, as Bloomie was grinning very excitedly. 'I'm trying not to think about him too much, because I haven't even seen him in like, months. And he's a smartarse. And too funny, too confident, too alpha, and the sexual tension was just ridiculous . . .'

'So?' exclaimed Bloomie. 'I thought you liked that kind of guy!'

'I do!' I exclaim. 'That's the problem, you know, I don't trust my judgement. He's almost certainly a bastardo underneath it all and would make me even more crazy and unhappy and I can't go back there.'

'I really don't believe he's like that,' she said, finishing her beer and signalling the waitress for another. 'Why are you being so negative? What makes you think that you couldn't keep your new life changes and, you know, get some action at the same time?'

I shook my head. 'It's not negative, I'm just . . . I'm not willing to risk everything. Not when my life is going so well. I could fuck everything up again.'

'Well, can you wait to see how you feel after this weekend? Just promise me that. Don't just rule it out.'

I nodded. 'I promise.'

She grinned gleefully. 'Sass loves Jakeeey!'

'Shut up, Susan,' I said.

The bar was hitting its busy peak right about then, and a nearby table of guys were drinking the house cocktail: the Flaming Ferrari. (This is a cocktail the size of a puppy that looks and tastes like diesel fuel – oh, and yes: it's lit on fire when you drink it. As you drink it, the bar plays the sound of a Ferrari revving over the loudspeaker.) Bloomie and I started chatting about the upcoming weekend, just as two martinis arrived at our table – a present, apparently, from the guys.

We looked at each other. Even six months ago, we'd have downed them, joined their table, and at least one of us ended up snogging and/or dating at least one of them.

'I'm not up for it,' said Bloomie.

'Me either,' I said. I leaned over to call to the guys, who were drunkenly waving at us.

'Thanks, but no, thanks . . . We're leaving soon.'

They made some drunken protestations, but when we couldn't be persuaded, they shrugged and turned back to their table. Soon afterwards we called it a night. It was a great Thursday: fiscally undemanding and emotionally rewarding.

Now I have a slight Tiger hangover mixing with the asking-for-a-raise nerves. God, a hangover from four beers. I must be getting old.

At 3 pm, I get up and walk slowly over to Cooper's Chinese screen.

'Um . . .'

Bad start. Never start negotiations with um.

'Cooper?'

'Yeah-llo?'

'Got a minute?' I poke my head round with a tentative smile.

'Come on in.'

'Can we go to the conference room?'

Cooper frowns. 'Sure.'

We walk from his desk to the conference room in silence, and I can feel everyone in the office looking at us.

The second we get in, he turns to me.

'Don't worry, he's going.'

This throws me.

'What?'

'Andy. Andy is leaving.'

'That wasn't what I . . . wait, Andy has resigned?'

'I thought you knew . . .' I shake my head. Cooper sighs.

'I talked to Scott about it. Andy came to me on Monday and said either you go or he goes.'

I'm speechless.

'It was after some email you sent, questioning his creative route. I saw the work, and the email, and backed up your right to ask those questions, though I thought the creative was strong enough to go over anyway . . .' I nod my head. He's talking about the 70s postcards.

'So he told you to fire me?'

'Not exactly,' says Cooper. 'He just said he couldn't work with you. Said you were too inexperienced, too green.' I feel the blood rush to my face, and the inevitable tears to my eyes – ah, yes, weepy-anger. Cooper leans back. 'I told Andy that if he felt that way, he should take a week to consider it, and let me know if he still wants to leave. Because there is no way I'm getting rid of you.'

Now I really feel like crying. Be professional, goddamnit. You're about to ask the man for more money. I clear my throat and smile at Cooper.

'Thanks, Cooper. That's just . . . so good to hear. He's such a—'

'I know,' interrupts Cooper.

'So – he's leaving?'

Cooper nods. 'He put a letter of resignation on my desk this morning. He misspelled resignation . . . anyway, I thought you'd like to know.'

I giggle at the spelling thing, but my mind is racing. What a roosterprick. I'm trying to remember if he's been especially rude to me this week, but I've just done my usual thing and stayed out of his way.

'Well, that's very interesting. Who will we recruit?'

'I'm having a drink with Chris tonight,' he says.

'Chris!' I say excitedly. 'Would he come?' He's my old art director, the one Coop and I worked with at the big agency.

He's brilliant, easy to work with, and would fit in here perfectly.

'He will if the money is right,' says Cooper. 'I called him last night. It's almost a done deal.'

I cough. It's now or never. Time for my speech.

'Speaking of money, Cooper, I would like to talk about my remuneration. I know we're in a difficult economic climate, but I'm sure you'll agree that I'm being substantially underpaid for someone of my experience and position. The agency is financially very stable, and I am working on every single account, and I think you know the substantial contribution I made to the pitch last week.' Phew.

Cooper is nodding, but saying nothing. I think he wants to see how long I'll go on for before I peter out.

'I've done some research, and the average copywriter with my experience is paid between . . .' Here, I'm going to have to block your ears. You don't mind, do you? Talking about money in public is so icky. '. . . and I know we're in difficult economic times, but well, this company is doing very well indeed, and I think I'm a major factor in it doing well.' Whoops, that was off script, I sort of repeated myself. Never mind. I take a deep breath and look at him.

'I agree,' says Cooper. What? I thought he'd argue. 'I have been wondering if you'd ask me this. How much?'

Shocked, I tell him.

'Done.'

'And I want it backpaid to my last review, when it should have been given,' I add. This is a semi-improvised bit. Kate suggested it the other day when she helped me write out my speech, but I scoffed at the time, as it seemed so outrageous.

'Done.'

'OK,' I say. 'Wow. Thanks.' I'm speechless for the second time in five minutes.

'Now. When Chris arrives, we're reorganising the company.

243

You two are in charge of creative.' I open my mouth. 'No official title change yet, but we're about to double in terms of revenue and work, and since I'll be travelling a lot more, I can't be as hands-on as I'd like, so I want you to manage the creative department. We'll be recruiting more copywriters and designers, and you're in charge of that, too. You've really brought everyone together in the past few weeks, and the way you handled Andy the morning of the pitch was really great. I thought a bit of sink or swim would be good for you . . . I think you'll be fantastic. Then, in three months, we'll talk about official promotions.'

I am still speechless, and in fact, my mouth is slightly open. Cooper stands up, and we shake hands. I start to grin.

'Wait,' I say.

'What?'

'Why . . . why me over Andy?' I've never wondered this before, but why has Cooper kept Andy around all this time?

Cooper sighs. 'Andy joined this company on practically no pay, back when I first started it. I felt like I owed him. And he is a good, solid designer. He's just . . . not much more than that.'

I follow him out of the meeting room and back into the office, still grinning. I look over and see Andy staring at me with open dislike. I smile back as broadly as I can.

I got a raise and a promotion. Kind of a promotion, anyway. And definitely, definitely a raise. I sigh with content. Now this is what I call inside-out happiness. I should have done this ages ago. Why didn't I believe in myself enough to do this before?

I wonder what it'll be like when I see Jake tonight.

Oooh, hello, random Jake thought.

I sit down at my desk, and am instantly hit by a full-stomach-jump of nerves.

Think about work, damn you.

I can't, asking for a raise was the only thing that was distracting me – and now Jake and the weekend at Eddie's is all I can focus on.

I try to deep breathe and summon the calm, contented feeling I achieved last Sunday. No good. I try to call Kate for comfort. No answer. I call Bloomie. Obviously the financial world is having a quiet day, because she answers straightaway.

'Mushi mushi?'

'I'm DYING with nerves about seeing Jake. I might vomit,' I whisper.

'WOO WOO!' she crows, then clears her throat and says quietly, 'Jeez, the looks I get in this place when I don't act like a robot . . .'

'Halp,' I say. 'Pleeeees halp.'

Bloomie is never impressed by my *The Fifth Element* impression.

'You don't sound anything like her. So have you changed your mind? Are you going to break the Sabbatical for Jake?'

I think about actually changing my status from 'unavailable indefinitely' to 'girlfriend' and for a second, I think I'm going to throw up. It would all go badly badly wrong. I know that in my heart.

That's not inside-out happiness. That's outside-in chaos.

'No fucking way . . . I mean, no. I'm just telling you I'm nervous.'

'Well, at least you've properly admitted having a crush on him, after all that "Jake . . . is . . . interesting . . ." bullshit last night.'

'Crush is the right word,' I say. 'I feel like an orange going through a juicing machine.'

'OK . . . so wait, why did you call me?'

'Can you distract me?' I say in a whiny voice.

'Poor baby,' she says, giggling. 'I'll email Eddie asking exactly what we're doing tonight. He'll just think I'm being bossy. Then he'll be prompted to send a group email and we can get some e-banter going. That should distract you and you can channel your nerves into that.'

'Brilliant,' I say.

True to her word, about half an hour later an email arrives from Eddie.

245

Subject: The Best Weekend You'll Ever Have.

Hmm.

Most of the email is about how to get to his parents' house. I don't have to worry about that, since Kate's driving. (I don't know how to drive. I know, I need to sort that out, don't nag me.) Then I see he's added a PS.

PS: If you're wondering about the plans this weekend, it's something like this: Boys do a wine tasting, followed by a beer tasting, then a spirit tasting. Girls cook. Boys watch girls cooking. Boys eat. Girls clean up. Repeat for each meal of the weekend, interspersed with sleep. Hakuna matata, beeetchez.

Ha! I know he wrote that specifically to annoy us, and I am obviously not a particularly emotionally intelligent person, because it's worked. I contemplate replying all and scan the email list. Bloomie, Eugene, Kate, Fraser, Ant (Ant? Oh, for fuck's sake), Tory. So far, so predictable. And then I see it. J.Ryan@proxicol.co.uk. His last name is Ryan? It must be him, he's the only J I don't know.

I look at the email for a few minutes, then decide to draft my reply.

(Yes, email replies really are this important.)

Edward. I'm so thrilled that you're taking so much time to worry about the happiness of the women fortunate enough to be attending your party.

Nonono. Straight sarcasm won't work. I'm just going to have to be sexist back.

Edward. The plans have been redrafted. The men will taste the wine, guzzle the beer, and ruin our spirits.

Pfft. It's not that good. Sending a group email is like being a standup comic. You have to be pretty damn sure your material is not going to tank in front of your audience.

I delete both drafts and press 'send and receive' on my email to see if anyone else has replied all.

One from Bloomie:

246

Thrilled, Edward. I'll be sure to pack my own rubber gloves, as you know how much I love to scrub. Then again, you've always loved scrubbers too, haven't you?

Ha. Clearly his email irritated Bloomie too.

One from Mitch:

WTF? The girls are allowed to sleep?

Haha. Funny Mitch.

I press 'send and receive' again. Nothing. Jake must be busy. Maybe he's not coming. Maybe he thinks funny reply-alls are stupid.

Stop thinking about it.

I decide to go and have a long lunch, and decide to lie in Golden Square with takeaway sushi from Kulu Kulu and a Diet Coke and listen to Aerosmith on my iPod.

Golden Square on a sunny day is exceptional for people-watching. I see a couple on a lunch date, flirting gently: the guy pretending nonchalance, his nervous date having trouble maintaining eye contact, a palpable air of excitement between them. Another couple are snoozing in the sun, and she's using his tummy as a pillow as he enjoys the freedom to check out other women. Across the grass I see a girl on the phone, crying and smoking.

Ah, the three stages of dating. Flirty excitement, ill-judged happiness, lonely misery. Sigh. I look across the other side of Golden Square, and see two guys walking together through the centre of the square holding hands. I wonder what the gay dating scene is like, I think. I bet it's more straightforward than the straight one. I peer closer. Oh my God. One of the holdy-hands guys is Clapham Brodie.

You have got to be fucking kidding me.

I duck down flat on the grass and stare at the two guys through my sunglasses. They're too wrapped up in a bubble of happiness to even glance my way, oblivious to everyone around them, laughing and talking as they walk through Golden Square. He's

247

wearing really nice jeans, I think irrationally. And his boyfriend is gorgeous.

They walk out of Golden Square, and I sit back up, looking about me in shock. Fucking hell. Clapham Brodie is gay. No wonder we watched so many DVDs, lying chastely side-by-side. Hang on. This means that in the last six weeks, I've seen every guy that I've ever dated for more than a month. Except Arty Jonathan. I'm not likely to see him. He probably took my £200 quid and moved into a squat in Brighton, or wherever it is talentless artists end up.

What is the universe trying to tell me? Is it reminding me that every past mistake is alive and well so that I adhere to the Dating Sabbatical? Or is it showing them to me so I can see that they've ended up fat, boring, evil, in love with someone called Belly or, well, gay? Or is it just saying that I need to explore new areas of London to hang out in?

I think I'll have to have a little cigarette, which I wouldn't ordinarily do without even the pretence of a phone call to make it 'social smoking'. But honestly. Clapham Brodie is *gay*.

When I get back to the office, my inbox is filled with reply-alls from just about everyone attending the weekend. I scan the list . . . Bloomie, Ant, Mitch, Eddie, Ant again, blahblahblah . . . Everyone seems to be offering to bring different things. (Starting with food, alcohol and blow-up mattresses, which then led to contribution offers of blow-up dolls, a blow-up sheep and the ability to tie a cherry stalk in a knot in one's mouth. That last one was Tory.) I feel oddly tongue-tied. This is not like me. Then a reply-all arrives from Jake Ryan.

My contribution to the weekend is my ability to scale sheer mountain walls. I can also skipper a yacht and make a hot air balloon out of a paperclip and snot.

Heehee. I decide not to reply-all just yet, though. I'll just wait and see what happens. Over the next hour, the email reply-alls become even giddier. Fraser offers to show us how to take apart and put back together a rifle in less than a minute, Tory says she'll do the splits, Mitch – predictably – says his contribution is a naked Extreme Worm tutorial. Then, at 4.52 pm, another email arrives from Jake.

He sent it to me. And only me. My heart jumps.

Taptaptap . . . Is this thing on? Tough crowd . . .

I wait for just under ten minutes – you have to, with this kind of email, or else you look too keen – and then reply:

I was waiting till someone said something funny.

He replies (almost eight minutes later):

You and your cocky silences.

I reply (nine minutes later):

Stop it. I'm blushing.

He replies (six minutes later):

Uh . . . that wasn't a compliment. And I thought you knew the meaning of words n stuff.

Heh. I reply (eight minutes later):

So I hear you were talking to your cousin about me. Am sure you know he's a congenital liar.

He replies (four minutes later):

Anyone who throws a glass of wine in someone's face has to expect to be talked about.

Shit.

I think about what to reply and (nine minutes later) settle on:

That was bar theatre. You wouldn't guess it, but everyone involved was an actor. Even the wine was acting.

He replies (six minutes later):

Wow, Oscar-worthy performance. Especially the guy playing the arrogant ex-boyfriend.

I reply (seven minutes later):

Yes, they nailed it when they cast him. Sadly, he hasn't been booked for any repeat performances.

He replies (less than two minutes later):

No great loss to the illustrious world of bar theatre. He didn't look like the type anyone would want to get the girl.

Oh, my gosh. I'm sweating slightly. This is fucking brilliant. I look at my watch. It's almost 4 pm.

I reply (six minutes later):

Well. This has been charming, but I have to go home now and pack. Toothbrush, pyjamas, paperclips, snot . . . the usual. Will you last the afternoon without me?

He replies (immediately):

Only time will tell, Minxy.

I feel euphoric, albeit clammy-palmed. I wonder if he's coming tonight, or if he's in the group arriving in the morning. I guess I'll find out.

I stand up and pack up my desk, and grab my jacket and clutch. As I start walking towards the door, and see Andy get up from his desk, I pretend not to see him, open the front door and walk out.

'Sass,' he says, following me out and shutting the door behind him. Oh God, what now.

I turn around and look him straight in the eye. 'Oh, Andy. I'm just on my way home . . .'

'Can I have a quick word?' he says.

'I'm in a hurry. Can you make it very quick?' I say, and see his eyebrows raise in surprise.

'Shall we go into the conference room?'

'Here is good,' I say. Yes! Score one to me. I don't care what nasty things he might say to me, I realise. Bring it on.

'Uh, well, you may not know, but I'm leaving Cooper. I just wanted to say, I think you'll be a great head creative in a few years. You've got a bright future ahead of you, as they say.'

Not nasty. Just patronising.

'Yes, I know you're leaving,' I reply, smiling broadly. 'Cooper told me everything. Shame your ultimatum didn't work. And thanks, but I know I'll be great, because I'm fucking brilliant at my job. Thanks for the chat, Andy. I'll see you Monday.'

Andy stares at me, open-mouthed. He doesn't say anything, so after a few seconds I smile at him again and turn around. I skippy-bunny-hop down the stairs and out into the evening sunshine. Self-high-fives all round.

Chapter Twenty-Five

I get to Kate and Bloomie's house at 6.30 pm after a whirl-wind dash home to change, and I'm now mentally, physically and sartorially ready to face Jake and whatever else the weekend throws at me. I'm dressed in perfect country weekend wear (Road Tripper theme: pale blue skinny jeans, Converses, dark grey top, Bloomie's leather jacket). My hair is clean. My make-up is understated. My eyebrows are doing just what I asked them to. I have an overnight bag packed with a selection of comfortable, yet rather sexy clothes. If you think well-worn T-shirts are sexy. Which I do.

'And where were you on the emails this afternoon?' asks Bloomie as a greeting. She's standing outside her house, leaning against Kate's car. Kate's inside getting her bag. 'After all that fuss . . .'

'Stage fright sucks,' I shrug. I'll tell her about the emails with Jake later.

'Fag for the nerves, darling?' asks Bloomie, fishing Marlboro Lights out of her bag. She's wearing my white jeans. I think they look better on her. Damn.

'I think my jeans look better on you,' I say to her by way of response.

'I think my jacket looks better on you,' she nods, lighting two cigarettes and handing one to me.

'Is The Dork coming up with us?'

'He has a family thang,' says Bloomie. 'His cousin is here for the night after a school trip all week, so they're going to a musical. I cried off on the grounds that musicals make me homicidal.'

'Fair,' I nod.

'He's coming up first thing in the morning. With that guy Benoit who chatted you up at Montgomery Place that night.'

I raise an eyebrow. Great.

'Let's hit the road,' says Kate, coming out of the house. Bloomie and I immediately start arguing about who gets shotgun. I win. It's nice being 'the three of us' again. Aside from being around more, Kate's Tray-induced uptightness (not a word, never mind) is fading and she's back to being fun and silly. She'll always be a bit obsessive-compulsive, mind you. She spent an hour today plotting and printing the perfect driving route on viamichelin.com and Google Maps, and cross-referencing it with Bloomie's roadmap.

As we drive through Notting Hill, I remember to ask Kate something I've been meaning to all week.

'Any news from the hot Aussie, by the way?'

'Didn't I tell you? He texted me at 4 am on Saturday night – I mean Sunday morning, really – asking if I fancied a nightcap back at his place.' She shakes her head. 'As if.'

'Shame. Le Rappel Du Booty, I believe that's called.'

'Silly man,' says Bloomie. 'He just got overexcited and blew a little early, so to speak . . .' She pauses. 'God! Sorry, that was filthy of me. Mitch must be rubbing off on me, so to speak . . . God! Sorry! There I go again!'

Kate and I start giggling.

'I've been wondering if maybe I wasn't flirting very well,' says Kate. 'Or flirting so obviously that he thought I'd be up for a 4 am sex-request. Can you watch me this weekend, see how I do?'

'Of course,' Bloomie and I reply. 'Though I think you flirt very well indeed,' I add.

Kate shrugs. 'Perhaps he was just drunk. I've deleted his text and number, obviously.'

'Obviously,' we agree in unison. We fall into silence and listen to the radio for awhile. Then I remember I haven't told them my news.

'I got a raise today. And a promotion. And I saw Clapham Brodie in Golden Square and he's gay and has a really hot boyfriend.'

'WHAT?' Bloomie and Kate explode with excitement, and I tell them everything. After several minutes of excited questions, we fall silent.

'Gosh, I wish they'd just tell me I've definitely got a job,' says Kate. 'I had lunch with my boss, though, and he talked to me about my six-month objectives and stuff. So that must be a good sign.'

'I'm sure everything is fine,' says Bloomie. She's lying.

'Me too,' I agree. So am I.

'What would you guys do if you lost your jobs?' Kate asks.

'I . . . wouldn't think about it till it happens,' I say.

'I'd take some time off,' says Bloomie. 'I'd come back in six months, or a year, and see where things are.'

'Can you afford to do that?' I ask.

Bloomie shrugs. 'I have savings.'

I always forget that everyone has savings except me.

Kate sighs fretfully and starts nibbling her cuticles – a first; her nails are usually pristine. I'd better change the subject to distract her.

'Does anyone know if Jake is coming tonight or tomorrow?' I blurt out. Nice distraction. Idiot.

'Tonight, I think. Eddie said Mitch "and that lot" are driving down later . . . so that would include your LUVUH!'

They start teasing me like we're ten years old. Bloomie clearly told Kate my 'Jake . . . is . . . interesting' speech when she got home last night, which is par for the course with the three of us.

'So, do you love him?'

'Do you want him to be your boyfriend?'

'Would you kiss him?'

'Would you touch his THING?!'

'If you don't shut up, I'll be forced to smack you both. In the mouth. With my fist.'

'She would! She would like sooo touch it.'

'Ew, I KNOW.'

They're giggling hysterically at themselves.

'I was going to tell you about the emails today, but now I won't,' I say airily, looking out the window. How quickly London turns to green countryside. It's kind of weird, because when you're in the middle of it, it's hard to imagine that the countryside even exists.

'Tell us!' They both shout at once. 'TELL US. NOW.'

'Tell us or I'll pull over and you can walk to Eddie's,' says Kate.

'OK, OK,' I say. I tell them all about it. They giggle at his witty emails (Kate also comments on his rather polite and sensitive way of dealing with seeing the Botanist Incident, which I hadn't even thought about) and get even more excited about me seeing him tonight.

'He's pretty slick, alright,' I say, voicing a thought that's been in my head since the emails. 'It reminds me of Rick.'

Silence.

'Jake is nothing like Rick,' says Bloomie. 'Jake is nice, for a start.'

'Jake is much better looking,' adds Kate.

'Jake is a Boy Scout. And a prince,' says Bloomie.

'Jake *is* a prince,' agrees Kate.

'Jake is a pony. You should take him for a ride . . .'

Kate shrieks with laughter.

'Jake is an ice cream. And she should lick his pointy end,' adds Bloomie.

'Ooh! Jake is a chocolate bar she'd like to melt in her mouth,' says Kate.

'Jake is a fish that she'd like to bone,' says Bloomie.

255

They're both laughing helplessly. They know wordplay is one of my favourite things, damn them.

'Jake,' I say, despite myself, 'is a roast dinner. And I want to taste his meat and two veg.'

'Jake is . . . a chutney and you'd like to scoff his pickle!' screams Bloomie. Kate is laughing too hard to speak now.

'Jake is . . . a builder, and I'd like to admire his marvellous erections.'

'Jake is . . . a fry-up. And you'd like to nibble his sausage.'

'Jake is . . . a Royal Mail depot, and I'd like to get my hands on his package.'

The drive to Eddie's is meant to take an hour and a half, but what with the silliness, snack stops and Friday traffic, we don't make it till past 9 pm. As we pull up the long driveway to the house, I feel a fizzle of nerves in my tummy and my heart starts pounding.

I wonder if he's here yet. I wonder if he knows about the Dating Sabbatical. I'd be embarrassed if he did. It does kind of make me seem like a serial dater. And a basket case.

It's a perfect May night, and the sky is not quite dark, and everything is still and clear. I love this house. It's old, very big, and surprisingly cosy. The outside is all covered in greenyvineythings, and the inside is a divine mess of sprawling rooms and fireplaces and photos and sculptures, with over-spilling bookshelves absolutely everywhere. I take a deep breath as we walk in . . .

. . . and exhale as we enter the kitchen. Only Eddie and Ant are here.

They're sitting at the long kitchen table drinking beer and talking loudly. They're already rather pissed. Within a few minutes we've dropped our bags in our rooms upstairs, and are at the table opening a bottle of wine.

I feel like I'm home when I'm in this kitchen. Half of it is taken up with the table, which sits about 24, the other half with a walk-in pantry, an Aga (but of course), an enormous fridge and a kitchen island for preparing food, and what seem to be dozens of cupboards over big country sinks. One entire wall is windows and big double doors looking out to the huge expanse of perfectly manicured garden and lovingly tended flower beds, leading down to tennis courts. The rest of the house is delightful, too, but this room – this is kitchen porn.

'What have we missed, then?' says Bloomie.

'Nothing appropriate for pretty little ears like yours,' grins Ant. 'It was boys-only talk. We'll have to clean it up now.'

I roll my eyes.

'I've been made redundant, if you must know,' says Ant.

'Oh, gosh . . . how awful,' I say. 'I'm sorry.' Bloomie and Kate chorus this.

'Don't be. I've been expecting it for months. Anyway, anyone who wants to work now is a chump. It's the perfect time to go and hide on a desert island for two years. Then come back and take over the world.'

'Can you afford to do that?' asks Kate reasonably.

'No, of course I can't,' he says. 'But it's a fucking brilliant idea.'

He's such a prat. He's not saying anything Bloomie didn't say in the car, but it's all in the delivery. I turn to Eddie.

'What's new, pussycat?'

'I'm getting dry humped at work,' he replies, leaning back in his seat and surreptitiously letting out a gentle beery belch. 'Nothing new there.'

'Actually, the term is "frotted",' says Kate with an angelic smile.

'Speaking of dry humping, I would like to tell a story about a girl with a pet snake,' says Eddie.

'Oh, God,' says Bloomie.

Eddie launches into a long and entertaining story I've heard several times before. It takes him 15 minutes to tell it. I'll tell it to you in 15 seconds. A girl he knows had a pet snake, and it stopped eating and kept going all rigid for hours like a tree log.

And she took it to the vet and he said 'Well, it goes rigid to measure itself against the length of you, and it's stopped eating because it's getting its appetite big enough to eat you. And it's a good thing you came in because it has just dislocated its own jaw on purpose, which indicates it would have attempted to eat you within the next 12 hours.' (Everyone always screams at this point.) Eddie swears this is a true story. I'll leave it up to you to decide.

I hear a car pull up outside.

'I need to use the . . . euphemism,' I say, and dash upstairs.

As I'm washing my hands, I hear new voices in the front hallway. My heart starts pounding with fear slash excitement, and I peek over the stair banisters to see if it's him. Nope, it's just more of Eddie's engineering friends, Neil and Harriet, who've arrived with Fraser and Tory. Fraser and Tory are back together, apparently, which is slightly worrying. Harriet is one of those heavily competitive women who thinks she knows everything about sport and tries to ensure guys pay her attention by talking to them about cricket. I find it very hard to warm to her. She spends most of her time telling Neil what to do. He is skinny and has never had a good haircut. He also has yet to reveal anything remarkable about himself and never contributes anything to the conversation, but Eddie seems to like him . . . Of course, he's probably absolutely hilarious and brilliant and thinks I'm a total arsehole. He and Harriet are going out, I think.

Oh God, the waiting is killing me.

I go back into the bathroom and point at myself in the mirror. Calm the fuck down. He's probably not even a good person and you are practically forcing yourself into a crush that would kill you. You can't trust yourself. And he's a slick, funny, charmingly bossy, ultra-confident alpha male and you know how it would end: tears, misery, disappointment. That is why you are on a Sabbatical. So take a fucking chill pill. (A chill pill? I think as I walk down the stairs. Sheesh, I am a dork.)

'Hello everyone,' I say, coming back into the kitchen.

'Hello, treacle,' calls Fraser. I lean over and give him a kiss on the cheek as I walk past to my chair, and my eye is caught by Tory's grubby little foot toeing his groin. I look over at her and we smile at each other. You need a pedicure, I think. And a muzzle, I add, as I sit down at the other end of the table and she launches into a loud story about her birthday last year. I'm not really paying attention – Bloomie and Kate are making fun of each other as roommates, which is quite diverting – until Tory says:

'And I thought, you know what, I deserve a birthday bang.' The entire table falls silent. 'Really, it's what every girl deserves . . . Sadly, I didn't know about young Fraser's abilities, else I would have booked him for the night, yeh?' I glance at Fraser, who is puce with embarrassment or possibly – though I hope not – delight. Tory continues: 'So I spent a hilarious night phoning every single man I've ever been with, yeh? And every single one is now in a relationship and couldn't oblige! Can you imagine? I must be some kind of graduate school for relationship-ready men . . .'

'Graduate school? That's the first time I've heard her call it that,' says Bloomie under her breath to me.

'Call what that?' says Kate equally quietly.

'Her hoohoo,' murmurs Bloomie. Kate guffaws, spraying red wine all over the table. Everyone looks up at us.

'Sorry! She has a drinking problem,' says Bloomie, and we hurry to the sink to get sponges and towels, laughing hysterically. Suddenly, I feel far more relaxed.

By 10.30 pm, we're a few more bottles of wine down, Bloomie, Kate and I are happily tucking into fags and the very good cheese and bread brought by Tory and Fraser. I keep intercepting very heavy glances from her to him. Fraser couldn't give a heavy glance if his life depended on it, bless him, but he's staring back as hard as he can.

Ant, Kate and Neil are talking at the other end of the table about the room allocations for the weekend. Well, Ant and Kate are talking. He grabbed her hand after our last fag break and wouldn't let go until she sat next to him. God, I hope she's only practising her flirting.

'I don't see why the bedrooms should be single sex,' says Ant. 'We're all grown-ups, after all. I mean, I've seen thousands of breasts. What makes you girls think I'd be so keen to see yours?'

Eddie makes a coughing sound that sounds like 'bullshit'. The old jokes are often the best.

Kate starts to laugh. 'But I don't want to share a room with a guy. The snoring, the bodily functions . . .'

'I can go a weekend without touching little Jimmy and the boys,' says Ant.

Ew.

Kate is laughing even more now. 'That's not the function I was referring to.'

'Come on, I know it's all you girls think about . . .' he says, leaning towards her. 'I'll have you know, there's a very high criteria for girls to make the J-list.'

'Two feet and a heartbeat?' I call down the table.

'Oh, hello, look who's getting involved now!' he calls back. 'Private conversation here, thanks.'

'Privates conversation . . .' quips Kate, and Ant laughs far harder than he ought to.

I hope she's not confusing his sleaze with naughty charm. It's a classic pitfall for the newly single. Then again, she's a big girl, and I'm not about to tell her what to do. I turn back to Eddie and Bloomie, who are having a serious conversation about whether you could pack blue cheese on a skin infection and it would work like penicillin.

'Guys . . . seriously. That's gross. I was just thinking that I'm hungry. It's gone now.'

'We've already eaten dinner,' says Eddie. 'But I was about to cook up some sausages as a bit of a late supper.'

Love men and their perma-hunger.

'Is Maeve coming this weekend, by the way?' asks Bloomie.

'Uh, she has to work,' says Eddie.

I turn to look at Eddie and frown thoughtfully. He catches my eye and frowns back, and gets up to go to the fridge. I follow and stand right behind him as he rummages in the fridge pulling out sausages and butter, turns around and jumps.

'Jesus, woman!' he exclaims. He clearly didn't realise I was there.

'Are you still going out with Maeve?' I ask quietly.

'Why would you ask that?' he replies.

'Answer me.'

There's a long pause. He looks at me, sighs and says, 'We broke up two months ago. I just haven't been in the mood to talk about it.'

'Are you serious?' hisses Bloomie, who's propped herself against the back of the kitchen island, facing us. Everyone at the kitchen table is now very involved in the bodily-functions conversation and not listening to us.

'Oh fuck, and you wonder why . . .' Eddie shakes his head and hands me a bag of onions. 'Chop these, please.'

I grab the onions, a board and a knife and start chopping. 'Teddyboy, what the hell? What happened?'

He shrugs, pouring oil into a large saucepan and putting it on the stove. 'It just . . . fell apart. I haven't been crying myself to sleep about it.'

Bloomie shakes her head. 'That's so repressed.'

'It IS,' I agree, wiping away a tear. 'Sorry, it's the onions, though obviously I am devastated about Maeve, too . . . Do you want to talk about it?'

'Do you want a hug?' asks Bloomie. She looks genuinely tearful. Yikes, love is making her squishy.

He starts to laugh. 'Fuck off, girls,' he says affectionately. 'I've already got two sisters.'

Bloomie and I look at each other and shrug, and start frying up the onions and sausages. Eddie slices and butters baguettes, and within 15 minutes, we're all at the kitchen table again, tucking into huge sausage sandwiches.

'Holy shit, do you want some food with your mustard, love?' I hear Ant saying to Kate, and she laughs in response.

'Hands up who wants to play touch rugby in the morning?' exclaims Harriet. Everyone ignores her. 'Well, I'm going to try to catch the highlights of the cricket on TV. I was watching it all afternoon on my computer at work. It was so exciting!' See? So annoying. She stomps off towards the other room with her sausage sandwich, followed closely by Neil. Heavy calves. (Both of them.)

All I can hear for a few seconds is the sound of happy munching.

'Ahh . . . I love a good sausage,' says Tory archly, raising an eyebrow at Fraser. Why do some people think their private jokes are, ahem, impenetrable to outsiders? Bloomie and I collapse laughing, and then simultaneously remember the conversation in the car and laugh even harder. Tory looks over and has the grace to look embarrassed.

Eddie's mobile rings. He looks at it and says decisively, 'Mitch. Lost.'

He answers it.

'Mitch . . . No kidding. Well, it's an easy turn-off to miss . . . Yeah, totally. Well, that makes sense. And . . . Sorry? You're where?'

He starts to laugh.

'Oh . . . man. I'll see you in like, four hours.'

He hangs up. 'They are lost in Wales.'

'Who's that?' calls Ant from the other end of the table.

'Mitch, Jake, some guy called Sam.'

I sense Kate and Bloomie looking at me meaningfully and ignore them. Bugger. He's not turning up anytime soon, then.

We start clearing up. The so-called Friday night party is a bit of a fizzle. Neil and Harriet are glued to the cricket on TV, Tory and Fraser go to bed almost immediately, and Ant is practically humping Kate's leg.

'Well . . . I'm turning in,' I say.

'Me too!' chorus Bloomie and Kate.

'We are so old these days,' grumbles Eddie. 'Three years ago we'd be, like, hammered by now.'

'Come on, let's play strip poker!' exclaims Ant. 'Katie, kitten-pants, are you game?'

'Tempting!' says Kate brightly, looking at me with 'help me' eyes. I knew she wasn't interested.

'I'm stealing her, sorry, Ant,' I give him a beaming smile. He gives a very obviously fake smile back.

Bloomie, Kate and I head upstairs to my room and flop down on the bed.

'Was that good? With the flirting?' asks Kate.

'What, darling?' says Bloomie. 'Just then? With Ant?'

'Yeah . . .' she says. She's looking so hopeful.

'You were definitely flirting a bit,' I say. 'But to be honest, he's kind of like . . .'

'. . . a randy dog?' finishes Kate. 'Yeah, I know. But I thought it was good practice. He's not that bad, underneath all the bull-shit. He said he's probably going to have to sell his house and move back in with his parents, because of this whole redun-dancy thing.'

We hear a car pull up outside. We all look at each other and gasp dramatically, and scurry to the window. Love being imma-ture sometimes (all the time). Bloomie pokes her head out.

'Tara Jones, I think,' she says disappointedly. 'With . . . is that Perry?'

Tara Jones is one of Mitch's ex-girlfriends, and Perry is her baby brother. She's very quiet and sweet, though I haven't seen her in over a year. (That's what happens when someone moves to North London.)

The outside light goes on as Eddie goes out to greet them. Bloomie looks out again.

'Yup, Tara . . . and holy shit . . . Wow, he certainly has grown . . . up . . .'

Kate and I start giggling and push her out of the way. Tara and Perry look up and wave, and we wave back. Perry was always boyishly handsome, but he's now less boyish and more very, very handsome.

'How old is he?' murmurs Kate under her breath.

'Not sure,' I say. '23 . . . 24?'

'Mmmm . . .' she says distractedly.

I pull my head in and start to giggle. 'Kate's just seen what she's having for dinner tomorrow night.'

By the time they leave my room, it's past midnight. I lie in bed for awhile thinking.

I know I shouldn't overthink things, and I know I often do, but I need to remind myself that the odds that Jake is a rooster-prick like Rick are high. I think back over every time that I've met him. He's always been pretty suave and confident, which is probably a bad sign. He approached me in the kitchen at Mitch's party with no shyness at all. Only a bastard would be that cocky. He's Mitch's cousin, and Mitch is such a player and it probably runs in families. And Jake hasn't ever really done anything to make me think he's a nice or thoughtful person. He's just a bit funny, that's all. If it's Jake versus the Sabbatical, then the Sabbatical wins every time. And with these thoughts, I drift off to sleep.

Chapter Twenty-Six

Waking up at Eddie's, I have a moment of where-am-I confusion till I look around the room and remember. A huge double bed, a big cupboard, sunshiney light escaping around the edges of satisfyingly thick double curtains, a vanity table (God, I've always wanted one of those), and a little ensuite. I've always had this room when I come here, and I've come to think of it as mine.

The morning starfish stretch and sigh that I noticed on that first Saturday of the Dating Sabbatical is back and, thanks to inside-out happiness, more enjoyable than ever. This morning I'm halfway through it when I remember that today I will, absolutely positively definitely, see Jake, and my nervous stomach kicks in again, hula-hooping away. I tell it to shut up, and remind it about the Dating Sabbatical and what I decided before I went to sleep last night. It ignores me and starts hopscotching.

I look at my watch and decide to go downstairs to the kitchen, get some coffee and have a little sit in the garden. It's huge and stunning, the kind of garden you never, ever see in London, and Eddie's mother's pride and joy. I think she's even won awards for it. This early in the morning there'll be birds and things to look at. Ooh! Maybe butterflies. (I'm so at one with nature, you know?)

No one else is up yet – it's just past 8 am – and I pad happily around the big kitchen finding a cafetiere, a tiny saucepan, some Illy coffee, and some milk. I put the kettle on to boil, pour some milk in the saucepan and put it on a low heat, spoon exactly three and a half tablespoons of coffee into the cafetiere, pour the boiled water gently on top, and stir it exactly three times anti-clockwise, three times clockwise, and then three times anti-clockwise. I poke my little finger into the milk and tap it on my wrist to check it's the right temperature, stir it briskly and take it off the heat. Finally, I press down the plungey thing on the cafetiere and pour the coffee and milk in the biggest mug I can find, till it's absolutely the perfect colour. I hum to myself happily throughout all this.

'Yet again, you are looking completely crazy,' says a voice from the corner.

I let out a scream – I know, I know, it's so girly, but I can't help it, I thought I was all alone – and turn around. It's Jake.

'Oh, God! You scared the . . . you scared me.'

'Sorry,' he says. He's sitting right at the other end of the long kitchen table, reading a book. He's looking – well, sorry, but it's true – delicious. His hair is a bit longer than last time I saw him, and he's all clean but dishevelled, like he woke up, showered and then didn't look in a mirror. He's wearing a rather loved-looking pale pink T-shirt with a hole on the collar. It takes a strong man to wear pale pink, I always think.

It has to be said, that after convincing myself he's a Rick-esque slick, smooth-talking, smartarse bastardo for the past few weeks, seeing him sitting here in boyish scruffiness, reading quietly, brings my over-active brain fluttering to a halt. My stomach, in the middle of hopscotching, falls over and skins its knee, and my heart starts hammering.

Ooh, the heart thing is new.

'No problem,' I smile back. I feel flushed with self-consciousness, and remember I'm wearing Ol' Grey and a pair of very baggy black boxer shorts. Goddamnit, why don't I own decent sleeping gear? 'One moment please,' I say, and dash into the little bathroom next to the pantry to quickly check myself out. My eyebrows are practically AWOL, my hair is all over the place, and I definitely have morning breath. I spy a tube of toothpaste under the sink and quickly eat some. On the good side, I don't have any mascara panda eyes, my eyes are clear and my skin looks alright, so bugger it. Do I need my mantra? No. I haven't needed it in ages, come to think of it. Not since that night with Rick at the Botanist when I couldn't even remember it. I point at myself in the mirror. You are still on a Dating Sabbatical. Jake is probably a bastardo so it's absolutely fine. I blow my nose quickly and run out.

'Dratted hayfever,' I say, as an excuse.

'Right,' he says. 'May I have some of that coffee?'

'Yes, of course,' I say. 'Milk? Sugar?'

'I want it exactly how you're having it,' he says. 'I have a feeling it's something you've worked out over a long period of time.'

'Perfection takes effort. You couldn't possibly understand,' I nod, pouring out a mug of perfect coffee.

He grins up at me and stands up as I walk to the opposite side of the table. I sit across and one down from him, and hand over his coffee. I grin back at him, but now we're up so close, I'm having trouble sustaining eye contact. I try to hide it by pretending to rub my face sleepily. Damn, my heart won't slow down. And the sun coming in the kitchen window is making this room awfully hot. Just chat to him. Don't flirt. Remember Rule 3.

'So I heard you had navigation issues,' I say, glancing up at him through my fingers.

'Navigation issues, petrol issues, Mitch snoring all night issues . . .' he says, taking a sip of his coffee. 'Oh Minxy. Thank you. That is amazing coffee. Amazing. I am so impressed.'

I smile back, and am about to reply something flip when my eye is caught by his book.

'*Lucky Jim*! Oh my God, that's my favourite book.'

'You're kidding,' he says. 'My sister just sent it to me . . . She thinks I'll like something she called "the hangover scene".'

'That is particularly hilarious,' I agree. I've read *Lucky Jim* about 20 times, and could quote the opening lines of the hangover bit to him verbatim, but that's a bit showponyish, even for me.

'I love it so far,' he says, and clears his throat. 'She sends me books to "de-stress" me. And I had a thing at work that was a bit crazy the last few months, so this is . . . relaxing.'

I can't think of what to say, apart from ask way too many extremely uncool questions (What's your sister's name? Do you think I'm insane after the Botanist thing? What's your relationship history? What do you do? Do you like it? Why was it crazy? What's your favourite food? Do you like me? Can I sit on your knee and smell your neck? Are you a bastardo?) so I just nod and smile at him.

'So, how have you been?' he asks. Yes. Time to make small talk.

'Uh, great,' I say. Throwing glasses of wine over ex-boyfriends, you know, the usual.

'Did you drive from London last night? . . . from your house? Where do you live, anyway?' he asks. I tell him, and tell him about the trip down with Kate and Bloomie, my inability to drive and various botched driving lesson attempts by friends over the years. He laughs at the appropriate moments and makes funny little comments that make me giggle. I don't think Rick ever, ever asked where I lived until he wanted to get into my pants and needed to tell the taxi driver where we were going. He never asked anything about me at all, really. Why have I been comparing Jake to Rick all this time? My nervous tummy is suddenly calm and still as a yoga master. I look at Jake's smiley, crinkly eyes as he takes a slow, deliberate sip of his coffee. I can hear birds singing outside. How fucking Disney.

'So what's the plan for later?'

'I'm not sure . . .' I say. 'Last night didn't really take off. Eddie will probably go into host overdrive now and try to make it the best weekend party ever, TM.'

'Oh, no, I meant for me. For me and the men. I figured you and the rest of the girls – sorry, women – would be preparing food all day.'

'But, damn, I forgot to pack my favourite pinny . . .'

'I'm sure we can rustle one up from somewhere in this enormous kitchen. Or . . . one of your little friends would have packed a spare, surely?'

'Well, one would assume so . . . after all, Bloomie likes to close billion-pound deals in her favourite apron. But you don't think it might, like, undermine this whole "cool" persona I've set up, you know? I mean, the Fonz doesn't cook.'

'True. And he is the coolest of the cool . . .' Jake says. He takes another sip of his coffee and makes an exaggerated, satisfied 'ahh' afterwards. I giggle. We lapse into silence again for a few seconds, smiling at each other. This feels familiar and just so . . . lovely.

He stands up. 'Would you like to help me make breakfast for everyone?' That's not something a smartarse bastardo would say. 'Then we'll be able to bunk off cooking duty and go to a local pub and play cards all afternoon.' Hmm, *that* is. But it is a good idea.

'Perfect plan!'

We head to the kitchen and in unison start pulling breakfast ingredients out of the fridge and pantry. Bacon, sausages, eggs, tomatoes, mushrooms, baked beans, bread. Jake starts by putting bread in the toaster.

'I wouldn't put the toast on yet, it'll get cold . . . Do the mushrooms instead like a good boy,' I say, filling up the kettle with water.

'You're even bossier than I am.'

'I said it charmingly,' I protest.

'I've never been bossed around so charmingly,' he says. He

leans over and puts the radio on. It's Jason Donovan's 'Sealed With A Kiss'.

'I love the music they play up here in the sticks,' I say, lining up sausages and bacon to put on the grill.

'We're in Oxfordshire, darling. Not Far East Kentucky,' replies Jake, chopping mushrooms briskly.

'When I first heard this song, I thought it was about sea eels,' I say. 'Because it's about summer, which means swimming, and I'd just found out that sea eels even existed, and it seemed to make sense.'

'Sea eeled with a kiss?' repeats Jake, and starts to laugh. 'What about . . . like a sturgeon?'

I laugh, and immediately go through fish names in my head to match up with song titles. All you have to do is think of a fish, sing the name in your head, and a song usually appears. 'What about . . . hake a chance, hake a chance, hake a ch-ch-ch-chance . . .'

Jake throws the mushrooms and a load of butter into the saucepan, and leans over to turn the radio off. 'Salmon chanted evening . . .' he sings.

And then, as breakfast comes together in a whirl of chopping and frying and toasting and buttering, I discover that Jake is irritatingly good at wordplay.

'When the moon hits your eye like a big pizza pie, that's . . . a moray?' (Me.)

'Pollack in the saddle again!' (Him.)

'Prawn in the USA!' (Me.)

'Who let the cod out?' (Him.)

I groan. 'Oh, dude . . .'

'Uh-oh, Minxy, looks like you can't think of one . . .' he says, chopping bread. 'My turn again. Prawn to run!'

'I just said Prawn in the USA. You're just repeating my fish and my artiste!'

'Different song. It's a song game, not a fish game. Sing a song or accept defeat.'

'Ummm . . . Shark the herald angels sing . . . ?'

'I see you, baby . . . shakin' that bass . . .' He starts shaking his bottom extremely unmusically.

'Oh dear, you're rhythmically challenged . . .' I say sadly. 'Ooh! Who let the dogs trout?'

'Not allowed, I actually used that exact song title. It has to be a different song. Same fish is OK, not same song. Don't look at me like that, Minxy, you know the rules as well as I do . . .'

'OK, OK. Let me think . . .' I pause for a minute. 'Get troutta my dreams?'

'Accepted! Hooked on an eeling?' Damnit, he had that one ready. I need to think.

'The hills are alive . . . with the flounder music?'

'We are whaling . . . we are whaling . . .'

That one really makes me laugh, and I can hardly get out my response: 'Cod put a smile upon your plaice . . . two fish! One song!'

'Bream a little bream of me . . . also two fish in one song,' he smiles smugly.

'That's the same fish, dude. That doesn't count!' I'm outraged.

'I'm not even sure I want to ask what's going on here,' says a voice behind us. I turn around and see Bloomie. She's all showered, dressed and pretty, and leaning against the kitchen table with her arms folded across her chest.

'We're cooking breakfast, clearly. And having a fish-song-title competition. Just as clearly,' says Jake.

'Clearly,' agrees Bloomie, coming over to give him a kiss and hug hello. As she leans over his shoulder she gives me an excited-child face.

I suddenly remember that I'm still wearing Ol' Grey and my boxer shorts.

'Well, I'm going to go and, uh, clean up. Can you take over from here, Blooms? I'll be back in 20 minutes.' I fill up my coffee mug and hurry upstairs to my room. I feel all smiley and giggly.

271

Ignoring that I had just woken up and looked like shit, that was just . . . so goddamn fucking nice.

I take a long hot shower with the usual routine. (I won't go through it, you must know it by now.) Make-up is Country Lite: fresh-faced and pink-cheeked. I am dressed as No Theme today. Battered old jeans, Converses and a thin-rib white Henley top. You can't have themes in the country. What would be the point? You'd just look a bit mad. (You have to have a theme in the city. Otherwise you'll just get lost in all the people.)

When I go back downstairs, everyone, apart from Jake, Tara and Perry, is sitting at the table having breakfast. Mitch, as usual, is holding court.

'I suppose, though, that the upshot of the story is that Wales is surprisingly pretty,' he nods sagely. 'You'd never think it, looking at the Welsh.'

'I'm half Welsh, Bitch!' shouts Bloomie, throwing a mushroom at him.

'Well, it can't be the top half, darling,' Mitch says, smiling a Cheshire cat grin.

I get myself another coffee and a banana from the fruit bowl, and sit down at the end of the table next to Kate and the new guy. He's tall, like Jake, but has a mess of pale brown hair and huge black-framed Harry Palmer glasses. He politely stands up as I sit down, causing much heckling from Mitch and Ant. Kate introduces me quickly – it's Sam.

'Oh, hi!' I say. 'I met you, briefly, at Montgomery Place that night.'

Sam looks confused. 'Oh, the night of Claudette's dinner party! It was fucking traumatic! She actually corrected my table manners at dinner. Twice.'

'Maybe they needed correcting?' I grin, taking a bite of my banana.

'No, I assure you, I have exemplary manners. Thank God Ryan was so keen to get us out bar-hopping.'

Ryan? Jake Ryan?

'Really?' I say. 'Did you make a bit of a night of it, then?'

'We just started at the end of Kensington Park Road and had a drink in each bar till we found you lot, actually. Hell of a coincidence, really.'

'Hell of a coincidence,' agrees Kate, glancing quickly at me.

'Can you all please stop talking about things that don't involve me?' shouts Mitch from the other end of the table. 'What the devil are we going to do now, anyway? No, Harriet, we are NOT playing touch rugby,' he says, closing his eyes and holding a hand up to stop her before she can speak.

'I'm going to get the papers and lie on the couch,' says Ant. 'A Saturday is a Saturday, after all.'

'Well, let's ask Edward what delights he's got planned for us this weekend then,' says Mitch. 'Edward?'

Eddie takes a long drink of orange juice, swallows it slowly, makes a cow-chewing-cud motion with his mouth and blinks a few times. 'Not much,' he finally says.

'Must I do everything around here?' says Mitch to the ceiling. 'Booze, tick, can buy that today, BBQ tonight or dinner party if it rains, tick, ditto, music, tick, everyone has iPods, right? What else could we need? A bouncy castle? Playing cards? Drugs?'

'No drugs,' says Eddie firmly.

'Fine, no drugs, which is good as I didn't pack them . . . though if you can't get ripped whilst enjoying God's countryside then where can you, I'd like to know.'

'No,' says Eddie.

'Fine. Have you written a list for food for tonight?' asks Mitch.

'Um . . . no,' says Eddie, eating a piece of toast. Everyone is watching this repartee like a tennis game, back and forth.

'Fucking useless. Well, you can do that now.'

'Can I finish my marmalade toast, please?'

'Who eats marmalade?' exclaims Mitch. 'Except Paddington Bear and my grandmother?'

273

'You guys are like a married couple,' says Kate.

There's a pause, and the boys look at each other with distrust, as though one might actually be secretly in love with the other. It's true: as we get older, Mitch is ever more highly-strung and naggy, and Eddie is ploddier and lazier, but they're still tied together. It is like a married couple.

'Someone has to clean up breakfast,' says Eddie. 'And someone has to drive into Banbury to get supplies.'

'No problem,' says Sam. 'Happy to do whatever is needed.'

'Me too,' chorus Bloomie, Kate and I.

'But Jake and I cooked,' I add. 'So, according to the rules of Eddie's Weekend Parties, we are not on cleaning duty.'

'We most certainly are not,' Jake agrees, walking in the kitchen door. I glance up and meet his eyes and we exchange smiles. His hair is wet from the shower, and he's wearing a navy shirt and old jeans. Mmm.

My attention is pulled away by Mitch saying, 'Right. I'll clean up. Then I'm going to do nothing all day till it's time to start drinking. Someone else can drive to Banbury for the food.'

'I'll do it. I just need some decent directions,' says Jake. He's standing behind the big island in the kitchen making himself a bacon sandwich. He catches me looking at him and makes a 'want one?' question with his eyes and hands. I shake my head no quickly and resolve to stop looking at him for awhile. Having him around with all these people is making me nervous. I need to wee.

'I'll help clean up. I've got to wait here for Eugene and Benoit,' says Bloomie. 'They'll be here in the next hour or so.'

'Looks like it's us four,' says Jake to Kate, Sam and I.

'And us!' says Harriet loudly. God, no. I can't take cricket talk and poor whipped Neil.

'Oh, do you really have to go, Harriet?' says Bloomie quickly. 'I was hoping you'd give me a quick rundown on the cricket last night. I was really sorry to miss it . . .' What a trouper. Talk about taking a hit for the team.

'Yeah, wicked!' says Harriet happily. 'Neil, we're staying here,' she says, without even looking at him. Poor whipped Neil nods.

'Oh dear,' says a clear voice. 'Have we missed breakfast?' It's Tara and her little-but-not-anymore-brother Perry. Tara is looking incredibly pretty. Her dark blonde hair is tumbling over her shoulders in shiny waves and makes her black tank top and black jeans look about a thousand times more glamorous than they ought to.

'Course not!' says Mitch quickly, getting up from the other end of the table. 'I'll make you a bacon sandwich, if you like.'

She nods and smiles. 'Hi, Mitch.'

There's a sudden tension in the air. Interesting.

'I'll have two, thanks, mate,' says Perry with a grin, walking into the kitchen. He and Mitch exchange some kind of masculine handshake slash hug, with a 'Good to see ya!' or two thrown in for good measure. I glance at Kate and see her staring at Perry with unabashed lust, and accidentally snort with laughter. The entire table looks at me, including Jake, so I quickly fake a coughing fit.

'Sorry . . .' I say, patting my chest.

'Dratted hayfever,' says Jake. I raise an eyebrow at him in response as Tara introduces Perry to everyone.

'We're going to go into the local town to get some food and drink for tonight, if you're keen,' says Kate to Perry and Tara. (Mostly to Perry.)

'Sounds good,' he says, smiling at her amiably. Tara's attention is taken by Mitch asking her how she likes her bacon, so Perry sits down and we all start chatting. It turns out he's just finished his law degree and is starting as trainee at a law firm in London in a few months.

'Lucky bugger. What are your plans for the summer?' asks Sam.

'I'm going to Florence, actually,' says Perry.

'Omygodispentayearthere!' exclaims Kate excitedly, before composing herself and adding, 'It was uh, pretty good. You'll love it. I mean you'll probably enjoy it . . . It's OK.'

I'm fighting the urge to giggle again, but I think Jake is looking at me, so I frown and make a 'how fascinating, do go on' face instead. Behind me in the kitchen, I can hear Mitch talking to Tara.

'So, how did you, uh, sleep last night? You're in the attic rooms, right?'

Hmm. I've never heard him make attentive small talk, ever. Down the end of the table, Bloomie is making her own version of the 'how fascinating, do go on' face at Harriet, who's talking about cricket, again.

Jake clears his throat. 'Well, no point sitting around here,' he says. 'Let's go and discover what Banbury has to offer. Someone make a list. Me. I will make a list. OK, shoot.'

'Why don't we just make spaghetti bolognese?' suggests Eddie. 'It's so easy and my recipe is awesome.'

'No,' say Jake and I in unison.

'It's the sundried tomato paste! And cashew nuts. And just a pinch of cinnamon.'

'No,' we say again. I meet his eye and grin. I wonder if he hates spaghetti bolognese as much as I do.

Everyone starts calling out ideas for tonight. The general plan is to have a BBQ – the weather forecast is warmish, a bit sunny with a chance of rain (ie, pretty much the same forecast you'll get anywhere in England from May to September) – which means we need meat, fish, salads, bread, alcohol, and more breakfast supplies for tomorrow. Jake writes everything down.

'How many people are definitely coming?' I ask.

Eddie starts counting on his fingers and pointing at people around the table. 'You, me, Kate, Mitch, Jake, Sam, Bloomie, Harriet, Neil, Tara, Perry . . . Eugene and the French dude Benoit are on their way now, plus the Irish guys are arriving from London tonight and let me think ... who am I missing?'

'Morning all,' says a booming voice. 'Where's the scran?' It's Fraser. He's showered and dressed, and looking smug, if slightly fatigued.

'Fraser and Tory,' I say flatly. 'You forgot them.'

Tory walks in behind him wearing an obscenely short, tight pair of pale-brown velour shorts and a matching tight velour zip-up hoody. Juicy Couture via Primark. Her hair is in a very obvious I've-been-fucked-all-night hive, and her chin is red from stubble rash. She's clearly not showered, and smiling coquettishly, sits down in a chair in the middle of the table near Sam and Jake, who both do the polite standing up thing. Nice manners.

'I'm Tory,' she says to them with a lascivious smile, pulling one knee up to her chin in what is clearly meant to be an unintentionally sexy move. 'I slept SO WELL!' she adds, yawning and stretching so her top unzips slightly, revealing some rather veiny boob.

'Toto,' calls Fraser from the kitchen. 'How do you like your eggs, darling?'

'Unfertilised, I imagine,' I say under my breath to Kate.

'Shopping expedition meeting outside in ten,' Jake says, standing up.

'Shotgun,' I say.

'You can't call shotgun until you see the car,' he says.

'I pre-call it.'

'You can have the damn shotgun,' says Kate, rolling her eyes.

'I can take our car, too,' suggests Perry. 'More room.'

'Great idea!' exclaims Kate.

Kate and I head out of the kitchen together and upstairs to get money and jackets. As soon as she closes my bedroom door, I turn to her with a dirty smile.

'You were undressing that boy with your eyes.'

'I know!' she crows delightedly. 'It's so much fun. Am I flirting well?'

'Perfectly,' I say. I flop down on the bed and sigh deeply.

Kate sits down next to me and mimes flipping a coin. 'Heads, Jake . . . Tails, the Sabbatical. Heads, Jake . . . Tails, the Sabbatical . . .'

Either way, it's a gamble. I pointedly ignore her, and close my eyes. Kate prods me.

'Please make me pretty for Perry?'

I open my eyes and get up off the bed. 'I saw Sam looking at you quite a bit.'

'Seriously?' she says. 'I was too busy gazing at my soon-to-be-preciousssss to notice . . . Tell me more about Jake. Have you talked to him about the Botanist thing yet?'

Urgh. The Botanist thing. I grab my make-up bag from the vanity table, and we sit on the bed.

'No, I have not . . . Touch of blush, bronzer, mascara? All very natural, obviously . . .'

She nods and I get started.

'So your Sabbatical is totally over now . . .' she tries again, trying not to move her face or lips.

'No!' I say. 'No, no, no. I just think Jake is a bit, um, good looking . . . that's all. It would all go tragically, epically wrong if I actually dated him.'

'Very healthy way to approach things, real positive. If you wouldn't end it for Jake, who would you end it for? Or do you want to end up bitter and alone and miserable?'

'I will anyway, because my relationships always end,' I shrug. 'I am doomed to it.' I don't feel as nonchalant as I'm pretending to be. If not Jake, then who indeed? Can you be on a voluntary Dating Sabbatical your whole life? Is voluntary romantic and sexual solitude better than certain heartbreak and crushing disappointment?

'Can you be serious for one fucking second?' snaps Kate. I thought

I was being serious. 'Do you want to never ever fall in love, never have sex, never get married and have kids, anything? Because that's how you sound.'

I sit down next to her on the bed and hide my face with my hands. 'I don't . . . I don't know . . . I feel so stuck . . . I . . . I . . .' I can't finish my sentences. I don't know what to say. No, I don't want to be alone forever and ever, and I certainly don't want a life without sex (sex. God! I miss thee), but I couldn't take another rejection either. 'Let's not talk about it,' I finally say.

'Just don't reject Jake automatically, OK? Just . . . just judge him on his own merits. Not on everything that all the other fuckwits did. Especially not Rick.'

'OK,' I mumble.

Kate hurries off to get a jacket for the shopping trip, and I clean my teeth, put on some lipbalm and grab Bloomie's leather jacket. I'm feeling a little low all of a sudden, but I force myself to skippy-bunny-hop down the stairs and through to the kitchen. Eddie and Mitch are washing up and singing happily along to Elton John's 'Don't Go Breaking My Heart' (Mitch is tackling the Kiki Dee part with gusto), which is a sight a little too strange to even comment on. Fraser and Tory are still tucking into breakfast and smirking at each other. Bloomie is still at the end of the table with Neil, listening to Harriet talk about cricket. I have to save her.

'Oh, Bloomie, there you are . . . ! Sorry to interrupt, Harriet, but Eugene just texted me that he's lost. You may want to give him a quick ring, Bloomie.'

'Really?' she says, her face brightening. 'I mean . . . oh, dear. Men! Sheesh!' She gets her phone out of her pocket. 'Oh yes, it's been on silent, silly me, five missed calls . . .'

She dashes outside quickly. I smile at Harriet, then quickly turn and walk out of the kitchen to the cars outside, where everyone else is waiting.

Chapter Twenty-Seven

The drive to Banbury only takes about 25 minutes, and Sam and Jake regale me on the way with stories about their journey last night, till my stomach aches from laughing. It turns out Mitch was in charge of directions, with Jake driving.

'And finally, Mitch asked for directions in some tiny town at about, like, 11 pm,' says Sam.

'Usually I am anti-direction-asking, as it's part of the contract of being a man,' interjects Jake.

'But it was getting ridiculous,' says Sam. 'So Mitch gets out and asks "Where are we, mate?" and this guy says "Bryngwyn". And Mitch says "Where's that?" and the guy says "Way-ales".'

'And Mitch says "FUCK. OFF," and gets back in the car,' says Jake.

'It was another half hour before we established that we were, in fact, in Wales,' finishes Sam.

'Never again,' Jake finishes. 'My cousin, apart from having the sexual morals of a stoat, has the sense of direction of a brick. And he said he's been here dozens of times.'

'He has,' I say. 'Though in his defence, we don't come that often these days.'

'It's an amazing place.'

'Yeah. It's the perfect weekend party house. We spent almost every university holidays here.'

'Is that back when you and Eddie were an item?' asks Jake lightly.

'No!' I say, laughing. 'That was 12 days of true, true love in October of first-year university.'

He shakes his head. 'Yikes. Tough break-up.' He looks over at me quickly. 'Why'd you kids end it?'

'Hmm . . . because we didn't fancy each other, I guess,' I say. 'It was the first time either of us had met someone of the opposite sex we found funny. Anyway, we got along so well, we just thought we ought to go out. But the kissing was just . . . ew.'

Jake smiles, but doesn't laugh like I hoped he would. 'Are you from around here originally?'

I shake my head. 'Born in London. My folks moved to Berkshire in my teens, and I moved back as soon as I possibly could. You?'

'Somerset,' he says, glancing over at me.

'Oh, tough break . . . I'm so sorry . . .' I say.

'Somerset is really very beautiful, I'll have you know,' he retorts huffily. 'Certainly more beautiful than Latimer Road or what-ever pothole area you were born in.'

'I'm from Surrey,' pipes up Sam in the back. 'If anyone is talking to me anymore.'

Double yikes, we were almost having a personal conversation there. Jake must think the same thing as he quickly veers back to driving-with-Mitch stories. I look at his hands on the steering wheel as he drives. Is there anything about him I don't find impossibly attractive?

Banbury is busy enough to be cheerful (nothing is more depressing than a lifeless English town on a Saturday), but we're here early so we easily get a parking spot.

'I know it's radical of me, but isn't there a Sainsbury's out here in the wilderness? Do we have to go to market, to market?' says Sam as we get out of the car.

'We're supporting the local economy,' I say, pursing my lips to look pious. 'Farmers. And butchers. And . . . fishers.'

'Fishers?' says Sam.

'Is this one of those choose-your-own-rose-oak-smoked-duckling-non-denominational-co-operatives farmers' markets?' says Jake. 'I've read about them.'

I nod, thinking quickly. 'Lemongrass-infused balsamic vinegar . . . laced with lavender poo. Hand-crushed albino-watercress pesto. Made by one-legged widows in the next town over.'

'Are you serious?' says Sam.

'Sausages with the name of the pig that they came from handwritten on the package. By the pig itself,' says Jake.

'Jeez, Sam, I thought you'd know this stuff,' I say, shaking my head in disappointment. 'It's pretty basic.'

'God, where did you two find each other?' groans Sam. 'It's too much.'

I can feel my face going red.

'How about this?' says Jake, as Perry and Kate walk over to meet us. (She's looking pretty giddy with excitement. I'd say she's been practising her flirting.) 'We tear the list in half and split up. Meet back here in half an hour.'

'And we'll take care of drink,' says Sam.

'Ooh! Champagne!' says Kate excitedly.

'Too much champagne gives me a terrible stomach ache,' says Jake. 'Especially that pink Laurent Perrier one.'

'Laurent Perrier makes you ill? How ghastly for you,' I say sympathetically.

'It is,' says Jake. 'It's a living nightmare.'

'And does your bed of money make you itch?' I add, and start giggling helplessly at myself. I know I'm breaking one of my rules by laughing at my own joke, but the tension of the car ride seems to have gotten to me.

Jake raises an eyebrow at me. 'Yes, and the clock in my Rolls-Royce makes a terrible racket.'

'Enough, enough,' says Sam, prodding both of us to start walking. I'm still giggling, but I calm down soon as we start the serious matter of food shopping. Every now and again I catch

282

sight of Kate flirting with Perry, smiling kittenishly and asking his opinion on everything she picks up. I'm grinning to myself as I go to skip to the next fruit stall, trip over Jake's foot and fall sprawling on the ground.

'Are you OK?' says Jake. Sam is off talking to a stallholder about asparagus season.

'Ow! Ow. Ow. Ow. Ow,' I say, sitting up and brushing gravel off my palms. They're a bit grazed but not really bleeding.

'I'm so sorry,' says Jake, crouching down next to me. 'Is anything broken?'

'No . . . don't worry, happens all the time,' I say, getting up and pretending not to see his outstretched hand. 'I'm not very spatially aware.'

Forty minutes later, our cars are groaning with food and alcohol, and we set off back to Eddie's. On the way home Jake and Sam tell me stories about their friendship.

'We met at six, but Jake was the school dork,' explains Sam in a matter-of-fact voice, 'and his sister gave me two pounds to talk to him during breaktime for a month, so he'd be popular . . .'

Jake nods. 'It was like *Can't Buy Me Love*, you know? Only without the ride-on lawnmower. And it was Ribena I spilled on my white suede fringed cowboy outfit instead of red wine.'

I crack up, and slap my thigh with glee. Ha! Some men really do know their 80s films.

We get home to discover Eugene and Benoit have arrived, and they join Jake, Sam and Perry to ferry in the shopping. As soon as we start unpacking, we realise that both teams have picked up 'a few extras' that the other team either already had on the list, or also thought necessary. As a result, we now have enough food to feed four hundred people.

'Ça va?' I say to Eugene and Benoit in the kitchen, kissing them on both cheeks hello.

'Ça va,' they chorus. 'Tu parle Français?' adds Benoit.

'Non,' I say apologetically. Benoit looks crestfallen, and goes back out to the car to get the last loaves of bread.

'What's for lunch?' calls Eddie from the lounge room.

'Four kinds of ham, five different cheeses, two pasta salads, three roast chickens, some pâté, and about nine loaves of bread.'

Eddie wanders in yawning, with one hand under his shirt scratching his tummy. He and Ant have clearly been festering all morning in front of the TV. 'Shouldn't we save some of that for dinnerofuck?' he says, as the sight of his food-filled kitchen greets him. 'Lunch buffet it is.'

My eye is caught by a couple drinking tea and chatting at the garden table outside the kitchen. It's Mitch and Tara. I can see Harriet and Neil playing croquet on the far side of the lawn – God, does she do anything that doesn't involve competition – which leaves only one couple unaccounted for.

'Don't tell me Tory and Fraser are back in bed,' I say.

'I'd rather they were in bed than in here,' Bloomie replies. 'Her breakfast attire was enough to put me off my food. And the irony that those shorts were a colour oft-called "camel" . . .'

'Toosh! Haut cinq,' I say, and we high-five each other.

Jake looks over from the kitchen quizzically.

'It's "high-five" in French,' I explain. 'We're, like, totally bilingual.'

'Mon dieu,' he says. 'Ou est le fromage, anyway?'

'You speak French, thank God,' says Benoit, coming back in to the kitchen, and launches into a question about English cheese. Jake follows extremely politely, and tries to answer as best he can in schoolboy French.

'You don't speak French,' says Benoit blankly, when Jake finishes with an 'erm, oh, bof'.

'Non,' Jake hangs his head in shame.

'Dommage,' says Benoit. 'No French, no dating . . .' he adds, gesturing at Jake and then me. Benoit turns and leaves the kitchen again. I can feel myself blushing again.

Jake turns to me. 'I'm so ashamed. How does he know no one wants to date me?'

Perhaps Jake doesn't know about the Sabbatical after all. Perhaps Mitch didn't tell him.

Within 20 minutes, the kitchen table is piled high with food, and we all take our plates outside to sit in the garden and on the outside table and chairs. The day has turned sunny and still, and birds are twittering happily. It's the picture of an English garden in early summer.

'Mmm. Bucolic bliss,' says Jake contentedly as he chews the last of his sandwich, leans back on his chair and puts his hands behind his head.

'You must be drowning in this kind of thing in leafy Somerset,' I say.

'Oh, yeah. Drowning. It's boring. So boring,' he murmurs, closing his eyes.

I want to gaze at him, but force myself to turn to talk to Bloomie, Benoit and Eugene. Mitch and Tara have slipped quietly inside and are sitting at the kitchen table eating sandwiches with Kate and Perry. Sam appears to have fallen asleep on the grass.

Eugene and Bloomie seem to be in good form, with lots of secret hand-holding and cheek-nuzzling. Bloomie is not carrying her BlackBerry – for the first time in years – and has deliberately steered away from any work or recession conversations. It might be obvious, but at least she's trying to show him that he's more important than work.

There's something almost magical about a weekend away like this. It's like stepping outside your life and all its stresses and worries, like they can't touch you. Bloomie is laughing more than I've seen her in ages, and Kate's little worried frown that she wears in quiet moments lately – thinking, I'm sure, about the chances of losing her job – has disappeared. Even I feel more relaxed than usual. It's just so easy.

I lean back on my chair, tuck my legs under me and gaze up

at the perfect, pale blue sky above my head. Then I look over at Jake again, and stare for a second at his quiet sleeping face. His eyes are still crinkly at the sides, even when they're shut. He must smile a lot, to have crinkles like that. Suddenly, Jake turns his head and looks straight at me. For about two long seconds, we lock eyes, and then I lose my nerve and look away. The heart-hammering thing is back.

Eugene and Benoit are telling a story about a previous driving holiday they took together in Biarritz in France. The holiday started with Eugene swimming in the sea with the car keys in his pocket, thus losing them, so they had to wait two days for Hertz to arrive with a spare set. They then drove over three chickens on the road, again Eugene's fault, so the car was covered in feathers and blood. Then Eugene lost the map, his wallet, and Benoit's phone, all separately, but all in the same day. And finally, over breakfast on the sixth day of the holiday, Eugene ate the last of Benoit's carefully-prepared Nutella on toast. 'That was it,' says Benoit. 'He was on my nerfs.' Apparently Benoit stood up, pushed everything from their breakfast table onto the floor, walked out of the hotel and drove back to Paris alone.

We're all laughing so hard by now that Mitch has come out with Tara to see what's going on.

'I waited for two days for him to come back,' says Eugene in a sad voice. 'And I'd lost his phone and the hotel didn't have wifi. So I couldn't call or email him.'

'God, life was tough back then,' sighs Bloomie. 'No wifi in hotels. Coal for breakfast.'

'Right, full story, please,' says Mitch, ambling over with Tara. 'I didn't think it would be funny, so I didn't listen, but now it sounds very funny and I want to hear the whole thing.'

'Hello, treacle,' I say, smiling up at him. 'You're awfully smiley today,' I add, glancing pointedly from him to Tara, who's chatting to Bloomie, and back.

'So are you,' he retorts, glancing equally pointedly from me to Jake, who seems to be dozing again, and back.

I stand up.

'I'm . . . going to stretch my legs,' I say.

'I'll come with you, Sass,' says Kate.

'I'll come too,' says Sam. 'Didn't someone say something about an afternoon in the pub?'

'I'm in,' calls Tara.

'Me too,' says Mitch quickly. 'Come on, Ryan,' he adds, prodding the reclining Jake with his toe. 'Get up.'

Eddie and Ant have already agreed to play tennis with Harriet and Neil, and everyone else says they're going to have a nap (winkwink) instead or really going to have a nap. So the six of us head off for the local pub on foot.

Chapter Twenty-Eight

The local pub is only a short walk away, but Mitch, of course, won't listen to Kate and I and insists he remembers exactly where it is. Twenty minutes later, we're still walking.

'I was confused!' he says. 'Now I know exactly where we are. The Rat and Reacharound is along this road and to the left.'

'The pub is called the Rat and Reacharound?' says Sam.

'No,' I say. 'It's just that Mitch can't remember the name of it, so he always makes up a revolting little nickname.'

'We're giving you five minutes,' says Jake. 'Then the women are in charge.'

In case of speeding Aston Martins and Porsches arriving unexpectedly, a genuine concern in this particular part of Oxfordshire, we're walking in twos along the side of a little road. Mitch and Tara first – she keeps looking around and giving Kate and I amusingly worried looks as Mitch strides confidently ahead – Kate and I in the middle, and Sam and Jake behind us. The sunny morning has become a little bit cooler and cloudier, but they're fluffy kids-drawing clouds that nobody could possibly mind.

After a few more minutes Mitch stops short.

'Fine. Where do YOU think that the Parrot and Pudenda is, then?'

'It's back about 500 metres and then we take the road the other way and then turn left after a wooden sign,' says Kate quickly. 'We walk down a little road behind some trees and we'll be there in about two minutes.'

She's right, and we are. The pub is actually called the King's Arms and it used to be a scabby old place that smelled like beer and urine. On our trips to Eddie's during university holidays we made ourselves very unpopular with the two old men who drank there quietly every night by being too raucous. There was a threadbare pool table and uncomfortable wooden seats. The two old men didn't talk to each other, just sat on opposite ends of the bar and stared at us. The landlord told us that they'd had a fight in 1963 and never made up.

Then, a couple of years ago, the landlord sold it to a Londoner looking to move his family to the countryside, and now it's just delightful. If you hate pubs being gastro-ed, I'm sorry, but you might just tolerate this one if you saw it: they've restored the original fireplaces, stripped out the deathly carpets and put in some long handmade tables and comfortable chairs. It still has soul. But now it smells good.

The happiest news of all, Eddie told us a year or so after the refurb, is that the two old men who hadn't spoken since 1963 bonded over a shared hatred of the new decor and owner, and now sit together happily every night talking about the good old days. So that's nice.

Mitch stops outside. 'Ah, the Frog and Fisting,' he sighs happily. 'Two rules. Girls have to drink beer. And secondly, girls have to drink beer.'

'Women,' I say.

'Whatever.'

The pub is almost empty, with a table of two older couples taking a much-earned break from a day of walking. We set ourselves up next to the fireplace – which has a little fire in it, which is wonderful as even though it's summer, it'd be depressing to sit next to an empty fireplace – and Jake and Sam go to the bar. I find myself gazing over at them absent-mindedly.

'Enjoying the view?' says Mitch. I look quickly at him and at Kate, who was apparently gazing dreamily in the same direction. We both start to laugh, and have to calm ourselves down before they get back with the drinks.

'This is great,' says Sam happily. He's sitting on one side of me, and Tara is on the other. Jake is sitting opposite, and we have a quick but surprisingly painful bumping-knees incident under the table.

'Sorry,' I say.

'Oh, no, my fault, I sat down on your knees, I'm sorry,' Jake replies quickly.

'Oh, but my knees were lying in wait, so I'm sorry,' I say.

'No no, the fault was all mine. Stupid knees. I curse them.'

'Calm down, you two . . . Cheers everyone,' says Mitch, holding up his pint. We all toast and Jake catches my eye as he clinks my glass. Yikes. Whoops. Rule 3. Obvious flirting.

'I haven't been here since that summer right after university . . . remember?' says Kate. 'Mitch was so hammered that he started to have a fight with someone in the bathroom. We could hear him arguing and calling someone a tosser, and we were about to go in and sort it out . . .'

'No, no, no, didn't happen,' interrupts Mitch, putting his arm around Kate's head to smother her mouth and looking at Tara anxiously.

'And it turned out he was fighting with himself in the mirror,' I finish.

'It was very dark in there and the guy wouldn't get out of my way,' says Mitch, as everyone cracks up. 'I've matured a lot since then, anyway, you know.'

'You did the same thing last Christmas at my parents' house,' says Jake.

Mitch turns to Tara. 'This is a total character assassination,' he whispers. 'Don't believe them. I'm so much better than that.'

'Don't worry,' she whispers back reassuringly. 'I know.'

'Let's talk about someone who isn't here and can't defend themselves. Like Tory,' says Mitch.

'I can't believe Fraser brought her,' I say.

'That man just wants to be in love,' says Mitch.

'Can't blame him for that,' says Sam.

'Yes, but he should pick someone who isn't such a bike,' says Mitch.

'Is she?' says Sam and Jake in unison.

'I guessed by her breakfast attire,' says Tara. 'And by the way she was making eyes at poor Perry. He was petrified.'

'Why is it that a girl who sleeps around is a bike, and a guy is just . . . a guy?' says Kate. I think she wants to get off the subject of making eyes at Perry.

'That's not entirely true,' I say. 'I don't care who she sleeps with, it's her business, but she makes it ours by always talking about it.'

'She does seem to do her best to look rather . . . oversexed all the time,' admits Kate delicately.

'Exactly,' says Mitch and I in unison. 'And she brags about her exploits in a way that makes *me* blush,' he adds, glancing at Tara with a wide-eyed innocent look.

'Yeah, that's true, too,' says Kate. 'Last year she cornered me at a party and began asking if I'd ever considered swinging – I thought she meant swing-dancing, and said yes, and she got thoroughly overexcited and introduced me to her boyfriend.'

Everyone roars with laughter at this.

The conversation, from here, predictably moves to gossipy sex stories, of which Mitch has many. As usual with beer on an empty stomach, I start feeling a bit light-headed after just one pint, and Kate, Tara and I switch to red wine on the second round.

'I love Malbec,' says Kate dreamily.

'I know. And I love that you get change from a tenner for it here. In London . . .' Tara shakes her head. 'I'm thinking about giving up wine for the rest of the recession. I'll drink cooking sherry instead.'

'No mentioning the recession,' says Mitch. 'It's too depressing.'

I glance over at Kate. She has her little worried frowny face back. Oh no, I hope this doesn't destroy everyone's blissful weekend-escape feeling.

'Everything will be fine,' says Jake. 'Two of my brothers were caught in the last recession, in the early 90s, right out of university. And they were fine.'

'Like fuck they were, I remember those years,' says Mitch. 'They babysat me constantly to earn extra cash. I swear sometimes my parents were just driving around the block all night and pretending to have a social life. I mean, they're not that popular. Dad especially.'

'They credit your parents with keeping them in beer and cigarettes,' nods Jake. 'Helped them survive.'

Everyone is silent for a moment, contemplating what we might have to do to survive this recession. We've all always had it so easy.

Jake attempts to lighten the mood.

'One day, sooner than you think, it will be over,' says Jake. 'We just have to sit tight and wait.'

Kate looks slightly relieved. 'Really?'

'Yes,' he says. 'And it can be a good thing . . . Patrick – my eldest brother – worked as a bartender to earn cash, and volunteered at a charity for six months. Great experience.'

'And, if you want to be cynical, it looks very worthy on his CV,' interrupts Mitch.

'The point is everyone will be absolutely fine,' says Jake pointedly. Kate looks deeply reassured. I smile at Jake gratefully, and he gives me a barely perceptible wink. I've decided that he is, in fact, a very nice person and not like Rick at all. This does not mean I should go out with him. Perhaps we can be friends. Oh shit. Rule 7. No new man friends.

Sam produces a pack of cards, and we start playing poker. The conversation continues in its usual funny, silly way. Mitch's getting louder and more outrageous every minute. He's drinking wine with us, whilst also enjoying his beer 'for propriety's sake'.

'Flush!' I say proudly.

'That's not a flush, Minxy,' says Jake, leaning over me.

'Yes, it is,' I say.

'No, it's not,' agrees Mitch. 'Why are you calling her Minxy? . . . Oh! I know!'

'Dash it,' I say, trying to think of a way to distract Mitch so he doesn't continue the Minxy route of conversation. 'I hate poker. I'm going for a fag.'

My ruse works.

'How I wish you girls wouldn't smoke,' says Mitch petulantly. 'You smell like a betting shop in Birmingham half the time. The other half of the time you smell like angelic flowers.'

Kate and I look at him in astonishment. 'We don't really smoke!' we chorus indignantly.

'We only smoke when we're drinking!' I say.

'That's simply not true,' says Mitch.

'Or in a crisis,' adds Kate.

'Ah, you chicks and your crises,' sighs Mitch affectionately. 'Speaking of, I completely forgot to ask about the Botanist Bust-Up!'

I feel Jake and Sam glance up at me and I shoot Mitch a warning look. God, he's annoying today. 'No. It's not a conversation for today. Possibly ever.'

'Can I have a cigarette, too?' says Tara quickly, standing up and putting her hand on Mitch's shoulder. He looks up at her adoringly. Perhaps that's a secret way of getting him to shut up. I must try it.

'Of course!' I say. 'Come on. Let's go and have a lovely smelly nicotine cancer stick.'

Kate, Tara and I head outside to a little seating area that must be wonderful on the few days a year when it's hot and sunny enough to eat outside. It's late afternoon now, and getting cold. The fluffy white clouds we saw earlier have had dark grey, angry-looking babies, and they're taking over the sky. I shiver and zip up Bloomie's leather jacket.

'What is the Botanist Bust-Up?' says Tara. 'I can see you didn't want to talk about it inside but . . . Do you mind if I ask?'

'Not at all,' I say, smiling. I really don't. 'Um . . .' I start, handing Tara a cigarette and lighting it for her. 'I had a drink with a fuckwit ex last week, and he was, yes, a fuckwit, and we had a fight, and I threw a glass of wine in his face.'

'Fantastic!' she grins, exhaling quickly. Amateur smoker. 'Fuckwit ex-boyfriends should have their eyebrows shaved or something, so we can identify them easily and avoid them.'

'I agree,' says Kate. 'But what about when their eyebrows grow back? Then they'll be mingling in normal society.'

'Maybe they should have a finger cut off for each woman they've messed around,' I suggest. 'So you'll know how mean he is by how many digits are left.'

'I love that idea,' says Tara. 'It would have helped me avoid my ex. He had a rap sheet as long as . . .' She stops, searching for the right word.

'His johnson?' I suggest.

'A lot longer than that,' she says, laughing.

'So what's with you and Mitch?' I've been dying to ask, and it finally feels like the appropriate moment.

'I don't know . . . I fear he has his own rap sheet I wouldn't want to see,' she says.

'Not at all,' says Kate loyally. 'Mitch hasn't messed around any girls, per se. He never leads anyone on.'

'He just avoids . . . entanglements,' I agree. It's the nicest way I can think of for saying he's a tart. 'I've never seen him act like he is with you, though.'

'Oh, really?' she smiles. 'Um, yes . . . well, he's been very . . .

we've been talking a lot over the past few months, for the first time in years.'

'Why did you guys break up, anyway?' I say.

She shrugs. 'I was still at uni, he was working in London . . . you know. It was a perfectly pleasant break-up. Well, at the time I was miserable, but I've gone through enough break-ups since then to know that there are degrees of misery.'

'Absolutely,' Kate nods.

'I'm not over-thinking it, anyway . . . I'll just wait and see.'

We finish our cigarettes and head back inside. The boys are in the middle of a very intense conversation, and all look up and around at us guiltily.

'Gossiping, boys?' I say disapprovingly.

'Never,' says Jake. 'We were just talking about, um, films.'

'Yes,' says Mitch. 'I was talking about *Terminal Velocity*. Such an epic.'

'Which one is that again?' says Kate, sitting down and taking a sip of wine. 'Those action films all have the same names these days.'

'Oh, I agree. Like . . .' I think for a second and then put on a deep, American-film-voice-over voice. '*Final Termination* . . . followed by the sequel, which is actually a prequel: *Penultimate Obliteration*.'

Jake starts to laugh, and puts on his own American-film voice. 'What about . . . *Fatal Demise*, and the sequel, *Incurable Fatality*.'

'*Sovereign Autonomy*,' I say, still in my deep American voice-over. 'Anything you say in the voice works, really. *Conjugal Matrimony*.'

Jake shouts with laughter. '*Collateral Repercussion* . . . is that good? What about . . . *Imperfect Conjugation*?'

'*Subliminal Deliberation*,' I say, almost laughing too hard to put my voice on. '*Imaginative Delusion* . . .'

'*Confessional Disclosure*,' says Jake.

'You two are nuts,' says Kate.

'*Unforeseen Revelation*,' says Jake. '*Unassailable Certainty . . .
Implicated Ramifications.*'

I laugh so much at these that I can't think of any more.
Everyone else is just looking at us. Not only are they not talking,
but they're not even laughing. Jake slowly stops laughing, too.
There's total silence.

'Well, I'm going to the bar,' I say.

'I'll come with you,' he says.

We walk over and smile at each other whilst waiting for the
bartender, an indie-looking dude who seems hungover as hell.
(You know what? I'm officially declaring Rule 3 null and void.
Obvious flirting is my Achilles' heel.)

'What the hell is that Hoxtonite doing in deepest darkest
Oxfordshire?' I whisper to Jake as the bartender ambles down
to the cellar to get another bottle of red.

'I think he must have taken a wrong turn at King's Cross,' says
Jake. 'I wish I was that cool.'

'You're definitely not,' I say sadly.

'I listen to totally cool music,' he says. 'Like, um, that Blunt
guy and oh, and The Stereophonics . . .'

I look quickly at him, trying to ascertain if he's joking. He is.
I grin, relieved.

'So, I thought you dealt with Mitch well back there.'

'Hmm?' I say, not really following. The ambling hipster is now
pouring the slowest beers I've ever seen anyone pour.

'The Botanist Bust-Up . . .'

I look quickly at Jake and flush. 'Uh . . . yeah. I can't believe
you saw that. It wasn't my finest hour.'

'I'll make sure to toe the line around you . . .' he says, grinning.
'Actually, Minxy, I saw that guy – do I call him your date? – arrive.'

'Not a date,' I say hurriedly. 'Your email was right. Ex-boyfriend.
Wanted a chat.'

'I figured . . . He bumped into my friend Peter and knocked
his drink all over him, and then instead of apologising, he called

him a twat. So when the crowd parted and we suddenly saw you throwing the wine at him, we were thrilled.'

'Oh God, he's awful . . . I thought I saw some guys laughing from my cab. Was that your friends?'

'Yeah, that was them. I thought you saw me as you were pulling up into Sloane Street, but I wasn't sure. You should have stopped . . .'

'I did, but I was not in great shape that night. You wouldn't have wanted to see me.'

'I always want to see you,' he says lightly, pushing my outstretched arm clutching my debit card away and giving the bartender a 20-pound note. 'Why do girls always pay everything with debit cards?' he asks.

'I'm pretty sure it's got something to do with menstruation,' I say, putting my card back into my wallet. 'Thank you, Jake.'

'That's the first time I've heard you say my name,' he says lightly, picking up two of the beers and turning around to head back to the table. I pick up the bottle of wine and the third beer, look up at him and smile.

Back at the table, everyone's somehow swapped seats, which means I'm now next to Jake. Kate and Sam are in a deep conversation about Italy, and Mitch is entertaining Tara with some private joke.

'OK. Do you want to play Snap?' says Jake.

'Maybe . . . Can you play Spit?' I ask.

'Is that a made-up game where no matter what I do, you'll still win? Because my little sister does that, and it's really annoying . . .'

'No, no, no,' I say. 'Look. You lay them out like solitaire, but only five rows, not seven . . .' I explain to him the rules of Spit, and we start playing. I beat him the first three times, but then, irritatingly, he starts to win. He gets faster and faster and the 'SPIT!' call and handslap at the end gets louder and harder, till I am laughing in mildly hysterical anticipation of the painful drubbing I'm about to get as we approach the end of each round.

'I am winning! I am winning!' he shouts.

'Change of rules,' I say quickly. 'Continuous Spit. When you finish, don't wait for the other person to pick up their cards, just deal and go.' As I say this, obviously, I am picking up my cards, dealing and starting the next game of Spit before he's had a chance to catch up.

'Get you, changing the rules,' he says. 'You're so dead.'

Ten minutes later, Jake has caught up and won every round, and has just two cards left to play with.

'You have to call him the winner sooner or later,' says Kate, looking over.

'I know, can you believe this?' says. Jake, gesturing at me shuffling my enormous hand of 50 cards. 'Although you have to admire her "never say die" attitude.'

I slam all the cards down. 'Fine. I'll let you win this time. Goddamnit, I hate losing Spit. It's the only sport I ever really play.'

'I don't know how to tell you this, but . . . it's not a sport,' says Jake. I'm about to retort, when I'm interrupted by Mitch stretching and making a big lion yawning sound.

'Once more unto the breach, dear friends . . . It's nearly cocktail hour. They'll be expecting us.'

I glance outside as I reach for my jacket on the seat behind me. It looks unnaturally dark for 5.30 pm. I look harder.

'It's not . . .' I say.

'It is,' says Jake. 'It's just started to rain.'

'If we run, and follow me, we can beat it,' says Kate. This is absolute rubbish, at least the beating-the-rain part is, but we all scramble out of our seats anyway.

'Natural born leader, aren't you?' says Sam admiringly, helping her on with her coat.

'After a pint and three glasses of wine, I'm lots of things,' she smiles coquettishly.

We stand in a huddle at the door of the pub looking out at the grey countryside. The rain is coming down a bit faster now, in quite fat drops.

'When I say go . . . GO!' says Kate, and starts to run. I follow her, with Jake and Sam at my side, and Mitch and Tara following behind, with Mitch calling, 'You didn't say go! You have to say it again!'

We run up the little road that the pub is on, and hit the bigger road, where Sam strides ahead to be side by side with Kate and Jake stays next to me. The rain is coming down harder and harder now, and the sky is getting darker and darker.

'You OK?' says Jake to me after a few minutes.

'Fine!' I call back, trying not to pant too much. The wine is sloshing around my tummy a little, but not too badly. The games of Spit slowed my drinking down.

Suddenly, Kate makes a decisive left turn.

'Are you sure?' calls Mitch.

'YES!' we all shout back. Ever noticed how brilliant it is to run in heavy rain? Seriously, try it. I'm completely drenched now, my Converses squelching and covered in mud. I look up at Jake. He's frowning to keep the water out of his eyes and his hair is all stuck to his forehead. Holy shit, he's sexy.

A sudden bolt of sheet lightning with an almost simultaneous crack of thunder makes us all jump and Tara lets out a scared giggle. The thunder was so loud that the storm must be almost on top of us.

'Nearly there, guys!' shouts Kate.

I hear a stumble behind us, and the sound of crashing into bushes. Jake and I stop and turn around. Tara tripped over something and is now lying on her back on the side of the road, laughing helplessly and looking up at Mitch in the rain. He's smiling down at her, with a look on his face that I have never seen before. I realise with a jolt that he's in love with her.

'Are you OK?' shouts Jake.

'I'm fine!' she calls back. 'Keep going!'

I turn and look at Jake. Simultaneously, we turn back and start running again. Kate and Sam are about 25 metres ahead now, and I recognise where we are. Only a few more minutes to go.

'Still OK?' says Jake.

'Yes!' I say, smiling up at him and noticing that the rain is getting even heavier when suddenly, Jake trips over something. He's about to go flying when I grab his hand to steady him.

'Thanks,' he says, slowing his running down slightly so as not to let go of my hand. For a second, I enjoy the sensation of my cold wet hand in his big warm wet one, and the feeling that we're running in unison. Then I start to feel like a retch-inducing scene in a romantic comedy, so I purposely take my hand away and pretend I needed it to wipe the snot off my nose.

We turn up the driveway to Eddie's house. It's really bucketing down now, and we sprint as fast as we can and crash through the open front door. We join Sam and Kate in the front hallway, dripping water everywhere and laughing breathlessly.

'Try not to mess up the hallway too much, children,' says Eddie, walking down the stairs with some towels for us. 'We've been having a really sophisticated time back here. Talking about art and literature, and whatnot.'

'Really?' I say disbelievingly, taking a towel and sponging off my face. I look at the towel. Yep, mascara is everywhere. 'I have to shower,' I say, and run up the stairs before Jake can see my panda face. (I know it's vain, but you know, one has to have standards.) As I get to the top I hear Mitch and Tara arrive.

'What is with the rain in this hellhole, hmm, Edward?' I hear Mitch opining noisily as I shut the door to my room. My drunky head wants to lie on the bed and think about Jake, but I'll just mess it up (the bed and my head), so I go straight to

the bathroom and strip off. Oh God, Bloomie's leather jacket.
I drape it carefully over the radiator – which isn't on, I'm not
that silly – lie the rest of my clothes over the bathtub to dry,
and have a long, hot shower.

Chapter Twenty-Nine

Next time it's raining outside, get all clean and wrap yourself in towels, and then get into bed. It's so goddamn cosy. I'm going to let myself have a little lie down and indulge in thoughts about Jake, without any guilt at all. I don't care if it's against the Sabbatical, I'm a little tipsy and I want to think about how lovely, lovely, lovely he is. I wonder if he has any hair on his chest. I wonder what his lips taste like. I w—

Just as I'm about to get stuck into some rather exciting thoughts, Bloomie bounces in, followed by a bathrobed Kate.

'It's meeee, darling!' Bloomie says, jumping on my bed. She's a tiny bit pissed, too.

'Hello Bloocinda,' I say. 'How did you survive the afternoon without us, then?'

'Well, it was ah-paw-leng, obviouslahhh,' she drawls, Posh-Mark style, and flops down on the pillow next to me. Kate stretches out at our feet. 'Eugene and I had a little nap . . .'

'Mm-hmm. Nice and restful, I'll bet,' I say.

'Yes, very restful, thank you, darling, how kind of you to ask . . . Fraser and Tory have also been in bed, pretty much all day, though, do you know, I think they may have been having intercourse rather than napping. And Ant and Eddie ditched their tennis with Harriet and Neil pretty fast, and started drinking with Benoit . . . How was the pub?'

'Ace,' I say.

'Mitch is in luff with Tara,' says Kate. 'And her him.'

'And I think Sam is in luff with Kate,' I say.

'Well, I think Jake is in luff with you,' she retorts.

'Rubbish!' I scoff. 'Though he is . . . nice.'

'How intriguing all this sounds,' says Bloomie archly. 'I can't wait to see it for myself. Now. I've volunteered us to cook dinner, so be snappy with the changing, hmm?'

Kate scrambles off the bed. 'Back in seven minutes for make-up, please,' she says.

'You got it,' I reply, as she closes the door behind her. 'Bloomie, about your leather jacket . . .'

'I already guessed, darling,' she says airily. 'A little rain is just going to give it more character.'

Bloomie flips through the American *Vogue* I packed (whenever I am staying somewhere remote, I need a really good fashion glossy to hand, it's like a security blanket) as I quickly change into some old-but-nicely-tight-around-the-bottom jeans and layer grey and white long-sleeved T-shirts. I add little pink ballet slippers, as my Converses are downstairs and absolutely sodden. Mmm, comfy. Theme-free but comfy.

I flip my head upside down to quickly blowdry my hair, and am slapping on some make-up just as Kate comes in to collect us.

'The Irish have just arrived,' she says. 'I love those guys.'

'Name?'

'Conor. Spud. The rhythmic gymnastic guys.'

'That guy's name is *Spud*?'

Kate shrugs.

After a few minutes, we go downstairs and into the kitchen, where everyone, except Jake and the Irish guys, as far as I can see, is sitting at the kitchen table with a few bottles of wine. Tara is sitting next to Mitch holding his hand.

He looks impossibly happy with himself, and whenever he says anything he glances at her to see her reaction. It's extremely endearing, and I'm just thinking about this, when out of the downstairs loo steps—

'Laura!' I exclaim.

'Ooooooooooh my God!' she squeals delightedly, rushing forward to hug me. It turns out my little Mac monkey from work, the one who entertains me with her dream-chatter every morning, is cousins with Spud.

'This is SOOO weird!' she says. 'Oh my God! How are you? It's so nice to see you! I mean, I saw you yesterday. But it's nice to see you again, you know?! This is the most amazing house! On the way up I was saying to Spud, this is so different to London. Like not in a bad way. But just so different! You know? It's no wonder there was always a country mouse and a city mouse. Because a city mouse would like, totally never survive here. I had to get a cup of tea the minute we arrived just to calm down!'

I grin at her and look around at Bloomie and Kate's speechless faces. The rapid-fire delivery of Laura's cuckoo commentary is remarkable when you first hear it, it's true. Then my eye is caught by Eddie. He's gazing at Laura with a slightly dopey grin on his face, and offers to show her to her room. Interesting.

Mitch stands up, holding his wine glass.

'I'd like to take this opportunity to thank you all for coming,' he says. 'I feel that it's incumbent upon me to take charge, as Edward will just sit back and get drunk. I'd like to propose we have a progressive dinner party.'

'We're going to swap partners?' exclaims Tory excitedly.

'No, my little flower,' says Mitch fondly. Tara and I snort with laughter and exchange a look.

'We're going to sit boy-girl around the table, and when I say, the boys will all move down two spaces.'

'So it's like musical chairs . . . but it's totally dependent on your mood?' says Bloomie.

'Gekko gets it,' he nods.

'Whimsical chairs,' I say, laughing and slapping my own thigh at my joke. No one else laughs. Sigh. I wonder if Jake would get it.

'Why?' asks Ant. 'In case one of us gets stuck with a dud all night, I suppose?'

Every woman in the room scowls at Ant in tandem, except Laura, who's peering myopically into her glass of wine. It's still pouring with rain outside, and any plans for a BBQ have been long cancelled.

'Boo!' shout two girlish voices in unison, and Eddie's twin sisters, Emma and Elizabeth, jump into the kitchen. Everyone shouts at once, and they start giggling. Apparently 'Mummy and Daddy were being so boring,' that they decided to come home early from Spain.

'Do Mum and Dad know you're here?' thunders Eddie.

'Yes,' says Elizabeth, rolling her eyes. 'We're only here for tonight, and then we're heading up to Ali's place in Scotland for the week.'

Emma is smiling shyly at Mitch. Oh dear. The last time she saw him was that night in Montgomery Place, months ago. Mitch turned up just as I ran away from Jake, and ended up snogging Emma. It caused a huge fight between Mitch and Eddie. Mitch now has a deer-in-headlights look on his face. Eddie, who never holds a grudge, seems to have forgotten about the whole thing. Thank God. Uber-protective big brother doesn't make for a fun party host.

The twins rush upstairs to unpack and shower for dinner, as they've come straight from the airport.

Bloomie, Eddie and I start cooking, and we're quickly joined by Tara. Actually, it's equal parts talking, changing the music on the iPod (lots of the Killers and MGMT), cooking, drinking and ducking to the covered part of the garden for cigarettes.

I'm coming in from one of our cigarette breaks when I notice Jake has arrived, and is sitting down the other end of the table next to Mitch and Sam, laughing at something Mitch is saying.

The twins come back in, all radiant expectancy. Then Laura arrives, followed quickly by the Irish guys, Conor and Spud, freshly showered and changed.

'This shindig can start now. The party facilitators have arrived,' announces Conor, looking around the room and making deliberate eye contact with every female except Harriet. Conor pulls up a chair between Emma and Elizabeth and starts twinkling at them, and Spud gets caught in a conversation with Harriet and Neil. Poor Spud.

Eugene and Benoit come over to help us cook, which seems to mean adding butter and salt to everything.

'You guys are such clichés,' I say.

'You cannot steam a steak, chérie,' replies Benoit.

Feeding a crowd this size verges on ridiculous. We've thrown all the sausages in a few pots with some beans, tomato, onions and garlic to make the biggest stew you've ever seen, roasted approximately 322 new potatoes, and grilled a few steaks, in case anyone thinks that stew isn't real food. And we've got enough bread to kill good Dr Atkins (were he still alive, God rest his soul). When it finally comes time to eat, it's past 9 pm. We've already drunk a case of wine, the crowd is nice and rowdy, and I'm keeping an eye on the various little dramas around the table.

Tara is sitting on Mitch's lap up the other end of the table, so Tory immediately jumps on Fraser, though she's considerably larger and Fraser doesn't seem particularly comfortable. Emma noticed the Tara-Mitch situation, of course, is very obviously surprised and upset about it, and is now whispering dramatic-ally to Elizabeth.

Eddie and Laura are in fits of private laughter. Perry, Conor and Spud are all flirting with Kate. Sam and Jake are talking to Tara and Mitch. Ant's been trying to talk to the twins, but they keep ignoring him, so he's sulkily cutting up bread. Harriet and Neil are talking to each other.

With dinner just about ready to be served, Mitch stands up,

tings his glass with a spoon and starts bossily arranging everyone. There's nine women and 12 men, which means some of the guys have to sit next to each other. I'm up one end of the table, near Bloomie, Kate and Tory, and for the first course, I'm sitting between Fraser and Sam. I look down and see Jake is next to Laura and Elizabeth. Eddie is down the end too, between his sisters, and trying not to look too put out about it. Emma is guzzling wine miserably and casting cow eyes at Mitch. Elizabeth is being chatted up by Benoit, and loving it.

'God, I'm shagged,' says Fraser, leaning back in his chair and taking a long drink of wine.

'Wrong tense, darling, you mean you were shagging,' I say.

He smiles at me and lowers his voice. 'Gosh, yes, Toto . . . She's so amazing. I think . . . I think she's the one.'

I smile back, thinking, oh, God no. Toto is so very not the one.

'That's wonderful, darling, I didn't know you two would have so much in common,' says Bloomie.

'Yah, and it's so nice being up here in the countrah,' he continues, gesturing at the pouring rain outside. 'I love it, I can see myself living up here, you know.'

Tory is sitting across and down a few seats from Fraser, and is now deep in conversation with Spud. Her voice floats up to us: 'I hate the country. The only thing I like about it is that you can shag outside and no one's around for miles. But that's kind of a shame too – it defeats the purpose of shagging outside!'

Fraser grimaces, and Bloomie and I get the giggles. 'Shut up, girls. Pass the bread.'

Mitch stands up again, and tings his glass to make another speech. 'Right. Before we start, I'm going to open some bottles of wine to save time for later. Hands up for red. Hands up for white. Hands up for beer . . . Eugene, mon dieu, you can't have both, this isn't bloody France, you know . . .'

I turn to Sam. 'This could go on for hours. Bonsoir, Sam, how's your evening? Would you help me carry the food to the table?'

'Very well indeed, actually, and I would love to,' he smiles. He's quite drunk, I think, and whispers as we get to the kitchen, 'Your friend Kate is lovely.'

'I know,' I whisper back. 'You should make a play for her.'

'I think I will,' he replies, and we start ferrying the big pots of stew and potatoes and the steaks in to the table. It all looks, I have to say, pretty damn good.

As everyone starts serving and eating, I sit down to discover Bloomie, Fraser and Eugene talking about online dating.

'If I hadn't met you the old-fashioned way – over a conference call – and I'd been single a few months, then I'd totally do it,' says Bloomie.

'No way! It's too weird,' says Eugene. 'The person you're meeting could be a serial killer. They could be a sex maniac.'

'Really?' interjects Tory excitedly, tuning in to the conversation.

'Dude, seriously,' I say. 'The odds are that the person is simply tired of meeting people drunk in bars, and has already tried it on with all their friends.'

'And friends' friends,' adds Bloomie helpfully. 'When you've exhausted all the options, why not try to meet someone online?'

'It's like . . . internet shopping. For a man,' I add. Then again, the old drunk-in-a-bar way always worked for me, I think, but don't add. I don't want everyone to start talking about me and dating. Or me and not dating.

'You should go to the Gumtree website. In the friends/dating page. That really is internet shopping for a man, and it's instant gratification – just find someone who lives near you . . .' says Tory dreamily. She sees Fraser looking at her, aghast, and quickly adds, ' . . . uh, I've heard,' and reaches for the wine.

Our attention is suddenly drawn by Mitch shouting at the Irish guys. 'Why do you guys keep picking on me? Huh? All I'm getting is shit from you. You just turn up, with your accents and your Irish charm, and – and your – and your . . .'

'Shut UP, Bitch,' says Tara affectionately. Everyone starts cheering and wolfwhistling at this, and Mitch stands up and bows.

Fraser raises a hand to get our attention back. 'Right-o. What sites would one, er, use, then? If one were to internet date?'

I start listing the ones I can think of, then notice he's surreptitiously typing the names into his BlackBerry and get the giggles again.

Sam clears his throat, and says, 'I had an internet date once', getting the attention of me, Bloomie, Fraser, Tory and Kate in one fell swoop.

'What happened?' says Bloomie.

'She was alright,' he says. 'I decided to try it a few months ago after I kept seeing girls for one date and either the conversation sucked, or I didn't fancy her, or vice versa . . .'

'. . . yes, yes, and then what happened? What was she like?'

'Nothing much,' he says. 'She was really nice, actually. Pretty, too. But then, I didn't really make an effort to see her, and she didn't make an effort to see me . . . and it fizzled, really.'

'Oh. So you rejected her,' I say.

'What? She could have contacted me!' he exclaims.

Bloomie, Kate and I shake our heads. 'Oh, no. You always have to call her. Always.'

'I would never, ever call a guy, or text him first,' says Kate, looking to me for approval. Yikes, I hope she hasn't really committed my tipsy dating wisdom from last weekend to memory.

'Oh, me either,' I say. 'Although Bloomie dared me to give my phone number to a bartender who looked like Andrew McCarthy when we were 24. I wrote it on a scrap of paper with eyeliner and handed it over and said "Give me a call if you wanna pull something other than beers sometime . . ."'

Everyone laughs.

'You did not!' shouts Sam in disbelief.

'OK, I didn't say that. But I did give him my number. And

309

obviously he didn't call. Which just confirmed my natural instinct that men have to do all the chasing.'

'Perhaps he didn't fancy you,' says Sam.

I frown at him in mock-confusion. 'How do you mean? "Not fancy" me?' Everyone laughs, which buys me a minute to recover. I'd rather fake arrogance than admit that the thought had never occurred to me. Is that genuine cockiness or simple stupidity? Or is it just that I've always said yes to dates, even if I didn't really fancy them?

Sam rolls his eyes. 'I thought you chicks were all, like, girl power and shit.'

'Of course,' says Kate. 'But feminist or not, it's programmed in us to let the guy chase.'

'I am a feminist,' I agree. 'But I still want the guy to make the first move. I just do.'

'Would you have called me after our first date, if I hadn't called you?' Eugene asks Bloomie.

She shakes her head. 'Never. Ever. And I also believe all that feminist shit,' she says.

'Wow,' says Sam thoughtfully. He stares at his plate, probably thinking about all the dates he didn't call, and we all focus on our food for awhile.

'OK . . . would you say "I love you" first?' says Eugene.

'You said it first,' grins Bloomie.

'I know. That's what I'm thinking,' he says. 'What if I hadn't?'

Bloomie shrugs. 'The guy always says it first.' Then she realises what she's said, and looks at me apologetically. I smile at her. It doesn't matter. Telling Rick I loved him was not only a mistake, it was a lie.

Sam looks up from the stew he's rather noisily enjoying. 'Now, that is ridiculous. Whoever says it first is brave. That's all.'

I'm silent for a second. That's a new way of looking at it.

Mitch stands up. 'Everyone, can I have your attention please! Men: pick up your plates and drinks and move down two spaces. Ladies: relax, make yourselves at home, you look great, I love your hair.'

'Already? But we haven't even finished eating . . .' protests Bloomie.

'We only have one course, darling, in case you haven't noticed,' says Mitch. 'Come on everyone, mush, mush.'

I'm now between Mitch and Benoit.

'Right. Tell us everything about Tara,' I say to Mitch.

'Nothing to tell, darling,' he smiles.

'You've gone and secretly fallen in love with Tara, fool!' exclaims Bloomie.

'Shhh!' he hisses. 'Don't fuck this up for me. It took six months of phone calls to get her to even see me. We only had dinner for the first time last week.'

'But you went out, like, years ago,' I say.

'It took me this long to realise no one else can ever compare to her,' he shrugs. I fight the urge to say 'aw'. 'And I'm not going to let anything fuck it up this time. She's perfect.'

'If you've been in love with her all these years . . . then why've you been such a slut?' asks Bloomie.

'Well, sex is sex, and I was single,' he smirks.

'More power to ya!' shouts Tory, who overheard his last comment. She leans up the table to high-five Mitch.

'That's all over now,' he says, looking up the table at Tara.

'What about Eddie's sister?' I say. 'She really likes you. You idiot.'

'That was a huge mistake, yes, but also, it was just a drunken snog in a bar,' he says, sighing. 'I feel bad but . . . what am I supposed to do about it now?'

'Just be sensitive,' I say to him. 'Don't snog Tara in front of her or anything.'

'I shall separate Tara from the party the first opportunity I get,' he says decisively. 'We'll go to bed.'

'The problem with this cassoulet is there is no duck,' interrupts Benoit, looking sadly at the stew.

'I'll toast to that,' says Sam, leaning across the table with his glass. It makes no sense, but we all join in.

I look up the table. Jake's now between Elizabeth and Perry. I do some quick calculations in my head. He'll be beside me next.

The room is getting noisier and noisier, and the kitchen windows are fogging up. A heated debate about g-strings versus pants starts up our end of the table. Ant, predictably, is very pro g-string, largely based on the airbrushed bottoms he sees in the lower-end lads' mags. Mitch is pro-pants, 'especially red ones, you know, the little red ones'. Benoit professes a liking for no pants at all.

'How's your lovelife, then, Ant?' asks Bloomie, as Mitch gets up and goes to sit near Tara again. I look anxiously at Emma but she's now talking to Perry. He's flirting with her, I think. He's a much better catch for her, and he's only 23.

'That's a rather personal question,' he replies. 'How would you like it if I asked you how your sex life was?'

'I'd slap you.'

'Well, exactly,' he says, buttering another piece of baguette and taking a big bite. Why can men get away with eating so many carbs? Why?

'Is that a single thing?' says Kate. 'You wouldn't believe how much I get asked if I've met any men yet . . . I thought it was just me.'

'Nope,' says Ant. 'It's singlism.'

'But I've only been single a month!' says Kate. 'It's so . . . odd. Like they're obsessed with my lovelife now whereas before they couldn't have given a damn.'

'Exactly!' says Ant, reaching his arm behind Kate to try to give her a hug. She squirms out of his sleazy grasp by hopping up to fetch a white wine glass.

'Oh . . . I didn't mean it like that,' says Bloomie. 'Sorry, Ant darling. I don't really give a damn about your lovelife, or your sex life.'

312

'Thank you, Bloomie darling,' he smiles sweetly. 'Likewise.'

'I love this wine,' I say, in a thinly veiled attempt to change the subject. 'Could you please pass another bottle, Benoit?'

Benoit rocks his chair sideways to reach the wine bottles on the kitchen bench and falls over. Elizabeth hurries over to see if he's OK, and Benoit, who had been looking quite fine and slightly embarrassed, immediately feigns pain in his shoulder.

'I did biology for A-level,' says Elizabeth earnestly. 'I think you should probably go to A&E.'

'I think it just needs a little rub,' says Benoit hopefully, and Elizabeth immediately starts massaging his shoulder.

'Cheers,' I say to Sam, and we clink glasses and drink.

'Mmm, this is nice . . . I did a wine-tasting course once,' Sam says. 'To meet girls.'

'Did it work?' I say.

'Not in the least,' he said. 'I just discovered that almost everyone who does that sort of course is a wanker. Or doing it to meet girls.'

We all start laughing, and then it's time for the guys to move again. The iPod is now playing French cover versions of 60s pop songs. We take all the plates into the kitchen as the guys move places, put all the cheese on a few wooden boards, and empty the huge bags of mixed sweets (Jake insisted on buying them at the market today) into large bowls. I look up the table at the crowd. No one is sitting where they're supposed to, the noise levels are higher than ever and I'm starting to feel a bit drunk. Emma is now in reluctant conversation with a very hopeful Ant and a confident Conor, though she's still casting sad cow-eyes at Mitch, who has his back to her and is sitting on Tara's lap. Tory is running the rim of her wine glass around her lips and throwing hot looks at Fraser, who seems to be trying to ignore her by eating all the cheese within forking distance and talking to Harriet and Neil about cricket. Laura is singing a filthy ditty up the end, causing Eugene and Spud to laugh hysterically, and Eddie can't stop looking at her and grinning from ear to ear.

'Hello,' says Jake, sitting down next to me, glass of wine in hand.

'Hello,' I reply. I can feel my stomach buckling. Goddamnit, I thought I had that shit under control.

'Delightful to see you again,' he says.

'You too. How's your evening been so far?'

'Marvellous,' he replies. 'I met the lovely Laura, who told me at length how totally like, lovely, really really amazing you are to work with, and how you stood up to some guy at work, and everyone thinks you're a superhero.'

'Ha,' I say, taking a handful of mixed sweets from the bowl.

'Ha? Well, I can see your conversational skills don't improve with wine, unlike my own . . .'

'OK . . . I was just thinking how lovely Laura is, and I've never really gotten to know her. And that I must look after her more at work, as I'm worried she's left out a bit. And that I'm so glad I stood up to that cockmonkey – the guy she's talking about – and that it's something that, until recently, I could never have done. And that I love liquorice allsorts, and I'm going to eat them first.'

'That's all you needed to say,' he replies, laughing. 'Is your brain always going in different directions like that?'

I nod. 'Sometimes it calms down . . .'

'That's good,' he says, and smiles at me.

And boom, my insides are tranquil again. It's about time. 'Tell me more about that end of the table, then.'

'Well,' Jake continues confidingly. 'Then I sat next to Perry, who makes me feel very, very old, and Tara, who seemed more interested in trying to hear what Mitch was saying. And the only other people near me were Neil and Harriet . . . who are just . . . I . . . words fail me.'

I stifle a laugh. 'No words needed. How fortunate for you that you're up here now.'

He nods in agreement. 'Extremely fortunate. I talked to Eugene a bit before dinner, too. Nice guy.'

'He's lovely,' I nod, chewing a liquorice allsort. 'Would you like an ersatz Malteser? How old are you, anyway?' I say. The wine and I have decided it's time to find out the answers to the questions I've had for weeks.

'Yes, thank you, and I'm 32,' he says, chewing.

'That's pretty old, dude,' I say, eating a sugary banana. 'What do you do for a living? And how the sweet hell do they make these things?'

'I thought we'd never ask each other this stuff,' he says. I smile. I really do feel completely relaxed. 'I work for a bank. But I'm not an arsehole. And I believe it's made from sugar, toxic e-numbers and fairydust.'

'Why would I think that you're an arsehole?' I say, trying not to laugh. 'Fairydust is my favourite.'

'I just have a feeling it's the kind of thing you'd think about bankers. And you, how old are you, what do you do, can I interest you in another glass of wine, and do you have any birthmarks?'

'I'm 28. I work for an ad agency. I'd love one. And yes, I have a birthmark the shape of Madagascar on my inner thigh.'

'How intriguing—'

'Hey! You two,' interrupts Bloomie. 'We're taking a vox pop here. Worst first date ever. Kate?'

'Um, well, one guy was like 20 minutes late to meet me, and when he got there he said . . .' Kate stops, and I grin, knowing what's coming next and how hard it is for her to say it. '"I'm sorry I'm late, I had to have a dump."' She shakes her head. 'Seriously.'

Everyone howls with laughter.

'I had a date with a girl who kept muttering and acting like something was landing on her,' says Eddie. 'Like this—' He starts nodding his head in a nervous tic, and slapping himself on the shoulder. 'Looking back, I realise she was completely mad.'

315

'Well, this isn't *that* bad, but I had a date once with a guy, and I didn't know his first name,' I say. 'I mean, I met him in a bar, and I didn't catch his name, and then we talked for awhile and he asked me for my number and then it was too late to ask . . .'

'Did you get caught?' says Jake, laughing.

'Yes. He asked me out for dinner, and after a few hours, he must have twigged, so he asked me outright if I knew his name and I said ". . . Ben?" He got up and walked out.'

'God, it's no wonder you're off dating, if that's an average night for you,' says Ant. I shoot a sharp look at him. I don't want to talk about the Dating Sabbatical right now. Not in front of Jake. Not at all, actually. And it's not just because of Rule 4.

'Alright, alright,' says Jake. 'A girl I was on a date with fell asleep in the toilet of the restaurant. I would like to say she was narcoleptic . . .' he pauses, and waits for everyone to stop laughing. 'But I think she was just drunk and bored. I had to ask the waitress to go and look for her.'

'Ooh, I've got one,' says Tory. 'I took this guy to a party on our first date, yeh? I had a great night, but then the guy I woke up next to the morning after wasn't my date. And get this: they'd been wearing the exact same shirt! Isn't that weird?!'

I laugh so hard at this that I get tears in my eyes, and even Tory starts to giggle at herself. The kitchen has reached new noise levels, and it's boiling. I take off one of my long-sleeved T-shirts and, out of the corner of my eye, see Jake looking at me as I do it.

'OK, my turn,' says Benoit. 'When I first moved to London, I dated a girl who told me on the first date she was into "the rough stuff",' he says. We all start to laugh. 'But I didn't know what she meant – I thought she was talking about a band. And then a few weeks later we . . .' he pauses delicately – '. . . went home together . . . and she asked me to pull her hair and smack her bottom as hard as I could.' He relates all this with almost no expression on his face at all, till we all fall about laughing and he starts to chuckle.

'Bloomie! You're up!' I say.

'Um . . . I was on a date with a guy and got a funny feeling he wasn't single . . . I don't know why, just a feeling. So I asked him, and he said "To be honest, I've been casually dating this girl for a few months". I found out, a month later, that he was married with a kid.'

Everyone gasps.

'Oh, shit. Should I take my wife and kids on my dates?' asks Jake.

'Ooh, and one more bastardo story, though it's not a date one,' adds Bloomie. 'But I was seeing a guy and he dumped me by simply deleting my Facebook profile and changing his profile to "single". Not that I could see his profile. Because I was deleted.'

'What kind of dysfunctional fuckwit would do that?' says Jake. 'And what kind of person feels the need to update their status every day? Jake is . . . eating porridge. Jake is . . . paying council tax. Jake is . . . chewing.' He drops his head to his chest and starts to snore.

As we're laughing, Bloomie leans over and whispers 'Jake is . . . a fish I'd like to bone' to me. I give her a shut-the-fuck-up face.

'You only hate Facebook because you're so old!' shouts Emma from down the table.

'Yeah!' shouts Elizabeth. They high-five each other. Emma looks cheered up, but how much is from wine and Conor's arm around the back of her chair, I'm not sure.

'Ouch,' says Jake.

'You like Facebook?' Ant says, turning to Emma. 'I'd poke you.'

Eddie looks thunderously at Ant and then to the windows, which are almost steamed up. 'I think it's stopped raining . . .' he says, craning his neck. 'It has! Everyone, outside! It's too hot in here.'

We all spill onto the damp lawn outside, lighting cigarettes, talking loudly over each other and laughing at Mitch trying to get everyone to arrange the dining room chairs outside so we can all sit down in order.

'Come on, people! It will be funny!' he's shouting.

Eddie runs back inside to turn on some outside speakers that his parents specifically hooked up for their many summer parties. He puts on someone's 80s mix, and Ray Parker Jr is singing 'Ghostbusters'.

Everyone is pretty drunk by now, and Bloomie and I start dancing, 80s-style (jerky finger clicks and kicks, lots of shoulder action) and singing loudly (badly) along to the music.

I look over and see Jake laughing at Sam, who is jumping up and down on the spot singing with his eyes shut.

Next on the mix comes Pat Benatar rocking out to 'Love Is A Battlefield'. Bloomie jumps on the long outside table and starts walking up and down it and miming as though it's a stage.

And then comes one of my favourite songs of all time: Guns N'Roses, 'Sweet Child Of Mine'.

Now, you may have the impression I have slight wallflower tendencies, because of the mantra and the nervous tummy and all that, but let me clear that up right now by telling you that when it comes to Slash, I am the air guitar queen, and nothing can stop me.

Within two seconds of the song starting, I'm on the table next to Bloomie, my air guitar down groin-level just like Slash and my head bowed in contemplation of the perfect wailing my instrument is giving me. Bloomie is Axl, singing along and leaning in to me like the perfect stage partner. As the song ends, I look up. Jake is talking to Sam and Eugene, and they're all looking up at us occasionally and laughing. In the back of my head a little voice tells me I might cringe tomorrow at the memory of this. I ignore it.

Still holding my air guitar, I glance around. Kate is over near the window having a bad 80s dance-off with Spud, Emma is leaning against the wall of the house drinking wine and talking to Conor and Perry, and Benoit is talking to Elizabeth and making pained, brave faces as she rubs his shoulder again. Everyone is talking and drinking and laughing. Shouts from down the other end of the garden draw my attention. Ant and Harriet are playing some form of tennis on the tennis court. I'm glad someone is finally doing something Harriet will like.

I look back to the house, as the next song starts – Billy Joel's 'Only The Good Die Young'. Bloomie and I glance at each other, wordlessly agree we don't know this one well enough to perform on stage, and get down from the table.

Eugene, Sam and Jake walk over to us, clapping. We smile and bow.

'No autographs, no press, no comment,' I say, holding up a hand.

'Where the groupies at?' says Bloomie in her best imitation of an American rock star. (Not very good.)

Sam and Jake start doing what appears to be a groupie impression, and Bloomie makes them pretend to kiss her shoes. Eugene is laughing.

I smile at him. 'I'm so glad . . . about you two,' I say. It's the wine talking slightly, but it's true. They really seem to fit together so well.

'Me too,' he says. 'I've never met anyone like her. She's incredible.' Again, a little of the wine talking there, but I know he really means it. He's not a dork at all, I think, looking at him. He's gentle and smart and just right for Bloomie. I hope they do get married.

Eddie and Laura run out from the kitchen carrying four bottles of different flavoured schnapps, a bottle of tequila and a bottle of Sambucca.

'LAYBACKS!' shouts Eddie.

Oh dear.

'Darling . . . really?' says Bloomie.

'My party, my rules,' says Eddie firmly.

319

'Atta boy,' says Mitch, who promptly takes Tara's hand and walks into the house.

'Right! Everyone! Sit down on the bench and lie your heads back on the table,' says Laura firmly. Wow, I hope she starts taking charge at work like this.

'Aren't you supposed to, like, make margaritas in someone's mouth?' says Kate, walking over with Spud.

'Not in Oxfordshire,' replies Eddie. 'Here we just drink the damn drink.'

Everyone comes over and sits down on the bench obediently, our backs to the table – I'm between Emma and Kate – and Laura scrambles up to stand on the table with one bottle of schnapps in each hand.

'Apple! Peach!' shouts Laura.

'Oh gosh, I hope we don't have apple,' murmurs Kate.

'Where's Mitch?' says Emma. Only it sounds more like 'wheresh mish?' She's hammered.

'GO!' shouts Laura. She pours the first two people's open mouths full of schnapps, and then moves to the next, and the next. When she gets to me I push my tongue up to block half my mouth so it fills up quicker and I get less schnapps. (Clever, huh?)

When I'm gargled, gulped, gasped and done, I stand up and nonchalantly look around for Jake. (It's an automatic reflex this evening, I'm more or less aware of where he is and more or less what he's doing at all times, without even thinking about it.) And wouldn't you know it, he's walking over to me.

'Did you enjoy that, Minxy?'

'Oh, terribly much,' I say.

Jake walks a step closer to me and reaches his hand out to my face. I look at him in alarm. He's going to kiss me? Now? Here? In front of everyone? Then he just wipes the side of my mouth with his thumb, and puts his thumb in his mouth.

It isn't as sexy a move as it sounds there. It's just sort of sweet.

'Sloppy schnapps pouring,' he says by way of an excuse.

I'm about to say something back when it starts raining again. Like this afternoon, but it doesn't do a gradual drizzle-drop-trickle-rain-pour-bucket-cats-and-dogs ascension of intensity this time, it just rains very, very hard, immediately. It's the kind of rain you can actually hear.

The song playing changes from Hall & Oates 'Maneater' to the Jackson 5 'ABC' in the same second that the rain starts, and everyone – obviously, truly drunk now – screams with delight and starts dancing in the rain. And then Conor takes a run from the other side of the lawn, drops to his knees and skids about five metres. That must hurt, but he jumps up and starts cheering himself.

And then it's all on.

The lawn is a blur of zigzagging people skidding, sliding and skating. Eddie runs into the house and runs out with a bottle of washing up detergent and a bottle of vegetable oil. (This is probably the moment at which the party gods named the weekend 'out of control'.) Within five minutes the lawn is a bubbling, oily mess; I'm skidding and sliding with the best of them. Conor – clearly a practised lawn slider – runs into the kitchen and returns a minute later carrying garbage bags.

'Lawnboggan! Lawnboggan!' is all he can say. Spud nods, grabs a garbage bag and slicks up one side with oil and detergent. He puts the oily side on the ground, sits on it and Conor bends over to push him towards the slight hill that leads down to the tennis court. As they reach the hill, Conor stops, and Spud skids down on his garbage-bag toboggan, shouting 'WEEEE', very butchly, all the way. Naturally, everyone else wants their own lawnboggan, too, and a good 20 minutes passes before we tire of it. Then it's time for more laybacks, and then more lawnbogganing.

It's still raining, we're all absolutely soaked, there's grass and mud everywhere, and no one seems to care.

I can see Jake, Kate and Sam stuck in a flower bed at the end of the garden, laughing helplessly. Eugene and Bloomie are in a

321

hedge behind a tree, snogging. And – I squint – it looks like Laura and Eddie are kissing against another tree. Elizabeth and Benoit are on the verge of snogging. Emma is serving herself and Perry more schnapps shots. Around them everyone else is sliding and laughing and falling over. All is chaos: it's like some hedonistic frat party from an 80s movie. Any minute now a girl will accidentally-on-purpose lose her bikini top, and a geek will lose his virginity.

I need a break. I turn around and start walking towards the house.

'Hello, princess,' smiles Conor, the man who started it all. He's now sitting happily on the garden table in the rain, covered in mud and grass, surveying the chaos he's created. 'Come here to me you, and have a little seat right here.' Crazy Irish syntax. He flashes a perfect smile, and pats the bench next to him. Ah, now I remember. He's rather successful with women. And knows it.

'You really are quite the party facilitator, aren't you?' I say, declining the seat.

'I have a gift for it,' he replies. 'And isn't everyone having fun?'

I laugh and decide to head inside for a cigarette, as it's raining too hard to smoke outside and the smell of a few cigarettes won't do much damage after everything else the kitchen has been through. Kate's also walking towards the house, so I make a smoking gesture at her. She nods and we go into the kitchen together.

Chapter Thirty

We sit down at the end of the kitchen table.

'I love smoking inside,' Kate says happily. 'Such a treat.'

'What's the story with Perry?' I say, lighting her cigarette and then my own. We can still hear shouts outside and the iPod has moved on to Glen Frey singing 'The Heat Is On'. Kate has a branch of some kind of plant stuck in her hair. I remove it silently and she frowns at it as though she can't for the life of her imagine where it came from.

'Not much,' she shrugs. 'He's drinking with Emma, apparently she had a fling with a friend of his in Verbier this year so they're mates . . . I still think he should be my first post-break-up kiss.'

'What about Sam?' I ask.

'He's too pissed,' she says. 'And he was a bit too . . . cuddly during the lawnbogganing when we crashed into each other.'

I start laughing. Too cuddly. Poor Sam.

'How's my mascara, by the way?' asks Kate. She has mud all over her face.

'Not too bad,' I say, licking a napkin and fixing a streaky bit of mascara. 'Me?'

'Here . . .' she says, doing the same for me. 'All pretty again.'

The music outside just changed to George Michael's 'Faith'.

'So. Jake?' she says, ashing her cigarette carefully.

I shrug. 'I don't . . . We'll have to wait and see, won't we . . .'

At that moment Jake comes in to the kitchen. Thank goodness he wasn't three seconds faster.

'May I join you for a cigarette, please?' he says.

'Of course,' we chorus, and he sits down with us.

'Enjoying the evening, ladies?' asks Jake, lighting his cigarette with practised precision.

'Are you an ex-smoker?' I reply.

He nods. 'You have to quit at some point. For me it was 30. That's when everything hits you and you have to grow up a bit.'

'How dull,' I say.

'It is,' he agrees.

'Is Sam the same age as you?' asks Kate. Outside, all the guys have started a game which seems to involve tackling each other as hard as they can. Sam is yelling at the top of his voice.

Jake starts to laugh. 'He's having a messy night, but yes . . . he's the same age as me. He's 32. He's not normally the drunkest person. I think he may just be a bit carried away with the excitement of it all.'

'He was a bit cuddly on the grass,' says Kate disapprovingly.

'She means gropey,' I explain.

'Oh, God, not really? Not groping the A-list bits?' says Jake in a shocked tone.

'No, it wasn't like that . . . it was just . . . cuddly.'

'He's a cuddly kind of guy,' says Jake. 'But he'll be mortified tomorrow if he finds out he made you uncomfortable. He's really not like that.'

Suddenly, Emma crashes into the kitchen. She's covered in mud and grass and is swaying slightly.

'Shashwhereshmish?' she says wildly.

Oh shit. 'Oh Em, I think he's gone to bed.'

She looks as if she might cry, but then starts convulsing and runs to the toilet off the pantry. A few seconds later follows the sound of violent vomiting. I shoot a horrified look at Jake and Kate and I run in after her.

'Darling, just get it all out and I'll put you to bed,' I say. 'You'll feel better in the morning.'

She can't reply, but I can hear her crying between her vomit-coughs. I pat her back as she vomits for awhile. Oh, being sad and drunk is a horrible thing.

'I'll look after her,' says Elizabeth, coming in behind me. 'She's OK. What a bastard Mitch is.'

'I know he seems that way, but I really don't think he ever meant to hurt her . . .' I say. 'He's carried a secret torch for Tara for years, and they went out years and years ago. He's far too old for Em, anyway. She can do much better.'

Wow. That's pretty fucking sound advice. Did I just say that?

Emma stands up and looks at me tearfully, and Elizabeth wipes the vomit off her face with toilet paper. 'Tara's his ex-girlfriend? Not new?'

'Yep,' I say. 'From years ago. But they only started even talking again really recently. So please don't be upset about it. It's no reflection on you.'

Emma nods tearfully, and she and Elizabeth pad back out of the kitchen and head upstairs to their rooms. I feel all motherly towards them. I hope Emma feels better.

I sit down at the table and light a new cigarette with a worldly sigh. 'Kids today! So. Where were we . . . What are the A-list bits, then?' I ask.

'Impressive work, you should be a Samaritan,' says Jake.

'I am the mistress of break-ups,' I sigh. 'Poor Emma. She's probably had a crush on Mitch since she was eight.'

Kate nods, and drops her cigarette into a wine bottle. 'Right. Speaking of crushes, I'm going to find my little precioussss, then it's time to get this first kiss over and bloody done with.'

She stalks out of the kitchen purposefully and Jake turns to me.

'What on earth is she talking about? She's kissing a . . . what, a hobbit?'

I explain briefly about Kate's recent break-up and decision that the first person she kisses will be Perry.

'That's a shame. I think Sam has a bit of a thing for her . . .' says Jake. 'And Perry, really? He's so . . . young. He should be with one of the twins.'

'We like them young,' I say airily, dropping my cigarette into the wine bottle. I suddenly remember that I am covered in mud. It's starting to crust and I'm freezing. I ought to go upstairs and change, but I really don't feel like leaving this table. Ever.

'Do you,' he says, grinning at me. I grin back. I've forgotten what he's just said. We're sitting in an empty kitchen, at a food-and-wine-strewn kitchen table, mess everywhere . . . but the only thing I can see in sharp, perfect vision is Jake. Mud-covered, impossibly desirable, crinkly-eyed Jake. Everything else is fuzzy. (This could, of course, be the drink.)

The song ends, finishing the 80s playlist, and everyone outside is too drunk and busy creating chaos to notice. Apart from the odd scream and shout, and the sound of the rain, the kitchen is almost completely silent.

Gosh, you could cut the sexual tension in here with . . . some kind of cutting instrument. Hmm . . . Huh? What – oh dear, my mind is wandering . . . I can't stop looking and smiling at Jake who is looking and smiling at me and we're looking and smiling at each other and it's very . . . tingly and nice.

'Come hither, please,' he says, leaning forward over the table.

'You're so masterful . . .' I sigh mockingly, but – I told you I like being bossed around charmingly – I lean my head towards him.

This is the best bit. This is the five seconds when you know, without doubt, that you're about to kiss someone for the first time, and you're not sure what it'll be like, but you're pretty sure it's going to be great, and you're smiling at them, and they're smiling at you, and it's just . . . the best bit. The anticipation is sometimes better than the kiss, in fact.

Not this time.

Because the kiss doesn't happen. With a crash, Tory storms into the room and I snap my head back just in time. She stomps through the kitchen without acknowledging either of us and goes straight out the door to the garden.

Jake and I look at each other. That was weird.

I'm hoping that we're about to pick up where we left off, when with a stompy huff, Fraser marches in after her.

'Oh, hullo, chaps,' says Fraser, looking surprised to see us. 'Haven't seen Tory, have you?'

'She's outside,' I say, hoping he's going to follow her.

'Good. I'll hide here with you two, then,' he says, ambling over to the table. Jake turns back to me and makes a what-the-fuck face that Fraser can't see, then turns back.

'Trouble in paradise, Fraser?'

'Uh, yes . . . can I have a fag? Cheers. Yes, she is very, um, demanding. And I was trying to talk to her the whole time, trying to well, end things, but she wouldn't listen. And then after she'd . . .' He pauses, exhales his cigarette smoke, and looks embarrassed.

'Had her wicked way with you?' I suggest, taking two more cigarettes from the packet, lighting them and handing one to Jake.

'Yes, after that, she said she was sick of me, and wanted to break up. And I said, that's what I've been trying to say, if you'd just listen rather than ordering me about like a sergeant bloody major. And she put her knickers back on and stormed out.'

I make a sympathetic face at Fraser, but out of the corner of my eye, I can see Jake holding his hand up to his mouth, hiding silent mirth. I start to giggle, and try to cover it with a cough. Jake is then completely unable to hide it anymore and collapses loudly in laughter, and I immediately follow.

Fraser, after looking perplexed for a second, starts laughing too and saying, in between guffaws: 'Well, I can see how that's . . . quite amusing, and I said to her "You don't have to take it like that", but you know, she always knows how she wants to, uh, take it . . .'

'Fraser!' I exclaim. 'You smut-monster. Don't be so rude about your girlfriend.'

'Ex-girlfriend,' he says. 'Definitely ex . . .'

Eddie walks into the room holding hands with Laura. 'We've run out of layback juice,' he says.

Sam staggers in almost immediately after them, looking nearly cross-eyed.

'Where's Kate?' he says with a light slur, before ambling to the other end of the table and crashing into a chair.

'What's going on here then?' says Eddie. 'Tory just came outside and made a beeline for the tennis courts . . . where I have a feeling a game of strip tennis is being played with Ant and Harriet, watched by Neil.'

Jake and I look at each other and start laughing again.

'Laura, can you do that thing we talked about?' says Eddie, standing up and going to the kitchen counter. He gets a large pair of scissors out of a drawer and brandishes them excitely.

'Yes!' she squeaks delightedly, running over and kneeling beside him. She starts cutting his filthy, mud-encrusted jeans off at just below crotch-level, making him a tiny pair of jeans shorts.

'See? See? Don't I have good legs?' says Eddie to her, pirouetting and flexing his calves happily.

She nods. 'Yes! Really nice.'

Eddie looks over at us all staring at him open-mouthed (except Sam, who has fallen asleep up the other end of the table), looks at his two jeans legs lying dead on the floor and shrugs. 'They were never going to recover from all that mud anyway. And I was finding it really hard to walk.'

'I want jeans shorts too!' exclaims Fraser.

Laura starts cutting his jeans into shorts, with Eddie supervising.

I look back at Jake. These guys aren't leaving for ages.

'Didn't you say you saw some gin and, uh, cooking sherry in the pantry earlier?' says Jake to me, raising an eyebrow.

'I did . . .? Oh. Yes, I did. Here, I'll show you where it is,' I say.

I get up, and followed by Jake, walk over to the pantry. Eddie, Laura and Fraser are still talking about jeans shorts, and don't even seem to notice. Soft snores from Sam confirm he won't be cuddling anyone again tonight.

The second we get inside the door of the pantry, I quickly turn around and look up at him. We're standing so close that I can almost feel the warmth of his body. My heart is thumping inside my chest and I feel shivery with nerves or cold or mud – I'm not sure which. For two long seconds, the delicious anticipation from earlier is heightened about four hundred million times. Then he leans forward and we kiss.

Now, I'm not going to go into detail about the kissing. You've kissed someone. You know it's one of the best things in the world, especially when you're doing it with someone with strong, warm lips, long arms he's wrapping around you, and your kissing instincts are perfectly synchronised. Just the right amount of tongue, pressure, mouth-openness, interspersed with the odd chin, jaw, lip and ear-nibble. And that's what we have.

After a few minutes of said perfect kissing Jake leans back and grins at me. Rule 8 is smashed to smithereenies.

'About fucking time,' he says.

'I think you should know that I'm only kissing you because of the fish puns,' I say. 'If you hadn't come up with "Shakin' that bass", I'd be playing strip tennis with Ant, right now.'

'Shh, Minxy . . .' he says, and starts kissing me again, pulling me further into the pantry. For the next few minutes I just think about kissing him, and get lost in the pleasure of putting my hands in his hair – softer than I'd have thought – and feeling his back, neck and arms. (Oh, stop giggling at the back. When you've been thinking about kissing someone as much as I've been thinking about kissing him, you do the same thing, I'm sure.)

'What tomfoolery is going on in there?' calls Eddie. 'How long does it take to find fucking cooking sherry?'

'We're just climbing up to reach it!' calls back Jake.

Then (as you would, too, if you were kissing someone really hot in a pantry) we start getting a bit more passionate, pushing each other against the shelves. Quite roughly, actually. It stops being passionate almost immediately, of course, and becomes funny, yet still – don't judge me on this – kind of sexy. The amusing snogging/shoving goes on for a few minutes, till he pushes me one too many times against the shelf behind me and it collapses, sending rice and flour and icing sugar and brown sugar and spices and a large long jar of dry linguini clattering to the floor. I gasp with horror, and after a three-second pause we both start laughing so hard that we can't actually get any sound out.

The ground is heaped with high mountains of multi-coloured powders. Maple syrup is dripping slowly down one mountain. Linguini is making its own little pick-up sticks game.

Fraser, Eddie and Laura open the door to the pantry.

'Christ,' says Eddie. 'That's a first.'

'We can clean it!' I exclaim. 'There's a dustbuster somewhere in the kitchen!'

'That thing died seven years ago,' says Eddie. 'Holy shit, what a mess.' He seems, unsurprisingly, to be freaking slightly about the pantry. I wonder what he'll do when he realises what has happened to the garden. And his jeans.

'Right . . . what about a broom?' says Jake. I look at him covered in mud and grass and flour, and start cackling helplessly at the idea that a broom will help. He turns to mock-frown at me and I quieten myself with difficulty. I have those hysterical giggle-hiccups that you get sometimes.

'We'll get someone in to look at this tomorrow,' says Jake decisively.

'Yes!' I say. Brilliant idea.

'You're going to fucking well clean up as much as you can first,' says Eddie.

'We'll all muck in,' says Fraser. 'First things first. Where's the vacuum contraption, then, Edward?' He becomes wonderfully military in a crisis.

'I'll pick up the linguini,' I say, still getting a mini giggling fit now and again whenever I look at the floor of the pantry.

'I'll help you,' says Jake. Eddie and Laura go into the kitchen to show Fraser where the vacuum cleaner is, and Jake and I pretty much immediately start kissing again, laughing at the same time. (It makes breathing hard, but I'm happy to sacrifice oxygen for the laughing and the kissing.)

A minute or so later, a purposeful clearing of the throat from Fraser, holding a vacuum cleaner at the doorway, wearing aviator sunglasses and still in his homemade jeans shorts, reminds us to spring apart.

'Linguini!' I exclaim, and quickly try to pick it all up. Amazing how hard it is to pick up a single strand of dry linguini.

'Out,' orders Fraser. We exit the pantry carefully. Jake and I are shedding flour with every step. I look down at my feet. My little ballet shoes are, without doubt, dead, suffocated by muck. We turn around to watch Fraser at work: he wields the vacuum cleaner as though it was a WMD, and within a few minutes almost all of the mess is gone . . . just as the vacuum cleaner makes a coughing, chugging sound and dies.

'Bloody thing is jammed,' says Fraser, wiping the sweat off his forehead.

I think. 'Did you suck up the maple syrup?'

'Was that the runny stuff? Yes. Everything. I got everything.'

Well, that explains it. 'Mmm,' I say. No point worrying about broken vacuum cleaners for now. Fraser steps out of the pantry and takes off his sunglasses, panting as though he just finished a marathon.

Eddie and Laura hand Jake and I gloves, wipes, kitchen

towel and kitchen spray. 'See you two later. Come along Laura. Come along Fraser,' says Eddie, shepherding them towards the garden.

'Oh, Eddie, we are sorry. Are you really pissed off? I promise we'll clean it as best we can now and again in the morning . . .'

'That's alright, darling,' he says, winking at me. 'You two have fun . . . I'm taking this lot outside.'

'He's fine,' I say, turning back to Jake, as they all leave the kitchen. 'Shall we finish cleaning up . . .?' This isn't the messiest party this house has ever seen, but it's in the top five.

Jake pulls me to him and we start kissing again.

'I need to be alone with you,' he says abruptly. 'It's all I've thought about for fucking months, and I want it, now. If we stay here, there'll just be interruptions all night.'

'Oh, gosh, OK,' I say. We throw down the cleaning things and leave the kitchen, kissing and stumbling as we go. The only private place I can think of, obviously, is my bedroom, which sets my mind racing again. We leave our shoes in the front hallway, where my sodden Converses are also drying out. Halfway up the stairs I stop and turn around. We start kissing again. 'Wait . . .' I say. 'Just so you know, we're going to my room, but I'm not going to – we're not going to—'

'Shut up, Minxy darling,' he says. 'I only want to be alone with you. I'm not going to try to get in your pants.' We keep walking up the stairs and he adds, 'Well, I am going to try, obviously, but I'm pretty sure you're not going to let me.'

We get to my room and stand in the doorway kissing, and well, I'm not going to go into detail about the kissing again, but it's really very good indeed.

'I need to . . . get out of these wet . . .'

'That is the worst line I've ever heard,' says Jake, shaking his head. 'What kind of boy do you think I am?'

I start laughing. 'I'm serious! We can't make the room dirty on top of everything else.'

'Who said anything about being dirty?' says Jake as we walk into the room.

I roll my eyes, grab a T-shirt, pants and my third and final pair of jeans from my overnight bag, and head for the bathroom.

'Need a hand?' says Jake.

'NO!' I say. 'Go and get some clean clothes.'

I get into the bathroom and look at myself in the mirror. What are you doing? Don't think about it. He's not Rick, don't think about the Sabbatical, just go with it. When I get out of the bathroom, dry and (of course, this is me we're talking about) make-up thoroughly checked, Jake's lying on my bed wearing clean jeans and a T-shirt.

I go over and sit down, and lie down next to him. We're on our sides, side by side, but not touching.

'I've been thinking about this since Mitch's party,' he says.

'So have I,' I say.

'No more running away,' he says in a stern voice. 'You always run away before I have the chance to talk to you properly . . .'

'OK,' I say. 'No more running away.'

And we get lost in the euphoria of kissing again for about an hour. He's good with the compliments, too. You'd think I'd cringe, but it's actually extremely nice when someone takes a good ten minutes to explain in detail and with amusingly silly anecdotes, why specific parts of one's body are perfect, and kiss them. Extremely nice.

'I want to see Madagascar,' he says, after a soliloquy of why he adores my left earlobe more than my right one. (The right one never looks him in the eye and he doesn't trust it, but he's willing to give it another chance.)

'No,' I say.

He makes a pretend huffing sound, and we lie back on the bed for a second. It is just lovely being this close to him. He smells very, very good, by the way, a little bit lemony around the jawline, and all soapy and clean everywhere else. He wraps his arms around me.

'I wonder if anyone's noticed we're gone?' I say.

'I'm sure they've been expecting it,' he shrugs, kissing the insides of my wrist. 'I can't stop looking at you. I can't even hear what other people are saying half the time, because I'm trying to read your lips from across the room. I only came here this weekend to see you, because it's been three fucking months and I couldn't wait any longer. God, I only made everyone leave that dinner party and bar crawl through Notting bloody Hill, in the hope of running into you.'

I sigh happily. Is there anything more flattering than an orchestrated coincidence? But I can't seem to say anything back. I can't process the magnitude of what he's telling me, so I try to make a quip to lighten the tension.

'Ah, there's nothing like a little stalking on a Saturday night.'

'Stalking?' he raises his eyebrows. 'That's charming. Right. Come here . . .'

We start kissing again. After a few minutes, I pull away. 'And what was with the Homer Simpson thing?'

He smiles. 'Criteria to see if you really were as good as you seemed.'

He lies back on the pillow and pulls me half on top of him, so I'm sort of leaning on his chest and we can talk face-to-face-ish. Finally I have the nerve to say what has been echoing loudly in my head since his wrist-kissing speech.

'Why . . . why do you like me so much?' I ask, and immediately think, God, why did I ask that? Never ask them how they're feeling or why. 'You hardly even know me.' Goddamnit, shut up, woman! Vino veritas. Truth in wine.

Jake looks up at the ceiling and thinks for a few seconds. 'You just always look like you're having fun being you.'

Good answer.

But he doesn't really know what I'm like yet, I think. He

couldn't, this is just a beginning. A lovely beginning, but a beginning, nonetheless. Right now, all he knows is what he likes about me, and he'll end up getting to know me better and then dumping me. Just like Rick, and Posh Mark, and every other guy I've ever dated. Never mind. Don't think about that right now.

'When Mitch told me you and Eddie used to date I was beside myself with jealousy,' he continues, gently pinching my earlobe. 'I wondered if you two were best friends destined to end up together . . . it was torture.'

'You stupid man,' I say, taking hold of his hand and kissing the palm. I want to tell him I think he's lovely and how he makes me laugh more than any other guy ever has, but the idea of saying how I feel aloud makes me feel sick. Blame the mistaken-love-confession to Rick, blame years of self-taught dating dos and don'ts, blame whatever you like, but I just can't. So I kiss his hand some more instead and hope for a subject change.

'Tell me about the guy you threw the wine at,' says Jake.

Why that subject? I groan and press my forehead into his chest so he can't see my face. 'He was a guy I, um, dated last year. The Pink Lady guy. I'm not proud of it. He is, um, an arsehole.'

'I wondered if that was him. Mitch said it probably was.'

'Mitch is a terrible gossip,' I say.

Jake nods. 'He told me he never liked your ex.'

'Why didn't he ever tell me that?' I say.

'He probably has a policy to never get involved. I do with all my friends' bad relationships.'

'Yikes,' I say. Bad relationships. God. I sigh. 'Well, I should have seen through him last year. But I didn't. I don't seem to be able to see things very well sometimes . . . I'm starting to think that I'm a bit of an idiot, actually,' I say. Hmm. Vino veritas strikes again. I don't feel drunk, but I've had about two bottles of wine, so I must be.

335

'I don't think you're an idiot,' Jake smiles. 'Were you . . . really heartbroken afterwards?'

'No, I was just plain miserable,' I say. It feels oddly natural to talk to him about this. 'Not heartbroken. I felt like . . . I was unbalanced. It sucked.' Ah, well put. Real eloquent.

He nods. 'I know that feeling. You have to just take a step back and a few deep breaths.'

'Exactly,' I say. A step back, a few deep breaths and a Dating Sabbatical. We start kissing again. We kiss rather passionately for quite a long time, actually, and I get all lost in lust for awhile. Then I remember I want to know more, much more about him, and pull away.

'What about you? Any mean girlfriends?'

'You're thinking about my ex-girlfriends at a time like this . . .? Yes, of course . . . everyone has battle scars by my age.'

'"Battle scars". I like that,' I say. 'It makes them sound important and trivial at the same time.'

'That's exactly what they are. I've been cheated on. Twice, in fact. And I've been dumped for no good reason. Everyone has.'

I sigh. I haven't thought about this stuff much today.

'It's a little depressing, isn't it? And things never change.'

'That's a silly thing to say. Everything changes.'

'Really . . .? I don't think it does,' I say. 'Like, look at our group. We're getting hammered and having wild parties and we were doing this ten years ago. It just seems like nothing will ever move on.'

'Of course it will. Take it from me. I'm older and wiser. It happens when you least expect it. Suddenly everyone you know is at a new stage . . .'

I look at him doubtfully. '*My* friends?'

'*Your* friends,' he nods.

'I found out recently that Bloomie and Eugene talk about marriage, which really surprised me, and then I felt like such a dork to be so surprised,' I admit. 'I just can't imagine being there.'

Jake nods. 'One of my oldest friends is married with a child and when it all happened about four years ago, I really couldn't understand how he was ready for that life, as I felt so . . . not ready. Then I decided I'd felt that way before,' he continues, tracing a line down my temple and jaw as he talks. 'Remember when you're a little kid, and you see your cousin's homework from school and think, I'll never be able to do that . . .?'

I grin. 'Yes. My babysitter used to do calculus study while I watched TV. The idea that I'd have to go to big school some day really stressed me out.'

'Exactly! It's like that. Suddenly, what seems impossible is the next natural step. My friends are in the middle of it. Marriage, babies, and everyone enters a different phase of their career, and just, you know, sorts their shit out.'

'Maybe I'm just a bit slow,' I say. Jake smirks. 'Seriously. I've only started to feel in control of my job and money and you know, life, in the last few months.' I think for a second. 'I like my place in the world at the moment . . . But I don't know where any of it is going.' All I know is that in exchange for that control, I had to give up dating, I think to myself. So what am I doing here snogging Jake when I'm on a Dating Sabbatical? Don't think about it.

'My mother,' says Jake, 'is a total hippie, and says that one can create self-fulfilling prophecies, but they can go both ways. So you have to create positive ones. Imagine your perfect future and make it happen.'

I grin. 'She sounds like my mother.'

'God bless baby boomers,' smiles Jake, wrapping his arms around me for a kiss, which turns into quite a long, grabby snogging session. 'OK – thank you, very nice kissing, by the way, well done . . . OK, so let's take your career. I know you're a copywriter . . .'

'Oh, you did do your homework, and you pretended you didn't know at dinner . . .' I say adoringly, and we start kissing again.

'So . . .' he pulls away. 'You're a copywriter. Do you like it? What next?'

337

I think. 'Yes, I like it. I love my company and my boss, and I want to help him do well . . . But I don't know what next. At some point in the next 30 years, writing ads to sell people shit they don't need is going to get boring.' I stare into space for a second. 'But I try not to think about that.'

'So what do you like doing?' says Jake, kissing the inside of my palm. 'You have lovely hands, by the way.'

'Thank you. You should see my feet. Well, the only thing I like to do is write. And that's good, since I get paid to write. But I don't want to be a journalist, which is what everyone suggests, and I don't know what else to do. So I just . . . try not to think about the future. At all.'

Jake shakes his head. 'You are a ball of negativity. You love to write. That's awesome. So start a blog or write a book or something.'

I look at him and laugh. 'Write a book? About what?! It's not that easy . . . But . . . yeah, you know, I've recently been writing these little short stories . . . They're nothing much, but maybe you're right. I could start a blog and post them . . . and then a publisher could snap me up and voilà, eternal happiness.'

'We have just created your self-fulfilling prophecy. You will find eternal happiness as a writer,' says Jake.

'That's a relief,' I say.

'Can I read your stories?'

'No,' I reply. 'Absolutely not.' He smiles at me and we start kissing again. After a few minutes I pull away again. The talking is almost as good as the kissing, and I want more of both.

'I adore you,' he says, then looks a little shocked at himself. 'Sorry, that was a bit, uh . . .'

I smile at him, and a warm feeling rushes through me. 'Good. I should hope so.'

'Cocky . . .' he murmurs and we get lost in kissing for awhile, till I pull away.

338

'Tell me more about you, then . . . what do you do?'

'Oh, Minxy, my job is so boring, it makes 30 years of writing copy to sell shit look like a night at Studio 54 in 1979.'

I laugh. 'Well, why are you doing it, then?'

He thinks. 'I'm quite good at it. And I do enjoy it most of the time, though I've been travelling too much recently. I was trying to lightly stalk you for the last few months and I couldn't, and Mitch wouldn't even give me your number, he said you'd castrate him if he gave it out again . . .'

'Aww, how sweet,' I say. We start kissing again.

Jake pulls away and continues. 'Where was I? Oh yeah, my job . . . and it'll get me where I want to be, which is living around the world, you know, meeting people . . . I lived in New York for three years, I'd love to go back there. I'm not sure this pesky recession will help me do that, though.'

'Oh lucky you. I'm dying to live in New York.'

'You'd love it,' he agrees.

'Where did you live?' I ask.

'Well, I lived in the Upper East Side at first, then I moved in with a friend from uni who works over there, Paul. That was downtown, in the West Village.'

'How awesome,' I sigh enviously.

I'm overcome by the urge to know everything about him. We talk and talk and talk, about our families, and our child-hoods, and books, and movies, and music, and our friends, and London, and travel, and holidays, and tell funny stories, and tell sad stories, and then kiss some more . . . We talk, and kiss, and talk, and kiss and then kiss quite a lot more, until the grey dawn starts peering in the sides of the windows. It's an unwel-come reminder of reality. I feel like we've been in some kind of surreal dreamworld all night.

At some point around 5 am, we get very sleepy and cuddle up under the duvet together.

'I was going to try to take all your clothes off and ravish you, just so you know,' mumbles Jake as we fall asleep.

'You say the sweetest things,' I mumble back. And then we're asleep.

Chapter Thirty-One

When we wake up, we're snuggled up tightly together under the duvet. I'm wrapped in his arms. The sun is up, and the room is depressingly light. It's almost 9 am. My head feels like someone is hammering nails into it.

'Mmm, this is good goddamn snuggling,' says Jake, kissing the back of my neck. 'We fit together like Pringle crisps.'

'Is that seriously the best you can come up with?' I reply. My head, ow, ow my head.

'Well, spoons are boring.'

'Spoons ARE boring,' I agree. Oh my God, why did I drink so much wine?

We lie in silence for a few minutes. The intenseness and intimacy of last night's soul-baring session are gone. I feel sleepy, extremely hungover, kind of uncomfortable, and very shy. He knows practically everything about me now; even more than Bloomie or Kate. At least I didn't tell him how I feel about him, thank fucking God for that. And yet I've never felt so completely exposed – and no, I'm fully dressed. (Dude, you know it wasn't that kind of night. Which I'm glad about now, as I'd feel even worse.) I pull the duvet over my face to hide in it a little bit. Oh alcohol remorse, how I hate thee.

We lie in silence for a few moments.

'So,' says Jake, nuzzling my neck again. 'I want to see you tonight. And every night this week.'

Just for a week? Then what happens?

I think this and almost say it aloud. And in a split second, I am hit by what I can only describe as emotional vertigo. I feel like I'm about to jump off a cliff with no safety net, no bungee rope, no parachute, nothing . . . Every instinct I have, every instinct that made me invent the stupid, stupid Dating Sabbatical crashes into me and all I can think is: this is never going to last beyond a few weeks or a few months, it never does, so why take the risk?

It's not just that I'm blindly obeying the Dating Sabbatical. But I couldn't bear to be dumped by Jake. And I couldn't bear to lose everything I've worked so hard to achieve. My happiness at work, my emotional equilibrium, the quiet satisfied feeling that seems to have appeared entirely as a result of not having any kind of dating distraction . . . I need it. If I date Jake it would all disappear. And I'd have to start again from scratch when he dumped me and build myself back up. I can't do that again.

Better to not start anything with Jake. Far, far better. Better to stay single and alone for a little bit longer, so I can protect the rest of my life and keep it just the way I want it.

I'm very awake now. My heart is racing and I'm dying to get the hell away before anything can happen. Or not happen. Or happen. Or not happen. Definitely better for it not to happen.

'Darling . . . are you awake?' he says, pulling me in to him tightly. I pull away and bury my head in the duvet. Oh God, get me out of here. 'Minxy?' he says, pulling the duvet away. 'Are you OK?'

'Yes . . .' I can't open my eyes. He'll be able to see how I'm feeling. 'But I can't see you this week.'

'Why not? Busy? Cancel your plans, I am infinitely more important . . .'

'No. I – I can't see you this week.'

'Why?'

'I just can't . . .' I take a deep breath. May as well pull out the big guns. 'I'm on a Dating Sabbatical.'

'Oh, come on . . . after all this? Mitch told me about that at his party and I almost didn't believe him. Still?'

'Yup.' Fuck. He knew the whole time.

'Don't tell me it's because of that jackass . . . the Pink Lady guy?'

'No, it's not him, it's really not. I just – I'm not ready. I'm simply not ready.'

'That's rubbish. You are ready. I know you are.' He pulls me towards him and starts kissing me. I kiss back for a few seconds, – well, it's pretty damn good kissing, as I think I've mentioned once or twice – and then pull away again.

'No. I'm serious, Jake. I don't want a relationship. I don't want to get involved.'

'You're already involved,' he says. 'Come on—'

'No,' I say firmly, sitting up in bed. 'No. I don't want to. I don't want to.'

'Look,' he says, sitting up and taking my hands in his. 'No one wants a shit relationship. No one. You don't need a Dating Sabbatical to believe that. But everyone wants a good one . . . Don't you think we should see each other again, just to see – to see what happens?'

'No. I can't – I just can't.' I snatch my hands away and get up off the bed. 'I think you should go.'

'You're kicking me out?' He looks shocked.

'Yes. Yes, I don't know what – I'm – this is all too – too fast.'

'Fast? Are you fucking serious?' I don't say anything. I really don't know what to say. Jake looks at me and shakes his head. I've never seen him look like that before. His habitual crinkly-eye smile has disappeared into a frown of disbelief and disappointment. 'This is . . . pathetic. You're just . . . I don't know . . . scared.'

'What! I'm not scared!' I say, raising my voice. 'I just don't want to get involved with you! Why can't you understand that?'

'Bullshit!' he shouts back. 'You're fucking petrified. You just want to bumble along and ignore life and not aim for anything and not risk anything, ever again. And all it boils down to is that you don't trust me because of every other idiot you've been out with who dumped you.'

I can't believe he's saying this. 'How dare you take things I told you and turn them back on me like that?' I scream. 'You don't even fucking know me! I have no fucking reason to trust you. And now I have a reason to absolutely *not* trust you. You're a jackass.'

'I thought the term you always used was bastardo,' he snaps, getting off the bed.

How dare he. And bastardo. That clearly comes from Mitch, the fucking bigmouth.

'Fine. Bastardo. You're clearly a total fucking bastardo. And better I found out now than later, that's all I can say.'

'You're the fucking bastardo,' he interrupts. He's standing in the middle of the room looking at me. I can't bear to look at his face, so I get back on the bed and bury my head in my hands. 'Every time I've seen you, it's amazing, it's fucking amazing, we had that click from the beginning and you know it . . . and then you ran away. Every time we met. And now you're doing it again.'

How can he say these things? How can he shout at me like this? I don't know what I expected, but not this . . .

I feel like bursting into tears, but I'm also furious. The two emotions battle it out for a second. Fury wins.

I look up at him and start talking, as clearly as I can through my anger. 'Look. It's my business, damn it, if I don't want to date you. I don't want to rush into anything. You should fucking well respect that.'

'This is pathetic and . . . you – are an idiot – I can't believe . . .' He throws his hands in the air as if searching for the right word. But I don't want to hear any more.

'Get the hell out of my room, Jake. Get. Out.'

'Fine.'

He turns and walks out of the room, slamming the door behind him.

I flop back down on the bed, and stare at the ceiling.

Fuck.

Chapter Thirty-Two

I don't know how long I've been lying here for.

Hours.

OK, probably not hours.

I keep running over the past day in my head. The car trip, the pub, the dinner, the kissing, the talking ... everything was ... perfect.

And then in about one minute and thirty seconds he lost his temper and I lost mine and boom, all over. I start to cry, but then stop myself. What am I crying about? It's fine. It's so fine. It was kind of like an entire relationship in fast-forward. The thrilling anticipation, the flirtatious banter, the kissing, the insecurity, the shouting, the break-up. Thinking that makes me laugh. Almost.

It's not fine. I feel ill. Seriously, I have an ache inside, in my chest and feel like I've been punched. Not that I know what that feels like, obviously, but I imagine that if someone punched me really, really hard in the middle of my chest, it would feel something like this. Oh, fuck.

I hear the front door slam, and then a car door slam. I jump off the bed and hurry to the window. I see Jake's car speeding down the driveway.

Oh, fucking fuck.

I scrabble through my overnight bag for some Panadol, have a quick, very hot shower, and put on clean jeans and a hoodie that I only wear with turbo hangovers. My face is a blur of stubble rash and red, mildly puffy eyes, so there's really no point in make-up. If there was a theme today, it would be Blister.

I look in the mirror and point sternly at myself. One night of conversation and some kissing. That's all it was. So just get over it right now and do not feel bad for one goddamn second.

I walk into the hallway the same second I see Laura coming out of Eddie's room.

'Hi!' she whispers elatedly. 'Oh my God, your friend Eddie is so, so nice! How are you feeling? Did you kiss that Jake guy last night? He's so nice too! Oh . . . oh no, what's wrong?'

I sit down on the top step and bury my face in my hands again, willing the tears not to come out. Oh, God. I can't face this.

Laura sits down next to me and reaches over to give me a side-hug. I lean against her and sigh deeply.

'I kind of fucked it up.'

'I think you guys can work it out . . . whatever happened,' she says, hopefully. 'I mean, I think . . . he's so nice and funny, and a bit sharp, you know, but I don't mean that in like, a mean way. He's . . . I just thought he was just like you.'

'Oh, God,' I say. That was so not the right thing to say. 'No, no, I don't want a boyfriend, you know, so it's good that nothing is happening. Or that it happened and it's over. It's a good thing.'

'Maybe you should talk to him . . .?' says Laura.

I take a deep breath. 'He's left. I can't.' I turn to look at her, and smile. 'Thank you, though. You and Eddie is exciting, isn't it?'

She smiles shyly. 'Yes! He's just lovely! We're going out on Tuesday.'

I smile as sincerely as I can, though it feels like it's hurting my face to try. 'That's great.'

Bloomie comes out of her room. She looks very pale. It must be the hangover. 'Hello, darlings. I hope you slept better than I did. Anyone for breakfast?'

'Oh, thanks, but I'm going to have a shower! I'll see you down there in a bit!' Laura scurries off.

Bloomie walks over, looking closely at me. She's very good at reading my face. It's annoying. 'So I guess you should tell me where you disappeared to last night and everything that's happened since.'

I sigh. 'You have no idea. Why didn't you sleep?'

She sighs back, and I notice that her eyes are bloodshot. 'You have no idea either. Let's go downstairs and talk.'

The kitchen is, predictably, chaos. Plates, food, glasses, bottles, clothes, mud, grass, cigarette butts, sweets, and a disturbing amount of floury footprints (I guess we didn't clean up as well as we thought we did) are everywhere. I fix Bloomie and I some (perfect) coffee as she makes a token attempt at cleaning up, and we head outside to the garden table with the pack of cigarettes Bloomie always stashes in her bag for the morning after. We settle down, light up, and both look up at the same exact moment.

'Oh . . . my . . . God . . .' we say in unison.

The beautiful garden has been garrotted. It would appear someone undertook trench warfare overnight, moved all the troops out by dawn and left a quagmire of filth-encrusted misery behind. The slope where the tobogganing took place has a deep, muddy crevasse straight down it. The grass is a heap of mucky little hills, with dirty dried detergent lather here and there. The flower beds look violated. Entire bushes are torn up and upended. Bottles and glasses and discarded bin-liner lawnboggans are everywhere, some broken, some whole. Eddie's mother is going to have a fit.

'That garden looks like my head,' I comment.

Bloomie turns to me. 'So what happened with Jake?' I tell her everything. At the end of the story I wonder what she'll say, but she doesn't say anything very much.

'Did you touch him in naughty places?' is about all she asks.

'Not really,' I say. 'I kept thinking we'd get around to that later, and we just kept talking and kissing. And then we fell asleep. Drunk, I guess.'

'Mmm . . . So what next?' she asks.

'Nothing,' I say. 'Dating Sabbatical business as usual. Every man I touch turns into a bastardo, it would appear, I'm like some kind of fucked-up Midas person.'

She gives me a frowny-smile and shakes her head. 'If I had the energy, I'd tell you what an idiot you are.'

'So what happened to you last night?'

She shrugs and takes a deep breath. 'Eugene and I . . . He caught me checking my BlackBerry in bed last night. I thought he was asleep. He lost his temper and said he doesn't think I really meant what I said about him being as important as work. 'Cos I promised him I wouldn't bring it this weekend. I don't even know why I checked it, I swear, but to him it means I lied . . . And I told him to get a fucking grip . . . And he said I was selfish and ridiculous . . .'

'Fuck,' I say. 'That's awful. Are you OK?'

Bloomie puts her face in her hands and starts to sob. 'We broke up. He slept in Benoit's room and I think he's already driven home to London.'

'Oh, fuck,' I say again, and put my arm around her heaving shoulders. Bloomie crying always freaks me out. It's like seeing your mum cry. We finish our cigarettes, light new ones, and she keeps crying.

'I don't know what . . . to do. I just don't know what to do,' she keeps saying, through her tears. I don't know what to say, so I just keep my arm around her shoulders and every now and again take her cigarette from her hand and ash it for her. After a few minutes, she seems to run out of tears. She sits up, takes a deep breath, and wipes her eyes with her sleeve. 'Let's clean up the kitchen and get the fuck out of here,' she says. 'Don't tell anyone yet. I can't take it.'

'Why don't you just call him?' I say. Today is the day of speaking my mind. 'For God's sake, Bloomie . . . he just lost his temper. And you broke a promise . . .'

'Fuck him,' she says.

'He forgave you for storming out of Ziani's like a dick last week. You should forgive him. He was drunk. It was a wine fight.'

'He's an idiot.'

'He's not, he just wants to know he's important to you . . . You're the idiot, darling. Every time someone does something you don't want them to, you lose your rag. That's not how life works. You have to give a little . . .' This is possibly the harshest thing I've ever said to Bloomie, so I try to make it sound as nice as possible. She stares into space for a few seconds. 'Come on, Bloomie. You know he loves you. Be a man. Call him.'

She looks at me. 'Be a man?'

'Whatever.'

She reaches to her back pocket, pulls out her phone, and calls him. I get up off the table and start walking back into the house to give her some privacy.

'Hi . . . it's me . . .' is all I can hear her saying.

My God, none of us have a clue what we're doing. I'm sure it's not meant to be this hard.

Back in the kitchen, I find Kate hunched over the cafetiere, muttering '98, 99 . . . 100'. On '100', she presses the plunger down.

'Freak,' I say. I look around quickly to see if we're alone and I can tell her about Bloomie, but we're not; I can see figures in sleeping bags over in the living room. So instead I whisper: 'Perry?' and she nods a quick yes. We do a little high-five and pour ourselves coffees.

'What else is gossip?' I ask.

'Well, Eddie and Laura snogged . . . Fraser broke up with Tory and then she went to bed with Conor. That's probably the biggest news . . .'

I can't help laughing at this.

'Two men in one night? God, she really is a ho . . . Poor darling Fraser.'

'Mitch and Tara, obviously. And you and Jake.'

'Yes,' I sigh. 'Me and Jake.' I try, in as few whispered words as possible, to tell her what happened last night and this morning. She interjects 'No!' and 'Really?' at the appropriate moments, and when it comes to the end, she starts doing her worried frowny face.

'It's better to not chance it, I think, rather than risk losing everything else I've achieved,' I finish. I do feel a teeny bit self-righteous about it, and I'm surprised that Kate and Bloomie aren't acting more impressed with my decision. Isn't it great that I'm taking control of my life? How much better my life is without the distraction and worry of dating? I'm about to ask Kate this, but as if she can read my mind, she simply sighs and shakes her head.

'You're an idiot. That's not how life works.'

Isn't that exactly what I just said to Bloomie?

My thoughts are interrupted by a soft purring sound.

'What the sweet hell is that?'

We look around the kitchen, but no one is there. I glance down into the living room, and see a few bodies huddled under sleeping bags, but the purring sound isn't coming from there, either. Suddenly, it gets louder. Kate holds her hand up for silence, listening intently.

'Wait . . . it's coming from under the . . .' She bends down, and starts giggling. 'Oh dear.'

Underneath the table is Sam, fast asleep, fully dressed, using a loaf of bread for a pillow and with a teatowel tucked under his chin. This cheers me up greatly, for some reason, and I crawl under the table and start prodding him.

'Wake up . . . wake up.'

'Mum, I'm wearing my retainer . . .' he mumbles, and then opens one impossibly bloodshot eye. 'Oh, it's you. Oh God, the pain. The paaaain . . .'

I lie down on the floor next to him. 'Me too.'

'Where's Ryan?'

I sigh. Jake Ryan. Jake goddamn Ryan. Anything I say will get back to him, I know, so I decide to not say too much.

'He left.'

'He what? How the dickens does he think I'm going to get home?' He opens both eyes, and tries to get up, then closes them and lies back down on his bread pillow. 'Oh God. Not moving for awhile.'

'Can I get you a coffee?'

'Yes. One of those perfect ones Ryan was telling me about yesterday. He says you are mistress of the caffeine.'

Oh, hell.

I make the perfect coffee for him, and he sips it under the table loudly, saying 'Ow' every now and again. Kate and I start to make breakfast and tidy some of the mess away as everyone trickles down from their rooms and the living room. I think back to yesterday, and the fishpun breakfast making, and everything seems very dull and grey in comparison.

Fraser strides into the kitchen, still wearing his new jeans shorts. They're so short that I can see he's a boxers man.

'It's the only pair of jeans I had,' he says, as we all fall about laughing. 'Fantastically comfortable. I might wear them more often. Right, I'm going back to London.'

'You OK, darling?' asks Kate, giving Fraser a hug as he heads out the door, fried egg sandwich in hand.

'Oh, yes. Think I dodged a bullet with Tory there,' he says. 'But I've already got an internet date lined up for Thursday, so all is not lost.' He smiles at me, and I try to smile back. 'You OK, treacle?' he asks. I nod, then shake my head, then shrug. He pats me on the shoulder, which is Fraser's equivalent of a hug. 'Last I saw you, you were wrapped around a young man,' he says to Kate.

'Mmm . . .' she says, a combination of pride and sheepishness.

'I saw him as I went to the khazi earlier. He was leaving with the twins.'

'I'm devastasted,' says Kate lightly, but I can tell she is relieved. Sometimes you kiss someone just to have done it, rather than to do it. If that makes sense.

Suddenly Bloomie runs in from the garden, sprints through the kitchen and into the hallway. I can hear her feet pounding up the stairs. Then a door slams.

Kate looks at me quizzically. 'I'll tell you later,' I mouth.

Neil wanders in from the living room. 'Morning, girls! That smells fantastic. Can I help? I'd love some toast. Oh, and I'll put the kettle on for tea. Lovely.'

I'm amazed. I've never heard him say so much in one go before.

'Hi, Neil . . . Uh . . . how are you this morning? Where's Harriet?'

'I wouldn't know,' he says cheerfully. 'She went off with Ant last night and I haven't seen her since.'

'What? I mean . . . gosh. I thought you two were . . .'

'Nope,' he says, filling up the kettle. 'She acted like it, but I've never even kissed her. Felt obliged to stick with her though. She's quite bossy when she wants to be.'

'No kidding,' I say.

'Yep!' he says, jauntily buttering some toast. 'Anyway. Had an excellent night. Ended up playing poker with Benoit over a bottle of whiskey. I'm going to pop out now and get another one to replace it. Toodles.'

I get the giggles at this, for some reason, and with all of my strength put myself on auto-pilot. I just need to keep quiet and enjoy everyone else's hangover till it's time to go home, and then I can think about Jake and everything that's happened. Oh hell, Jake. I wonder what he's thinking. I mean, I'm so glad I chose the Dating Sabbatical so I don't have to wonder what he's thinking.

'Kaaaaaaaaaaaaate,' bleats Sam from under the table. 'Can I have a cuddle?'

'No,' she snaps. 'You smell.'

'Pleeeease.'

'No.'

Sam puts a long arm out and grabs her ankle as she walks past, and she shrieks and starts to giggle. Ah flirting. How I will miss thee.

Eddie and Laura come in, hand in hand. Eddie's reaction when he sees the garden is not as extreme as I'd expected.

'Thought as much,' he says, gazing at it from the kitchen window and chomping a croissant like a peeled banana. 'I'll call Murray and he'll have it right by the time my folks get home.'

'Murray?' I say.

'Mum's gardener,' he replies. 'She pretends to do it all herself, but it's a total lie. He'll fix it up and she'll never even notice.'

'I'll help pay for it,' I say, and everyone else pipes up that they'll help too.

Ant slinks into the kitchen, ignoring the catcalls about him and Harriet, as there's the thunderous sound of heavy footsteps down the stairs. The front door slams.

'Harriet's going home,' Ant mumbles.

Mitch and Tara come into the kitchen, holding hands and looking smugly happy, until they discover that Jake and Perry have both left with the cars they were supposed to be going home in. Mitch calls Jake immediately.

'What the bollocks do you think you're doing, cuz? Leaving me stranded here in far north England . . .'

'It's fucking Oxfordshire,' says Eddie, rolling his eyes.

Mitch is listening now. I wonder if Jake is saying anything about me. Mitch's eyes flick up to me and then flick away.

'Alright mate, uh, talk later.'

'You can both get a lift with me,' says Eddie.

Benoit wanders in and sits down silently at the kitchen table.

354

Odd, I would have thought he'd have left with Eugene this morning. He's wearing very dark sunglasses and seems to have a nuclear hangover.

'Do you want breakfast?' I ask. 'Le petit dejeuner? Oui?'

He moves his head towards me slowly and says 'un café, s'il te plaît', then slowly turns back to look at the garden.

Kate, Laura, Eddie and I spend the next hour eating and tidying. Sam is still under the table, making loud requests for more toast or coffee now and again. Benoit doesn't speak or move. No one else asks me about Jake, so I just try to let the hangover banter distract me.

Oh for goodness' sake, stop wondering if he's OK.

Tory and Conor come in together, and immediately take seats at opposite ends of the table. Conor looks mildly embarrassed. Tory looks euphoric. I busy myself frying up bacon and eggs and making toast for everyone. Busybusybusy.

Spud comes in from the garden.

'Thanks, team,' he says. 'I just woke up in the rhodo-fucking-dendrons.'

We all fall about laughing at this. I'm a bit worried about Bloomie, but I pop upstairs at one point to knock on her door, and all I get is a shout of 'I'm fine! Down soon!' so I leave it. Neil pops in to drop off the whiskey, and leaves at the same time as Tory, Conor and Spud. Then, at about midday, Bloomie and Eugene come downstairs together, hand in hand, both flushed with happiness, post-sex exhilaration, and – sorry, but it's so obviously true – love.

I smile at them both. 'I owe you,' whispers Bloomie as they pass me. I guess Bloomie apologised. It turns out that Benoit refused to let Eugene drive when they woke up this morning, saying he was still drunk.

'I said he should stay and sort it out,' nods Benoit. Bloomie and Eugene start kissing again.

Bloomie, Kate and I decide to head home at about 2 pm and

offer Sam a lift. Eugene is driving with Benoit, as they have to stop off and see Benoit's aunt on the way. Eugene and Bloomie spend about ten minutes kissing goodbye and saying 'I love you . . . I love you . . .' It's pretty disgusting.

'Is that the "French" kissing I keep hearing so much about?' shouts Sam from the backseat of Kate's car. 'Can you please do it in slow motion so I can take notes?'

Eugene keeps kissing Bloomie, extending one arm to give Sam the finger.

'Le oiseau,' says Sam to Kate and I. 'That's the bird, ladies. Il a flippe le oiseau.'

Sam has progressed to a very loud, silly, still-a-bit-pissed type hangover. Kate's in an equally silly mood, though hers is from first-pull-after-a-break-up elation, and they sit in the back together giggling.

'I can't believe you snogged that child last night,' he says.

'He's all man, I'll have you know,' she retorts.

'Seriously. Did he feel your breasts and say "Mummy"?'

We all shout with laughter.

'You know, he's only going out with you so you can teach him how to drive. And shave.'

'I'm not going out with him,' says Kate. 'I snogged him in the living room for about 20 minutes and then he passed out and I slept in my bed, alone. I don't want to date him. He's too young and pretty.'

'Good, you can go out with me then.'

'But you're too old and . . . not pretty.'

'That really hurts my feelings . . . Want to kiss them better?'

'Oh, would you two stop flirting,' says Bloomie.

'Well, she broke my heart. When she went off with that child, she broke my heart.'

The drive to London continues like this, and by the time we get to Notting Hill they've decided to go to the Walmer Castle to start drinking.

'I love these lazy Fridays!' says Sam excitedly.

'It's Sunday,' says Kate seriously.

'My sweet, sweet darling . . . we're going to have to let me be the funny guy, and you can be the straight guy, OK?'

Sam then texts Mitch, who's driving with Tara, and they agree to it too, as do Eugene, Benoit, Laura, Fraser and Eddie. Sam also says he'll text Jake. He doesn't say what the reply is.

'Do you want to come to the pub, darling?' says Bloomie as we pull up to her house.

'Nah,' I say. 'I have an urgent date with a hot bath and bed.'

When I'm finally home alone, the silence is ringing in my ears. My insides are aching. It's probably just the hangover.

Oh fuck. I have lost him.

And that's what I want. I chose myself over Jake. I chose my new life and stability over inevitable heartbreak and disappointment.

On the way upstairs, I hear soft murmurs from the living room. I walk in and see Anna curled up on the settee with a man who – I think – must be Don. He's late 30s, got a lovely big smile, and seems to be reading her an article about Jennifer Aniston from *Look* magazine. She's giggling and smiling from ear to ear. There's several chocolate wrappers strewn around them. They look very cosy and happy.

'Hello!' I say, trying to sound as happy as I'm sure they undoubtably will.

'Hi, honey!' says Anna, and introduces me to Don. 'I was hoping we'd see you!'

'I've heard so much about you,' says Don, standing up to shake my hand. 'The famous Dating Sabbaticaller.'

'Oh . . . that stupid thing,' I say, a bit pointlessly.

'Can I get you a cup of tea?' asks Don. 'I'm just making one for Anna.'

'Um, I'd love one,' I say.

He hops up, tucks Anna back in with the duvet, and walks through to the kitchen, calling on his way, 'Peppermint OK?'

'Yep, fine,' I say, and turn to smile at Anna. She grins and puts her finger to her lips, beckoning me to come and sit down.

'Everything is perfect,' she whispers. 'He called me on Thursday and told me he had just needed a few days to sort his head out . . . like his own Dating Sabbatical. And that it's me he loves, and he wants me to move in with him! I'm so happy! Don't worry, I won't move out for a few months yet!'

I barely have time to process all this, and make the appropriate 'oohs' and 'wonderfuls' before Don is back with our tea.

'Something to nibble?' he says, offering me a biscuit. 'I am trying to feed this one up. She's too thin.'

Anna smiles at him ecstatically. I really could not have imagined seeing her this happy.

'I'd love to,' I say, standing up, 'but I had a very late one last night . . . I'm dying for a bath and bed . . . thank you for the tea. I'll take it up with me.'

'Anytime,' says Don. 'Lovely to meet you.'

I smile at them both as they rearrange themselves together on the couch, and head upstairs. As I get to my room, I look at my watch. It's almost 6 pm. I'm exhausted. I have a very hot bath, get into bed, and start reading *Pride and Prejudice* for comfort.

It doesn't work.

'Damn it, Austen,' I say aloud at one point, as I try for the ninth time to start a paragraph. I keep thinking about last night. I keep thinking about the talking and the kissing. And the dinner. And the pub. And the kissing again. And all the lovely, kind, funny things that Jake did and said.

Except, of course, when he called me a bastardo and an idiot and pathetic and a jackass. That was not lovely at all.

I pull my pillow over my head and let out a wail. It feels nice and dramatic. Then the irritating little voice inside my head starts talking.

I have damn good reasons for not seeing Jake again. Shall we go over them?

No, no. I know the drill, I do.

Good. Repeat after me.

I choose to not see Jake again.

I choose to not have my heart broken.

I choose stability over uncertainty. And safety over risk.

I choose the Dating Sabbatical. I don't want Jake. I choose the Dating Sabbatical. I don't want Jake.

Chanting this in my head, I fall asleep.

Chapter Thirty-Three

On Monday morning, I wake up, feel fine – in fact, pretty great since I've just had a marathon sleep – remember everything that happened, and feel my insides turn to stone.

I open my eyes and look around. My room is a mess. I still haven't unpacked from the weekend yet. In more ways than one: my overnight bag is a mess of floury, rain-sodden, mud-encrusted clothes, and my head is an equally revolting mess of Jake memories and thoughts. Get out, damned Jake.

It was the right decision. It is what I want. It's over.

I don't even have to attempt my happy starfish stretch and yawn to know it won't be happening today, so I just get out of bed, unpack and put some washing on, then shower (yada yada yada) and dress as quickly as I can, which isn't that quickly.

You know what's the cherry on this morning's fucking cake? I've lost my clothes mojo completely. In the end I dress like a farmer in a checked blue shirt, high-waisted flares, brown belt, and christen it Yee-ha. I don't think I could actually say Yee-ha aloud today if my life depended on it.

Then I grab my lucky yellow clutch (note to self: investigate alternative handbags, this fucker isn't lucky at all) and head out the door to work.

It's drizzling today, and colder than it should be for summer. Stupid London's stupid weather. I stomp up to Victoria angrily, realising halfway there that I forgot my iPod. Bugger. Then Victoria is shut because of overcrowding on the platform. As per fucking usual. Stupid Victoria line. I wait outside the gate, finally get downstairs, and discover that the Victoria line is suspended.

Of course.

I walk back up the stairs, getting bumped by every other pissed-off commuter on the way, and finally get on the 38 bus, but when we get stuck in traffic on that big road leading up to Hyde Park, I start feeling like I'm hyperventilating. Is this the universe telling me I'm heading in the wrong direction?

What a stupid thing to say.

I squeeze my way up the end of the bus and beg the driver to let me off. The hysteria in my voice must tell him I'm serious, and he decides to use the little power he has in life benevolently and flicks open the door without looking at me. Cockmonkey.

I walk the rest of the way to work frantically trying to peptalk myself into a mood of happiness and serenity. I am happy, I love being single, I love the Dating Sabbatical. It's the reason that my life is brilliant right now, why work has been so great and I'm in control of everything. I made a choice to be single, and it was the right choice for me, and I am happy. Ergo, I will always be happy being single. Suck that self-fulfilling prophecy, Jake.

Don't think about Jake.

I walk through scuzzy little Soho looking at everyone scurrying to work. My coffee is perfect. The rain has stopped and the clouds are trying their very best to clear the sky. I feel good. Yes, I do. I feel good from not thinking about Jake.

How, how, how am I going to not think about him today, this week, this month, forever? I'm already utterly exhausted from not thinking about him and it's only 9.15 am.

When I get to work, I have two surprises that distract me from my crisis. The first is that Andy isn't in, and will never be in again. He chose not to work his notice period, on the grounds that dealing with me is so far beneath him, I expect. Everyone is oddly giggly about it, especially Laura, who also gives me a little secret shy smile when I ask her about Eddie. 'We're going out tonight,' she whispers.

To distract everyone, and make Andy's absence less felt, I decide to rearrange the office. I'm tired of being smushed over against the wall; I want to be more involved with what's going on and create a real team atmosphere. I get everyone involved, and when Cooper gets back at lunchtime, we're all happily sitting in our new places: we're all a bit closer together, but no one can see over our shoulders so there's some privacy, too. All of a sudden, I feel like we're a real team.

And the second surprise is that Kate has been made redundant.

She emails Bloomie and I at 10.04 am.

It just happened! Redundant! So is my boss! My whole team! We're all out! Talking terms now! Call you later!

Oh, shit. I've never seen her use so many exclamation marks. Sign of hysteria, definitely. Bloomie and I both email her straight back telling her to call us when she can, and then Bloomie emails me.

Well, the fit's going to hit the shan now. I cannot imagine anyone that being made redundant suits less.

I reply:

Maybe there's a silver lining. She could get a massive payout.

Bloomie replies:

Three months at the most.

Three months' salary is pretty fucking awesome to most people, I think. Instead I reply:

Poor Katie . . . How was the Walmer?

Bloomie replies:

Pretty funny. Sam was hilarious. Everyone just pissed and silly. And The Dork and I are all better. In fact, we're perfect. Thank you darling. You were right.

I smile. I'm so glad she's happy.

Then I get a second email from her.

PS: I suppose now isn't the right time to do you the return favour, and suggest you ring Jake?

Ring him and say what, I think. I can't stop thinking about you but I still think I did the right thing? I don't reply to her email. I get rebriefed on the boiler job that caused the ruckus with Andy, and spend the rest of the day working with Laura and Danny on that.

In the afternoon, Kate sends a text saying she's fine, and inviting me over to her and Bloomie's place tonight. She sounds quite calm, surprisingly. Perhaps it's for the best. Perhaps everything is for the best.

The little clouds have completely disappeared by the time I leave work. It's so sunny that I decide to walk to Notting Hill through Mayfair and Hyde Park. Despite my best efforts on the way, my brain – inevitably – starts thinking more about Jake and the weekend. Hell, what a mess.

I hope he got home safe. I hope he understands my reasons. It's not him, it's not me, it's the Dating Sabbatical.

Why would he understand your reasons, you fool?

Self, please shut the fuck up.

I walk through Berkeley Square. The last time I was here was that night at Nobu. That was only ten days ago, but it seems like an age. Sweet ol' Lukas, I think. He's coming back from Germany on Thursday. I feel fine about seeing him. It was a kiss, and a mistake, but there are worse mistakes to make.

Yes, there certainly are.

Out of nowhere, Cooper's words from that same night with the Germans pop into my head. They are played on some kind of irritating loop for several minutes.

Cooper said: 'You'll meet someone you prefer to everyone else in the world. If he's being a bastardo, you'll just . . . call his bluff. And he'll call yours when you're playing up. You'll love it.'

I wonder if Jake called my bluff.

No, he did not. Of course he didn't. I am right. I know I am right. I don't regret it. If something had happened with him, it would have ended anyway. It always does. I am completely sure of that. I'd feel unsure about him, and that would make me act insecure and be unable to relax, and he'd decide it wasn't worth the effort and would end things anyway. Or some variation on that.

Thinking this, I walk quite happily for at least 30 seconds. I choose to be alone. I don't want Jake.

Maybe I could write all this down and just reread it every few minutes to save time. Or tattoo it on my arm.

Snippets of our five-hour soul-baring perfect-kissing conversation keep sneaking into my head. We talked about everything, absolutely everything. And the kissing. Hell, the kissing was good.

I haven't talked to someone like that – let alone someone new and male – in years. And unlike every other time I've met someone I was even slightly interested in, I didn't spend the night just hoping he'd ask me out. I simply enjoyed talking to him . . . I enjoyed him being near me, and the tingles I got when I met his eyes, and the kissing and soul-baring conversations . . .

Thanks to the fucking alcohol! I remind myself immediately. I'd drunk enough wine – and shots – to make anyone seem funny and interesting! And don't forget, young lady, that he woke up, assumed he already had me in the palm of his hand – because he is arrogant! And then we had a horrible fight and he called me names! The big roosterprick!

Yep, exclamation marks equal hysteria alright.

I am going to have to stop thinking about myself, immediately. Kate's been made redundant, and there are bigger problems in the world.

When I get to Kate and Bloomie's, they're knee-deep in cigarettes, red wine and a bag of pistachio nuts all bought from the off-licence around the corner.

364

'A £2.99 Merlot?' I ask.

'Desperate times, darling,' says Bloomie, lighting a cigarette. We only smoke inside during genuine emergencies. This is definitely one of those.

Kate looks almost impossibly calm. I lean over to give her a big hug.

'Are you alright?'

'Fine,' she says. 'I'm absolutely fine. In fact, I'm great!'

She tells us all about how it happened, and that she will probably get a three-month payoff. She spent the afternoon with Immie, talking about her options. It sounds like Immie has been pressing a few psychotherapy buttons, as Kate is being more introspective than I've ever seen her.

'I think it's time for me to reassess my life,' she says. 'I don't like being an accountant in a bank. I like the routine, but I don't know if it's good for me. I think it makes me more . . . controlling.'

I glance at the table in front of her and realise she's arranged the pistachio nut shells belly up in order of size.

'I think I'm going to try to get a contract job for a few months – I don't care where, anywhere that will pay me enough to stay living here – and then go travelling,' says Kate. 'Actually, I might do a teacher training course. Or yoga teaching. Or I might become a florist. I love flowers.'

I glance at Bloomie. Kate's calm exterior is a total front, clearly. Inside, she's spinning with shock. Bloomie shrugs and makes an 'I don't know what to say either' face.

'Well, darling, you don't have to decide now,' I say.

'I know,' Kate says cheerfully. 'That's the funniest thing of all. I don't have to do anything. I don't even have to get out of bed tomorrow.' Suddenly Kate looks tearful. 'I don't know what to do with myself.'

'This is a whole new start for you, Katiepoo,' I say, pouring her more wine.

'It's not a start. It's an ending,' she says, wiping a tear away from her eye. 'Another ending. First Tray, and now this.'

'Think of it as the start of something new!' I say, with slightly overcharged optimism. 'The last ten years of our lives have been all about university and getting jobs and surviving our 20s . . . Now we're almost 30 and it's time to find what we really need to make us happy.'

Bloomie and Kate are both looking at me oddly. Nothing this philosophical has ever come out of my mouth before.

I realise, as I'm saying it, that I really do think that. It's time for something new for all of us. For Kate to stop being a control freak and simply enjoy life, for Bloomie to focus on something – or rather, someone – other than her job, and for me . . . for me to not date men, ever again, so that the other areas of my life can work.

Sheesh, my something new sucks.

Kate drains her wine glass, which was almost full. 'It certainly is something new for me. I don't have a job.' She flops down on the floor and starts laughing and chanting, 'I have no job! I have no job!'

Bloomie and I look at each other in mild alarm. Oh well, at least she's getting it out of her system. We light a cigarette and pour more wine.

Kate suddenly sits up. 'Holy shit, my corporate Amex card. I've got enough points on it to fly just about anywhere. I have to use them before they take it away.'

'Oh my God,' says Bloomie. 'You really do. They'll never let you keep them.'

Kate stares at us. 'Where should I go? In fact . . .' She jumps up, runs to her room, and runs back with an envelope. 'I've got a free companion ticket. I could go somewhere, and one of you could come with me, for free. Let's go to Sri Lanka and lie on a beach for two weeks. No! Let's go to Croatia and hop around bankers' yachts.'

'Bankers don't have yachts anymore . . . And I can't take a holiday right now,' I say regretfully. Goddamnit, I haven't had a holiday all year.

'Let's go to New York for the weekend,' says Bloomie. I look over at her. What a wonderful idea. New York. New fucking York. It would get Jake out of my system, it would help distract Katie . . . it's perfect.

'When?' I ask.

'This weekend,' she says. 'It's perfect timing for your birthday! We'll go Friday lunchtime and leave Sunday night and be back for work on Monday morning!'

Oh God, my birthday. It's on Sunday. Turning 29 is the last thing I feel like dealing with right now. I hate birthdays.

'But there's only one companion ticket,' I say. 'And I can never repay the favour.'

'I don't care!' exclaims Kate. 'Take it!'

Bloomie shakes her head. 'I've got airmiles to use up, too. I can get my own free flight!'

We all start shrieking in a pathetic girly way. New York! Bars and shopping and skyscrapers and Central Park and . . .

'I can't afford a hotel,' I say suddenly. 'I mean really, guys, we can't do this. I don't have any savings and Kate has no salary. And the exchange rate isn't what it used to be. Even I used to be able to shop up a storm in New York, but not now . . .'

'I'm getting a three-month payout, I can find enough money for two nights in a hotel,' says Kate. 'And so can you, you've just had a raise. And we don't have to shop, we can just enjoy being there, all together . . . Please, darling? It's a last hurrah for us . . .'

Bloomie holds a finger up to silence us, and disappears into her room for a few minutes. She comes back with her laptop open.

'My company gets special corporate rates at half the five-star hotels in New York . . .' she says, typing furiously. After 30 seconds, she looks at us in triumph. '£84 a night. Split between three, we'll get a roller bed in . . .'

367

We all start shrieking again, and I'll spare you the scene.

When I realise that, actually, I really can afford this trip, and we spend the next hour booking and planning, my mood improves immeasurably. It's a highly successful distraction for both Kate and I. Kate's problem is, obviously, about ten times more serious than mine, I know, but it doesn't mean the fight with Jake isn't playing on a loop in a little TV screen in the back of my brain. I don't talk to the girls about Jake. Bloomie asks me once if I want to talk about him, and I simply shake my head. I don't. I don't I don't I don't.

All I have to do, in fact, is ask Cooper if I can have Friday off. I send him a quick text asking if it's OK if I call him, and when he responds 'no problem', I take a deep breath and bite the bullet. He picks up after two rings.

'May I take a half of Friday off?'

'Why?'

'Weekend away.'

'Yeah, that should be OK. Make sure the team knows, of course. And don't let anything slip.'

'I will and . . . um, won't.'

'Fine. See you tomorrow.'

And it's that simple. Odd how very easy it is to get what you want in life. All you have to do is ask for it. I wish someone had told me that earlier.

It's outside-in happiness, I know, but thank goodness we are going to New York. To keep my mind off Jake, and stop the weekend playing in a loop in my head, I start making packing lists and shopping lists and reading nymag.com the moment I get home on Monday night.

Tuesday isn't a great day. I get to work to find Cooper in a foul mood. He seems to be regretting his decision to let me take Friday afternoon off. We've had whiny emails from two long-term clients: they feel they've been neglected recently. Since we've been focusing on the German pitch so much over the past few months, and Andy was in charge of ensuring that everything else was up to scratch, this isn't surprising. Cooper immediately tells me I'm personally responsible for everything that goes out to those two clients from now on. So the week is pretty high-pressure, and brings me back down to earth. I may have got a raise, but in return, I've also lost my hiding-in-the-corner status.

The next few days spin by. I wake up at 6 am, and bloody Jake is always the first thought in my head. I banish him, and then go for a run. I don't try to write. I'm just not in the mood. The busy, Andy-free workdays spin by, and then when I get home I call Bloomie and Kate to talk about New York and read in bed till I fall asleep with my book on my chest. These are all excellent distractions. Just like vodka and clothes used to be. But much better for my liver and bank balance.

Kate's gone home to stay with her parents for a few nights, but she seems on excellent form, channelling all her control-freak skills into planning the perfect weekend for us. We've all been to New York enough times that we don't want to bother with too much touristy stuff and none of us can really afford to shop too much, which just leaves eating and drinking and walking. Three things that both we and New York excel at.

Kate also texts me at one point to tell me that the feeling you get when you realise you don't have to think about your job or your boss or your office politics ever again is like flying. I reply telling her to stop smoking crack. She replies that she can't keep replying to my texts as she's planning a practice pack. Yes, you read that right. Not just having a practice pack, but *planning* a practice pack.

Whenever I have a quiet moment and start thinking about Jake (maybe he'll know great places to go in New York? After all, he lived there), I slap myself in the face (metaphorically), and tell myself to get a grip.

I don't hear from him all week, of course. Not that I thought I would. (OK, I kind of thought I would.) (Well I hoped.) (No, not hoped. Wondered. I wondered if I would.) (It crossed my mind.)

(Like, once.) Late Thursday morning, the Germans come in for a meeting to look over our latest work. It's the first time I've seen Lukas since the Mahiki night, but with everything else that's going on, I can't summon the energy to be embarrassed about it anymore. Coop and I present the work together, with Sally, the schmoozy account director, looking on and making fatuous comments here and there. On their way out, Lukas lingers for a minute behind the others.

'Sass. Can I take you to lunch?' he asks. 'If it doesn't interfere with your Sabbatical, of course.'

I blink. Why would the Sabbatical stop me having – oh, shit. Rule 6, no accidental dating. Rule 7, no new man friends. I've started to think of the Dating Sabbatical as my shield from Jake, rather than a life philosophy like I did before. I ponder for a moment. What harm could it do?

'Come on,' he says. 'You look like you need something to eat. I am hungry. So let's have lunch together. It is so much better for the digestion than eating alone.'

'I'd love to,' I say. 'But Lukas . . .'

'I'm your client,' he says. 'I know.'

We walk out of the office and down to a little café near Golden Square, order at the counter and take a seat outside. Lukas tucks into a full English with all the gusto of a non-Englishman, and I take a bite of my Parma ham ciabatta.

'So, come on,' he says. 'Tell me what has happened. I can see something has. You're not worrying about what happened at Mahiki?'

If only that was it. 'No . . . not at all.'

'Good,' he says. 'I asked you for dinner, you said no, it was no big deal. I am not in luff with you.'

I grin at him.

'Actually,' Lukas continues. 'I am asking out every nice girl I meet at the moment. It is the opposite of a Dating Sabbatical. I am casting my net very wide.'

'A Date Trawl!' I exclaim. It's a bit weird talking to a client like this, but it's impossible not to like him and Coop wants everyone to get along. He's a good guy. Maybe he could ask Kate out. 'How's that going for you?'

'Not so bad,' he says. 'I have three dates lined up in London, and one back in Berlin. I'm moving here in two weeks, so it's time to concentrate more on London.'

'Nice work,' I say. Wow. And I thought I was a serial dater.

'I know,' he shrugs with false modesty. 'You should have dinner with me on Saturday night and I can tell you all about it.'

I start laughing. I do like him. He's fun. And very direct. 'No. I can't anyway. I'm going to New York for the weekend with my girlfriends. Sunday is my birthday, actually.'

Lukas leans back in his chair. He's finished the entire plate of fried English breakfast. I look down at my ciabatta. I've taken two bites.

'Do you mind if I smoke?' I say.

'Of course not,' he grins. 'You can smoke and I can tell you what I think you should do.'

I light a cigarette and raise my eyebrows at him. This bossy German thing is amusing. Still, he's not quite as charming as some people when they're being bossy . . . Damn it, stop thinking about Jake.

'You should go to New York with your friends. Celebrate the ending of the Sabbatical and have a lovely birthday. Then come back here and go for dinner with me.'

I smile at him and shake my head.

'It's only been three months,' I say. 'I think I need about three years off dating.'

We start chatting about London bars and restaurants, as he wants tips on the best new places for his dates. After 20 minutes I say I'd better get back to work, and Lukas wishes me a happy trip to New York before hailing a cab. I smile as I walk back to the office. He'd be easy to hang out with. Easy is good. Easy is better than men who call you names and call your bluff. Maybe we could be friends. To hell with Rule 7.

But then again, why bother to break one Sabbatical rule? Why not just break them all? And if that happens, why not break it for someone I really like? Why am I even thinking about breaking the Sabbatical?

I don't know.

I don't know anything.

Chapter Thirty-Four

I skippy-bunny-hop home on Thursday night – it was a slightly forced skippy-bunny-hop, I'll admit, and I have to use all my willpower to not think about Jake – and start packing.

We're hardly there at all, really – we arrive Friday night and leave Sunday night – but it's more than enough time to have a bit of fun and obviously I will need a wide range of outfits to choose from, according to the mood I'm in. I check the weather predictions online. Yay. It's 24° Celsius and sunny over there. It's already been arranged that Bloomie and Kate will be picking me up, from my house, in one of those cheap airport minicab services at midday tomorrow.

I'm all done in ten minutes. Goddamnit I am a good packer. I phone Bloomie to see how she and Kate are getting on. Bloomie is giddy with delight that she's managed to fit everything into an overnight bag. Kate is taking the biggest suitcase she owns.

'What are you taking, darling?' Bloomie asks.

'I am taking a very small suitcase,' I say. 'Although I do have approximately 21 possible outfits.'

'I knew you would, that's why I didn't pack much. Between you and Kate I'm completely sorted,' she says, then I hear her call to Kate: 'Kate! We don't need a first aid kit!'

I can hear Kate's voice in the background. 'In case of emergencies!'

'No.'

'Blooooooooomiiiiiiiiiieeeeeeeeeeeeeeeee.'

I haven't heard Kate whine like that in years.

'Sorry, Sass darling. How's your week been, anyway? You've been very quiet on email.'

'I'm great. Work. You know.'

'Haven't thought about Jake?'

'Nope.'

'The Sabbatical still on?'

'Yep.'

'Want to do anything special for your birthday on Sunday?'

'No, definitely not,' I say.

'Why can't you take your own advice?' sighs Bloomie.

I'm trying to figure out what she means when she suddenly says: 'I have to go. She's trying to pack a pillow . . . KATE! DROP IT!'

'What if I don't like the pillows in the hotel?' I hear Kate shouting back.

'I give up on both of you,' she says. 'See you at midday tomorrow. And get a good night's sleep.'

She damned me to a bad night's sleep with those words. I turn my light off at 11 pm and can't remember how to fall asleep. And it's because Jake is in my head.

Again.

I don't invite him in, you know. He just appears. I keep thinking about things he said, and stories he told me, and they remind me of stories I wish I'd told him, because I think he'd like them and they'd make him laugh. I think about him saying he adored me, and talking about my left earlobe.

And I think about our fight. I can't even remember it very well now, I've run over it so many times that it's like a scratchy, jumpy old VHS video tape in my head. A few not-nice things stick out, like him calling me pathetic and idiotic, and some nice things, I think, like about how amazing it was whenever he was with me. And at some point, he definitely said 'No one wants a shit relationship. No one. You don't need a Dating Sabbatical to believe that. But everyone wants a good one . . . Everyone.'

Hmm.

It must be 1 am. Is it 1 am? I look over at my clock radio. It's a 1.23 am! Sleep, damnit. Think about something else.

I'm 29 in three sleeps. Twenty fucking nine! That's depressing. That means I'm going to be 30. Which never really occurred to me before now. (I'm really not that bright sometimes.) I wonder if I'll still be on a Dating Sabbatical when I'm 30. Or 40. Or 50. God, that's a depressing, stupid idea, isn't it? And yet, what's the alternative? To keep having my heart broken and be dumped and be in an eternal date-dump cycle?

Rock, meet hard place.

Stop thinking about it. Sleep. Sleeeeeeeep.

And he said I was scared. And that I was pathetic and idiotic, which I know I've already mentioned but that bit keeps coming back to me. And a bastardo.

What did I say to him? OK. I definitely mentioned the Sabbatical. And I said I don't want to get involved. And he said that was bullshit, and that I was already involved.

I am already involved.

And pretty soon after that I kicked him out. And we lost our tempers. And he called me a fucking bastardo. And I told him I had no reason to trust him, and called him a bastardo and a jackass, I think.

I am a fucking bastardo.

Shut up, little voice.

If it was the other way around, and I'd met someone I felt a squirmy-warm-tummy with, and they'd run away every time I'd seen them and then kicked me out of their room after we'd kissed and talked all night, I'd . . . yeah, I'd probably think he was a fucking bastardo.

Please sleep, brain. Please.

I try to read for awhile to clear my head of Jake. Then at 1.57 am I turn off my light again. Jake is back immediately.

Please fuck off, I say to him.

You made a mistake, he says back. It's not me that you don't trust.

And then suddenly, I think I must be asleep, and dreaming, because I'm talking to Jake. (Remember that thing I said once about dreams and jobs being just about equal when it comes to boring topics? Well, too bad again. I still have the conch.)

I'm sitting on a sofa with Jake, outside a hotel. We're facing a beach, it's overcast and not too hot and there's a mild breeze. We're talking to each other, but the conversation keeps being whisked away with the wind. At one point I shuffle over from my side of the sofa to lean against him and he cuddles me under the crook of his arm. I relax into him, my legs stretched out next to his. 'I'm 5.9, you know,' I say. 'You're 5.8,' he replies. 'I'm not. I'm really tall,' I say. 'Oh, Minxy,' he says.

And with that, I wake up.

Sorry, I had to share that with you. Analyse it if you want. I'm damn well not going to.

It's 6.40 am. I still have almost an hour before I have to get up. I lie in my lovely cool room in the early June half light. How nice it is to lie here. And not think about Jake.

I'd like to think about Jake.

Well, you can't.

Chapter Thirty-Five

I drift back to a dream-free sleep for 50 minutes. When I wake up again, I feel reasonably refreshed. Forget Jake. Today is Going To New York Day. It's sunny outside. Let's go.

Work is blissfully uneventful, and I hurry home at 11.30 am, swiftly change into my travel clothes (old comfy jeans, white T-shirt, blazer – which is almost boring till I hitch the jeans up with a belt, add aviators, roll the sleeves up and decide I'm a Transatlantic Cindy Crawford circa '91), and am downstairs, with my suitcase, at 11.59 am on the button. At midday Bloomie and Kate roll up in the minicab, and with much happy yelping I put my suitcase in the back of the car and jump in.

'Passport?' says Kate.

'Yep.'

'Money?'

'Yep.'

'And here's your online check-in confirmation, the hotel's phone number and address and a map of the area around the hotel, and the phone number of the British consulate in New York.'

'What do you think is going to happen this weekend?' I say, putting it all in my lucky yellow clutch. It barely fits.

'I don't know,' she says. 'But it pays to be prepared.'

Bloomie pulls out her phone and calls Eugene. He doesn't pick up, so she leaves a message. 'I love you, darling. I'm just calling you to tell you that. I'll call you from the airport.' She hangs up, and sees Kate and I looking at her. 'Shut up.'

We get to Heathrow Terminal 5, which is a bright shiny spaceship of an airport, check our luggage and stroll through Immigration. We're lining up to put our bags through the security check when Bloomie gasps.

'There's Jake!'

'Where? Where?' I say, and immediately crouch down on the ground. (The machine operator sees me doing this but is too fat to get up and see what I'm doing. Great security, Heathrow. I feel really safe.)

'Is it him? Where?' hisses Kate.

'There!'

'No! That's not him!' says Kate.

'Where? Where?' I shriek, in an under-my-breath kind of way.

'Gone now, darling,' says Bloomie. 'He was walking that way. I'm sure it was him.'

'I'm sure it wasn't,' says Kate.

'Oh my God, why are you doing this to me?' I say, still crouched on the floor.

Well, now my nerves are completely shot. We have about half an hour before we board, and wander through duty free smelling the perfumes. I can't really enjoy it though, as every step I take, I am doing frantic 360-degree turns looking for Jake. I look like a paranoid ballet dancer. I don't see him. Of course.

'Got another surprise for you,' says Bloomie, as we start walking to the gate. 'Check your boarding pass.'

I check it. I haven't really looked at it since Kate checked us in. It looks totally normal. 'Is it OK?' I say anxiously.

'We're flying Club World, baby!'

'What?' I say. 'But—'

'Honestly, we realised on Tuesday that we both had the points and we were like, why not,' says Bloomie. 'It's just so much better.'

'How often does a girl lose her job, you know?' says Kate. 'Consider it an early birthday present!' I go into paroxysms of delight about flying Club World and thank them both profusely. This is going to be the best birthday ever.

Urgh, my birthday.

'We could go to the lounge, but it's not that great,' says Bloomie. I'm crestfallen at this. Hanging out in the lounge would be amazing for me.

We get to our gate and start lining up to board. After our intense chattiness and hyperactivity over the past few hours, we're hitting a little sugar low, and are all standing and shuffling in relative silence (with the occasional 360-degree check for any Jake-shaped men) when I get a tap on the shoulder.

'I told you I'd see you around.'

It's Rob, Mr America from Harlem-slash-the-Lonsdale. We all exclaim excited hellos and offer cheek kisses, and he joins us in the queue, politely apologising to the people behind us.

'I'm sorry, ma'am, sir, I just haven't seen these ladies in a while . . .' He turns to us. 'So what gives? A weekend in New York? Shopping, drinking, eating?'

'Can I pick D, all of the above?' I ask.

He laughs. 'Sure. You ladies staying in Manhattan?'

'Is there anywhere else to stay?' says Bloomie, echoing my thoughts. 'Oh yes, Brooklyn.' Damn, I forgot about Brooklyn.

'And, like, three other boroughs . . . and then there's a little thing called New York State . . .?' he says, shaking his head at us in mock-disapproval. 'How you doin', Kate? You look a little worried. Bad flyer?'

'No, no, I'm just checking things off in my head,' she says, looking up at him anxiously.

'I'm taking a couple of Valium the second I get on this flight,' he says, in a slightly lower voice. 'I need to rest up before the weekend. An old work buddy is having the 30th to end all 30ths tomorrow night. You guys should come. I mean, if you don't have any other plans?'

'We'd love to!' exclaims Bloomie. She's overcompensating for Kate and I being such freaks today, I think.

'We'd love to!' I add, slightly belatedly.

'Awesome,' he says. 'It's tomorrow night, downtown. You guys know the Meatpacking District, right? What's your number? I'll text you the details.' He looks at me expectantly. I tell him my number. 'Finally! God! That was like, harder to get hold of than my MBA.'

I start laughing, half at him as I don't know if he's being funny or is genuinely a bit of a wanker, and half because it is pretty funny that it's taken three separate meetings for me to acquiesce to handing over my sacred digits. A couple of years ago I would probably have fallen over myself to give him my number.

He sends me a quick text:

About freaking time, baby . . .

I can't think what to reply, so I don't reply anything at all, just nod at him. 'Got it.'

We walk through the gate and down the stinky little alley to the plane. I hope Rob isn't sitting near us. That would really be annoying. I want to giggle and be silly and I can't with him around.

'You guys flying coach?' he asks.

'No, Club World,' I say, trying not to sound too elated.

'Me too.'

Damn.

Bloomie, Kate and I settle in our seats and pretend to nonchalantly look through the free toiletry bag. Well, I'm pretending. The other two have flown Club World before, so their nonchalance could be genuine. It's pretty fucking awesome as far as I'm concerned. Kate is across the aisle by herself ('I'd much prefer it,' she said as we boarded, 'I don't like talking on planes. I need to concentrate to remain calm'), and Bloomie and I are sitting sort of top-and-tailed yet side-by-side.

I stuff my bag under my seat and look up to see Rob putting his bag in an overhead locker on the other side of the cabin.

'See you on the flip side,' he says, winking at me, putting two little pills in his mouth and washing them down with a gulp of water. Definitely a cockmonkey.

I catch Bloomie's eye and we both do a little jumping up and down in the seat dance. 'OK, I'm sick of you now,' she says, flicking up the fan-shaped thing separating us. A second later she flicks it down. 'PSYCH!'

The silliness continues until we're taxiing down the runway. I reach across the aisle to hold Kate's hand for take-off, as I have a feeling she'll appreciate it. After we've taken off, I slowly unpick each of her fingers hooked rigidly around my own.

'What do you do when you're flying by yourself?' I ask.

'You'd be surprised how many people are willing to hold hands during take-off,' she says.

Right after take-off, Bloomie pulls out her laptop.

'What are you doing?' I ask.

She looks over guiltily. 'I didn't get to work till half past nine today. It's the first time I've ever gone in past 8 am . . . I was in bed with The Dork . . . So I just have to review something and then send a quick email when we land . . .'

I watch three episodes of *Arrested Development*, then stretch out and try not to think about Jake. After last night's sleep antics, I'm exhausted. I fall asleep and don't wake up until we land.

After going through passport control at JFK, we get our bags, jump in a cab (a yellow cab!) and 45 minutes later, we're driving in the early evening sunshine across a bridge (I think it's the Williamsburg Bridge, but who knows) to MAN-GODDAMN-HATTAN.

We're all fizzing with excitement as the city, with its shiny sky-scraper-packed beauty, gets closer and closer. The buildings seem part of a single entity from far away, and then when you're near

381

enough you can see that each one stands alone and proud, with its own personality and history and attitude. It's almost over-whelming: too big, too beautiful . . . Then, three seconds later, Manhattan swallows us up and we're inside it, we're there, I mean – we're here!

See, this is just what I needed to distract me from Jake.

What do you mean, distract you from him? Nothing happened. A bit of a chat, a bit of a kiss, he's a roosterprickcockmonkey-bastardo, over.

But I miss him.

Shutthehellup.

Mkay.

The taxi pulls up at the Standard Hotel, which is a tall square building that appears to rather awkwardly straddle the High Line, a public park-slash-walkway on the far west side of the Meatpacking District.

'I thought we were staying at a boring hotel midtown?' I say, as we get in our cab. I've been so distracted that I didn't even hear Bloomie give the taxi driver directions. She turns to me and shrugs.

'This deal was better. And so is this hotel.'

She's right: it's an extremely cool hotel. We check in and the charming bellhop takes us to our room, which is huge, espe-cially in my limited experience of hotel rooms in New York. Our room has views over the Hudson and all the way uptown. I can even see the Empire State building, twinkling away in the dusky light. And there are views from the bathroom, too. So you can have a bath and look out.

'Wow,' we all say in unison.

I flop down on the bed and sigh. I'm suddenly shattered.

I miss Jake.

Shut up.

'I'm ordering us coffees on room service,' says Kate. 'It's only 7 pm, but it's midnight at home, and I think we need the caffeine because tonight we're going out to dinner. Now get dressed.'

Everyone should travel with a control freak at least once in their lives. It's so much easier.

Chapter Thirty-Six

An hour later we're ready to hit the streets of the Meatpacking District. In a non-hooker way.

In case you have some Carrie-Bradshaw-and-the-gals type thing in mind, by the way, we're not marching the streets of Manhattan in fabulous designer outfits, shoulder to shoulder, stride by stride, with a 'where shall the city take me tonight?' glow on our faces. We're British. We're not wearing designer clothes – my entire outfit is from H&M, actually, including my bra and pants (nothing special, I'm too distracted to really think about it, so I pair a red dress with my trenchcoat and red shoes and call it Flasher) – and to be honest, we probably look a tad too dishevelled to be New York women. Sexy and stylishly dishevelled, we hope, though probably just dishevelled. They do glossy so well in the States. I wish I did glossy. Anyway. Never mind.

'Minetta Tavern is from the guy who brought us Pastis and Balthazar!' exclaims Kate brightly, as we get in a cab. 'Corner of MacDougal and Minetta Lane, please,' she adds to the driver.

I exchange glances with Bloomie. Oh my God, she's a tourist guide.

'What do we eat there?'

'The steaks are sublime and the Black Label burger is famous,' recites Kate. From memory. 'It's classic New York with that famous McNally sheen.'

'Ace,' I say. As we're driving down, I'm looking out the window of the cab. I love how every single street here is alive and buzzing at 8 pm on a Friday night. In London, you have pockets of crazy-fun action, and pockets of lights-out sleepiness. Even on a Friday. I crane my neck to try to see into every shop (the shops are still open! How wonderful capitalism is) and bar and restaurant as we go past. People, people everywhere, walking and talking and laughing and eating. I wonder what they do. I wonder how much a copywriter earns here. I wonder where Jake's old apartment was. No I don't. I don't wonder about Jake at all.

'I love New York,' I say, turning to the girls. Predictably.

'Where are we going?' says Bloomie.

'The West Village, baby,' says Kate.

Bloomie and I exchange glances. When we pull up and see the front of the Minetta Tavern, I turn and smile at Kate. Yet again her obsessive tendencies have served us well. I've never been anywhere as divinely, stunningly New York as this: a small, packed bistro, with black and white floor tiles, caricatures on the walls and packed booths. It's simultaneously chic and cosy, warm and cool, and it's packed with people eating and enjoying themselves.

'The guys in here are so good looking,' whispers Kate, after we've ordered.

'They are?' I say. I have not seen a single man since we got here.

'I feel spaced out,' comments Bloomie.

'That's not surprising. It's almost two in the morning in London,' says Kate helpfully.

'OK,' says Bloomie. 'That's it. No more telling us what time it is in London. It just makes me miss Eugene.' Aww.

'Touchy!' says Kate, as the waitress arrives brandishing huge plates. 'Maybe I could be a waitress in New York,' she says dreamily. 'Maybe I could live in a garret and be a waitress and paint.'

'Garrets are in Paris,' says Bloomie helpfully. Which I was about to say, but the words got stuck in my head, somewhere behind thoughts of Jake.

'Ah,' says Kate.

'What is wrong with you?' Bloomie turns to me. Ah. Spiky Bloomie is back. 'You've barely spoken all day.'

I haven't? I feel like I have. My brain won't stop talking to me.

'See? You don't even say anything when I say you're a mute.'

I clear my throat. 'I'm feeling a bit, ah, you know, out of it. I didn't sleep well last night.'

'It's your birthday on Sunday. You haven't even mentioned it.'

'I don't want to make a fuss about it, that's all,' I say. 'You know I hate birthdays. We should just pretend it's not happening.'

'Is this a Jake thing?' says Bloomie.

Yes, it is.

No, it's not.

'No.'

'Liar.'

'Let us know when you want to talk about it,' interrupts Kate hurriedly, putting her hand on my arm and shooting Bloomie a shut-up face. I nod, and take another slug of my dirty martini. I don't know why I ordered it, but it seemed like the thing to do in a place like this. It's the size of my head. Kate starts wittering about our plans for tomorrow, and I let her words wash over me and try to keep my eyes open. The martini, which I hoped would be a heart-starter, is in fact a giant liquid sleeping pill.

'Ooh!' gasps Kate, waking me up. 'Food is here. Oh, thank you . . . Do you have any English mustard?'

Kate is having steak, Bloomie is having pig's trotter ('Why not?' she shrugs) and I'm having the burger. It's unbefreakingliev-ably delicious and the delightful sugar, salt and fat rush wakes me up for the first few bites. About halfway through, my body hits the 'done' button, and I can't eat another bite.

I miss Jake.

Didn't I already tell you to shut up?

Oh dear, I seem to be going senile. I have stopped eating and am staring into nothing, having this conversation with myself. I can't eat any more. As a matter of fact, all of us have gone silent and spacey.

'What shall we do now?' says Kate.

'I'm sorry to say this, but maybe we should go to bed so that we are more on form tomorrow night,' I say. My mood has gone through the floor, I feel tired and miserable, and I can't believe I'm wasting a weekend in New York feeling like shit. We get the bill (check) and walk back out to the street. I wonder if native New Yorkers can tell we're tourists. I feel somehow aggrieved to be a tourist, when I'm always rolling my eyes inwardly at them in London, especially the hordes of Spanish students that hang around Piccadilly Circus.

We light cigarettes and walk for awhile, but I am having trouble putting one foot in front of the other. I don't even know if Bloomie and Kate are talking, as my brain seems to be on the pause button.

We hail a cab and are heading back to the Standard when we get stuck in traffic. I'm leaning back against the seat, gazing out of the cab window, with my eyes nearly shut, and my brain tucking itself into bed for the night when I see him.

It's Jake.

It's fucking Jake. I can't believe it's Jake.

He's walking on the pavement, right across from the cab so I can see the side of his face perfectly. He's with a woman. He's wearing the same shirt he was wearing when I kissed him. It's him. It's definitely him.

'GET DOWN!' I hiss at the girls, and our cab edges forward about 20 metres and then stops again.

'Huh?' says Bloomie. She's been leaning on my shoulder with her eyes closed. Kate's looking out the other window.

We're now ahead of Jake, and I peer up from my (rather uncomfortable and cramped, actually, I wish they had nice big spacious black cabs here) semi-crouching position over the back window to get another look at him.

He's on my side of the road, walking towards us, so I have a very clear view: he's with a woman about my age, very pretty, with shiny brown hair and a gorgeous blue dress on. Glossy. Very glossy.

'Lookitshimitshim!' I hiss, interrupting their vague 'Why? What? Who?' questions. Bloomie slowly turns around and looks out the back window in the direction I'm staring obsessively.

'Ohyou'refuckingjoking,' she says under her breath.

We're all staring speechlessly. He's walking up towards us and is nearly parallel with the cab again when somehow, the traffic clears and we speed off. The last thing I see is him putting his arm around her shoulder.

'I can't believe that,' I say, in shock. I turn to face Bloomie and Kate. 'Did I imagine that?'

'No, that was him,' nods Bloomie. 'Definitely him. In New York. With a girl.'

'Well . . . wow,' I say.

We all sit back and stare straight ahead wordlessly.

I told you that you missed him.

Shut up. I'm thinking.

Well, it's all your fault. You told him to fuck off. Now he's moved on.

I said shut up.

The journey back to the hotel passes in total silence. We're all shattered, which would make us quiet anyway, but because I've refused to talk about Jake all week, I don't think they know what to say to me. Am I upset? Am I indifferent? They don't know. I don't know.

'I need a drink,' I say, as the cab pulls up. Opposite the Standard is a filthy-looking graffitied bar with a neon sign outside saying 'Hogs & Heifers'. 'Let's go there.'

'Oh, no,' says Kate worriedly. 'That's like one of those tacky bars where the bartenders abuse the shit out of you, but actually it's all a show.'

'I don't care what it's like,' I say. 'I just want a drink.'

We walk up to the bar, past a handful of smokers outside, and push our way in. The place is packed with drunk people singing to AC/DC and looking at two female bartenders dancing on the bar in nothing but jeans and bras. They are absolute skanks. The place is tacky, covered in graffiti and faux-dive-paraphernalia, and behind the bar hang about 5,000 discarded bras, like wild animal skins hung up to dry.

'OhmyGod,' I hear Kate say behind me.

One of the skanktenders looks over at us, and picks up a huge megaphone from behind the bar.

'Hey Sweet Valley Hiiiiiiiiiiiiiiiiigh,' she screams. 'When you're in my fucking bar, you take off the fucking trenchcoat, motherfuckaaaaah. That's a fashion faux-pas, bitch!'

I'm stunned. She's talking to me. Everyone in the bar turns around and smiles at us, partly in sympathy as they probably got abused when they walked in too, and partly because it's funny. In a split second I realise that I can either run away or stay and face the skanktender. I have a feeling she only bullies people who are either scared of or rude to her. Anyway, I have more important things to worry about and all I want is a drink.

I start taking off my trenchcoat and walk to the bar. Bloomie and Kate walk behind me.

'We don't have to stay here,' I hear Kate say.

I walk straight up to the bar and the skanktender jumps down and faces me, raising a drawn-on eyebrow.

'Shots only, bitches,' she says. 'What's your poison?'

I glance at the bar and read out the first bottle I see. 'Makers Mark.'

'That's my fuckin' drink, Sweet Valley HIIIGH!' she exclaims. 'You're alright. Hey, Enid, Regina, get the fuck up to the bar and drink with your pal Elizabeth.'

'I always wanted to be a Jessica,' I say. The skanktender glances at me and laughs.

'Fuckin' AY! Six shots!' she shouts, and then glances up to see a guy looking at her hopefully. 'What the fuck do you want, motherfuckaaaahhhh?'

'Uh, a drink?' he says hopefully.

She starts screaming abuse at him through the megaphone. I turn to Bloomie and Kate and we wordlessly down our shots.

'How do we get out of here alive?' Bloomie asks out of the corner of her mouth. I've never seen her intimidated by anything before. 'I really, really hate this kind of thing.'

'Can you believe we just saw Jake?' I ask in reply.

They both shake their heads, and we all do our second shot.

'I can't believe you're not scared of that . . . girl,' says Kate.

I glance over at the skanktender, who is screaming at some poor dude who is going to the bathroom. The Maker's Mark is making me feel eerily calm. 'She's alright, really. I wonder what Jake is doing in New York?'

'Can we please leave now?' says Kate urgently.

'Yes, seriously . . .' agrees Bloomie.

I catch the other skanktender's eye, and ask for the bill. She doesn't have a megaphone, but screams 'Why the fuck are you leaving, motherfuckaahhhh?' at me. Why are these women's vocabularies so limited?

'I'm jetlagged,' I say, looking her straight in the eye.

Unbelievably enough, she shrugs, gets me the bill, and winks as we leave. It's all a total show.

'Sweet motherfuckin' dreams, motherfuckaaahhhhs!' screams megaphone skanktender as we leave.

We get out of the bar, light cigarettes and start giggling helplessly as we walk over to the Standard. That was one hell of a way to get my mind off Jake being in New York with me, I think. I'm so drunk and tired that I can't think properly, and I fall asleep as soon as my head hits the pillow.

Chapter Thirty-Seven

I wake up in exactly the same position exactly seven and a half hours later. It's just past 6 am. I feel elated for a second – I'm in New York! – and then the memory of Jake walking along the side of the road with another woman hits me with a thud.

I open my eyes and stare at the ceiling. I'm wide awake now. OK.

I'm not jetlagged or drunk or tired. It's time to cut the crap. Forget the Sabbatical and Rick and dating and heartache and the fight and that it would probably go wrong and all that shit. Just be honest.

I like him. I really, really like him. I've missed him since the second I kicked him out of my room last Sunday. I liked – no, I *loved* talking to him, I loved being near him, I loved kissing him. I don't want him to be here with someone else. In fact, I don't want him to ever be with anyone else but me. I don't ever want anyone else but him.

Oh God.

Inside-out happiness, exit stage left. Enter stage right, inside-out chaos.

I groan aloud at my own fuckuppishness. Kate rolls over.

'Morning, princess,' she yawns. 'You OK?'

I put my face into the pillow and scream.

'Darling?' calls Bloomie from her single bed.

I sigh, and roll over. 'Jake.'

'I knew it!' pipes up Bloomie, bouncing out of her bed and onto ours.

'I knew, too!' says Kate, sitting up sharply and grabbing the phone. 'I'll just order us some coffees,' she whispers, and presses the room service button.

'I – oh, can I have two, please Katiepoo? – oh guys, I'm sorry to bring this up so early, but I . . . I've been trying to make it go away and I . . . I can't.'

'OK . . .' says Bloomie.

'I can't believe I said those things to him last weekend. I told him . . . that I wasn't ready, I didn't want a relationship, I didn't want to get involved, and then I think I called him a jackass . . . and a bastardo.'

Bloomie laughs. 'You don't do things by halves, do you, Sass darling?'

I try to smile, but I feel overwhelmed with sadness.

'I think – or rather, I *thought* I was doing the right thing. You know how much things have changed since I started the Dating Sabbatical, it's really changed my life . . . And I don't want to lose everything, I don't want to go back to the way I was before, to being unhappy . . .'

'Why do you think you'd lose that?' asks Kate. 'Even when you saw Rick again that night, you didn't lose that.'

'Really?' I say. 'But . . . but I got hammered that night. Just like the old days.'

'Yeah, and threw a glass of wine on him,' says Bloomie. 'You would never have done that before.'

'And Jake isn't like Rick, or anyone else you've ever been with,' adds Kate. 'He's just like you, actually. Bloomie and I were talking about it the other night. Hasn't that even occurred to you?'

I think for a second. She's right. He's not like Arty Jonathan, or Rugger Robbie, or Clapham Brodie, or Smart Henry. And he's absolutely nothing like Rick. Being with him was surprising, unpredictable and fun in the best possible way. Every time I saw

392

him, he was consistently honest and straightforward and kind to me and everyone else, and I told him he was an untrustworthy bastardo jackass and threw him out of my room.

'I think he's much nicer and kinder and smarter than me,' I say sadly.

Bloomie and Kate sit still, waiting for me to say something.

'Feel free to disagree with that, guys,' I say, and we all start laughing.

'God, this is intense for quarter past six in the morning. Let's just . . . chill out.' I flop down on the bed. How do I fix this? I can't. I can't fix this. He's here with another woman and I can't fix it and if I even tried to ask him if he'd give me another chance – or rather, a first chance – he'd tell me no way. So why bother.

'That's it? That's all you're going to say?' says Bloomie.

'That's all for now,' I say, turning on *The City*. I don't want to think about it. I want to look at Olivia Palermo's hair.

We drink our coffees and then decide to get up and explore the town. We're going to have breakfast at the Bonbonniere, a tiny, threadbare diner a few minutes' walk down the street. It's a perfect early summer's morning outside, and even the weather is bigger and better than in London: bluer sky, brighter sunshine. As we walk out onto Washington and head towards Eighth Avenue, I do a quick scan for Jake.

'He's not here,' says Bloomie.

'Let's not talk about it till this evening,' I reply. I want to enjoy my day. I don't want that little voice to start talking to me again.

But I want to talk to you about Jake and the Dating Sabbatical.

I said I want to enjoy my day goddamnit.

Fine.

We're up so early that the Bonbonniere is delightfully half-full, quiet and peaceful, with sun streaming in the open windows. I'm having pancakes with maple syrup and bacon. This I already know. I look around at the other diners, feeling happy for them that they're lucky enough to live in the West Village and walk here for brunch every Saturday. The bastards.

'Jello omelette. That sounds like a sexual position,' says Bloomie idly as she stares at the menu.

'No, it doesn't, you filthmonger,' says Kate, flipping through her notebook.

'Yes it does. You know, like an Angry Pirate,' says Bloomie.

'A Jello omelette sounds floppy, that's not sexy . . .' I say. 'What is an Angry Pirate?' I add reluctantly, as I know I'm supposed to. I don't know what it is, but it can't be good.

'Oh, no, please, not here . . .' says Kate.

Bloomie leans in to the table, gesturing to us to do the same, and whispers. 'It's when the guy, um, you know, finishes in the girl's eye and then kicks her in the shins. So she's got one hand on her eye and one hand on her leg, hopping up and down going "ARGGHHHH!" Like an Angry Pirate!'

I laugh so hard that latte from my last sip – taken around 'eye' – is coming out my nose, and I'm banging the table with my hand. That's the most disgusting thing I've ever heard. I love it.

'That's the most disgusting thing I've ever heard! I hate it!' says Kate in an agitated whisper. She's utterly horrified, or at least pretending to be. She turns to me. 'Shhh! How can you laugh at this? It's disgusting! And anti-women!'

'It's FUNNY!' I gasp.

'Well, there has to be at least one penis involved, darling,' Bloomie continues. 'But you can have a gay Angry Pirate. So it's not really anti-women.'

I'm laughing so hard that I start crying and nearly lose my balance on my chair. Breakfast – despite being phenomenally good, as ever in New York – never really recovers after that. Kate is mortified in case anyone around us heard, and almost stops speaking. I'm in a never-ending, barely contained giggling fit and for some reason I can't look at Kate's breakfast without losing control.

After breakfast, we decide to go down to visit Ground Zero. Admittedly, for an escapist weekend in New York, it's a slightly sobering thing to do, but we all feel that it's respectful and important to do so, and there's not much left in life that is respectful and important, so you'll have to bear with me.

Bloomie's cousin was in one of the Towers and just managed to get out before it collapsed, but most of his colleagues didn't make it. What a horrific way to die. The memory of watching it on TV still makes my stomach flip. I had recently started my very first job on 9/11. It was about 2 pm in London and we all piled into the boardroom to watch it. I went to yoga that night – which is unlike me but I didn't know what else to do with myself, and it was that year I told you about when Bloomie and Kate hadn't moved to London yet – and everyone in yoga started crying together. The teacher suggested we sit in silence and think of the families and friends of the victims. So we sat together, in a dimmed room, crying together.

After that sombre hour, we head back up to Soho and have a coffee whilst we discuss our options.

I'm in two minds as to whether to talk you through the rest of the morning or not. I think not, as it might be a bit boring if you're not that into clothes. So I'll just list the places we went in no particular order, and if you're really keen, then next time you're in New York, you can check them out for yourself: Theory, MAC, J Crew, Banana Republic, Barney's Co-op, Atrium, Sephora, Ricky's, Bloomingdale's, the MOMA shop, and a bunch of other Soho boutiques that don't have clearly marked names on the outside because they are too cool.

The shopping gods are smiling on us. I buy a few cheap little bits and pieces, but realise that really, I'm having a good time being in New York with my best friends, regardless of shopping. Isn't that bizarre?

By 2 pm, we're ready for lunch. Kate takes us to the Pearl Oyster Bar, where we manage to get seats at the bar.

'I can never get over how good the food is over here,' comments Bloomie, her mouth full of bread and lobster and fries.

'Me either,' I sigh happily.

'Maybe I could open a place like this in London, after my job is over,' says Kate thoughtfully. She looks over at us. 'Just thinking aloud.'

My phone beeps. It's Rob, the American, giving us the details about the party tonight. I confer with the girls and reply that we'll be there around 10 pm. We finish lunch with the best sundae I've ever eaten in my life, get the bill and wander down Cornelia and Bleecker Street with our shopping bags. Bloomie lags behind to call Eugene for a quick I-love-you, and Kate and I walk and people-watch in thoughtful silence. There are so many tall, glossy women striding along in heels that I feel inspired to start wearing heels every day myself.

We're all walked out but unwilling to go back to the hotel and waste a minute of our day. And New York – yes, yes, everyone says this, but it's true – has so much energy that you kind of soak it up. It gives me a weird excited feeling, like anything is possible and you never know what's around the corner. Thinking this, I do a quick skippy-bunny-hop. The Jake issue isn't settled, in fact it's pretty awful, but my life is good. It really is.

Suddenly, across Bleecker Street, I see someone I never thought I'd see again.

He's got longer hair, and a beard, and is wearing a lumberjack shirt and army combats, and orange-tinted aviators. He's leaning against a building, smoking a roll-up cigarette and pontificating on the phone. I can't hear him, but I know he's pontificating, because that's exactly what he looked like when I was 23 and he was lecturing me about Blek Le Rat whilst 'borrowing' money from me.

It's Arty Jonathan.

Without thinking about it, I cross the street and start walking towards him. I hear Bloomie and Kate calling after me, but I ignore them. This is the guy that started it all. This is the arsehole that borrowed money from me and took advantage of my naivety and dumped me to go and pick up his girlfriend and take her to Paris. Sure, it's not as bad as Rick. But it sure as hell wasn't that good, either. And I'm going to tell him that.

I stop right in front of him, take off my sunglasses and flash him a huge smile.

'Hi! Remember me?'

Arty Jonathan pulls his shades to the top of his head and stares at me, then mutters, 'I gotta go, man,' into his phone. 'Whoa . . .' he says. 'This is unbelievable.' He's got a slight rabbit-in-headlights look about him.

'I know!' I say, smiling from ear to ear. I glance behind me and see Bloomie and Kate a few metres away staring at us. 'Weird! You're living in New York?'

He nods, regaining his customary nonchalance by the second. 'Yeah, I was in Brooklyn, but now, you know, I'm in Queens.'

'Still doing the arty stuff?'

He looks surprised and a bit affronted by this. 'Yeah, I show in a gallery in Woodstock. And I'm managing a band.'

'Of course you are,' I say, still smiling. He's such a poser. And he's not even good looking – his teeth are so yellow. I can't believe he ever impressed me.

Suddenly a girl comes out of the shop that he's been leaning against. She's in her early 20s, with long, long dark hair and is wearing high-waisted jeans shorts and a little prairie girl top. An indie princess if ever I saw one.

'Thank you sooo much for waiting, Jono!' she says, then smiles at me, showing perfect American teeth. 'I'm Keira, are you a friend of Jono's?'

'An old friend,' I nod, smiling at her. Poor girl. I lower my voice and look her in the eye. 'Never lend this man money. Never trust him. And don't be impressed by his bullshit. He has no talent.'

'He's friends with Damien Hirst,' she retorts.

'No, he's not,' I say gently. 'He just used to drink in the same pub.' I turn to 'Jono', who looks like he might cry, and smile. 'You owe me more than you'll ever fucking know, not to mention the money you borrowed to take your girlfriend to Paris, you lying piece of shit. But I don't care about that anymore. Just stop taking advantage of nice young women. We deserve better.'

I turn and walk away, leaving Arty Jonathan speechless and his girlfriend shouting 'Screw you!' after me (classic New Yorker, a Brit would never have the cojones to do that), followed by Bloomie and Kate.

'Who the fuck was that?' asks Bloomie in shock.

'The guy who started it,' I say. I feel fantastic; light and happy and completely clear. 'Arty Jonathan. The one who set me on the path of knee-jerk reactions and rejections. If only I'd said that stuff to him years ago.'

'I always thought you hated confrontation,' says Kate. She's looking at me in a slightly scared way.

I frown. 'I did. But I don't anymore.'

'No shit.'

'What was that about Paris?' asks Bloomie. I've never told them that story.

'He borrowed money from me and then dumped me to take his girlfriend to Paris,' I shrug.

'Fuck off,' says Bloomie disbelievingly. 'I knew we hadn't gotten to the bottom of the Arty Jonathan story.' She turns around and looks back up the street. I turn too, and see Arty Jonathan and Keira getting in a cab the other way. 'Yeah, run away, dickhead!' she screams, and turns back to us, smiling. 'I could *so* be a New Yorker.'

We all start laughing. Kate decides that since we haven't eaten in about two hours, we must be starving, and directs us around the corner to a café. We sit down and order Diet Cokes and cupcakes. (Because, you know, the calories saved by having a Diet Coke practically cancel out the cupcakes.)

'You know what's funny?' I say thoughtfully, nibbling at the icing. 'I've seen all of them in the past three months. All the ex-boyfriends. And none of them were really bastardo cockmonkeys. They were just figuring themselves out.'

'Except for Rick,' says Bloomie, biting her cupcake like an apple.

'Except him,' I agree. 'And Jonathan, really, he is a cockmonkey too. But none of the others were worth crying over. They just weren't right for me.'

'They really weren't,' agrees Kate, using a knife and fork to eat her cupcake.

'And I don't feel angry at myself for dating them anymore, either,' I say. 'They were simply part of what had to happen to get me to the Dating Sabbatical and all the good things that have come from it.'

'Why are you so fucking philosophical lately?' demands Bloomie.

I think for a minute. 'Because I'm happy with my life, I guess.' Except for the Jake thing, I add silently.

'Are you going to try to get in touch with Jake?' asks Kate gently, reading my mind.

'The Sabbatical is officially over,' chimes in Bloomie.

'No,' I say honestly. 'I'm scared.'

Bloomie and Kate look at each other and start laughing. 'If there's one thing you're not, ever, anymore, it's scared,' says Kate finally.

We sit and eat in silence for a few more minutes.

Bloomie looks at her watch. 'Shit, it's nearly time for the last surprise I booked . . . A woman in my office works here half the month and swears by a hair salon near the hotel . . . I've booked us all for a blowout at 4 pm.'

It's the perfect end to the afternoon. We get to relax in peaceful silence without wasting a second of our time in New York. After all, we could not get a proper New York blowout anywhere else but here. Obviously. Half an hour later, we're all sitting in a row in the salon, wet hair hanging around our faces, looking up hopefully at the stylists behind us.

'So, straight but with body at the roots? Glossy?' they ask.

'Yes,' we say.

The hairdryers are switched on, and Bloomie and Kate pick up *Us Weekly* and *People* magazines and start reading. I look straight ahead at myself in the mirror and sigh. The confrontation euphoria has disappeared. I'm alone with my thoughts.

What am I going to do?

Usually, I can't bear to look at myself in hairdressing mirrors, as the lighting is awful. Today I face myself and start talking.

What's wrong with you?

What?

Everything you said to Jake was wrong.

So?

You just don't want to think about it. You were wrong. He was right. You were a bastardo cockmonkey. He wasn't. And you don't want the Dating Sabbatical anymore. You want him.

Shut up. I'm scared. I've been dumped six times in a row. I'm battle-scarred. I can't trust men.

I am so sick of hearing about those battle scars. You admit none of them were worth the agony. It's not men you can't trust. It's you.

What?

It's YOU that you don't trust. Don't be scared. Take a risk. Trust yourself. That's all you have to do.

Holy. Fuck.

I feel like a thousand lightbulbs have switched on in my head. Is that all that ending the Dating Sabbatical comes down to? Trusting myself?

It is, I realise. It really is. Because I didn't trust myself before. I'd let myself down too many times, with the wrong decisions and the wrong men . . . But that's all changed. I trust myself to do anything I want to do. All I have to do is decide I want it, and I can make it happen.

I trust myself to find Jake and tell him how I feel about him. And I need to do it right now.

I turn to Bloomie and Kate. Our heads are all being pushed and pulled by our stylists and huge hairdryers are blasting noisily in our ears. Kate's reading a magazine and biting her cuticles, and Bloomie, judging from the faraway smile and furiously texting fingers, is getting a little textual healing from Eugene.

'I NEED TO FIND JAKE!' I shout above the racket of hairdryers and music.

'WHAT?' shouts Bloomie. Kate is still reading, completely oblivious.

'I NEED TO FIND HIM AND TELL HIM I WAS WRONG!' I shout. My stylist looks at me quizzically.

'WHAT?' she shouts again. Kate looks around the salon, frowning vaguely.

'I NEED TO FIND JAKE AND TELL HIM I LOVE HIM!' I scream as loud as I can, at the exact second that all of our stylists turn off the hairdryers. Whoa, I love him? Where did that come from?

Bloomie and Kate, the stylists, and all the other women lined up at the mirrors are staring at me in shock. Even the receptionist is looking over. There's total silence. My screaming voice is ringing in my ears. (And probably everyone else's.)

'I'm going to text Mitch and get his number,' I say quietly.

I get my phone out and text Mitch immediately. It's late Saturday night back in London, but he'll be up. I think about explaining, then realise he doesn't need, or probably want, any details:

Dude. Can you please forward me your cousin's mobile no?

I stare at the phone for a few seconds. No reply. I look over at Bloomie and Kate anxiously. They're still staring at me as the stylists flip and flop their hair around. My stylist is flipping and flopping my hair very gingerly, as though I might bite him at any second.

'Done!' he exclaims brightly. 'Beautiful! Amazing!' he adds quickly and scurries away.

I look in the mirror. I am not exaggerating: my hair has never looked this good in my whole entire life. I look over at Kate and Bloomie. They look incredible, too. Suddenly, all of us have full-bodied, perfectly shiny hair. We're glossy.

We stand up to go. I'm in a daze, staring obsessively at my phone every few minutes. Nothing. Nothing. What the hell? Mitch is a phone addict. He always has the damn thing on, always, he even puts it on the table when we're in a restaurant.

We pay, leaving tips for the stylists – I leave mine extra for the emotional trauma I must have caused him by screaming under the hairdryer – and jump in a cab.

'What the fuck was that about?' exclaims Bloomie, the moment Kate closes the cab door.

'I trust myself!' I say.

'What?' she says. 'Are you OK?'

'I need to find Jake and tell him how I feel about him. It's the only way to make up for being a fucking bastardo and prove that I trust him and that I trust myself and the Dating Sabbatical is over!' I gabble.

Bloomie and Kate look at each other. 'You're hysterical,' says Kate.

'No, I'm not, I'm fine for the first time in weeks!' I exclaim.

'Calm, darling. Breathe,' says Bloomie.

I turn to look at them both, take a deep breath, and talk as slowly as I can. 'I know I made a mistake. I know he's the guy I want to be with. And I can have everything, I can have my new happiness and Jake, I just have to trust myself to make it happen and I will.'

'OK . . .' says Kate.

402

'I was a fucking bastardo to him. What if he's here getting back with his ex-girlfriend right now because I was a cockmonkey? Every second counts!'

'Well . . . shit,' says Bloomie. 'Let's find Jake, then.'

We get back to the hotel and race through the ground-floor lobby to the lifts. 'I'm going to find him tonight and tell him how I feel,' I say confidently. 'Even if he was with another girl last night. Even if he's not in New York anymore. I'm going to do it. Where the fuck is fucking Mitch?'

'I'll text him,' says Bloomie. 'Maybe yours didn't get through.'

'I'll text Sam!' says Kate.

'Why do you have Sam's number?' say Bloomie and I in unison, after a second's pause.

Kate grins. 'He asked me for it last Sunday at the Walmer Castle. We've been texting and . . . we're going out next week.'

'Oh my God,' I exclaim. 'That's so great!'

'That's fantastic!' says Bloomie.

She grins. 'Yeah, well, it's nothing, it's just dinner. I like him.'

The lift stops at our floor and we race to our door.

'Why are we running?' I say.

'I don't know,' says Bloomie. 'It seems like an emergency.'

I'm in love with someone I told to fuck off six days ago. And now I have to get him back.

It is an emergency.

Chapter Thirty-Eight

We get into the room, hearts pounding from the unnecessary running, and look at each other. There's really nothing we can do except wait for Mitch or Sam to text back with Jake's number. There was no reason to run.

'Do you want to talk about it?' asks Kate.

'All I've done is talk about it for days,' I say. 'To myself, at least. I'm sick of talking about it. I just want to fix it.'

'High-five to that,' says Bloomie cheerfully. 'I'm breaking out the minibar.'

An hour – and several mini bottles of vodka – later, we're slowly getting ready for the evening ahead. The boys haven't texted yet, infuriatingly. We've all showered (it's the first time in my life I've seen the point of a shower cap. When your hair looks this good, you want to nurture and protect it, like a baby) and are halfway through make-upping, and anxiously checking our phones every few minutes.

'It's almost midnight in London!' I exclaim. 'Where the fuck is Mitch? He's clearly in a bar somewhere with no phone reception, the fucking drunk.'

'That's it,' says Bloomie. 'I'm calling him.'

She rings, but it goes straight to voicemail.

'ARGHH!' she screams, and then looks up at me with a smile. 'This is fun.'

'We could get the concierge to call other Manhattan hotels asking for a Jake Ryan,' says Kate helpfully.

'There are hundreds of hotels in New York,' says Bloomie.

'What if he's staying with his ex-girlfriend and that was her last night?' gasps Kate, then claps her hand to her mouth at saying something so unsupportive.

I look at her and reach for a mini bottle of Wild Turkey. I need a little kick to help me deal with this much tension.

We've all agreed that the best thing for us tonight is some potent drinks. Kate booked a chic little restaurant in Nolita called Public, but Bloomie suggests a place in Gramercy called ¡Vamos! for the excellent reason that it has margaritas. I think Kate was hoping for a slightly more sophisticated evening, but she says she appreciates the importance of tequila-based cocktails at a time like this.

'You'll love it,' Bloomie says cheerfully. 'It's good, dirty fun. Eugene recommended it. Now, if you'll excuse me, I'm just going to call him . . .'

She steps outside into the corridor, so she can mew sweet nothings to him in private.

'What are you wearing?' says Kate, looking into her suitcase anxiously. Hers is still perfectly packed. Bloomie and I have basically thrown all of our clothes around the room. Some landed on hangers. Most did not.

'Um . . .' I say. I'm wrapped in a towel, and have just finished my make-up. 'Something short and slutty, I guess. Are we going to meet Rob later for his friend's party?'

'Absolutely,' says Kate. 'I want to meet American men. I hear the dating scene here is brutal and I am ready.' She pauses. 'Unless you'd rather, I don't know, comb Manhattan for Jake?'

'I'll get his number and find him, or I won't,' I say calmly. 'Either way, we *will* have fun. And that means you meeting American men.'

Kate whoops and opens a mini bottle of Jack Daniel's.

Unexpectedly, Kate ends up in my short and slutty black mini dress. I'm in a classy knee-length, vaguely Grecian gold one-shouldered dress of Bloomie's. Bloomie is in a demure white shift dress of Kate's but she's much taller and with high red shoes, it somehow looks kind of sexy on her. It's so warm tonight that we won't need jackets.

'I'm not sure what to christen this . . .' I muse.

'Huh?' says Kate.

Bloomie looks me up and down. 'Lovely. You don't need to christen it anything. You can borrow my Loobs, too.'

'OK,' I say. I'm in floppy-dolly mode suddenly. I'll do anything I'm told. (Being told to wear skyscraper gold Christian Louboutins isn't that bad, obviously.) God, I really have decided I'm in love with someone I told to fuck off six days ago. And now I have to get him back, possibly wrestling him away from another woman in the process. My stomach contracts in a ball of terror.

'Shut up,' I tell it. 'You're just going to have to ride this one out with me. I am in control and I know what's best.'

My stomach immediately relaxes.

That's better.

Bloomie hands me her four-inch-high gold Christian Louboutins. They're – there is no other way to say it – fucking gorgeous. They're matchy-matchy with the gold dress, but I don't care.

'And for fuck's sake, don't wear that yellow clutch.'

'But it's lucky!' I protest half-heartedly.

'It's clearly fucking not, darling,' she replies. 'Katie, did you bring your red evening bag?'

Kate snaps to attention. 'Yes! I did! The tiny black clutch? Do you need it? Here you go! Don't forget to pack passports, girls! They won't let you drink in bars without one!'

I transfer everything from my (un)lucky yellow clutch into Kate's tiny black clutch. 'I feel like you,' she comments, looking in the mirror at herself in my little black dress and black shoeboots.

'Fabulous, you mean?' I ask, squishing in lip gloss, credit cards, passport, cash, room key, cigarettes and chewing gum. The only thing I leave out of the clutch is the old, tattered piece of paper with the Dating Sabbatical Rules on; the ones Bloomie and I made up on that drunken night at Sophie's Steakhouse all those months ago. I won't be needing them tonight, I think. I rip the paper in two, then fold the halves together and rip again, and then one more time for luck. Goodbye, Dating Sabbatical, I think. I don't need you anymore.

Kate and Bloomie are staring at me curiously. I shrug. 'Everyone ready?' I ask, glancing at my phone. Where is Mitch's text with Jake's number, goddamnit?

'We could call Eddie,' says Kate helpfully. 'He might know where Mitch is. Then we could track him down and get the number.'

I look at my phone again. 'No. I can wait. I'll do something next week when he's back from New York.' I'm not sure what. But I'll figure it out.

'If he's coming back,' comments Kate thoughtfully.

'What?' I say.

'Um . . . nothing,' she says. 'It was just something Sam said last weekend . . . I wasn't going to bother to tell you . . . Sam said Jake was thinking about leaving London. I didn't even think about it, but now that I do, I wonder if he meant for New York.'

'Shit!' I say. 'What if he's already decided and he's here looking at places to live and that's why he's thinking about getting back with his ex?'

We all look at each other, aghast.

'Don't overthink it. Let's go and get a margarita,' says Bloomie.

We get to ¡Vamos! and get a little table to the three of us, near a large and extremely noisy group of New Yorkers our age who seem to have been here for several hours. We quickly take advantage of the last 15 minutes of happy hour and order two-for-one margaritas: The Classico for Bloomie, Lemon Basil for Kate and Frozen for me.

'Fuck me,' gasps Bloomie after she takes her first sip.

'Fuck me,' echo Kate and I as we take ours.

'I can actually feel it careering through the meridian lines of my body,' adds Kate. 'Like heroin.'

How does she know what heroin feels like?

Halfway through my drink, I relax and look around. The large group is ordering more drinks. One guy is shouting 'I cannot have another frozen one. I have an ice cream headache. Don't you people care?' He's the Mitch of the group, I decide. Up the end are three girls snickering together about a private joke. That's me, Bloomie and Kate. And down the other end of the table is a tall, good-looking guy who seems to be eyeing up one of the Bloomie, Kate or me girls. That is Jake. Or maybe it's Rick. It's hard to tell.

I sigh deeply, and take another slug of my frozen margarita.

Bloomie looks up. 'Darling, for God's sake. You're in New York. Cheer up.'

'I am cheered up!' I say, stirring my margarita thoughtfully. 'I'm just pensive.'

'About Jake?'

'No,' I say. 'About me. I thought being dumped six times in a row made me hate dating and you know, the whole thing. But that wasn't it. I lost trust in myself. Somewhere among every smashed hope and fucked-up choice, I lost the only thing I needed to be really happy: trust in myself.'

Bloomie and Kate start applauding.

'Good speech!' says Bloomie. 'I love new philosophical you!'

'Oh shut up,' I say, laughing.

'I thought the Dating Sabbatical was just about not being dumped,' says Kate.

'Well, it was. I didn't want to be dumped, in fact I didn't want to try anything in case I failed, because I always, always failed . . . and then, on the Sabbatical, the reverse happened. Everything I tried, I succeeded at. You just have to decide what you want in life, and trust that you can make it happen.'

408

'I completely agree,' says Bloomie. 'Create a self-fulfilling prophecy.'

I smile to myself. That's what Jake would say.

'OK!' I hold my hands up. 'That's enough navel-gazing . . . thank you for this trip, you guys. Here's to you.'

We clink and drink.

'And here's to the end of the Dating Sabbatical,' I add.

We clink and drink again.

'Here's to me being made redundant,' says Kate. 'If I hadn't been, we would never be here.'

We clink and drink yet again.

'Here's to me showing Eugene he's more important to me than work,' adds Bloomie.

We clink and drink.

'Here's to Tray. May he find happiness and love,' says Kate. That was nice of her.

'Here's to Arty Jonathan. May he remain poor and unsuccessful,' I say, raising an eyebrow.

'Here's to Facebook guy. May he forget his login details,' says Bloomie.

'Here's to Rugger Robbie. May he never sleep-piss again,' I say.

'Here's to The Hairy Back. May he discover the joys of waxing,' says Bloomie.

'Here's to Clapham Brodie. May he come out of the closet earlier next time,' I say.

'Here's to Fuckface. May he . . . stop being a fuckface,' says Bloomie. She shrugs, and whispers, 'I can't remember why we broke up.'

'Here's to Smart Henry. May he find deep joy in being truly shallow,' I say.

'Here's to the Missing Link. May he evolve,' says Kate.

'And here's to dear Posh Mark. May he find everlasting happiness with Belly,' I say.

'Here's to Rick,' starts Kate gaily, and then we all pause. There is nothing good to say about Rick. 'May he rot in hell?' she says tentatively, and we all start laughing.

Then I raise a tiny silent private toast. To Jake. May you forgive me for being a cockmonkey bastardo.

Another half a jug of margarita later, and the world seems a much happier place. Love lovely New York. Love Kate and Bloomie. Love fajitas and fish tacos and quesadillas, even though I genuinely don't know which is which when they're placed in front of us. In the middle of ordering our next round of drinks – we decide to make it easy for them, and go for a pitcher of frozen margarita – I get a text from Rob.

Hey kitty! Party at tenjune! Text me when you're here!

I read it out loud to the girls.

'*Kitty?*' says Bloomie.

'Tenjune is a nightclub,' says Kate. 'It's near the hotel.'

'Are you sure the Meatpacking District won't be like Covent Garden on a Saturday night?' I ask.

'Leave your London snobberies at home,' says Kate. I text him back that we'll be there by 10 pm.

'Ooh, Katie, tell us about Sam,' I say to her. 'Come on. Don't be shy.'

'Well . . . you weren't at the Walmer last Sunday,' says Kate. 'It all got a bit silly and drunken and I told them about the pretend speedskating. And so then Sam had a speedskating competition with Mitch. And before the competition, he said to me, if I win this competition, you have to give me your number and go out on a date with me.'

'No!'

'Yes! And then he won! So obviously I, um, had to give him my number.'

Bloomie and I crack up.

'Are you laughing at me?' says Kate. 'I do know it wasn't a real competition, you guys. I do know that. But I thought he should be rewarded for trying and . . . and for ingenuity.'

'So true,' smiles Bloomie. 'That was such a fun day . . . I miss Eugene.' She pouts slightly.

'Aw . . . darling. Next time we come, let's bring him too,' I suggest.

'Great idea,' she grins. 'Actually,' she clears her throat. 'Kate, I'm sorry I didn't tell you before but I couldn't tell one of you without the other and, um, well . . . I'm moving in with him.'

Kate and I both squeal in delight and immediately stifle our squeals (so not cool) and start whispering excited congratulations. It turns out Eugene asked her to move in with him last Sunday after the night at the Walmer, and they've been discussing it all week.

'I decided yes,' she says. 'I love him with all my heart. Almost losing him last weekend . . . was the worst thing that ever happened to me.'

'Daring, I'm so happy for you,' I say.

'Me too,' says Kate, though I can see she's also thinking about something else.

'Don't worry about the flat, Katie, or about a new flatmate or anything,' says Bloomie quickly. 'Take as much time as you want to figure out what you're doing next and we can take it from there.'

Kate immediately looks relieved. 'Actually, I have figured out what's next, I was just waiting for the right time to tell you guys about it,' says Kate. 'I'm going to go back to university and get a Masters in fine arts and museum management. And then I'm going to try to work in fundraising or financial management or something, for an art gallery or a museum . . . I don't know. I haven't planned that far.'

'Oh, my God,' says Bloomie. 'What a brilliant idea.'

'That's perfect for you,' I agree.

'I know!' she says happily. 'Anyway, I've worked it all out, and I can just afford to keep living at Bloomie's place, just. And I'd hate to move out. I'm so happy living there. I've saved some money, and I may have to get a part-time job, and it'll be a tough year, but that's OK,' she shrugs. 'I don't mind.'

'I'm so glad you want to stay!' exclaims Bloomie. Suddenly she and Kate both turn to look at me.

'What?' I say.

'Isn't it obvious? Will you move in with me? Please?!' says Kate.

I'm surprised. I've been living with Anna for years. It's cheap, and convenient – and it's time for a change.

'Of course I will,' I say. 'I would love to.'

We all clink margaritas again and start discussing moving plans immediately.

After getting the bill (check), we slip outside for a cigarette and hail a cab. We text Rob we're on the way, and find Tenjune pretty fast. As I get out of the cab, I notice there's a big queue of people lining up to get in, and a very small queue on the other side that seems to be a guestlist. What's more, everyone in the guestlist queue is in a costume.

I turn to Bloomie and Kate. 'I think the shorter VIP queue is for the party. And I think it's a costume party. I can't believe we're not dressed up for this.'

Bloomie nods. 'What's the theme? Something to do with music. I definitely saw a Michael Jackson and a Dolly Parton.'

'Perhaps it's a plastic surgery theme,' I suggest.

'Goddammit!' says Kate. 'I can't believe we're going to be the girls at the dress-up party who look hot, but not funny! That is completely not us!'

This sounds so un-Katelike, and so conceited, that Bloomie and I crack up.

Rob appears at the doorway next to the bouncer, and points at us. The bouncer nods. Feeling kind of special, dorky though it is, we skip past both queues and walk into the club. Rob's wearing normal clothes, with just John Lennon glasses on. Shit effort. He is good looking, though.

412

'Thanks again for the invite, Rob . . . but how about a heads-up about the theme, dude?' I say, after we've all kissed hello.

'It's Real American Idols . . . Nah, you wouldn't have dressed up, would you?' he says. 'You look way better in normal clothes! Love the outfits! So London!'

We thought we looked so New York.

Tenjune is small, rammed and noisy with the happy sound of drinking and fun. We turn left and walk up a step to a slightly separated area, and I nearly bump into a guy dressed as Vanilla Ice talking to another guy improbably dressed as early Diana Ross.

'I had to get the haircut, but dude, it was so worth it,' says Ice.

'Where the fuck are my Supremes?' says Diana.

I am going to enjoy this party.

We get a drink and Rob starts introducing us to people. Underneath the costumes, I can tell that we are surrounded by rather good-looking, clean-cut types. They're all excruciatingly charming and polite. And as soon as we've made a few minutes of small talk, they're funny as hell.

Around us I can see Axl Rose, Jim Morrison, Michael Bolton, Prince, Marilyn Manson, Barbra Streisand, Joni Mitchell, several Britneys, a Madonna from every era (except, unsurprisingly, the baffling 'American Pie' period), and three Elvises. I'm chatting to a bowler-hatted-and-waistcoated Debbie Gibson, as Bloomie and Kate are laughing at Jim Morrison and Axl Rose arguing over which of them has had a greater influence on rock music. '"Paradise City", man! Did you not HEAR the subtext in my lyrics? Come on!' says Axl.

These New Yorkers know how to throw a dress-up party.

Every now and again, Rob pops over to say hi, though he's spending most of his time chatting up a Nancy Sinatra. (I can't be absolutely sure, but the beehive and the white go-go boots kind of give it away.) He's a very good host. We're clearly only invited here as the ratio of guys to girls is about three to one, but that suits us just fine.

He also introduces us to the party boy, who insists we call him Birthday Paulie. It turns out he's English and has lived here for about six years. He's dressed as Kurt Cobain, in a blond wig and blue-and-white-striped top, and keeps buying everyone shots, especially Kate.

I catch up with the girls, mid-mingle.

'I can't BELIEVE we didn't dress up for this,' I say.

'I know. It's almost ruining my night,' replies Bloomie.

'I like Birthday Paulie,' says Kate thoughtfully. 'I wonder how we'd make a long-distance relationship work, though?'

I find myself, at midnight, dancing to '9 to 5' with Kate, Bloomie, Cyndi Lauper and MC Hammer. The DJ is amazing, playing new music and old music and rap and everything, all at once. I love this party, I think happily. I bet Jake would love it, too. I'll have to tell him about it one day.

'Anyone for another shot?' shouts Birthday Paulie.

'I want shots, I want beer, I want champagne, I want the whole thing. I want the fairytale,' says MC Hammer. Bloomie and I laugh so hard at this that I drop my little black clutch.

And then, as I pick it up, out of the corner of my eye, I see Slash standing at the bar. But it's not Slash.

It's Jake. A frizzy black wig covers half his face, so I can only see his mouth, but I know it's Jake. And he's looking right at me.

As well as the wig, he's wearing mirrored sunglasses and a top hat, with a sleeveless black T-shirt and black leather trousers. He also has a guitar strapped around his chest, which is a nice touch.

I turn to Bloomie and Kate. 'Thank you again for bringing me to New York,' I say quickly.

I walk over to him. Neither of us can speak for a second.

'You own black leather trousers?' I finally say. No response. He just looks at me, slightly stunned, with his mouth open. It adds to the Slash impression, actually. Very impressive.

'What are you doing here?' he finally asks, taking off his sunglasses and wig.

414

'Um – I kind of know that guy over there. Rob,' I say, pointing. 'I'm here with Bloomie and Kate for the weekend—' I turn the other way to point them out and see they're clutching each other by the arm and staring at us. 'Why are . . . why are you here?'

'I'm spending the weekend with my sister. She lives in Brooklyn,' he says, and I look behind him and see the girl he was walking with last night. She's dressed as Jon Bon Jovi, which I really have to respect, and talking to Billy Ray Cyrus. She's not his girlfriend. Thank God.

'I shared a flat with Paul when I lived here. I worked with half these guys,' he continues, clearly trying to make small talk.

'Nice,' I say.

Jake finally meets my eye. 'I decided that another weekend away was a really good idea. So I booked it on Monday and flew over yesterday.' He's being dry, or wry, or something. I can't tell.

'About last weekend,' I say. This is it, time to do it. Am I ready? I haven't even thought about what I am going to say. I should have made notes. Kate would have made notes.

'Don't worry,' he says quickly, looking at his drink. 'I'm really sorry I . . . called you all those things. I . . . I totally misinterpreted the situation. I wish I could take it all back.'

'No! No . . .' I say. 'I was wrong. I was totally wrong.'

I take a deep breath.

'I was a jackass and, um, and a bastardo. And I know that. And it wasn't that I didn't trust you. I didn't trust myself to know what was really right for me,' I say. 'But I do now. And I'm . . . I'm crazy about you,' I falter, and then clear my throat. He's staring at me, his lovely crinkly eyes locked on my face. I try to ignore a tear escaping down my left cheek. 'I didn't mean those things I said, and I regret it so much . . . I want to fix it, if you'll let me . . .'

I'm starting to babble, and am trailing off when Jake gives me that huge smile and says, 'I'm crazy about you too.'

'Really?' I say, quickly wiping away the tear.

'Yes, Minxy, I am. And I don't think you're really a jackass,' he replies. 'So really, no more Dating Sabbatical?'

'It's over,' I say honestly, and then look at his watch. 'It's past midnight. It's my birthday.'

'Happy birthday,' he says, smiling at me.

I decide that's enough talking.

'You should kiss me now,' I say.

'So bossy . . .' he sighs happily and, smiling, leans in to kiss me.

After a few seconds I pull away from him, take a deep breath, and jump off the cliff that I almost jumped off that morning after Eddie's houseparty.

'I love you.'

I don't think I would have the cojones to say that if I hadn't just had the best kiss of my life, if we weren't in New York, if I wasn't sure – absolutely sure beyond any modicum of doubt – that I love him with all my heart and that telling him is the most important thing I could ever do.

'I love you, too,' Jake says.

And then we kiss again.

We kiss and kiss and kiss. I can hear Bloomie and Kate cheering in the background, and we kiss some more. I'm sorry to be romantic, but there have never been any other kisses like this, ever. This is outside-in happiness and inside-out happiness all mixed up together in a blissfully, impossibly happy explosion.

Epilogue

PSYCH! Like I'd leave it there.

It's eight months later, and Jake and I are, um, yes very in love. I feel bashful when I say that. I'm tracing little circles in the ground with my big toe. The rest of the weekend in New York was amazing. I had the best birthday of my entire life. Jake and I got our own hotel room at The Standard and smashed Rule 9 to smithereens and then, on Sunday, took the ripped-up Dating Sabbatical Rules and threw them into the Hudson. Inside a coffin of the (un)lucky yellow clutch.

I've never been so happy in my life. I can't believe I could ever have come close to mistaking the feelings I had for previous boyfriends for this . . . He's just– perfect for me.

As to what's in store for us next . . . well, I couldn't possibly say. But let's just say I understand calculus now and we discuss it all the time.

OK, stop retching. Sheesh. You've come this far with me. I thought you'd like to know how it worked out.

Everything else is kind of brilliant, too. I've been promoted, officially, to deputy creative director. I'm still taptapping away at my own stuff. It's terribly easy to write when you're happy. At least, it is for me. I haven't finished anything worth talking about yet, but I'll get there eventually.

Now, about everyone else: Kate is studying fine art and working part time for a small art gallery in Mayfair. She's not sure what she'll do next, and doesn't seem to mind that much. She's also dating Sam, whom she finds funny and baffling in equal measure. He absolutely adores her. Bloomie is living with Eugene. She's still working hard, but has thrown away her BlackBerry entirely. So I guess that's a small, but significant, change.

Eddie and Laura went out for a few months before she decided to go travelling for a year, which he tried not to take personally. He seems to be enjoying the single life. Mitch and Tara just moved in together. Fraser is internet dating and having the time of his life. Cooper and Marlena are having a baby. Lukas is in love with a girl called Alexa. Tory is still single. Rick, I heard a few weeks ago, was made redundant from his job. And everyone else I know is in different states of love, lust, misery, happiness, hope and chaos, trying to figure out what they want and how to make it happen. It's fantastic.

Acknowledgements

Thank you to Keshini Naidoo, who loves a man named Steff in a rolled-sleeve linen suit almost as much as she loves Sass; Maxine Hitchcock for her fantastic support; Alex Stone, Alice Sumpster, Alida Stewart, Bennary Smith, Amy Eastall, Catherine Ryan, Caroline Morrison, Sarah Gibson, Jackie Cook, Devi Govender, Jean Cahill, Yvette Quane, Elsa Stewart and Valerie Nestor for their enthusiastic feedback, encouragement and/or participation in 'Name That Bastard'*; Conor Barry for insisting on a cameo; Victoria Hannon and Matt Hallett for their copysmarts and support; Cat Cobain at Transworld for her brilliant advice; Laura Longrigg at MBA Literary Agents for her wise guidance and general loveliness; my parents Sue and Bill Burgess for being hilarious and wonderful; Paul Barry for being so damn perfect and most of all my beautiful sister Anika Burgess who read it first and thought it was funny.

* For details of 'Name that Bastard, Part Deux', go to www.gemmaburgess.co.uk

The Dating Guide

There are hundreds of dating guides out there. This one is different.

You see, I'm not about to tell you how to act, what to wear, what to talk about and where to go. If I did, your date wouldn't be dating you. They'd be dating me. And not even the real me, but the imaginary me. (Much better than the real me, who would probably get drunker than she intended and knock over her wine glass laughing at her own jokes.)

This also isn't a guide to meeting someone and/or getting asked out on a date. That's a whole different guide. I shall write it one day. (I shall call it 'Why You'll Never Meet A Man At A Salsa Class'.) One quick thing about getting asked out, though: lots of girls complain they 'never meet any single men'. These are usually the same girls who refuse to go out on Saturday night because 'I'm just really tired' and when they are finally out at a party or something, will grab their two best friends and sit in the corner laughing at private jokes all night, not even looking up to see if any men are in the room. Think of it this way: if you needed a taxi cab, you wouldn't simply stand there, hope one would read your mind and stop for you. You'd go to the road and put your hand out to stop one. It's the same with men. Just make eye contact, make him laugh, and make him feel funny. He will ask you out.

Anyway, back to the point. So, think of this dating guide as a magical catalyst to help you be the best possible version of yourself. The well-dressed, funny, impressive, intelligent, flirtatious, warm, attractive, kissable, self-assured, memorable Super-You. Primped and primed to get out there and date like you've never dated before. Like performance-enhancing steroids . . . for lurve.

And even more importantly, this guide will give you a few tools to help you enjoy dating. Because – and this is what people forget – it's fun. You get dressed up, drink and eat good things and talk to someone who's never heard your best lines before. What's not to like?

Now that I've completely oversold everything I'm about to write, let's get started.

Getting ready

Men like red. Men hate red. Get the puppies out. Cover the puppies up. Blah blah blah. Yawn yawn yawn. If I had a pound for every time I've read some rubbish article about the psychology of dressing for dates, I wouldn't be here right now. I'd be on the Med, making eyes at the boatboy over my whiskey sour.

Dude, wear whatever you want. Something that makes you feel taller and thinner is good. Keep non-boob bulges to a minimum. Don't wear those bras with the see-through straps. (They look cheap.) Make sure you can walk in your shoes. Check for peanut butter on your top. You might have peanut butter on your top because of my next tip: eat peanut butter on toast, or similar, before you leave the house. Two vodkas + nervous excitement + no dinner yet = drunky. And nothing makes a date more unlikely to succeed than getting drunk and falling over. I can back that statement up with statistics. Where was I? Yes. Wear whatever the sweet baby jane you like to wear. If you like it, you probably look pretty damn ace in it. Have a trying-on session the night before, preferably to music so you can make your own chick flickesque montage.

Anyway, ask the average guy what he likes women to wear,

and he'll respond 'as little as possible'. He'll think he's funny and original for saying it, too. As long as your outfit is girl-shaped and not too out-there or mumsy, you can't really go wrong. A failsafe date outfit: a black pencil skirt, a black top and extremely high shoes in a bright colour. When conversation runs out, you can say 'I was hoping you'd wear canary yellow peep-toes, too. Then at least we'd have something to talk about'.

The first two minutes . . .

A key part of your night, and one that will dictate how the next hour (or five) will go. That's why you need to meet him with your game face: a carefully-arranged facial expression that doesn't reveal how nervous / excited / thrilled / bored / disappointed you really are to be there. One that helps you appear the Three Cs: Calm, Cool and in Control. A basic game face: unfurrowed brow, chin up, mouth arranged in a serene nearly-smile.

Don't worry about talking straight away. Not rushing to fill a silence shows self-assurance. Plus, wittering undermines the Three Cs. I should know. I am one of nature's witters: on dates, at work, in lifts, anywhere. As I've gotten older I've learned to shutthehellup. It turns out the world doesn't stop turning if no one is talking. Who knew?

Having said that, try not to be a total mute for the entire night. If you can't think of anything to say, try something like 'Can you make conversation for a while? I don't think I'll find my funny until the second drink'. If he laughs, and you're feeling cocky, add 'And try to be interesting, okay?'. Faux-arrogance is amusing. And it'll keep him on his toes.

Anyway, he should ask what you want to drink, and that's an easy conversation-starter. I'm assuming you're meeting for a drink, and perhaps dinner. If you're meeting for a game of rounders in the park, then more power to you, sister. This guide will not be of any help to you at all. If he seems stuck for words, take charge: arch a knowing eyebrow and say 'Oh, I'll have a [insert favourite drink here], thanks for asking'. This is a funny, kind icebreaker, and the Three Cs. Jackpot.

And if you can't do any of the above, then laugh. Because you have a long night ahead of you, sweetcheeks.

The date

When it comes to conversation, don't just lie there. I know you're special, you know you're special, but unless you show or at least hint at how unique and hilarious and memorable you really are, then he'll never know . . . because he'll never bother to find out. He'll end the date, go home, watch the sports recap and never think about you again.

If you say you like 'going out to dinner, going to the cinema, having a bit of a laugh, hanging out with my friends, going to the gym' then frankly, you sound like everyone I've ever met. Including my mother. If you say 'I like watching Sex And The City with the sound turned down so I can dub in my own conversation. I like eating burgers layer by layer. I like painting guyliner on my male friends when they are drunk and easily influenced' then you sound like someone I'd remember. And frankly, want to see again. (Actually, what are you doing later?)

However, being unique doesn't require revealing absolutely everything about your life and history. I've learned, through trial and ohGoddidIjustsaythat error, that dating someone is like the dance of the seven veils. At every date, you drop a veil and *ta-da!* reveal a little more. You are a meal of many courses to be savoured, not a pureed foodshake to be gulped in one. So don't unzip your chest, pluck out your heart and soul and lay them naked and pulsating on the table between you. Everyone's got sad stories and heartbreak and gripes and secrets. Keep all that juicy stuff till later.

Just talk. You're good at it. You've been doing it since you were two. Ask questions. Tell stories you know are funny, like the time that you reverse-parked into a dumpster during your driving

422

test. Be coy. Be confident. Be wry. Be unusual. Smirk, frown questioningly, arch your eyebrow and laugh freely. It's called flirting and damnit, it's fun.

Troubleshooting 1: Nerves

From the heart-hammering, hand-shaking school of nervousness? I feel your pain. Nerves suck. Sometimes there is nothing you can do but ride them out. They will disappear eventually. You're smart, ridiculously good-looking and totally in control, so just smile and wait for him to talk. And remember to breathe.

Troubleshooting 2: Unwelcome discoveries

So he's got kids. Or scabies. Or suggests you head to his for a nightcap at 8.41pm. Or he voted for the BNP, and tells you – at length – why you should too. Or his table manners make you want to vomit, or he still lives with his ex-girlfriend, or he spends all night looking at himself in the mirror above the bar. Shit happens, my friend. Discovering you don't like him on the first or second date is nothing to get upset about. Chalk it up to experience.

Troubleshooting 3: Bad dates.

Some dates will be bad. This is a fact. Frankly, some men will be bad, too. Just keep your wits about you, and figure out what he's really like rather than what you *want* him to be like. A lot of time is wasted wishing/pretending a guy is smarter/keener/kinder than he really is. You need to look out for signs. They're not that hard to spot. One idiot wore a tshirt saying 'I taught that girlfriend that thing you like' on a date with me. Such a hilarious lack of judgment just made me laugh till I had tears in my eyes. He probably thought I was mad. Hey ho.

The point is that every guy is the wrong one until he's the right one. That doesn't make it any easier, especially if you feel stupid for liking him when he wasn't that nice, or used if he seemed to like you and then stopped calling, or – heaven forbid – in love with him when he's not with you. Don't worry about it, and don't focus on it. Some men simply aren't very nice. Some dogs aren't very nice either, but that doesn't mean you should never pet one again.

Thinking about bad dates, bad men and bad feelings is addictive, like picking scabs and playing with candle wax. But you are stronger than you think, so just put those bad thoughts down, flip them the metaphorical finger and look ahead to the next guy/night out/drink. Batter up.

The last two minutes

The last two minutes of your date is just about as important as the first two minutes. If you want to kiss him, and you haven't, and you are bored of watching him work up the nerve to make a move, just look him straight in the eye and say 'I think you should kiss me now'. Seriously. Yeah, it takes some cojones – the drink will help with that – but I think you can do it.

The point of it all

You need to decide if you like him. That's the only thing that really matters. Not if he likes you (he does), not if you look good (you do) or if you're being funny (you are). But if you'd like to spend a Sunday morning lying in bed with him, if you can laugh adoringly at him and he at you, and if he can make you gasp and moan like a hot bath.

So once the date starts, forget how you look and whether you've got the Three Cs. They're just there to help you feel prepared, so you don't work yourself into a frenzy of pressure and nerves. Does he seem kind? Smart? Funny? Interesting? Interested? Do you want to rip his clothes off? That part, no guide can help you with. That part is up to you.